STATE OF ALERT

FIRST FAMILY SERIES, BOOK 8

MARIE FORCE

State of Alert
First Family Series, Book 8
By: Marie Force

Published by HTJB, Inc.
Copyright 2024. HTJB, Inc.
Cover design by Kristina Brinton and Ashley Lopez
Cover photography by Regina Wamba
Models: Robert John and Ellie Dulac
Print Layout: E-book Formatting Fairies
ISBN: 978-1958035863

The First Family Series

More new books are always in the works. For the most up-to-date list of what's available from the First Family Series, go to *marieforce.com/firstfamily*

CHAPTER ONE

L ieutenant Sam Holland was silent during the ride from Metro PD headquarters to New York Avenue, where the body of Navy Lieutenant Commander Juan Rodriguez had been found in a clothing donation bin. She and her team had been riding high off an arrest in the murder of U.S. Attorney Tom Forrester—after Sam took down murderer Harlan Peckham on a city street—when the word came that the missing naval officer's body had been found.

Sam had experienced a crushing wave of grief on behalf of her husband, President Nick Cappuano, who'd worked closely with Juan at the White House.

Her partner, Detective Freddie Cruz, sat next to her in the back seat of her Secret Service SUV, while Sergeant Tommy "Gonzo" Gonzales was across from her. Apparently sensing her tension, her two closest colleagues and friends were quiet, too.

How would she ever tell Nick that Juan, the military attaché who'd tipped him off about a possible military overthrow of his administration, had been found murdered? Nick had been inconsolable, and had barely slept in days, since he'd learned Juan was missing. His stress was her stress, which meant neither of them had been getting much sleep while MPD officers and multiple federal agencies searched for the missing officer.

Nick had spoken to Juan's mother and learned she'd raised him as a single mom. She owned a hair salon in Philadelphia that'd supported them. He'd also learned that Juan was her only child, which had only added to his despair.

Vernon, Sam's lead Secret Service agent, brought the black SUV to a stop about a block from where Patrol officers had taped off the box where Juan's body had been found by a volunteer from the agency that collected used clothing.

"Hang on for just a second." Vernon and his partner for the day, Agent Quigley, got out of the SUV to confer with other agents who'd arrived ahead of them.

This was the part of having a detail that drove her crazy. She was a highly trained police officer capable of protecting herself, but she had to wait for the Secret Service to ensure the scene was safe for her to do her job.

"You guys go ahead and get started," she said to Freddie and Gonzo. "I'll be right there. I hope."

Her colleagues got out of the SUV and closed the doors behind them.

Sam watched them go as she acknowledged that one of them would have to take the lead on this case since she'd known Juan personally. As one of the keepers of the "nuclear football" briefcase that went everywhere the president did, Juan had been a frequent presence in their lives over the last five months since President Nelson died suddenly, giving Nick a promotion neither he nor Sam had wanted. Him being the vice president had been more than enough for them.

Everything had changed since they got the phone call about Nelson's untimely death.

Well, a few things had stayed the same, such as the tight bond she and Nick shared as a couple, and the ones they had with their kids, extended family and close friends. Those ties sustained them now that they were under the most intense scrutiny of anyone in the world, with a level of attention on their every move that could make them insane if they allowed it to.

Sam refused to let that happen, which was much harder than it might seem with new piles of shit hitting the fan constantly.

In the hours since they'd closed the investigation into the murder of U.S. Attorney Tom Forrester and the shooting of FBI Special Agent-in-Charge Avery Hill, which had been tied to a single shooter, Sam had been oddly numb, especially as the search for Juan had intensified. She told herself the feeling was normal after having lost a close colleague in Tom and nearly losing another close colleague—and friend—in Avery. Thankfully, he would make a full recovery.

Eventually.

After nearly sixteen years on the job, she knew by now what was part of the drill and what wasn't. Total numbness wasn't normal, no matter how much she wished to believe otherwise. At some point, she'd have to do something about that, but with a new murder to deal with, now was not that time.

Vernon opened her door. "All clear."

"Thanks."

Sam got out of the car and walked over to join Freddie and Gonzo, who were leaning into the back side of the clothing donation bin. She didn't want to look in there and confirm what she already knew, that Juan was dead, that someone had killed him, possibly because he'd warned Nick about the Joint Chiefs' nefarious plan. The thought of another case that required wading through hip-deep bureaucracy exhausted her. She'd just done ten rounds with her husband's Attorney General and managed to eke out a victory of sorts after Nick fired Reginald Cox for stonewalling Sam and her team, and for being deeply in debt from gambling. They'd uncovered the gambling in the course of their investigation.

Her colleagues stepped aside to allow her close enough to the bin to see inside.

"Hold your breath," Freddie said.

Sam was thankful for the warning as she bent at the waist for a closer look. The sight of Juan's khaki uniform with the ribbons on his chest hit her like a punch to the heart.

This would devastate Nick, who'd become fond of the eager young officer. She could see only the left side of his face, enough to confirm his identity.

"I need to go home." She couldn't let Nick hear this news from anyone else. "Can you guys take the lead and keep me in the loop?"

"Absolutely," Gonzo said. "We're on it."

"I'm really sorry about this, Sam," her kindhearted partner said.

Sam gave Freddie's arm a squeeze. "Thanks. Me, too. Keep a tight lid until I have a chance to tell Nick and he can notify Juan's mother."

"Will do," Gonzo said.

As she walked back to the Secret Service SUV, the medical examiner's vehicle was arriving. She stopped to talk to Dr. Lindsey McNamara and was relieved to see that some of the pink had returned to Lindsey's cheeks after a recent illness had left her pale and listless.

"What've we got?" Lindsey asked as she pulled on latex gloves.

"Navy Lieutenant Commander Juan Rodriguez, military attaché to the president."

"Oh no. Sam... Is he the one..."

"Who told Nick that the Joint Chiefs wanted a regime change? Yep."

"Shit."

"Only child of a single mom."

Lindsey's deep sigh said it all.

"I'm going home to talk to Nick. I'll catch up shortly."

"Take your time. We've got this."

"Thanks, Linds. Keep it confidential for now."

"No one will hear about it from us."

"Appreciate it."

Vernon held the SUV door for Sam and then closed it when she was inside the vehicle.

"Where to?" he asked when he was back in the driver's seat.

"Home, please."

He gave her a curious look in the rearview mirror, but didn't ask any questions.

It was highly unusual for her to return to the White House in the middle of a shift, but there was nothing usual about finding the body of one of her husband's colleagues in a clothing donation bin on New York Avenue.

Enclosed in the back seat of the SUV, Sam wanted to punch something—or someone. She'd give anything to not have to tell her beloved husband this dreadful news, even if he'd been halfway expecting it for days now. His tenure as president had been far more traumatic than either of them could've anticipated when he took the oath of office on Thanksgiving.

Since then, they'd dealt with two mass shootings, the sudden death of her brother-in-law, the thwarted military coup, claims of illegitimacy because Nick had never been elected vice president or president and endless demands on their time, energy and emotions. That, and the relentless pace of a national campaign, was exactly why he'd announced his decision not to run for president when his tenure as vice president ended. He'd waited all his life for the family they now had, and he didn't want to be away from them for months on end campaigning for a job he didn't want.

Then Nelson had dropped dead, rendering that decision a moot point—and gave Nick's detractors even more to talk about by noting the country was "stuck with" a president who didn't even want the job. That wasn't what he'd said when he announced his decision to sit out the next election cycle, but they didn't care about the truth.

It'd been nonstop bullshit for five straight months.

And now this.

Her heart ached for him.

Juan had risked everything to inform Nick about the Joint Chiefs' rumored plan to overthrow the "illegitimate" president. How had Juan found out about what they were up to? Sam never had heard the answer to that question and would really like to know.

The Naval Criminal Investigative Service would be involved in this case, which would complicate things. Battling over jurisdiction was one of her least favorite parts of the job. The murder had occurred in DC, thus the case belonged to the Metro PD, but they'd be forced to play nice with NCIS.

Maybe it would work out in their favor if NCIS helped them quickly solve the case rather than engaging in a turf war that would detract from their common goal of figuring out who'd killed Juan.

Sam's anxiety spiked as they drove through the gates to the White House fifteen minutes later. She had to go in there and tell Nick the news he'd been dreading, news he would then have to share with Juan's devoted mother.

Vernon opened the car door.

Sam stared at the ground, summoning the will to move forward, to do what needed to be done.

"Sam?"

She looked up at him.

"Are you all right?"

"Nope. Not at all. The body in that bin was Juan Rodriguez."

"Oh no."

"And now I have to tell Nick that the man who took such a huge risk to protect him is dead, possibly because he took that risk."

"I'm so sorry."

"Me, too, Vernon. Me, too."

"Is there anything I can do for you?"

"No, but thanks for asking. I appreciate it."

She tried to find the fortitude she would need to do what had to be done, the same way she did in every new homicide investigation, but this was different. This one would hurt Nick, and that would hurt her, too. It would be better coming from her, she thought, as if anything could make this news more palatable for him. Nothing could.

After everything he'd endured before they were together, Sam wished she could wrap him in her love and protect him from ever being hurt again. She had no doubt he'd do the same for her if he could. But they were both painfully aware that life didn't work that way. All they could do was love each other through the crisis of the moment, and that was exactly what she would do.

Harold, one of the White House ushers, stood ready to greet her at the door.

"Afternoon, Mrs. Cappuano. Are you home for the day?"

She wondered what the staff thought of a wife, mother and first lady who spent most of a Sunday at work. "Unfortunately, only for a few minutes, Harold. I'll hang on to my coat."

"Yes, ma'am."

"Is the president in the residence?"

"No, ma'am, he's in the Oval."

"Thank you, Harold."

"My pleasure, ma'am."

Sam made her way to the West Wing, nodding to the few people she passed on the way. They all knew her. She didn't recognize any of them, which wasn't unusual. Even on a Sunday, scores of people worked in the people's house every day. She'd made a point of calling every member of the White House staff and as many of Nick's team as she could by name, whenever possible. Occasionally, a new person would sneak by her, but she tried her best to make them all feel valued.

The residence staff was the best part of living in the White House. They went above and beyond to make the family comfortable in their home away from home.

Outside the Oval Office, she stopped to speak with Julie, the admin who guarded the gates. Sam was surprised to see her there on a Sunday and wondered if Nick's team ever took a full day off. "May I please have a moment with him?"

"He's in a meeting with the cabinet. Shall I arrange for him to leave the meeting?"

Sam thought about what Nick would want and made the decision based on how tortured he'd been waiting for news since Juan had disappeared. "Yes, please."

"Yes, ma'am. If you'd like to wait inside the Oval, I'll send him in."

Sam was thirty-six years old and hated being called ma'am, but that was something she was learning to tolerate. Everyone called the first lady ma'am. The honorific was baked into the title, and it was pointless to expect people to call her anything else. Thankfully, she'd persuaded Vernon and his regular partner, Jimmy, to call her Sam when they were alone.

"Thank you, Julie."

Sam opened the door to the Oval Office and stepped into her husband's inner sanctum, the most famous office on earth, and took a seat on one of the sofas, hoping she'd done the right thing by interrupting the cabinet meeting.

She waited five minutes before he came in, stopping short at the sight of her, probably taking one look at her and figuring out why she'd called him out of the meeting. In deference to the weekend, he wore a navy V-neck sweater over a light blue dress shirt and gray dress pants.

Sam stood, went to him and put her hands on his chest as she gazed up at his handsome face and the gorgeous hazel eyes that looked at her with apprehension. "We found Juan."

His entire body tensed.

She didn't have to say anything else for him to know that since she was there in person, Juan hadn't been found alive.

"How?"

"I'm not sure yet. He was found in a clothing donation bin on New York Avenue." His sharp intake of oxygen had her holding on tighter to him, putting her arms around his waist. "I'm so, so sorry, Nick."

He dropped his head to her shoulder as he exhaled a deep, pained breath. "Who knows?"

She reached up to run her fingers through his dark, wavy hair, wishing there was more she could do to provide comfort. "Only us and you so far."

"I have to call his mother. I promised to keep her informed."

"I'll stay with you while you do that. I'll stay for as long as you need me."

"You can't stay as long as I'll need you."

"Yes, I can."

"Will you guys lead the investigation?"

"We have jurisdiction since he was found in the District. NCIS will want in, but they can be helpful in a situation like this."

"I'll make sure they're nothing but helpful."

She placed her hand on his face, compelling him to look at her. As she gazed into his beautiful eyes, she said, "Please tell me you know this isn't your fault."

"I didn't kill Juan, and I didn't shoot the service members at Fort Liberty. But like that, this happened because I became president, and somehow... Somehow, I have to find a way to live with that."

CHAPTER TWO

I t took every bit of self-control Nick could muster not to erupt into rage that would only upset Sam and wouldn't bring Juan back. The rage was tinged with agony for Juan's mother and everyone else who'd loved the sharp, funny, ambitious naval officer who'd risked everything to warn Nick of a nefarious plot.

Had he paid for his loyalty with his life?

Juan was the seventh member of the military to die since Nick took office. The other six had been killed at Fort Liberty by a disgruntled soldier who'd opted to take a voluntary dishonorable discharge for not being willing to serve under an "unelected" commander in chief. He'd responded to his outrage by shooting up a gathering of his fellow service members.

Each of those deaths weighed heavy on Nick's soul, but this one…

Juan Rodriguez had been one of the first people to enter his orbit as president, responsible for the nuclear codes that were carried by Juan and a rotation of other military attachés, one of whom was always close to Nick.

Most of them were quiet and reserved in his presence. Juan

had been the exception. He had been friendly and usually had something to say to Nick when they'd been in the same room. They'd discovered a common love of sports, baseball in particular, and had shared spirited conversations about the DC Feds, Juan's Phillies and Nick's Red Sox.

In a world where no one treated Nick like a regular guy anymore, Juan had, and Nick had appreciated that more than the young man would ever know. His heart was absolutely shattered that Juan was gone forever. And the thought of having to tell his mother... It was unbearable.

Sam sat next to him on the sofa and put her arm around him, leaning her head on his shoulder.

Nick had talked to Mrs. Rodriguez twice over recent days, heard stories of young Juan sweeping the floor of the salon for baseball card money from the time he was seven or eight. He'd heard her pride at Juan receiving a prestigious appointment to the Naval Academy, followed by his service to the president in the White House.

He'd promised to personally let her know the second they learned anything about Juan's whereabouts, but now that he knew, he wanted to delay giving her the devastating news for as long as he could.

Nick dropped his head into his hands.

Had one of the disgraced former Joint Chiefs murdered Juan to exact revenge for blowing the lid off their plot? They'd been dishonorably discharged from the military and were facing criminal charges as well as the loss of lucrative pensions. With their careers and reputations in tatters, what did they have to lose by killing the man who'd thwarted their plot?

Nothing. They had nothing at all to lose by killing Juan.

Nick had to pull himself together and do what needed to be done to get justice for Juan. He'd take five more minutes with Sam and the comfort only she could provide, and then he'd get back to being the president.

"What can I do for you?" she asked.

With his arm around her, he brought her with him when he sat back against the sofa. "This is what I need most." They both had a million things they should've been doing, but none of that mattered during the five minutes he was taking for himself.

She rested her head on his chest and kept an arm around his waist. "I wish there was more I could do."

"I'm sure you'll do plenty to find the person who killed Juan."

"Everything I can."

"Don't you need to get back to work?"

"Not yet."

"I heard you got Tom's killer."

"We did."

"I heard *you* did."

Sam shrugged, as if that arrest seemed like a lifetime ago now that a new crisis had arisen.

"I have to call Juan's mother."

"I'll be right here with you when you do."

"I don't want to make that call."

She tightened her arm around him. "I know, love."

"If I could go back in time, I'd say an emphatic *no* when Nelson asked me to be his VP. Then people wouldn't be getting killed because of me."

"It's not because of you. It's because people who kill other people are assholes."

"How can it not be related to their disapproval of me?"

"You know what I've learned after all these years on the job? Nothing is ever as obvious as we think it's going to be. It's always more complicated than it seems at first. As much as you liked and respected Juan, you didn't really know him. You didn't know what he did outside of work or who he was out of uniform. Anything is possible, right up to and including something totally random."

"This wasn't random. No way, and Juan wasn't the type to be

someone different away from work. He was a what-you-see-is-what-you-get kind of guy, which is why I liked him so much. One of many reasons."

"People show the world the person they want everyone to see. Behind the scenes is a whole other story—and that's true for everyone."

"It's not true for you. You're exactly who and what you appear to be in public."

"But there are sides to me that the public will never see. Just like there're sides to you they don't see."

"I guess."

"Juan was a great man and a distinguished officer who was excellent at his job. Other than the things he chose to share with you, we know nothing about him."

"I refuse to believe he was anything other than exactly what he seemed to be."

"I'm so sorry you lost someone you cared about. He was a wonderful guy from what I knew of him."

"He really was."

Nick sighed, realizing his five minutes were up. "I need to make that call."

He made no move to get up.

The thought of calling Mrs. Rodriguez made him sick.

He stared at the door to the Colonnade. "What do you think people would say if I walked out that door and never came back?"

"You probably wouldn't get too far before Brant and the other agents went after you."

"They'd bring me back, right?"

"Sorry to be a buzzkill, but I believe so."

"Is this what jail feels like?"

She looked up at him, offering the barest hint of a smile. "With many fewer amenities and no butlers."

"I'd miss the butlers."

"Would you miss me and the kids? I assume this breakout doesn't include us."

"Why do you think I haven't made a run for it?"

Sam turned his face toward her and laid a sweet kiss on him. "I love you so much, and I hate that this has happened."

"I love you, too. Thank you for coming in to be with me."

"There was nowhere else I wanted to be."

He took another deep breath and blew it out. "Let's get this over with."

They got up together and went to the Resolute Desk.

He dragged a chair around the desk so she could sit next to him.

When they were settled, he pressed the button on the phone that got him to Julie. "Could you please get me Linda Rodriguez?"

"Yes, sir, Mr. President. One moment please."

"Thank you."

While they waited, Sam reached for his hand and held on tight.

The phone beeped. "I have Mrs. Rodriguez for you, Mr. President."

He glanced at Sam before he pressed the flashing button. "Linda, it's Nick Cappuano."

"Mr. President... is there any news about my Juan?"

Nick closed his eyes against an instant surge of tears. "I'm sorry to have to tell you that he was found dead this morning."

Her screams pierced his soul.

He brushed at tears that spilled down his cheeks. "I'd give anything not to be calling you with this news. You know I thought the world of Juan, and I'm heartbroken for you and everyone who loved him." The words rang hollow to him. What difference would they make to his grieving mother?

"Th-thank you for your kindness. He... He adored you."

"Do you have someone with you?" Nick asked.

"My s-sisters, nieces and nephews are here."

He heard something in the background before a man said, "I'm sorry, but my aunt isn't up to talking anymore."

"I understand. This is Nick Cappuano. Please tell her I'll see to it personally that Juan is afforded full military honors."

"I'll let her know."

"Would you also mind notifying me of funeral arrangements?"

After a long pause, the man said, "Yes, of course."

Nick gave him the phone number to call to get the details to him. "Juan meant a lot to me. I'm very sorry for your loss."

"Thank you. What do you know about what happened to him?"

"Nothing yet, but there'll be a full investigation and more information forthcoming. Should I pass along your contact information to the officers in charge?"

"Yes, please. My aunt is in no condition to deal with police."

Sam released his hand to produce her notebook and pen.

"Go ahead and give me your number," Nick said.

Sam wrote down the number.

"And your name?"

"Francisco Alba."

"I'll make sure the police are in touch, and again, my heartfelt sympathy for the loss of your cousin."

"Thank you for calling."

Nick pressed the button to end the call.

Sam reached for him, and he fell into her embrace, thankful as always to have her by his side for the good times, the bad times and the truly dreadful times.

He held on to her and soaked in her love for a few minutes before he pulled back to kiss her. "Thank you for knowing just what I need."

She wiped the remaining tears from his face. "I wish it could be more."

"It's everything."

He pushed the button for Julie again. "Would you please

ask Secretary Jennings and Acting AG Conrad to come in? I'd also like to see Admiral Malin and NNSA Administrator Gilmore as soon as possible. Please get a message to Vice President Henderson and the cabinet that I won't be rejoining the meeting."

"Yes, sir."

"Thank you."

"What is NNSA?" Sam asked.

"The National Nuclear Security Administration. They oversee the safety of the nation's nuclear stockpile, and as the agency that acts as the first responder in a nuclear emergency, they work closely with the military personnel responsible for the nuclear codes."

"Just when I think I've heard of every federal agency, there're more."

"There're so many, it would make your head spin."

A knock on the door sounded.

"Come in."

Julie and the other admins had been instructed to wait for him to grant admission whenever Sam was with him in the office. Otherwise, his staff were on a knock-and-enter system.

"Secretary Jennings and Acting Attorney General Conrad for you, sir."

"Thank you, Julie."

"Do you want me to go?" Sam asked.

"Not yet."

"Thanks for coming in," Nick said to the others. "I've been notified that Lieutenant Commander Rodriguez has been found dead."

"Oh no," Defense Secretary Jennings said. He was tall, with silver hair and a normally stern expression that cracked with emotion when he heard the news. "I'm so sorry to hear that."

"As was I. I'd like you to instruct NCIS to work in tandem with Lieutenant Holland and the Metro PD to fully investigate his death."

"Is it being looked at as a murder?" In her mid-fifties, Conrad was a career prosecutor with shoulder-length brown hair and dark eyes. She'd been tapped to take over for former AG Cox, pending Senate approval.

"We don't know yet," Sam said. "Our medical examiner has his remains, and we're awaiting the results of the autopsy. He was found in uniform inside a clothing donation bin on New York Avenue."

"Good God," Jennings said softly. He seemed to take a second to recover his usual stoic composure. "I'll pass along the instructions to NCIS. I assume they should reach out to Lieutenant Holland?"

"Sergeant Gonzales on my team will be leading the investigation," Sam said.

"I'll ask them to get in touch."

"Thank you."

"Please also ask them not to turn this into a battle of wills over jurisdiction," Nick said. "We all want the same thing— answers for Juan's mother and family as soon as possible."

"Understood, sir."

After the secretary and acting AG had left the room, Sam fanned her face.

"What?"

"Hot. As. Fuck."

"Huh?"

"You, giving orders and taking charge. I dig it. And thank you for anticipating the jurisdictional battle that was brewing."

"Only you could make me smile right now."

"I don't mean to be disrespectful, but that was quite something."

"Knock it off," he said with his usual disdain for her finding him hot.

"I'll never knock it off." She stood and stepped away from the desk. "Come here and give me a hug so I can go back to work feeling as if you're going to be okay."

He stood and reached for her.

Sam stepped into his embrace and wrapped her arms around him. "Are you going to be okay?"

"What choice do I have?"

"I'd give anything to fix it for you."

"I know, and that helps. I'm just so angry and afraid that Juan's murder will be traced back to the former Joint Chiefs, which would result in yet another enormous shit show."

"Wherever it leads, it won't be your fault. Tell me you know that."

"I do."

"Remind me what you've got on the calendar the next few days."

"I've got that thing in Baltimore at the boys' school tomorrow." His younger twin brothers, Brock and Brayden, had invited him to appear at their elementary school as part of his outreach to students. He'd been looking forward to it until the news about Juan deflated him. "After that is lunch with the Maryland governor and Baltimore mayor, followed by a fundraiser for the Maryland Democrats. I'll make an appearance and get out of there. And I've got the West Coast trip on Wednesday."

"We're not discussing that until we have to."

He smiled. "I'll be back before you miss me."

"No, you won't." She held on for another minute before pulling back and looking up at him. "I love you, and I'm sorry you're hurting."

"Thanks. I love you, too." He gave her a sweet kiss and then buried his face in the curve of her neck, breathing in her familiar scent and clinging to the love of his life for another minute. "Be careful out there with my wife. She's my whole world."

"I will." She reached up to caress his face. "Be careful in here with my husband. He's everything to me, and the best person I've ever known."

He kissed her once more.

"I'm so, so sorry about Juan."

"Thank you. I am, too. His potential was endless. Whatever happened to him and for whatever reason, I promise you he didn't deserve it."

"That's often the case with murder."

A knock on the door had them stepping back from each other.

"Come in."

Nick's chief of staff, Terry O'Connor, walked into the room. "I'm sorry to disturb you, Mr. President, but you're needed in the Situation Room."

Ugh, Sam thought. *What now?*

"Thank you, Terry. I'll be right there."

"I heard about Juan, sir. I'm very sorry for the loss of such an outstanding young man."

"I am, too."

Terry nodded and left the room, closing the door.

Nick leaned his forehead on Sam's. "I've got to go figure out what fresh hell is brewing in the Situation Room."

"I know."

"I guess this'll be a late one for you."

"I'll try to get home at a decent hour. Call me if you need me? No matter what. Call me."

"I will. Thanks for coming to tell me yourself."

"I'd never have let you hear that news from someone else if I could help it."

"Means a lot that you have my back."

"Always."

"Never had that before I had you."

"Now you're stuck with me, and I want you to hear me when I tell you that if it turns out to be related to the Joint Chiefs, Juan knew he was taking a huge risk passing that info on to you. He'd probably tell you he'd do it again, because that's who *he* was."

"Yeah, he probably would say that. He was a proud American and naval officer."

"Hold on to that when the despair threatens to drag you under, okay?"

"Yeah, I will. Thanks for the reminder."

"You got it." She kissed him. "Now get to the Situation Room before you're marked tardy."

He gave a small smile. "They can't start without me."

CHAPTER THREE

Nick walked her to the foyer where they would part company.

Sam was about to head out the door when the vice president, Gretchen Henderson, approached them, wearing a sharp-looking red suit with sky-high heels that put her endless legs on full display. Sam suspected that was intentional on her part—she'd be one to play up her best features.

"Nice to see you, Sam."

"You as well," Sam said with a coolness only Nick would notice.

"Are you heading for the Situation Room, Mr. President?"

"I am. I'll walk with you."

"Excellent."

As Gretchen brushed by her, all glossy glamour next to Sam's workaday jeans and running shoes, Sam wanted to call out for the rest of this day and stick around to protect what was hers, even if he didn't need protecting.

Nick blew Sam a kiss as he took off with Gretchen, moving quickly toward whatever new crisis awaited his attention.

If there was one thing in her life Sam was certain of, it was that she never needed to worry about him and other women.

But any time she laid eyes on Gretchen Henderson, every Spidey sense she had went on full alert. Gretchen had never said or done anything to make Sam distrust her. It was just a feeling, and she'd learned to trust those instincts.

Knowing Nick would start an international incident before he'd ever do anything to endanger their marriage, Sam walked toward the exit confident in him and them, but with another reminder to keep an eye on the VP.

When she was in the back seat of the Secret Service SUV, Sam called Freddie. "Where are we?"

"Back at HQ, and Agent Truver from NCIS is here. I told her Gonzo is in charge of the Rodriguez investigation, but she wants to see you and only you. I told her you'd be back shortly, and she's waiting in your office."

"I'll be there in ten."

"I'll let her know."

"What's she like?"

"Seems nice enough, but she didn't have much to say to us. Said she'd wait for you."

"Anything else popping?"

"We're running Juan's financials and have requested warrants for his phone and apartment."

"Do we have the phone?"

"We have a phone that was recovered with the body. Archie is waiting on the warrant to get started. How did Nick take it?"

"Hard, even if he'd begun to expect it wasn't going to end well. I was with him when he called Juan's mother to tell her that her only child has been murdered."

"Ugh, I can't even."

"It was as horrible as you can imagine. He's wrecked over this. We've got to get him and Juan's mother some answers as quickly as possible."

"I hear you. We're on it."

"Be there soon."

Sam slapped the phone closed and stared out the window

at the city rushing by in a palette of color, people and cars. So many cars.

"Another tough one," Vernon said.

Sam's gaze met his in the mirror. "Yeah. Nick is beside himself."

"As expected. Juan was an outstanding young officer and was thrilled to be working in close proximity to the president."

"Nick thought the world of him."

"And vice versa. I got to know Juan a little over the last year, and while he was honored to work for President Nelson, he felt a true affinity for President Cappuano. He once told me that he appreciated how humble and normal your husband is despite the office he holds."

Sam smiled. "That's a wonderful summary of him. I'm worried about him, though. He's convinced Juan's murder is tied to the situation with the Joint Chiefs, which leads right back to him and his presidency."

"Juan wouldn't want him to blame himself for other people's actions."

"I said nearly that very thing to him just now."

"Keep reminding him of that over these next days and weeks. It'll help him to hear it."

"I hope so."

While Vernon dodged the endless traffic congestion, Sam stared out the window and watched the city she'd called home all her life go by in a bustle of activity. Her earliest memories included Saturday morning doughnut runs with her dad, followed by a couple of hours at HQ while he caught up on paperwork from the week before.

Her mother hadn't liked him taking her there, but she'd loved it from the start. He'd said she asked at least a million questions per week, and he'd answered every one of them with more patience than she would've had for a kid who never shut up. Her interest in police work had been sparked by those Saturday mornings with him.

Sam hadn't thought about that in a long time, and the memory brought back warm thoughts of her late father. She missed him so much all the time, but especially at times like this when he'd have words of wisdom about how to help Nick through this difficult situation.

While Nick hadn't known Juan for long, the close bond they'd formed had led Juan to take a huge risk on Nick's behalf. That kind of loyalty had become a precious commodity to Nick as he'd tried to determine whom he could trust among the officials he'd inherited from the Nelson administration. So far, the secretary of State, the Joint Chiefs of Staff and the AG had been forced to resign for unethical—and illegal—behavior.

In all her many years living adjacent to the national seat of power, she hadn't given the running of the federal government much thought until she'd had a front-row seat to Nick's work, first in the Senate, then as vice president and now as president. She'd decided she'd been better off not knowing so much. The things he dealt with on an average day boggled her mind, but somehow, he handled it with aplomb, class and grace that she greatly admired.

God knew she couldn't do it.

The thought of her as president made her laugh.

"What's so funny?" Vernon asked.

"I was thinking it's a good thing Nick is the president and not me."

"I think that's a good thing for all of us." Vernon's eyes glimmered with amusement as he looked at her in the mirror.

Quigley cracked up.

"You have been spending too much time with Freddie Cruz."

"He's taught me well," Vernon said. "What brought on these deep thoughts about you being the president?"

"I can't believe what he has to deal with on any given day. It can be anything from a bridge collapse in Minnesota to a fire in California to an avalanche in the mountains to violent protests in Chicago to a pipeline running through indigenous land to railway workers threatening to strike. It goes on and on and on without letting up. Every issue is as important as the one before, and every decision is filled with consequences bigger than anything any of us have ever faced. I worry about his head exploding or something equally awful happening to him when the stress gets to be too much."

"He's young and healthy, smart as a whip and surrounded by the best-possible advisers helping him manage it all."

"I know, but I still worry it'll be too much for him and that I won't see it coming."

"You'll see it. No one is more tuned in to him than you are."

"I hope so."

"You are, Sam. If he were buckling under the pressure, you'd see it. This situation with Juan is horrible, and it'll break his heart, but he'll be okay."

"Thank you for the reassurance."

"Any time."

"Vernon is right," Quigley said. "You two are hashtag couple goals."

"What does that even mean?"

The two of them lost it laughing.

"Come on, Sam," Vernon said. "Even I know what that means, and I'm a T. rex."

"Well, maybe you can explain it to me, T. rex."

"Yes, Vernon, let's hear you explain it," Quigley said with a smirk.

"It's when a couple are so awesome that everyone wants to be like them, and they're given the couple goals hashtag on social media."

"Oh, I see," Sam said. "I think."

"How'd I do, Quigs?"

"It was an admirable effort, sir."

"Is he patronizing me?" Vernon asked Sam, glancing at the mirror.

"I fear he might be, in the same way my grasshopper would've patronized me."

"We've lost control of all our grasshoppers."

Sam laughed. "I lost control of mine years ago." And she felt better, she realized, after talking it out with Vernon—and Quigley. "Thank you for the conversation, the levity, the friendship. I appreciate it very much, and Agent Quigley, I hope you'll respect the sanctity of the SUV."

"Of course, ma'am. What happens in the SUV stays in the SUV."

"Always a pleasure," Vernon said with a warm smile.

"You have to protect me. You don't have to be my friend, too."

"It's so much nicer to be friends if we're spending our days together, right?"

"Very much so."

They pulled up to the morgue entrance a few minutes later.

"Thanks for the lift."

"Have a good rest of the day at the office, dear."

Sam chuckled as Vernon held the door for her. "We'll be heading out again shortly."

"We're always ready."

"Thanks."

Sam popped into the morgue to check in with Lindsey, who had Juan's body on the table, thankfully covered by a sheet at the moment. "What've you got, Doc?"

"He suffered severe injuries throughout his body. I'm trying to narrow down which one killed him."

Sam fought through a tsunami of emotions as she listened to Lindsey. The person who'd killed Juan had made sure he suffered. Until his killer or killers were brought to justice, the Metro PD worked for Juan—and his family.

"I'll get you something as soon as I have it."

"Thanks, Linds. His mother and family will be eager for answers."

"I'm on it. Uh, I hate to mention this when we're both busy with far more important things..."

"Mention what?"

"Bridesmaid dress fittings."

It took everything Sam had not to grimace. She forced a smile for her close friend. "Of course. When do you need me?"

"Thursday around six p.m. at Shelby's studio in Georgetown?"

"I'll be there."

"Should I remind you again closer to the day?"

"That would be very wise."

Lindsey smiled. "Will do. I know this is the silliest, stupidest thing ever, but—"

Sam put a hand on her friend's arm. "There's absolutely nothing stupid or silly about your wedding to the love of your life. It's my great honor to be one of your bridesmaids."

"Thank you. I've got my fitting this afternoon. I'm unreasonably excited to see my dress again."

"Enjoy every minute of this, Linds. It's a once-in-a-lifetime thing."

"I'm trying. Thanks for being part of it."

"My pleasure. I'll see you in a bit."

"I'll be here."

After Lindsey's recent health scare, Sam would never again take her friend's presence down the hall for granted. Following the sudden, traumatic losses of her dad and brother-in-law in recent months, Sam had gotten painful reminders of how precious life was and how critical it was to be there for the ones you loved.

She loved Lindsey.

Did she love being a bridesmaid? Absolutely not, but since there was nothing she wouldn't do for Lindsey, she'd happily wear whatever dress her friend chose and stand by her side for the biggest day of her life and Terry's. They were a great couple who deserved all the good things. Nick was excited to be his chief of staff's best man.

Their wedding was something to look forward to this summer, but before they could get to fun in the sun, they had to figure out who'd killed Juan—and why.

Sam stepped into her pit, which was a beehive of activity with Detective Cameron Green standing over Gonzo's shoulder as he pointed to the screen of Gonzo's computer. Freddie stood off to the side, listening to Cam and Gonzo while Matt O'Brien sipped a soda in his cubicle.

"What goes on, gentlemen?"

They startled at the sound of her voice, which gave her great pleasure. Not that she'd ever tell them that.

Freddie used his chin to gesture to her office. "NCIS is getting impatient."

Sam rolled her eyes. Playing nice with others would never come naturally to her.

Sam stepped into her office, where a cool blonde with a chin-length bob and a don't-fuck-with-me expression awaited her. Sam usually appreciated that quality in other female law enforcement officers. She hoped this one would be one to admire and not revile. "Hi there, I'm Lieutenant Sam Holland."

The other woman stood to shake her hand. "Carleen Truver, special agent-in-charge, NCIS."

Sam appreciated that there was no first lady fawning or none of the other nonsense that had become routine since Nick became president. Truver had earned hard-to-come-by points with Sam right out of the gate.

Sam went around the desk to sit. "Sorry to keep you waiting. As you can imagine, Lieutenant Commander Rodriguez's murder has struck close to home for my husband and me."

"I understand. I need you to come with me."

For a second, Sam was too stunned to respond. Most people

didn't give her orders. She gave *them* orders. She tipped her head. "To where?"

"I can't disclose that. It's vital that you accompany me immediately."

"I have a Secret Service detail. I can't go anywhere without them."

"Then I'll go with you. Either way, we need to leave right away."

"I'm afraid you're going to have to give me more information before I go anywhere."

"I'm unable to do that." She stared at Sam with sharp blue eyes and never blinked or wavered. "I'm here to help you get answers for Lieutenant Commander Rodriguez's family and friends. In order to do that, I need you to come with me."

"Could I see some identification?"

Truver produced a badge that she handed across the desk.

Sam studied it carefully and determined it to be legit. She returned it to the other woman.

"This is highly unusual."

"I understand."

"What am I supposed to tell my team?"

"That you're going into the field with me."

"They'll want to know why."

Her left eyebrow rose ever so slightly. "They question your authority?"

"No, we work collaboratively, so they'll wonder why I'm leaving right when we've begun a new investigation."

"You're leaving for that investigation." Truver checked her watch. "We need to get going."

"Can you tell me where we're going?"

"Once we're on the way."

Everything about this was bizarre, but Sam's innate sense of curiosity won out. She stood, grabbed her coat and radio and went to the pit to tell Freddie she'd be back in a bit.

"Where're you going?"

"Into the field with Agent Truver."

Freddie eyed the agent, who'd followed Sam out of the office, suspiciously.

"I'll check in shortly."

"Please do."

Sam had taught him to be as wary about strange circumstances as she was. "This way." She led Truver toward the morgue. "What're we telling my detail?"

"We'll give them a destination and then ask for privacy."

When he saw Sam come through the morgue door, Vernon jumped out of the SUV to open the back door for her. "This is NCIS Special Agent-in-Charge Carleen Truver."

"May I see your badge, please?" Vernon asked her.

Truver handed it over.

Vernon studied it with far more intense scrutiny than Sam had given it before he returned it to the agent. "Where to?"

"Navy Yard DC," Truver said.

Vernon nodded and waited for them to get settled in the back seat before he closed the door.

"May we have privacy, please?" Truver asked.

Vernon shot Sam a look in the mirror.

She nodded.

He put up the divider to seal them off from the front seat.

"What's this about?"

"What you're about to learn is top secret and in the highest interest of national security."

"Does my husband know?"

"He doesn't and won't be told until the time is right."

"What does that mean?"

"I'm not at liberty to say anything further until we're inside a secure facility."

This had already become the craziest workday she'd ever had, and Sam suspected she hadn't seen anything yet.

CHAPTER FOUR

As they approached the Naval Yard, Truver made a phone call. "I'm with Lieutenant Holland, arriving at the gate in her Secret Service vehicle."

They were waved through security and driven a short distance to a nondescript white brick building.

"Right this way," Truver said.

"You want me to come?" Vernon asked Sam.

"I don't think so."

"This is weird."

"You're telling me." Because it was a secure federal facility, Vernon let her go in without him, but she could tell he didn't want to. They'd come to a fragile accord when she was on the job, and she appreciated him rolling with her even when he didn't agree with the plan. A less flexible lead agent would've made her life a living hell. She was thankful every day for him and the faith he had in her as a fellow law enforcement officer.

They went up two flights of stairs and down a long hallway that reminded Sam of every other federal building she'd ever been in. It was like the designers of these places had set out to make the workplaces as drab as they possibly could. Not that her cinderblock HQ was much better. It'd probably been designed by the same architect.

Truver stopped at the last door on the right side, keyed in a code and went into a generic office. It had four walls nothing on them, a desk, a chair and a closed laptop. Otherwise, there wasn't a single other item in the room.

"You've stepped into an ongoing investigation, Lieutenant. I need your assurances that everything you learn here will be kept in the strictest confidence. It's vital that you not tell anyone—not your colleagues or your husband or anyone else —what you're told here."

"How is it possible that I've stepped into an ongoing investigation when Lieutenant Commander Rodriguez's body was found only this morning?"

"Before I say anything else, I need your assurances that what I tell you will remain confidential. People's lives are on the line, including those of my team members. As a commander yourself, I'm sure you can appreciate my concern for them."

Sam had never been more confused or more curious as to what in the hell was going on. But she was also torn. How could she promise to keep stuff that might be material to the investigation from her team or from Nick if it involved Juan's murder?

"Do I have your word?"

From what Sam could tell, the woman seemed to barely blink.

"How am I supposed to give you my word before I know what I'm agreeing to?"

"If you want to know what's happening, you need to give me your word."

"You can see why that's preposterous, right?"

"I can."

Again with the steely stare.

"You're asking me to keep things from the people I'm closest to, including my husband."

"I assume he'd want you to protect national security. Am I correct?"

"Well, yes, but—"

"There're no buts when it comes to matters as sensitive as this is."

"Why did you bring me here if I'm not allowed to do anything with the information you give me?"

"Because I need your help."

Sam stared her down, but the woman never blinked. She was even better at the steely stare than Sam was, and that was one of Sam's best features. She'd seen a lot of crazy things on this job, but this—whatever this was—could turn out to be the craziest thing yet. What choice did she have but to cooperate with the agent who seemed to be holding all the cards at the moment?

"I give you my word that I won't disclose to anyone what I learn here."

"Including your team, your husband and his team?"

Sam swallowed hard, hoping that was a promise she could keep while not at all confident she could keep a big secret from Nick, national security or not. "Including them."

"Very well." Truver knocked on a door on the far side of the office.

The door opened, and Truver gestured for Sam to follow her into another basic room where Juan Rodriguez sat on a sofa under the watchful eyes of another NCIS agent.

Sam did a double take.

What the actual fuck?

Her head whipped toward Truver. "What is happening?"

"Juan is not dead."

"I see that." And holy hell, how would she ever keep that information from Nick? *Fuck!* "Do you mind telling me who's in my morgue?"

"I'm not at liberty to disclose that information at this time."

"You expect me to keep this a secret from my team, my husband and everyone else?"

"That's exactly what you just promised to do. We're in the midst of a very sensitive situation, and it's necessary to our investigation to make the rest of the world think that Lieutenant Commander Rodriguez has been murdered."

Sam zeroed in on Juan, who wore a gray T-shirt with basketball shorts. "I just stood next to my heartbroken husband in the Oval Office while he told your distraught mother and family that you're dead."

Juan's expression conveyed his agony at hearing that. "I'm so sorry, ma'am. I hate this as much as you do."

"Your mother wailed when she heard you were dead."

His dark eyes filled with tears. "I hope that when she learns the full story, she'll understand."

Sam doubted his mother would ever get over this. She wouldn't if someone told her that one of her kids let someone tell her they were dead when they weren't.

"Please have a seat, and we'll tell you what we need from you, Lieutenant," Truver said.

Sam glanced at the other agent, a middle-aged man with gray hair and a matching beard.

He was staring at her as if he'd never seen the first lady before, or something like that, which instantly irritated her considering the circumstances.

Sam sat on the other end of Juan's sofa.

"For the last four months, we've been coordinating with Lieutenant Commander Rodriguez and several other active-duty and civilian personnel who worked in close contact with the former Joint Chiefs of Staff after it came to our attention that they were having covert meetings and other conversations about the new commander in chief and whether he was qualified to oversee the military."

Sam's stomach began to ache the way it had before she gave up diet soda. The thought of keeping a secret like this from

Nick was beyond her ability to comprehend. How would she do that? She settled in to get the information she'd need to figure out what to do next.

Agent Truver laid out a winding, twisting story that spanned months and involved some of the highest-ranking officers in the U.S. military, who'd apparently revolted the minute they heard Nelson was dead and that Nick Cappuano would take the oath of office as the nation's next president. From what Truver said, they weren't even subtle about their objections to the young, inexperienced vice president suddenly becoming the commander in chief.

The sick feeling in Sam's stomach intensified with every word Truver said. She had names, dates, details of the plot to rid themselves and the nation of a man they felt was woefully unprepared to command the world's mightiest military.

"Needless to say," Truver continued, "there was widespread shock throughout the Pentagon and the military apparatus as word began to filter out, past the offices of the Joint Chiefs."

"So it was a badly kept secret, then?" Sam asked.

"Yes," Truver said. "And it had reached the rank and file, who were becoming confused about who was in charge if the Joint Chiefs were in open revolt."

"That's how I heard about it," Juan said. "A friend who knew someone who worked for the Navy chief heard there was talk of open revolt at the highest levels."

"What did you do after you heard that?" Sam asked him.

"I did some digging to confirm it wasn't just a rumor, and then I went directly to the president. As someone who works closely with him on a regular basis, I have no doubt about his fitness to hold the office, about his superior intelligence and grasp of the issues. Not to mention his decency and the kindness he has shown a low-ranking person on his team. As a naval officer who took an oath to support and defend the Constitution and to follow the orders of the president of the Unites States as well as the officers appointed over me, I was appalled by what I'd heard. It never occurred to me for one second *not* to tell him."

Juan earned a permanent place in Sam's heart with that statement.

"He appreciated what you did very much and worried about your safety afterward."

"Believe me, I was concerned about that, too. After I left the Oval Office, I went directly to NCIS to report what I knew and what I'd done with the info. I've been working with them ever since."

"We've had him under protection as he went about his normal routine," Truver said. "Which is how we determined he was being followed."

"By whom?" Sam asked.

"We were able to tie the tail back to Admiral Goldstein, the former chief of Naval Operations and member of the Joint Chiefs of Staff."

"How did you tie it to him?"

"We followed the money."

Sam nodded. That's what she would've done, too.

"Goldstein didn't try to hide the fact that he was paying a private investigator to follow Juan. Our team waylaid the investigator, brought him in and got him to confess to who'd hired him and why."

"And what did he say?" Sam hated feeling like she was pulling the story out of Truver.

"That they wanted to be aware of Juan's whereabouts and his routine."

"Did that lead you to believe he was in danger?"

"It did. Why else would they care where he was or what he was doing when they already knew he'd outed them to POTUS? We believe they were looking to possibly eliminate anyone who could testify against them. There's no paper trail. There were only rumors, nothing in writing."

"But rumors would count as hearsay and be inadmissible in court," Sam said. "How would that be valuable?"

"When added to the other evidence we've collected, the testimony would be allowed."

"What other evidence?"

"In addition to financials, we've got phone records and other surveillance that tied Goldstein, former Chairman Wilson and two others to the plot to overthrow the Cappuano administration."

Those words—*the plot to overthrow the Cappuano administration*—gave Sam chills from head to toe. She still couldn't believe such a thing had nearly happened. Without Juan tipping off Nick, who knew if the coup would've been thwarted in time?

"After careful consideration, the decision was made to make the former chiefs think that Juan had been murdered. We think it might be an opportunity to gather further intelligence as they communicate about the 'murder.' So far, we're seeing them turn on each other as they accuse one another of making everything worse, as one of them said."

"Where did you get a body?" Sam asked.

"A young officer who resembled Juan was killed in a motorcycle accident in Norfolk three days ago. With the permission of his family, after we explained there were national security concerns, we secured the body for this purpose. He'll be turned over to his family as soon as possible."

"Did you put him in the clothing donation bin?"

"I'm not at liberty to discuss that."

Which meant *yes* in Sam's mind. "What am I supposed to tell my medical examiner?"

"She'll have no reason to question the identity of her subject, as he was carrying Juan's identification."

"What about security-clearance fingerprints?"

"Those wouldn't be available to her through AFIS or IAFIS. We saw to that."

"I'd like to know why the president isn't being told about this," Sam said, pretending for a moment that said president wasn't her husband and the love of her life.

"We believe it's in his best interest to be able to say later that he knew nothing about the inner workings of the investigation," Truver said. "As he was the subject of the former chiefs' plot, it makes sense to keep him removed from the larger investigation for the time being so there can be no conflict-of-interest claims when our case goes to court."

"What exactly will you be charging in court?"

"Treason and conspiracy to commit murder."

Sam's brain spun as she tried to wrap her mind around what she was being told. "What do you want from me?"

"We need you and your team to investigate Juan's murder the way you would any other case."

"Why would I do that? And how am I supposed to conduct a homicide investigation for someone who isn't dead?"

"We'll leave that to your discretion to conduct the case the way you normally would. I imagine you'd pull Juan's financials, interview his roommate, talk to his family, his coworkers, friends, softball teammates."

"You're asking me to further traumatize people by interviewing them about a death that didn't happen."

"I'm asking you to help us make the case against the people who tried to overthrow your husband's administration."

"Which makes everything about this a conflict of interest for me."

"I fully expected you to name a member of your team as the lead detective on this case, which you've already done."

"You've thought of everything."

"We've tried to. As you can imagine, this is a very complex situation with numerous elements occurring simultaneously."

"You're also asking me to lie to my closest colleagues and my bosses, not to mention my husband."

Truver never blinked as she returned Sam's steely stare. "Yes, I am."

"I don't know if I can do that. I suck at lying. I always have. Nick will immediately know that something is up, and he'll be relentless in asking me what's wrong."

"Certainly, with everything you deal with in your line of work, you can think of something that would account for your distress, not to mention your sorrow over the murder of Juan."

This woman was too much like her, Sam decided, which was a scary thought. "I'd like to speak to Juan alone."

Truver glanced at Juan, who nodded. Then she stood. "I'll be right outside when you're finished."

After she stepped out, Sam turned to Juan. "Your mother is devastated. How can you put her through this?"

"I'm sick over that, but when NCIS presented this plan to me, they were emphatic that it had to look real, or it would be for nothing. That included my family going through the motions of mourning."

"What will happen when your mother wants to see her son before she buries him?"

"She'll be told that my injuries were so gruesome that it wouldn't be in her best interest to see me."

"And who will formally identify the body as yours?"

"You will. You knew me personally and can attest that the body is mine."

"You're asking me to lie to the people I'm closest to."

"I'm sorry. I understand it's a huge ask, and I hate it as much as you do. The thought of my mother thinking I'm dead... All I can say is I hope my miraculous recovery will make her so happy that she won't hate me forever for doing this to her."

"She's apt to. If one of my kids did this to me, I'm not sure I'd ever forgive them."

"If it was done for the good of the country, you would. They tried to *take down the president*, Mrs. Cappuano. They subverted the Constitution and the will of President Nelson when he chose President Cappuano to be his vice president and the Senate when they confirmed him. We can't let them get away with that." The young man's voice quivered with emotion and outrage. "Everything I stand for as a naval officer and an American is at risk in this situation."

His patriotism and courage were impressive, but the thought of lying to Freddie, Gonzo, Lindsey, Captain Malone and Chief Farnsworth—not to mention Nick—was unfathomable to her.

"You could always fall ill after you identify my body and step aside from the investigation," Juan said.

"The president is traveling this week. I could join him, I suppose." That was preferable to perpetrating a lie that would span days, if not weeks, as they made a case against a would-be killer. Thankfully, she'd never been in a situation even remotely close to this one.

"Please know that it's because of your dual roles as first lady and the Homicide commander that you were brought in on this. If you weren't the first lady, they would've let the case play out organically. I insisted you be briefed, or I wouldn't go along with it."

"Why?"

"I have tremendous respect for your husband and for you. He's been so good to me, so encouraging and supportive. He certainly doesn't need to invest his time and attention in me the way he has."

"That's who he is."

"Yes, and this is who I am, Mrs. Cappuano. I insisted you be told the investigation was a sham, or I wouldn't be part of it."

"I have no idea how to proceed from here."

"You're being asked to play a role in a drama far bigger than you or your team. I know it goes against everything you believe in, but if I didn't strongly feel it was in the best interest of the country, I'd never have done this to my mother." He leaned in, intense and focused. "They tried to *overthrow* the United States government, ma'am. Surely we can't allow that to stand."

"No, we can't."

"Can we count on your support?"

Sam held his gaze as a million thoughts spiraled through her mind in the span of seconds. If she agreed to this, how many different ways would it ruin her life? Too many to count. In the end, her decision came down to one consideration, one man, the one person on earth she'd do anything for, even help to perpetrate a massive deception.

They'd tried to dispose of him.

Of Nick.

Of the best man she'd ever known, other than her father.

Juan was right. That couldn't stand.

"Yes, you can count on me."

CHAPTER FIVE

S am emerged from the NCIS office where Juan would remain in hiding for as long as it took to make the case against the disgraced chiefs. She could only hope that would happen quickly, because it'd take everything she had to play her part as requested. Dishonesty didn't sit well with her. She was a straight shooter, raised by one. Skip Holland had hammered into his three girls the importance of always telling the truth.

Not that she didn't love a good white lie every now and then, but to be part of something like this? Never. She shuddered, imagining the many ways this could destroy relationships she'd spent years cultivating and valued above all else.

Vernon held the door for her. "Everything okay?"

"Yeah." She didn't look at him as she lied to his face. She'd have to get used to the despair that accompanied each lie.

"Back to HQ?"

"Yes, please."

How would she bear to keep this from Nick when he was suffering so profoundly over the loss of Juan?

As she stared out the window, the SUV whipped through

light Sunday traffic. She went over it all again, picking over the details shared by Truver and Juan and preparing herself to be involved in a fake homicide investigation.

She considered recusing herself and taking the West Coast trip with Nick. She'd been dreading his absence, the way she always did when she knew he'd be away. But how would she spend that kind of time with him and not come clean?

Juan had said they were protecting Nick by not telling him.

Would he see it that way when he found out she'd kept this from him?

Because he'd find out eventually.

Her stomach ached fiercely at the thought of disappointing him in any way, but not as fiercely as her heart ached. She hated this for her—and for him. She despised the way people wanted to tear him down after he'd stepped up for his country when Vice President Gooding had become ill and then again when President Nelson died.

If only they saw the sacrifice, the time, the commitment, the energy he put into the job. If only they knew how much he *cared*. From the first minute she'd learned of the Joint Chiefs' betrayal, she'd seethed with outrage on his behalf. She would never forget his hurt, bewildered expression as he explained the situation to her while trying to make sense of it himself.

It defied belief and would never make sense.

Juan had said military officers took an oath of office to support the commander in chief, even when they didn't share the same politics, religion or beliefs. That the highest ranking among them would attempt to kneecap their commander in chief had sent shock reverberating through the ranks as well as official Washington, the country as a whole and around the world.

Their actions had rattled the foundation under Nick's presidency, giving his many political enemies enormous fuel for their illegitimate fire.

Sam had grown to loathe that word: *illegitimate*.

She and Nick hadn't ever discussed it in detail, but she was painfully aware that the word stung him for more reasons than just the implication that he didn't belong in the Oval Office. He'd been illegitimate from the start, born to teenage parents who hadn't wanted him and raised by a grandmother who hadn't wanted him either.

I want him.

She wiped away tears that suddenly filled her eyes.

I want him more than I've ever wanted anything or anyone. I honestly think I'd kill for him if it came to that. I hope it never does... But lie to him? I don't know if I can do that.

Tears slid down her cheeks that she wiped away as quickly as they appeared. She couldn't show up to HQ looking like she'd been crying. The last thing she needed was more reason for people there to talk about her. She'd given them more than enough cause by keeping her job while being the first lady and a mother, too.

The push-pull of competing demands never let up, but today's events gave all-new meaning to the truly unique situation she found herself in.

Had she not been the president's wife, Juan never would've insisted she be told that she was investigating the murder of someone who was still alive and well.

"When we get back to HQ, I'm going to brief the media on what we know so far," she said to Vernon.

"Just give us a heads-up when you're heading out."

"I will."

"Are you sure you're okay, Sam?" Vernon asked with the fatherly concern he regularly directed her way.

Normally, she lapped that up like the fatherless girl she'd become last October. Today, she didn't like knowing that he could easily tell that something was very wrong. "Yeah, all good. Just reeling about Juan, like everyone is."

"I'm sick over it," Vernon said. "He did the right thing—the patriotic thing—and paid for it with his life."

"I know."

Her chest burned like it would with heartburn, but this felt an awful lot like shame. The lying had already begun. What she wouldn't give for ten minutes with Skip Holland right now.

His words of wisdom were always with her, and one thing he'd said to her at the beginning of her career echoed loudly now: *If you know something that your superior officers should know, tell them. Don't sit on any bombs, or they'll explode under you.*

Or something to that effect.

The pain in her chest intensified as they pulled into the parking lot at HQ, the two sides of the argument waging war inside of her. National security depends on your discretion. It's in his best interest that he not know about the inner workings of an investigation involving the plot to overthrow his administration. *Don't sit on any bombs, or they'll explode under you.*

In all the months since he'd passed, Skip's voice had never been louder than it was right now.

Outside the morgue entrance, Vernon held the car door for her. "Anything I can do?"

"No, but thanks for asking."

"Let me know if your answer changes."

"I will."

It was as if he knew, Sam thought, as she went inside, stopping at the morgue where Lindsey was performing the autopsy on the body that was not Juan Rodriguez.

"Just the woman I wanted to see. His prints aren't in the system, so I need a formal identification from someone who knew him. Then I can wrap this up."

"What was the cause of death?"

"Blunt force trauma. Every rib was broken, along with several vertebrae in his back and neck. He also suffered a severe head injury, which was the ultimate cause of death. Whatever happened to him was violent." Lindsey looked up at

Sam, who'd hung back, wishing she were anywhere but in the middle of this mess. "Can you take a look?"

"Sure." Sam swallowed the bile stinging her throat and stepped up for a closer look at the man who she could now see was not Juan Rodriguez, as another piece of the puzzle clicked into place. They'd rushed to waylay her before she could take a closer look at him under the bright lights of the morgue and say, *No, that's not him after all. Despite the name tag on his chest and the identification in his wallet when he was found, that's not Juan Rodriguez.*

"Sam?"

A part of her died inside as she said, "That's Lieutenant Commander Juan Rodriguez."

"Are you okay?"

She shook her head. "Nick loved him. He's distraught."

"I'm so sorry. Are you handing the investigation off to Gonzo or Cruz?"

"To Gonzo."

"What can I do for you?"

"Just the report when you have it." The rest she'd have to handle herself. Somehow.

"Coming right up. Are you sure you're all right?"

Sam forced a smile for her friend. "All good. Just another day in paradise."

"Ain't that the truth?"

Sam turned to leave, but stopped to turn back. "How'd your dress fitting go?"

Lindsey offered a sheepish grin, probably feeling silly over being so excited about things such as wedding gowns with Juan's body lying on the table in front of them. "It was good. I definitely picked the right one for me. I love it so much."

"I'm glad you're happy with it. I wish I could be there with you for all of it."

"Please don't apologize. You're the busiest person any of us knows."

"You're important to me." Sam hoped her words would offset the lie she'd told to one of her closest friends and colleagues, even if it was for national security purposes. "I hope you know that."

"Of course I do. Likewise." Lindsey gave her a curious look, as if she could plainly see that Sam was not all right. "If you need a friend, you know where I am."

"Thank you. That means the world to me."

Sam left the morgue, aware that she was leaving Lindsey with more questions than answers. That was the downside of being known by the people she interacted with every day. If something was off, she couldn't hide it from them. If there was any upside to the last couple of hours, the numb feeling she'd had after closing the Forrester case had been replaced with dread.

She made her way to the pit, where her team was hard at work on their latest case.

Probably sensing her arrival, Gonzo looked up. "What was that about with NCIS?"

"Just some backstory on the case with the Joint Chiefs. Nothing we can use."

"You were gone a long time for backstory."

"Trust me, I was hurrying them along. You know how it goes when the Feds are involved."

"True. We're ready to brief you on what we have so far."

Don't sit on any bombs, or they'll explode under you.

I hear you, Skippy. I hear you loud and clear.

"I have one thing I need to do, and then I'm all yours."

"Sounds good."

She went into her office, dropped off the lightweight jacket she wore in the early spring when it wasn't quite cold and wasn't quite warm. Then she walked toward the lobby and the chief of police's suite of offices where his faithful admin, Helen, guarded the gates, even late on a Sunday. Today had been an all-hands-on-deck kind of day with the culmination of the Forrester case. How was it possible that case would become the least of her concerns today? "Is he available?"

"He has a meeting in ten minutes, but you can go ahead."

"Thanks, Helen."

"You're welcome, Lieutenant."

Sam knocked on the door to the office of Chief Joseph Farnsworth, also known as Uncle Joe to Sam and her sisters.

"Enter."

She stepped inside and closed the door as the war continued unabated inside her—was this the right thing to do? If only she knew for certain.

He greeted her with a smile, full of the affection he'd had for her all her life. "How's it going with the deceased Navy officer? Is NCIS hassling you?"

Rarely did she not know what to do in any given situation. Her dad used to say that intuition on the job was something people had, or they didn't. It couldn't be gained along the way. He said it was either in the DNA or not and that she had it in spades. She could only hope it would serve her well in this unprecedented situation.

"I need to tell you something that you can't tell another living soul. I need you to swear on your life—and Marti's—that you'll keep this confidential." She hoped that by invoking the name of his beloved wife, the gravity of the situation would become immediately clear to him.

It did. He stood, came around the desk and stopped a foot from her. "What is it?"

"Do you swear?"

"Whatever it is, Lieutenant, you'd better start talking before I lose my patience."

"It's a big deal."

"I've already figured that out for myself."

"I'm only here because my dad once told me that any time something happened that you should know, I should never hesitate to come directly to you. But in this case, that's not as simple as it might seem."

He crossed his arms, tilted his head and studied her in a way he hadn't in quite some time. "It's obvious to me that you're upset. I hope you know by now that you can trust me with anything, and I'll always have your back."

She choked back the huge lump that suddenly appeared in her throat.

"You know that, right?"

Sam nodded. "Did you hear that NCIS came and asked me to leave with them?"

"Yes, and that your detail drove you."

"To the Naval Yard. They took me into an office, where I learned that Juan Rodriguez isn't dead, but they need me to run the investigation as if he is. They told me this after getting me to swear I wouldn't tell anyone else, including my husband or anyone here, that the body in our morgue is that of another man who resembles him, an officer who was killed in a motorcycle accident in Norfolk. I was told it was a matter of utmost importance to national security that I keep the information confidential and investigate Juan's 'murder' the way I normally would."

The chief's expression never changed.

"So far, I've lied directly to Lindsey when I ID'd the man in the morgue as Juan."

"Why?"

"Sir?"

"Why're they asking this of you, and why did they tell you the truth?"

"Out of respect for me and Nick, Juan insisted that I be told the investigation is a sham, and NCIS is insisting on full discretion. I think they brought me in and briefed me mostly because I'd be able to tell the body wasn't Juan's when I got a closer look at him in the morgue. They needed me to be on board so they could continue their investigation of the disgraced Joint Chiefs, all of whom will probably be pointing fingers at the others for the killing of the man who told the president of their nefarious plot."

The chief finally blinked as he sat back against the edge of his desk. Reaching behind him, he picked up the receiver for his desk phone. "Helen, please ask Deputy Chief McBride to take my meeting with Captain Greyson."

"Yes, sir."

He put down the phone and turned back to Sam.

"I came right to you when I returned to HQ, with only a stop in the morgue to give the false ID to Lindsey."

"Coming to me was the right thing to do."

"I know. Skip told me so."

A faint smile appeared on the chief's face at the mention of his late best friend. "He was right, as always."

"He's never steered me wrong."

"Will you tell Nick, too?"

"They were adamant that he not be told so he could later deny any knowledge of the investigation strategy if or, I suppose, *when* it blows up that Juan's death was faked."

"Okay, but will you tell him anyway?"

Sam held his gaze for a long moment before she looked away. "I don't know what to do."

"Yes, you do."

Surprised by his tone, she looked up at him again. "What do you mean?"

"You can't keep this from him, Sam. He'll never forgive you, even if your intentions are pure. I read the statement the White House released that said the president is heartbroken by the senseless murder of his aide, who'd also become a friend during the months they'd worked closely together."

"Nick likes him a lot, and Juan took a huge risk to warn him of what the Joint Chiefs were planning."

"How will you look him in the eye and keep this from him?"

"I don't know! They said it was in his best interest that he *not* know."

"What do you think is in his best interest?"

"How do I know how these things work in official Washington? They're already looking for ways to get rid of him. If they find out he knew that Juan's death was faked by NCIS, would they impeach him for going along with that?"

"His party has control of Congress. He won't be impeached."

"See? I don't even know how these things work. They'll find another way to tear him apart and undermine his administration."

"They'll do that for as long as he's in office, Sam."

"Do you see why he didn't want to run?"

"I've always understood why he didn't want to run."

Sam dropped into one of his visitor chairs. "I don't know what to do."

"Yes, you do."

"What if I tell him and he ends up caught up in some massive scandal or something that he could've avoided if I'd kept my promise to NCIS?"

"He'll know how to manage the information."

"The NCIS agent, Truver, said they felt it was in his very best interest to know nothing about this. Why would she say that if it wasn't true?"

"I don't know, but think of it this way... You tell him. He has the information. No one but the two of you will know he has it."

"That's true."

"Maybe they expect you to tell him, so they won't have to. They want him to be able to say later that he wasn't in the loop on the investigation that included him and his administration."

That possibility hadn't occurred to her. "You think?"

"No clue, but if I were you, and I thank God above every day that I'm not you, I'd protect my husband. He is national security, you know?"

"You're right, as always." She glanced at him, suddenly feeling emotional. "I appreciate you talking through the personal aspect of this as well as the professional."

"I'm always here for you. You know that."

"I do, and that makes all the difference, especially since October."

"I hope you know that works both ways. If I can't have my buddy around, having his daughter in my daily life helps to fill the void a bit."

"Really?"

He smiled. "Yes, Sam. Really."

"Wow, and here I thought it was always you taking care of me."

"We're taking care of each other without the man we both loved."

"Don't make me cry. Chicks crying on the job bug me."

He laughed. "You crack me up, Holland."

"I do what I can for my people. Speaking of my people... What do I do about this bullshit investigation?"

"You go forward the way you would with anything else. Work the case. Who knows what you might uncover in the process?"

"And that's not a waste of taxpayer dollars? To investigate a murder that didn't actually happen?"

"We can easily say later, if or when it becomes an issue, that we were acting in concert with NCIS and federal authorities."

"You're good at this."

He huffed out a laugh. "I sure hope so after all these years, and PS, so are you. Coming to me with this was one hundred percent the right call. It'll stay between us and only us. Understood?"

"Yes, sir. Thank you."

"I want you to brief me—in person. No paper trails between us."

"Got it." She took a deep breath and tried to get her game face on so she could go out there and do the job. "You're sure we're doing the right thing here?"

"Not one bit sure, but I guess we'll find out. Either way, we're in it together, kid."

She stood to leave. "That makes all the difference. I'll check in later."

"Sam."

Turning back, she raised a brow.

"He'd be so, so proud."

All she could do was nod, fearing she might still lose her composure. Nothing he could've said would mean more to her, as he knew. Making her father proud was one of her top goals on—and off—the job.

With the chief on board, it became more bearable to go through the motions. Hopefully, when the others learned the truth, they wouldn't hold it against her.

As Sam was leaving the chief's office, Jeannie McBride approached from the other end of the corridor, smiling when she saw Sam. Her white uniform shirt was untucked over her pregnant belly.

"Deputy Chief McBride, how goes it?"

Jeannie put her hand on the baby bump. "Getting bigger by the day and busy doing a million things I had no idea needed to be done around here."

"We miss you in the pit."

"I miss you guys, too, but this is the right job for me now. I'm so tired at the end of the day I can barely function. I wouldn't have the stamina to chase you around."

Sam laughed. "I barely have the stamina to chase me around."

"I heard about Juan Rodriguez. I'm so sorry. I know Nick was close to him."

Sam winced to herself. "He was. It's terrible." God, the lies just rolled off her tongue. "I need to get back to it. Come visit once in a while, you hear?"

"I will. Good to see you."

"You, too, Chief."

Back in the pit, she said, "Everyone in the conference room in five."

It was time to shift this phantom investigation into high gear.

CHAPTER SIX

S am walked into the conference room, ready to rumble. "Where are we, people?"

In addition to Freddie and Gonzo, Detective Cameron Green and his partner, Detective Matt O'Brien, were in the room, as well as Gonzo's partner, Detective Neveah Charles.

Freddie stood next to the murder board they'd started for Juan, which included photos of him alive and in uniform and one from the morgue.

NCIS had done a damned good job of finding someone who looked enough like him to play this most unusual role. While Sam could see subtle differences now that she knew the truth, the others wouldn't doubt the ID, especially since she wasn't questioning it. And how had NCIS managed that? This whole thing was too bizarre for words.

"Juan Rodriguez, age thirty-two, a lieutenant commander in the United States Navy, assigned as a special attaché to the president in conjunction with the National Nuclear Security Administration, was found in a clothing donation bin on New York Avenue after an intensive multiday search," Freddie said. "He was reported missing by his roommate, also a Navy lieutenant commander, named Isaac Erickson. We were waiting for you, Lieutenant, but Isaac was going to be our first stop."

"Agreed. What else?"

"We're running financials for Juan, and Archie has his phone," O'Brien said.

"Have you requested warrants for the phone?" They needed one for the device and another for the data.

"Yes, ma'am, and included computers, tablets and any other devices belonging to him, as well as the apartment itself."

"Excellent. What else?"

"We interviewed the people at the donation site," Gonzo said, "and requested security footage from the area. Their security camera stopped working about six years ago, and they've never gotten it fixed."

How often did they hear about malfunctioning cameras? Every day.

"What do we have nearby?" Sam asked, referring to the cameras the department had situated around the city.

"Archie is checking on that." Gonzo glanced at her. "Assume the family has been notified?"

"Yes, Nick called his mother. It was horrible. He's her only child."

Gonzo grimaced. "That's awful. How's Nick?"

"He's taking it hard. He considered Juan a friend since they started working together. Juan was the one who tipped off Nick to what the Joint Chiefs were up to."

"How hard are we looking at them?" Green asked.

"Very hard, but NCIS is handling that part of the investigation. They want us looking at the possibility of no connection to his work."

Cam gave her a skeptical look. "Do you think it was random?"

"I don't know. We're just getting started, and you've heard me say before that it's not wise to jump to conclusions. We'll follow the evidence like we always do."

"But you like the Joint Chiefs angle for this?" Charles asked.

"It stands out as a potential motive. Juan telling Nick about their plot ended their careers and put them in legal jeopardy, not to mention endangering their fat pensions. These are people who've been successful all their lives and have taken a mighty fall. But what would be the point of murdering Juan after he's already told the president what he did, and they've already been disgraced?"

"That's a good question," Gonzo said. "What's the rationale for taking him out now?"

"Maybe they just wanted someone to pay for what happened to them after he told Nick," Freddie said. "Pure revenge."

"That's possible," Sam conceded, "but I still say it's an awfully big leap to go from Joint Chief to murderer."

"Don't forget the stop at treason along the way," O'Brien said.

"Noted, but we're going to work this case the way we do all the others and follow the evidence. All other theories and hypothesizing should be kept to a minimum until we know more. Am I clear?"

"Yes, ma'am," they said as one.

Sam looked to her sergeant. "Due to Nick's close professional ties to Juan, you'll be taking the lead with the paperwork and the media."

Gonzo nodded. "No problem."

"Can you do a quick briefing of what we know so far?"

"Yep."

"All right, everyone, let's get busy. Cam, get on the financials, Neveah on Juan's social media, and Matt, get me those warrants the second you have them. Let's find some threads to pull."

"What's our plan?" Freddie asked her after everyone else except Gonzo had filed out of the room.

"I want warrants for Juan's apartment and electronics

before we leave here. Put Haggerty's team on notice that they'll be executing the warrant at the apartment."

"I'll do that and get with Captain Malone to see about expediting before I do the briefing," Gonzo said.

"Hey, Tommy?"

He stopped on his way out of the room and turned back. "Yeah?"

"Thanks again for taking the lead. I'll be right there with you, but I need someone else to be the face of this one."

"I get it. No worries."

After Gonzo walked away, she looked to Freddie. "I wish I didn't have to delegate so much lately."

"It's fine. We don't mind, so don't add that to your list of worries."

"I appreciate you guys."

"We know that. We get to work with the first-lady detective every day. Everyone in our lives thinks that's wicked cool. It all comes out in the wash."

"Wicked cool, huh?"

"Yes, you are, and that rubs off on us. Don't sweat the stuff that doesn't matter."

"When did my grasshopper become a wise owl?"

He rolled his eyes. "Puleeze. I've been wise all along. How's Nick doing?"

"Not well at all. He and Juan talked sports and kept it real, which is rare in his world these days."

"I'm so sad for him, especially right after Fort Liberty."

"Me, too. No president wants to see service members die on his watch, especially when he's the motive."

"Does that mean you secretly suspect the Joint Chiefs?"

"I don't know what to think."

"Did NCIS give you any insight into what they're doing?"

"Not much." Sam wanted to tell him the truth so badly, it hurt not to. The words burned the tip of her tongue, but she couldn't say them. Not even to him, one of the few people she trusted implicitly. She hoped he and the others would understand when—not if—the truth came out about this case. More than anything, she despised the idea of disappointing them in any way, especially when they did so much to make it possible for her to hold down multiple roles.

Without them at work, she couldn't even pretend to be first lady or try to be a halfway decent mother. Lying to them went against everything she believed in, but what choice did she have? If lying to them was next to impossible, what would it be like to lie to Nick's face when she got home?

Dreadful.

"Sam?"

She realized he'd been talking to her while she spaced out. "Sorry. What did you say?"

"Will you go to Juan's funeral?"

"I suppose so. Nick will want to be there." Dear God, would they have to go through the motions of a funeral for a man who wasn't dead? Sam had no clue how to manage this situation, and that was saying something. She almost always knew what to do. But this was truly unprecedented.

Her entire body vibrated with tension that she felt from her scalp to the bottoms of her feet. The tightness in her shoulders and chest was almost painful.

Matt O'Brien came back into the room. "We've got the warrants."

Relieved to have something to do other than freak out about lying to everyone in her life, she said, "Let's get going."

JUAN LIVED in a townhome in Adams Morgan, a trendy Northwest neighborhood known for history, culture, nightlife, entertainment and the arts. If Sam had been a single girl interested in living anywhere but Capitol Hill, she would've chosen Adams Morgan. Juan's building had the standard DC red-brick façade with black shutters and brass detailing. She pushed the button next to the label that said RODRIGUEZ/ERICKSON.

A few seconds later, a voice on the intercom said, "Yes?"

"This is Lieutenant Sam Holland with the Metro PD. We'd like to speak to Lieutenant Commander Erickson, please."

After a long pause, there was a beep followed by a lock disengaging on the front door.

They stepped into a foyer with a coatrack and hooks for backpacks and other bags. Several pairs of running shoes were on the floor under the hanging bags.

"Come on up."

Sam and Freddie climbed the stairs to where a young man with light brown hair and swollen blue eyes waited for them. He wore a gray NAVY T-shirt and athletic shorts. "Are you Isaac Erickson?"

He nodded.

"I'm Lieutenant Holland. This is my partner, Detective Cruz. We're very sorry for your loss."

"Thank you. I still can't believe it."

"Could we talk for a few minutes?"

"Sure, whatever I can do." Isaac led them into an open space with more brick and industrial ducting running across the ceiling. He took a seat on a sofa where he'd obviously been hunkered down. Takeout containers littered the coffee table along with soda cans and beer bottles. "Sorry for the mess. It's been a rough week."

Sam and Freddie sat across from him in leather chairs.

"No worries," she said.

"I still can't believe Juan is dead. It's surreal. He was just here."

"When did you last see him?"

"What day is today?"

"Sunday." Was it still the same day that they'd closed Tom Forrester's murder case with a high-profile arrest? Twelve hours later, Sam was running on fumes, and her knees and elbows hurt from tackling Harlan Peckham on a city street. She'd have bruises tomorrow, if she didn't already.

"I saw him when I got home from work on Wednesday. He was on his way out as I was getting home. He said he'd see me in the morning, but when I got up, he wasn't here. I hit him up but didn't hear back. Honestly, I didn't think much of it until I got to work and found out he'd missed muster for his morning rotation at the White House. That was when I started to get worried." His gaze shifted toward them. "Juan loved working with your husband." His voice took on a gruff, emotional tone. "He fucking loved that guy." He wiped tears off his face. "Sorry for the f-bomb."

"No need to apologize. Nick loved him, too. He's devastated by Juan's death." The guilt cut deep over what Juan's loved ones were being put through for the cause of national security. Sam hoped it would be worth it in the end. The tension inside her was similar to how she'd felt being wrapped in razor wire by Stahl and threatened with fire, a memory she certainly didn't welcome.

"Anyway, work sounded the alarm that he was missing. NCIS quickly got involved and interviewed me and everyone who interacted with Juan daily and started to search for him." With his arms propped on his legs, he held his face in his hands. "The whole thing is surreal."

"How long have you known Juan?" Sam asked.

"We went to Annapolis together. Were roommates after the first year. Kind of been together ever since. Our friends tease us about being a couple, but we're not. We're just great friends who enjoy hanging out and keeping it real. Or, I guess, we *did*."

The devastation on his face nearly broke Sam wide open. She wanted to howl. She wanted to tell him the truth and swear him to secrecy, but she couldn't. They'd made her believe the greater good was at stake in this situation, and she had to believe that was true, or she'd go mad.

"Did Juan have a girlfriend?"

"He had a friend with benefits who he was hoping to turn into a girlfriend, but she was playing hard to get."

"What's her name?"

"Jillian. I think her last name is Danvers, or something like that."

"Where will we find her?"

"She works at a coffee shop down the street. That's how he met her."

"What's the name of the shop?"

"Uh, I can't remember it. I don't drink coffee. That's Juan's thing. But it's on 18th, near the post office."

"We'll find it. Has she been told of his death?"

Isaac shook his head. "I haven't pulled myself together enough to reach out to her. It was early days between the two of them, but he was excited about her."

"Was he having problems with anyone that you knew of?"

Isaac looked up at her, seeming shocked that she'd ask that. "Uh, *yeah*. Ever since the thing with the Joint Chiefs, he seemed to have trouble with everyone. I told the NCIS people this. They know he was being hassled."

"Who in particular was hassling him?"

"Might be easier to say who wasn't. They knew right away that it was him who told POTUS what they were up to."

"How did they know that?"

"White House visitor logs. They were able to show him going in when he wasn't on duty, meeting briefly with POTUS and leaving in under fifteen minutes. They put two plus two together with what happened next, and the rest unfolded from there. Suddenly, he's being contacted by top staff to the Joint Chiefs, his own chain of command is under fire for letting him go rogue, there's talk of pulling his security clearance, he feels like he's being followed everywhere he goes, he's getting odd calls at all hours from unknown numbers with people telling him to keep his mouth shut or it'll be shut permanently. So yeah, in short, he was having some trouble with people."

Sam took note of everything he'd said. "If everyone was angry with Juan, should I take that to mean that the plot to unseat the president went far beyond the Joint Chiefs themselves?" The implications of that sentence made her almost as sick as the lying did.

"We'd begun to think so. Although, the chain of command was upset because Juan went right to POTUS, skipping about fourteen layers between them, which is generally frowned upon in the military. Juan said he'd do it the same way again because the only one he was sure he could trust with the info was POTUS. He had faith in him to handle the situation appropriately. He couldn't say that about anyone else in the chain. Who knew how pervasive the plot was or who else was involved or who would kill to keep it quiet? Juan said that even knowing how intense it would get for him, he wouldn't have done anything differently."

Isaac ran his fingers through his hair, which was already standing on end, probably from him doing that over and over as he absorbed the loss of his closest friend. "I just wonder if he would've done it if he'd known he'd pay with his life." He took a deep breath and released it slowly as he seemed to come to some conclusion. "Yeah, he would've done it anyway. He was all about doing the right thing, and telling POTUS was the right thing."

"Did he tell you about it before he told POTUS?" And yes, it was weird to refer to her own husband by his acronym, but everything about her life was weird these days. That they even had acronyms...

Isaac shook his head. "He didn't tell anyone. He went straight to POTUS. He told me after the fact, though."

"How did that go?"

"He came home rattled. Like, really undone. Pacing and drinking, which he rarely did when he had to work. Took an hour of me asking what the hell was wrong with him for the whole story to come pouring out."

"What did you think when you heard it?"

"At first? I thought he was making it up until I realized how seriously undone he was. Like, hands shaking and everything. He kept telling me to stay away from the windows, as if he was afraid someone would take a shot at us."

"Why was he afraid of that if he'd already told POTUS what he knew?" Freddie asked. "What point would there be in killing him after the damage was already done?"

"I guess because he was a witness with information that could be used against them."

"Why would that matter, though?" Freddie asked. "Heads were already rolling. The case against them was being built almost immediately after Nick... er, I mean, POTUS was notified. What did one naval officer know that would make it worth adding murder to the list of charges?"

"Other than revenge for messing up their plans—and their lives—I don't know the answer to that, but I sure do wish I'd done more to protect him."

"What could you have done?" Sam asked.

"I don't know, but I could've done more than go about my life like his hadn't been turned upside down."

"Did you ever feel personally unsafe after this started?"

"Not really."

"What does that mean?" Sam asked.

"I didn't feel like anyone was out to get me personally, but there was this... I don't know how to describe it. Like an aura of tension, I guess I'd call it. I kept my wits about me when I was out and about, and I know Juan did the same."

"Is there anything else you can tell us that you think might be relevant? We tell everyone to really drill down because often it's the smallest thing that can blow the lid off an investigation."

"I've been drilling for days and not finding anything other than the gigantic Joint Chiefs elephant in the room."

Sam put her card on the table. "Call me if you think of anything else."

He picked up the card and gave it a close examination. "Is it weird?"

"What?"

"To be investigating a case tied to your husband the president?"

"Every single thing about my life is weird. Everything."

"What she said," Freddie added, making the young man smile.

"I imagine it's about to get even weirder."

You have no idea, Sam thought.

"We're going to need you to relocate while Crime Scene detectives examine your apartment. Is there somewhere else you can stay?"

"Can I stay if I'm not in their way?"

"I'm afraid not. We have a warrant for the search."

Freddie handed him the piece of paper.

"I'll call a buddy and borrow his sofa."

They waited for Isaac to pack and then called a Patrol officer to deliver him to his friend's place, after getting a key and promising to keep him informed. They had walked out onto the street when Freddie's cell phone rang.

"It's Gonzo," he said to Sam. "Hey, what's up?" After a second, he said, "Let me check with her. He says we've been called to a homicide in Crestwood. What do you want to do?"

Sam thought about it. "Go see if you can track down Juan's FWB at the coffee shop while I go to Crestwood."

"What's an FWB?"

"Friend with benefits. I forget you never had one of those. You married the first woman you f—"

He scowled. "Do not finish that sentence."

Sam gave him a shit-eating grin. "Is any part of that sentence false?"

"Go to Crestwood. You're irritating me."

"Then my work here is finished." She handed him the key

to Juan's apartment. "Come back to let in Crime Scene and then go home."

"She's all yours," Freddie said to Vernon as he stormed off toward the post office to find the coffee shop.

"Oh, glory and praise," Vernon said with a smile for Sam. "What did I do to deserve this?"

"You won the lottery."

"Where to, my prize?"

Sam stifled a laugh so as not to encourage him. "Crestwood. Jump on Beach Drive toward the park."

"I might need a little more insider info than that."

"I got you covered."

CHAPTER SEVEN

S am directed him toward the "quick" way, as if such a thing existed in her city even late on a Sunday, the most endless day ever, and sat back to text Gonzo for specifics about where she was going.

He responded with an address on Webster Street Northwest, near the National Conservatory of Arts.

What do we know?

Husband came home from being gone all day to find the wife dead in the bathroom attached to their bedroom.

Reminds me of Ginny McLeod.

Funny, I said the same thing to Cam.

Ginny McLeod had been found dead in her garage by her husband when he returned from playing golf. She'd later been tied to a massive fraud that'd been the motive for murder. They'd closed that case right before Nelson died and their lives changed forever. *Ah,* she thought, *remember that?* And they'd thought things were crazy before. Haha. They'd been naïve babies before Thanksgiving made them her bitch.

She smiled at the thought of telling Nick that, but her smile quickly faded when she recalled what she was keeping from him.

Her phone rang with a call from Malone.

"You got the word on Crestwood?"

"Headed there now."

"I'm sending Dominguez and Carlucci to meet you. Turn it over to them and go home."

"Thank you, Jesus."

"That's Jake, but you can feel free to call me Jesus."

"Haha, everyone is a comedian today."

"Me and who else?"

"Cruz, as usual, and Vernon."

He caught her eye in the mirror and smiled.

"Where are we with the Rodriguez investigation?"

"Early days. We met with the roommate, and Haggerty's team is heading over to his apartment to execute the warrant for Juan's electronics and other evidence. Cruz is trying to track down the FWB."

"The what?"

"Friend with benefits. How old are you?"

"Old enough that I haven't had one of those in thirty-three years."

"You don't need one. You've got a wife, the ultimate FWB."

"Go home, Holland. You're getting punchy."

"Yes, sir. Thanks for sending the cavalry."

"Great arrest today, Lieutenant. Archie has footage of it from one of our cameras."

"Awesome," she said dryly.

"It was indeed. Wait until you see it."

"I'm picturing a water buffalo taking down an unsuspecting ant."

"That was my thought exactly! How'd you know that?"

"I'm ending this call."

His laughter echoed through the phone as she slapped it closed. Fools. She was surrounded by them, but thank God for the gallows humor that kept her mind off the secret she was keeping from almost everyone who mattered to her.

Her phone buzzed with a text from her stepmother, Celia. *Thinking of you! Had a nice chat with the kids earlier. They said you were working all day and had arrested a bad guy. Good for you. The gals and I are having a blast in LA. Today we did Rodeo Drive and felt very fancy. We pretended to be Julia in* Pretty Woman *and generally made a scene. Next to San Fran. Miss you all!*

Sam smiled at the vision of Celia and her sisters prancing around in Beverly Hills. *Miss you, too. So glad you girls are having a blast. You deserve all the fun and good things. Glad you got to chat with the kids. They miss you, too, but everyone is doing well, and Mom is holding down the fort for you.*

Glad to hear!

When you get back, I want to talk to you about an idea I had for Ninth Street. Nothing urgent.

I've got time if you do. What are you thinking?

Ever since the home invasion incident at Avery and Shelby's, everyone is looking for safer living situations. We're going to rent our place to Gonzo and Christina. I thought yours might be good for Freddie and Elin, but only if it works for you. Not sure if you're ready to cut the cord, so feel free to say no. Of course you'll have a home with us no matter where we end up afterward.

Afterward, Sam thought. After their time in the White House ended in the far-off future.

I like the idea. Let me think about it while I'm gone. I think I might be ready to cut the cord. I don't want to live there without your dad, and I love being with you guys and the kids. Seems silly to have the house sitting there empty if someone could be using it.

And you could make some $$.

True... I'll be back to you about this. It's a great idea!

Enjoy every minute of your trip. Love you!

Love you, too! Sent some pics to Scotty.

I'll check them out when I get home. Be safe and have a blast!

Celia and her sisters were spending a month touring the West Coast before their Alaskan cruise in May.

Sam would never admit to wishing she had a smart phone

so she could see the pictures now, but if she kept the thought to herself, no one would ever know she'd had it. As the long day caught up with her, she rested her head against the back of the seat. She could never wait to get home to Nick, but tonight she was filled with apprehension about how she'd handle things with him.

Her conversation with the chief ran through her mind. Maybe they'd told her not to tell him knowing she'd never keep this from him. Was that the case? Would she be doing the right thing for him and the country by telling him what she knew? She'd give anything to know what the right thing was, but she was sure of one thing—keeping this from him wasn't an option. If she did, she feared the very foundation of their union might crack beneath them. From the beginning, he'd hated when she kept things from him, even if she was doing it to protect him. She physically shuddered at the thought of real trouble with him. She'd never be able to handle that.

The SUV coming to a stop jarred her out of her thoughts.

"This is as close as we can get," Vernon said.

"Good enough."

"I'll go with you."

She wanted to tell him that wasn't necessary, but she knew it was pointless. There was no way he'd let her go to a murder scene alone, especially since Freddie wasn't with her. A few months ago, she would've chafed at that. Now she was comforted by his presence. Funny how that happened.

"What a day, huh?" he asked as they walked toward flashing lights a block and a half away.

"Yep. Sorry to keep you so late."

"Are you kidding? This is the most fun I've ever had on this job."

She turned to him, stunned. "Really?"

"Yes, Sam, really. Security is often super boring. Rote routine. Redundancy. There's none of that on your detail."

"Well, thank you. I think."

"You're more than welcome," he said with a low chuckle.

"I bet your other subjects haven't had you out running the streets at nine o'clock on a Sunday night."

"No, they haven't."

"I'm sorry to keep you away from your family all day."

"It's fine. My wife and daughters were away for a spa weekend, whatever that is, and weren't due home until tonight anyway."

"A spa weekend," Sam said with a sigh. "How do I get me one of them?"

"Ma'am... You're the first lady of the United States of America and a badass detective. If you want a spa weekend, have a spa weekend."

"I can just, like... do that?"

"I can't tell if you're being serious or not."

"I guess it never occurred to me that I could."

"When we get back in the car," he said, "I'm gonna tell you something important."

"Thank you for the warning."

Patrol Officer Clare lifted the yellow tape for Sam and Vernon, who ducked under it. "Good to see you, LT." He'd matured a bit since Sam had last seen him and now looked more like a man than a boy.

"You as well. What've we got?"

"White woman, age forty-six, found dead in the bathroom off the main bedroom on the second floor."

Sam glanced at the house, which was a large white colonial with black shutters. She'd known a few kids who lived up here when she was in high school and had envied them their leafy streets and grassy yards. There'd been no yards on Ninth Street. As much as she loved Capitol Hill, she could picture them living in an area like this after Nick left office. The kids would want a yard after living at the White House, with all its grass and open space.

She followed Officer Clare into the house, aware of Vernon

following her but giving her the space to work that she needed. He remained in the foyer while she and Clare went upstairs. "Have you called the ME?"

"Yes, ma'am. Dr. Tomlinson is on the way with his team, as is Crime Scene."

Haggerty and his people would be up all night with two new cases demanding their attention. "Excellent. Thank you. Where's the husband?"

"My partner is with him on the back porch."

He led her into the main bedroom, which was huge and lovely, with one of those cathedral-ceiling thingies. They cut through a massive closet with a fancy chandelier, custom built-ins and an island in the center with more drawers and cubbies. A robe was tossed over the counter on the island. They entered an opulent bathroom, where a naked woman lay on the floor in a pool of blood under her head. A bath towel was in a pile next to her, and slippers were on the floor, as if they'd been waiting for her to come out of the shower. Patrol had left her uncovered so Sam and her team could see how she'd been found.

As Sam approached her, she was saddened for a woman she'd never met and would never know. "What's her name?"

"Elaine Myerson. Mother of two teens. She works for a lobby firm."

"What's their issue?"

"The husband said oil."

"Do people kill over oil?"

"Um, I'm not sure, ma'am."

Sam missed Freddie. He would've known the question was rhetorical. She squatted next to the body for a closer look at the bloody injury to the back of her head that'd ended her life. "This feels personal. Overtaken while coming out of the shower. Vulnerable."

"Yes, I suppose so."

"Any sign of a murder weapon?"

"No, ma'am. We did a quick look through the house but

didn't see anything. And there was no trail of blood or anything like that."

"If it's in the house, the CSU detectives will find it. What about cameras?"

"We saw some positioned around the house and outside, but we'll need the homeowner to provide access. We haven't asked for that yet. We wanted to wait for you."

"I'll talk to the husband about that. Good job, Officer Clare. Thank you."

"Thank you, ma'am."

Detectives Carlucci and Dominguez arrived as Sam stood to her full height and swayed ever so slightly as exhaustion overtook her. She blinked them into focus, Carlucci tall and blonde, Dominguez petite and dark-haired. "Glad to see you, ladies. I'm ready to hand off to you."

"Thirteen hours later, you must be toast," Carlucci said.

"That's a good word for what I am." Sam caught them up on what she knew so far. "I'd like to talk to the husband while one of you takes pictures. The other can come with me."

"I'll do the pics," Gigi said.

"How're you doing?" Sam asked her.

"All good, LT. Thanks for asking."

"Glad to have you back to full steam."

"Glad to be full of steam."

Sam was thankful that most of the trouble caused by Cameron Green's ex-fiancée was now in the past for both her detectives and that they could get back to enjoying their new relationship. They still faced a wrongful death lawsuit from the ex's family, but no one expected that to go anywhere.

"Cover her up after you take the pics."

"Will do."

Sam went downstairs with Carlucci and Clare, who showed them through the spacious home to the back porch, where Officer Youncy watched over Mr. Myerson.

The young woman nodded to Sam and Dani as they came

out on the porch. "Frank Myerson, this is Lieutenant Holland and Detective Carlucci. They'd like to speak to you if you're able."

"Thank you," Sam said to Youncy.

She sat across from the man on furniture right out of the Frontgate catalog that used to make her wonder who could afford the stuff they sold.

"We're sorry to intrude at such a difficult time," she said, "but as you can imagine, the first few hours are critical in a homicide investigation."

He raised his head and wiped tears from his face. "Homicide?"

"Yes, sir." He had salt-and-pepper hair and wore a light blue dress shirt with dark trousers. "We believe your wife was murdered."

"That isn't possible. Who would kill her? Everyone loves her."

Sam wished she had a buck for every time she heard someone say that about a murder victim. She could retire early. "Was she having trouble with anyone in her life?"

"No, of course not."

"You say that like it's impossible for people to have conflicts with others."

"Elaine wasn't like that. She's a gentle, caring soul. When I say everyone loves her, I mean it." His eyes filled. "What am I supposed to do without her? She's my whole world."

"We're very sorry for your loss. Where were you today?"

"I was at a day-long staff retreat in Bethesda."

"Can someone confirm that for us?"

He glanced up at her, seeming surprised. "You certainly don't suspect me. I didn't hurt her. I adored her."

"I understand, but if you can help us establish your alibi, we can move on to other suspects."

"You can contact my assistant. She can confirm my whereabouts today."

Sam wrote down the name and phone number he gave her. "Was she with you?"

"Yes, she was there. The retreat began at eight, ended at five, followed by dinner. I got home about thirty minutes ago, and... I found her." He broke down again. "How can this be happening?"

"I know it's a lot to process all at once. We noticed you have cameras positioned around the house and grounds. Is there a way to gain access to the recordings?"

"There're no recordings. Our daughters are adamant about not being recorded in their own home."

Shit, Sam thought. *That would've been too simple.* "What was your wife up to today?"

"She went out to do some errands. She texted around three to say she was home."

"How did she come and go to the house?"

"Through the garage. She had an opener in her car."

Sam made a note of the detail.

"Officer Clare mentioned you have teenagers."

He nodded. "Two girls, fifteen and seventeen."

"Where were they today?"

"I... I don't know. Elaine manages them."

"It's getting kind of late. Where are they?"

"I'm not sure."

"Have you contacted them since you found their mother dead?"

"No, I haven't. I... I don't know what to say to them."

"We can call them for you if you'd like," Dani said.

"You can?" He visibly brightened and then crumpled again as he shook his head. "I can't let a stranger tell them this. I'll do it."

"Do you have somewhere you can stay tonight?" Sam asked.

"What? We can't stay here?"

"No, sir, this is a crime scene, and our detectives will need full access."

"I, uh… I have a sister in Bethesda. We can stay with her."

"We're going to need you to call the girls and ask them to come home right away, but don't tell them why."

He gave her a confused look.

"We'd like to be here when they're told."

She could tell he still didn't understand that they wanted to witness the children's reactions to hearing their mother had been murdered.

"Who else has access to the house?"

"No one. Just the four of us."

"No cleaning people or anyone who works part time for you?"

"Elaine likes to do the cleaning herself. She says it relaxes her."

"So no one else has the code to the door?"

"No."

"Would the girls give it to their friends?"

"They were told not to."

"I'll let you call your daughters."

"We can take it from here, LT," Carlucci said quietly while Mr. Myerson took out his phone to make the calls to his children.

"Are you sure?"

"All good. Go home."

"I'm going to leave you in Detective Carlucci's capable hands, sir."

He held his phone to his ear. "Elaine… My Elaine admired you very much."

"That's nice to hear. I'm sorry again for your loss."

"Thank you."

Sam walked back into the house, taking the weight of his grief and sadness with her. She knew what it was like to confront the sudden death of a loved one and wouldn't wish it on anyone.

Vernon stood inside the front door, waiting for her. "Let's go home, Vernon."

CHAPTER EIGHT

S am fell asleep on the ride home, coming to when the SUV glided to a stop outside the door at the White House. Home sweet home. *Hahaha, right.*

Every so often, she yearned for the simplicity of their lives on Ninth Street. Even after Nick had become vice president, not much had changed for them except for the presence of Secret Service. Even that had been an easy adjustment compared to the move to the White House.

Who was she kidding? Their lives had never been simple. It'd been one crazy thing after another in the two and a half years they'd been together. And just when they thought they'd seen everything, life threw something else at them, such as a dead guy who wasn't dead after all.

"There was something you were going to tell me when we got back in the car," she said to Vernon when he held the door for her.

"I wanted to remind you that life is short, and no one wishes they'd spent more time at work in their final moments. Make sure you're taking care of yourself in the midst of the craziness."

"That's good advice. Thank you."

"Have the spa day, you hear me?"

"Yes, sir."

"What time tomorrow?"

"Let's leave at seven forty-five."

"We're sleeping in."

Sam laughed. "Thanks for everything today."

"Always a pleasure."

Sam trudged through the door to home, her knees and elbows aching from the tackle earlier in the day.

"Evening, Mrs. Cappuano," George said as he held the door and took her coat.

"Hi there, George. Is the president in the residence?"

"No, ma'am. He's in the Situation Room."

"For how long?"

"About an hour now."

"Thank you." Sam hoped that whatever had taken Nick there wouldn't keep him all night, because she desperately needed to see him. She trudged up the red-carpeted stairs to home and was greeted by an excited puppy who wanted her undivided attention. Laughing, she scooped Skippy into her arms and gave her a good snuggle as she walked toward Scotty's open bedroom door.

"Found something that belongs to you."

"She's decided she has to approve anyone who comes up those stairs. It's easier to just let her than try to keep her contained."

"A woman needs to run free, doesn't she?" Sam asked the dog, who replied with a swift lick across her face that Sam never saw coming until it was already over. She put Skippy on Scotty's bed and wiped the dog slobber off her cheek. "You aren't, by any chance, doing homework at almost ten o'clock on a Sunday night, are you?"

"Of course not. I'm just getting a jump on the week."

The statement was so preposterous that she busted out laughing. "You're so full of it."

His shit-eating grin made her whole day. "Can't get nothing by you, Mama."

Her heart soared when he called her that. "That's my job. Sorry I was gone all day."

"You made a *dope* arrest."

She sat at the foot of the bed and was attacked by Skippy's tongue again. "You heard about that, huh?"

"Duh, it's all over the interwebs."

She winced. "Did they make me sound like Rambo or something?"

"Rambo is super dope, and so are you."

"I hear there's video of it."

"I want to see that."

"I need to approve it before anyone sees it."

His brown eyes glittered with delight. "When that gets out, you're gonna be even more famous."

"Oh joy. Just what I want." She handed Skippy back to him. "Get control of your woman."

"People say that to Dad, too."

"Hey!"

His laughter was the purest, most joyful sound in the whole world. More than anything, she loved that he was so comfortable with them that he'd ruthlessly tease her and never think a thing of it, which was exactly how she wanted it.

She bent to kiss his cheek and was pleased when he didn't recoil like a typical fourteen-year-old would. There was nothing typical about her son. "I love you, even when you're being mean to me."

"Love you, too."

"Let me see the pics Celia sent."

He pulled out his phone and called up the photos for her. "The ladies say they are taking California by storm."

"Looks that way," Sam said as she scrolled through photos of the sisters from Rodeo Drive and Beverly Hills. She handed the phone back to him. "You got any info on what took Dad to the Situation Room?"

"Something about Iraq."

"Ugh, not them again."

"If it's not them, it's the North Koreans, Iranians or Russians."

"Don't forget our old pals in China."

He laughed. "Glad it's not my job to deal with them."

"I'm glad it's not mine either. Don't stay up too late."

"I won't. Hey, Mom?"

Would it ever become routine to answer to that name? She sure hoped not. She wanted it to always be the greatest thrill of her life. "What's up?"

"Are you okay? You looked kinda sad when you first came in."

"It's been one hell of a day, but I'm okay. Thanks for asking."

"Get some sleep. My mom says that helps everything."

"Your mom is very wise."

"And humble."

She walked away, laughing. He was such a gift and had been from the minute he first came into their lives. Nick had spent thirty minutes with him as a Senate candidate and had immediately wanted more time with him. She kept waiting for Scotty to become a surly teenager, but she had reason to believe he wouldn't rebel the way so many teens did. Unlike many other kids who were raised in traditional families, he was thankful to have parents and a family. He would never take that blessing for granted—and neither would they.

In her and Nick's room, she turned on the shower and winced when the hot water washed over raw elbows and knees. Thankfully, they were only scraped and bruised, not cut. After the shower, she dabbed ointment on the scrapes and covered them with bandages. She changed into pajamas and then dried her hair.

Only when her stomach growled, loudly, did she realize she

hadn't eaten in hours. The last freaking thing she felt like doing was eating, but if she had any prayer of sleeping, she needed something. She picked up the phone and ordered a grilled cheese and tomato soup, the ultimate comfort food.

"Coming right up, Mrs. Cappuano."

"Thank you so much. Sorry for the late order."

"No problem at all, ma'am."

The White House butlers were amazing and always willing to get them whatever they wanted or needed. She feared they'd be spoiled completely rotten by the time they moved out. While she waited for dinner, she went to check in on Aubrey and Alden, who were sound asleep and wrapped up in each other. She ran light fingers over downy blond hair and soft cheeks. "Love you to the moon and back," she whispered as she kissed them both, sad for the day she'd missed with them.

On days like today, she seriously thought about leaving the department to become a full-time mother and first lady. What would it be like to no longer have to worry about chasing murderers and dealing with nonstop bullshit? It would probably feel pretty damned good.

Today had been a shit show from the get-go. First, she'd been stuck inside the comms vehicle while the rest of her team executed the operation she'd put together to capture Harlan Peckham. If their target had spotted her in the group outside the church where they'd used Federal Judge Corrinne Sawyer to lure him, he would've made them right away, so she'd had to be tucked away with Vernon while the rest of her team put themselves in harm's way.

That would never sit right with her and had her doubting every decision she'd made since Nick became president. Was she putting the people she cared most about on the job in danger every time she showed up to work a shift?

She'd taken down Harlan Peckham single-handedly when she'd spotted him walking down a city street after he'd failed to show at the church. In the end, they'd arrested the man who'd killed Tom Forrester and shot Avery, but she wouldn't soon forget the impotent feeling of being sidelined while her team handled the dangerous part.

Melding her high-profile personal life with her high-profile professional life had made perfect sense to her until she'd realized that choice would take her off the front lines on days like today—while the people who reported to her risked their lives.

LeRoy Chastain, one of Sam's favorite butlers, delivered her meal a few minutes later.

"Thank you so much, LeRoy."

"Always a pleasure, ma'am. You're all over the news tonight. Congratulations on the arrest."

"Thank you. I think."

He laughed as he set the tray on the coffee table for her. "I tossed in a couple of the cookies you like so much."

"You're the devil, but the good kind."

His chuckle was full of joy for a job he'd told her before he loved. "Can I get you anything else?"

"This is absolutely perfect. Please thank the kitchen for me."

"I'll do that, ma'am. You have a nice evening."

"You, too."

Sam's spirits lifted considerably when she heard Nick greeting LeRoy in the hallway. The two men laughed at whatever Nick had said. They would miss these people when they moved out, and she had a feeling they would be missed, too. Gideon Lawson, the chief usher, had told her the entire staff was in love with their family—and vice versa.

"Is that my husband, the leader of the free world, returning from battle?"

He offered her a small grin as he took a seat next to her on the sofa and leaned in to kiss her.

"Want some grilled cheese?"

"Just a bite."

She held half the sandwich while he took his bite.

"God, that's good. Why's it so much better here?"

"Because we don't have to make it ourselves?"

"That's possible. One more bite."

"Take this half. I'm happy with the other half."

He took his half, and they ate in peaceful silence.

"Everything okay with the Iraqis?"

"Define 'okay.'"

"Okay for now?"

"Yes, for now. But there's considerable unrest in the world tonight, which I've been fully briefed on at bedtime."

"Awesome." His insomnia was bad enough without the literal weight of the world on his shoulders. "Anything I can do?"

"This helps. Sitting here eating grilled cheese with you helps. Just having you here with me after a day like this helps."

"I wish I was here more. Thirteen hours today. It's ridiculous."

"That's rare."

"Still, it's a Sunday with my family that I'll never get back."

"It was for a good cause. I heard from several people tonight that there's tremendous relief at knowing Tom Forrester's killer has been arrested. People were on edge after he was murdered." He got up and went to pour himself a glass of the good bourbon that Graham O'Connor had bought for him and returned to sit next to her. "Any news about Juan's case?"

"Yeah, a little." *Tell him, Sam. Just tell him.* "Could I ask you something rhetorical?"

"Sure."

"If you had to choose between national security and our relationship, what would you do?"

He stared at her for a hot second. "How would that ever be a choice?"

"Answer the question."

"There is nothing, and I do mean *nothing*, that I value more than our relationship, and you know that. But would I risk the other three hundred and fifty million people in my care to save us? God, I hope I never have to make a call like that."

"I do."

"What do you mean?"

"Something was presented to me today as a matter of national security, something I was specifically asked to keep from you. Something that I think you should know and that I do not want to keep from you."

He put the glass on the coffee table and turned to face her. "Tell me."

"The people who asked me to keep it from you said it could cause you big trouble later if it comes out that you knew about it."

"Tell me anyway."

"Are you sure?"

"Yeah, I am."

"Juan isn't dead."

His face went slack with shock as he gasped. "*What?*"

In as few words as possible, Sam conveyed the series of events that had led NCIS to reveal Juan to her, alive and well.

"I told his mother…"

"Juan is in agony over that and the other people close to him who'll suffer over him, but he was very clear that a much larger investigation hinges on certain people thinking he's dead and out of the picture."

"What the hell, Sam? His mother has asked me to speak at his funeral next week." After a beat, he said, "NCIS told you they specifically didn't want me to know about this?"

"They did. They said it's in your best interest not to know so you can say later that you didn't. And if that turns out to be true, the only person on earth who knows you know is me— and maybe Uncle Joe."

"Why does he know?"

"Because there was no way I could oversee a fake

investigation into a fake murder without his awareness and approval. He's the one who said I needed to tell you."

"I can't fucking believe this."

"I've been in a state of disbelief for hours. I wanted to tell you the second I knew, but I needed to wait until we were in person."

"You did the right thing telling me and waiting until it was in person."

"I hate this so much."

"I'm so glad to hear he's alive, but his poor mother."

"They said it had to be believable."

"What the fuck is going on that they brought you into this but not me?"

"They only brought me in because of my dual roles. Juan insisted I be told the investigation was a fraud. Joe said he thinks NCIS wants me to tell you, that they're counting on that."

"And I'm not allowed to do a goddamned thing to find out more about this without throwing you under the bus."

"Something like that. Are they right that it might be in your best interest not to know?"

"It's better for me not to know the details so no one can later say I tried to influence the investigation into the attempted overthrow of my administration."

"Is it weird to be the chief executive of a government that has a million things happening that you'll never know about at any given time?"

"Super weird and a little unnerving. Like you don't know what you don't know, and is the unknown gonna be the thing that takes you down?"

"I understand that fear on a much smaller scale. I worry all the time about things like Stahl's madness or Ramsey taking down Joe and upending our lives."

"Because, like me, Joe is responsible for what every single person under him does, even if he has nothing to do with it."

"And people actually fight tooth and nail for your job?"

He offered a small smile. "Right? If only they knew the reality of it. No one would want it."

"They'd still want it. For some reason unknown to me—and probably to you, too—people crave power."

"I heard someone say once that if they had to choose between being the most powerful person on earth and never having sex again, they'd choose the power."

"What would you choose?" she asked with a grin.

He leaned in and kissed her. "Luckily, I get to have both."

Sexiest answer ever. "Let's go to bed. This day has been endless."

Glancing at his watch, he said, "I hate to tell you that it's almost tomorrow."

"Stop. I can't."

CHAPTER NINE

W hen they were settled in bed, facing each other, arms and legs intertwined, Nick released a deep sigh. "I'm so fucking relieved to hear Juan isn't dead."

Sam ran her hand down his bare back and over his equally bare backside, loving his smooth skin and the muscular contours of his body. "I was, too, for your sake."

"So how do you conduct a fake homicide investigation?"

"Carefully. We were asked to go through the motions, hoping to uncover information that'll assist NCIS in their effort."

"Did they say who they're targeting?"

"They believe Goldstein was the ringleader."

Nick's face lost all expression. "Damn. He was the one who was nicest to me while plotting to stab me in the back. Where'd they get the body?"

"Another military member who closely resembled Juan was killed in a motorcycle accident. The family has been notified and told the body will be turned over to them following an autopsy."

"Wouldn't there be fingerprints and stuff?"

"NCIS took care of that, and I gave an ID for Juan. It made me sick to lie to Lindsey and the others."

"I'm sorry. It's my fault you're in this position."

"It's not your fault."

"It is, Sam. Without me in the presidency, Juan would've had no reason to warn me about anything, nor would he have been in any danger. Thus you wouldn't be asked to lie to your closest colleagues and friends."

"It's hot when you use words like 'nor' and 'thus.'"

"Oh my God, did you hear anything I said?"

"I heard everything you said and focused on the hot parts."

"Samantha, I'm being serious."

"I know, and it's hot as fuck."

"My job has put you in a terrible spot at yours, and you want to make jokes?"

"Isn't that better than making myself sick over the lies I'm being forced to tell people I love?"

"Yeah," he said with a sigh, "I guess it is. But I'm still sorry about all this."

"Hopefully, they'll forgive me when the truth comes out."

"What if they don't?"

"I can't think about that right now. I just can't."

He pulled her closer, pressed his lips to her neck. "Sorry."

"Quit apologizing to me. It's annoying."

She felt his lips curve as he continued to kiss her neck before he shifted to hover above her.

"I regret putting you in this position. Is that better?"

Raising her hips to press against his erection, she said, "This is my favorite position of all the positions. You know that."

Oh, she loved that gorgeous smile of his, the way it lit up his lovely hazel eyes and relieved some of the burden that weighed on him so heavily these days. She loved that she alone could do that for him. "So are you going to follow through, or is this all tease and no action?"

"You must be exhausted after the day you put in."

She was tapped out, her elbows and knees hurt, and she craved sleep, but not as much as she craved him. "I am, but now you've got me all... interested." She rubbed against him suggestively. "It'd be a shame to let that go to waste."

"Indeed it would." His forehead landed on hers as he took a deep breath.

Sam ran her fingers through his thick, dark hair. "Are you okay?"

"Today's been a lot for me. I can't imagine what it was like for you."

"I'm okay if you are."

He pulled back to help her out of her T-shirt and then worked her pj's pants down her legs, going for maximum impact as he dragged his fingertips over her sensitive skin. When she was down to just panties, he took a long, perusing look at her, devouring her with his gaze.

"What happened to my favorite knees?"

"A few scrapes from the arrest earlier." She raised her arms to show him the bandages on her elbows.

"Ugh. Do they hurt a lot?"

"Not too bad."

"That's good," he said as he leaned forward to nuzzle her breasts.

She'd learned that it was pointless to try to hurry him along when he was set on giving her the full treatment, and since his full treatment was the best thing she'd ever experienced, she closed her eyes and settled in for the ride.

Her nipples stood up at attention, waiting for him to get to them. He didn't disappoint. He never did.

She gasped and buried a hand in his hair as he sucked her left nipple into his mouth. He ran his tongue back and forth over it. The combination had her clamoring for more. His lips on her skin set her on fire as he moved from left to right and back to do the whole thing over again.

This... This was the only thing that could wipe her mind clean of the daily stress and struggle. He alone could take her away from everything other than the two of them and what they were together.

His lips skimmed over her belly, making her shiver and squirm. "Samantha... My sweet, sexy, difficult Samantha..."

Her eyes flew open as she raised her head off the pillow. "Difficult?"

His low chuckle vibrated against her abdomen, adding to the fire building inside her. "Just making sure you're paying attention."

"I'm definitely paying attention. In fact, if you wanted to move things along—"

The swipe of his tongue over her clit shut her right up as she dropped back down to the pillow, her muscles gone liquid.

"You were saying something?"

"Forgot."

"Hmm, thought you might."

"Less talking, more—" A noise came from deep inside her that barely sounded human. "Holy *shit*."

Fingers, tongue, lips... He was the master and quickly had her biting back the urge to scream her head off, which would start an international incident, surrounded as they were by world-class security.

She ought to do something for him, but she couldn't have moved if she had to. "Nick..."

"Hmm?" Still in no apparent rush...

"*Please*."

"What can I do for you, love?"

"You know!" Only he could make her beg for release. Only he could make her want it that badly. She used to think there was something wrong with her that she couldn't quite seem to get there, but it turned out she'd been trying with the wrong men. After she found the right one, that'd never been an issue again.

"In good time."

She exhaled and then gasped when he doubled down, taking her up and over the edge so quickly, she never saw it coming until she was in the middle of it, shaking like a tree in a tornado.

Then he was pushing inside her, riding the waves of her release, taking her up again like the first time had never happened—another thing that'd been unthinkable before him.

"Hey."

She opened her eyes to find him watching over her. "Hey, yourself."

"What's up?"

Sam smiled. "You are." She ran her hands down his back to cup his ass and pull him deeper into her.

He gasped from the impact. "Way to almost finish me off, babe."

"I do what I can for my person."

As his laughter rang out, he never missed a beat, rolling them so she was on top, startling her out of her stupor to realize he'd turned the reins over to her.

She brushed the hair back from her face and then rested her hands on his chest, watching him closely as she pivoted her hips and made his eyes roll back in his head. Her aching knees made their presence known, but she ignored the pain to focus on the pleasure.

His fingers dug into her hips as he arched into her, nearly making her forget that she was in charge.

She recovered and took great pleasure in drawing out the suspense now that she was controlling the situation, even as her knees screamed from the friction of the bed against her bandages.

"Samantha..."

"Yes, Nicholas?"

"You're doing this on purpose."

"Doing what? Exactly what you did to me?"

"Yeah, only better."

"There's nothing better than you."

"I disagree."

"We can fight about that later. I've got work to do."

His laughter quickly became a groan as she picked up the pace, driving them both to explosive releases that left them panting in the aftermath.

"Holy moly," he whispered as he held her close to him.

This was her favorite part, the peaceful quiet that followed wild passion. Not that she didn't love an orgasm or two as well. The thought made her giggle.

"It's not polite to laugh when your husband is still throbbing inside you."

That only made her laugh harder.

"What is so funny?" he asked indignantly.

"I was thinking that I like this part the best, the aftermath, the cuddling, but then I thought a couple of orgasms don't suck either. That made me laugh, and then you made it worse by being prissy."

He rolled her so suddenly, she had no time to prepare before she'd landed on the bed with a large, still-aroused man on top of her. "Who you calling prissy?"

Sam laughed helplessly as he started to move again, showing her with every deep stroke that he was anything but prissy. She was as tired as she'd ever been, but what did sleep matter when your sexy, insatiable husband was gearing up for round two?

She woke in the morning to his lips on her back.

"Wake up, babe."

"Not yet."

"What time do you have to work?"

"I don't know."

"Yes, you do. Kids to get ready for school and shift change at eight, right?"

"I think."

"Samantha."

She forced her eyes to open. The bedside clock read six twenty. "Ten more minutes."

The next thing she knew, he was kissing her shoulder as the citrus scent of his cologne washed over her in a comforting cloud of home. "Your ten minutes are long up."

"Why are you being so mean to me today when I was very nice to you last night?"

He laughed. "Because I don't want you to get fired. We don't need the headlines."

"They need me too much to fire me."

"You worked a double yesterday. You could technically take the day off."

Sam turned over so she could see him, handsome and dressed for another day of world domination. "I would, but we caught a new case right as I was leaving last night."

"That your team can more than handle without you."

"They've been covering for me too much lately. I want to save that for when I really need it."

"Gonna miss you when I'm gone this week."

Just that quickly, her entire mood changed. "Where you going again?"

He rolled his eyes in pretend annoyance. "You know exactly where I'm going—three days and two nights out west."

"No."

"Yes."

She shook her head, despondent at the thought of it, as ridiculous as that was. "Don't wanna."

"You could come with me."

"I can't on such short notice."

"In fairness, I told you about this last week."

"I blocked it out."

He chuckled. "Of course you did."

"What are we doing about Juan's funeral?"

"His mother said they'll schedule it around my availability. In light of what I know now, I'll be unavailable until later next week. Do you think that'll be enough time?"

"I really hope so. I suppose you could come up with another delay if needed."

"Probably." He linked their fingers. "We have to make a solemn vow, you and me."

"I thought we already did."

"Another one."

"All right…"

"We can never, ever, *ever* tell anyone that we knew about Juan being alive. We have to be as surprised as everyone else when the truth comes out."

"I was planning to come clean with my team after the fact."

"You can't. If you do, it could take me down."

"Why do you say that?"

"Because I need to be able to deny that I knew, and no one who knows us, even a little, would ever believe you'd keep something like this from me."

"NCIS knows I know. Juan knows I know. Joe knows I know. That's a lot of people to trust with a gigantic lie."

He sighed. "Yeah, it is."

"How about if I come clean with knowing, but say I didn't tell you?"

"People who know us won't believe that."

"I could say I put national security interests ahead of my own marriage."

"People won't believe it, Sam. Even those who've never met us in person know how we are, thanks to *SNL* and all the mocking of our obviously close relationship."

"So what do we do?"

"I need to think about it, but in the meantime, I'll tell Juan's family that later next week will be my first opportunity. I just hope by then they'll know the truth."

"Why do I feel like this is going to turn into a gigantic shit storm?"

"Because it probably will, with me at the center of it."

"If I'd known exactly what I was going to have to keep from you before I went into that room and saw Juan, I would've said no way."

"I keep going back to them specifically asking you to keep it from me and Joe's theory that they were counting on you to tell me."

"You think it was intentional?"

"I do."

"Why don't you call the NCIS director in to explain it to you?"

"Wouldn't that give away the fact that you told me?"

"Or it could be something you picked up in the morning briefing that tipped you off to a bigger story."

"That's a possibility. I could hear about it from someone else. Let me see what I can do."

"I hope we can find a way to manage this. I absolutely have to come clean with my colleagues after it's over. There's no way I can let them think I lied to them for no good reason."

"Just when I think I've seen everything…"

"I know. I thought the same thing yesterday." She ran her fingers over the silk of his burgundy tie. "What's up for you today again?"

"Going to Baltimore for the thing at the boys' school." His brothers, Brock and Brayden, had invited him to their elementary school and would be interviewing him in front of the student body.

"Oh right. They must be so excited."

"Dad called yesterday to tell me they wanted new suits for the occasion and hair gel."

"Stop it." Sam laughed. "Oh my God. Please tell me it'll be recorded."

"It will."

"I can't wait to see it."

"I've got lunch with the Maryland governor and Baltimore mayor followed by a fundraising thing in Baltimore with the Maryland Democrats, so I'll be home late."

"I'm already in a pissed-off mood, and I'm not even out of bed yet."

"Should I warn Freddie?"

"You might want to."

He held out his arms to her. "Come here."

Sam sat up and fell into his warm embrace, soaking him in while she could. "I miss being able to pout like a five-year-old when I'm not getting my way."

"It'll be Friday night before you know it, and I'll be back for the weekend. We should go to Camp David for Easter."

"Do we have to?"

"I think we should. We've got a dedicated staff there waiting to welcome us back, and we need to make some new memories there."

The bucolic presidential retreat would forever be associated with the sudden, tragic death of their brother-in-law Spencer late last year. Until disaster struck, Nick had been relaxed there in a way he seldom was anymore. She would go back for his sake, even if it would be painful. "Let's do that."

"The family time away from here will be critical to maintaining my sanity."

"I know."

"I'll ask Dad if he and Stacy and the boys want to come. We'll change it up this time."

"Sounds good."

"We have the Easter Egg Roll on the South Lawn on Monday. I'll need you and the kids there for that."

"Lilia has it on my schedule, and I requested the day off."

"You're going to be okay today?"

"Yes, but I'm mad that you're going away."

"We have two more nights before I have to go, so we'll make the most of them."

"I'm still mad."

Smiling, he kissed the pout off her lips. "Have a good day, my love."

"You, too. Have fun with the boys."

"I'm sure it'll be the highlight of my time in office so far."

"Try to fully enjoy it, okay? You so rarely get to have fun anymore."

"I will. I promise." He kissed her again and went to don his suit coat. "If I get Scotty up and the twins dressed, will you do breakfast?"

"Yep, I've got it."

"Excellent. Then it's off to the daily security briefing, also known as the thing of nightmares."

"Have a blast."

"No blasts. We're hoping for no blasts anywhere."

"Ah, got it."

"Be careful with my cop. I love her more than anything."

"Be careful with my POTUS. I love him more than anything."

He blew her another kiss and was gone. She was glad he had the event with his brothers to look forward to. He loved connecting with young people and would truly enjoy that special time with his much-younger brothers.

CHAPTER TEN

S am rushed through a shower and got dressed in jeans and a top that could use ironing, but who had time for such things? She headed to the kitchen to whip up some French toast sticks for the twins and an egg sandwich for Scotty.

He was pouring coffee when she walked in.

She stopped short. "What is happening?"

"A man needs a kick of caffeine to survive the eighth grade. That's what is happening."

"A man does, huh?"

"That's right. My friends have been getting Starbucks for two years already. I promise it won't stunt my growth or whatever else you might think."

She held up her hands. "I've got no objection, but I'd recommend only one cup and none after noon if you want to sleep at night."

"Done. Excellent negotiation."

"It doesn't count as a negotiation if you're already doing the thing you know I'm going to object to before negotiations begin."

He gave her a shrewd look. "That's fair."

"Next time, we negotiate *first*, you got me?"

"Yes, Mother."

"French toast sticks for everyone," Alden yelled as he and Aubrey came running into the kitchen, wearing their adorable burgundy-and-gray plaid school uniforms.

Sam held out her arms to hug them. "How are my sweeties today?"

"Good!" Aubrey said with a fist pump that just missed connecting with Sam's jaw.

She gave a tug to the little girl's ponytail. "Nick did a good job with your hair."

"And it didn't hurt at all!"

Sam served their breakfast along with the syrup and confectioner's sugar they loved, as well as the orange slices she insisted they have so they'd get something healthy. She'd learned to tuck a hand towel over their school clothes to protect them from syrup and sugar.

Scotty sipped his coffee and scrolled through his phone as she made eggs and toast for his breakfast sandwich.

"What's going on in the world?" Sam asked him.

He gave her a look that was all Nick. It still took her breath away whenever she saw her husband in him, proving nurture was every bit as important as nature. "You really want to know?"

"Give me the highlights—or lowlights, such as they are."

"Troubles in Iraq, which we knew because Dad had to go downstairs last night."

"What are they doing now?"

"Warring factions causing concern for a wider conflict in the Middle East."

"I don't know what that means."

"It's not good."

"Ah, thank you for that succinct summary."

"What does that mean, Sam?" Alden asked. "Suc-cinct."

Sam put an egg sandwich in front of Scotty. "It means summing things up in just a few words."

"Oh, okay."

"Thanks, Mom," he said between bites, before continuing his recitation of the headlines. "There's flooding in upstate New York and talk of a labor strike in a chicken processing factory in Arkansas."

"Chickens come from factories?" Aubrey asked, wide-eyed.

"No, silly," Alden said. "They come from *eggs*."

"Wait, so if Scotty eats the egg that Sam made for him, will he have a chicken?"

Scotty and Sam tried not to laugh, but it exploded out of them anyway.

"No," Scotty said when he could speak again. "I won't have a chicken."

"Why do they need a factory, then?"

"That's a story for another time." Sam figured that telling her about chickens being slaughtered so they could be eaten wasn't the best visual to send Aubrey off to school with. "Go brush your teeth and wash the sugar off your faces."

After they took off, Sam cleared the table and loaded the dishwasher.

"Nice deflection, Mom. You know we haven't heard the last of that question."

"Probably not, but oh my God, when she asked if you would have a chicken..."

"Hilarious." He put his plate and mug in the sink and kissed Sam's cheek. "Have a good day."

"You, too. Love you."

"Love you, too."

She heard him talking to his detail, telling them he needed a minute and then he'd be ready to go.

The twins returned from brushing their teeth, and Sam loaded them up with backpacks and the lunch boxes Nick had packed for them the night before. Sometimes she could make herself believe they were just another ordinary American family going about their morning routine. That was, until

Secret Service agents came to collect the twins to deliver them to school.

Sam kissed them goodbye and waved them off, thankful for the agents who would see to their safety when she and Nick couldn't.

Glancing at the clock, she called Carlucci for an update before she and Dominguez punched out for the day.

"Hey, LT, I was just going to call you."

"How'd it go last night?"

"We waited at the Myerson home for the daughters to get home. As far as we could tell, they were shocked and devastated as well as confused about why they had to leave the house to go to stay with their aunt. We didn't get much of a chance to ask them where they'd been all day or anything like that yet."

"We'll get on that today."

"We knocked on doors up and down the street. None of the neighbors saw anything suspicious going on at the house during the day yesterday. Archie is working on getting film from cameras in the area. I printed out social media posts from both daughters and the mother, which was all pretty routine stuff. We didn't find anything for the father online. We started on the financials and have turned that over to Green to finish."

"Good work, Dani. Thank you."

"You got it. I'll check in later."

After she ended the call, Sam ate some yogurt and finished her coffee before heading downstairs to meet Vernon and Jimmy for another day in paradise, suspecting the best part of the day had already transpired with her loved ones. She couldn't wait to tell Nick about the chicken and the egg. The Littles never ceased to entertain them with their innocence and curiosity.

Speaking of Nick… Her phone lit up with a call from him. "Hey, I was just thinking about you."

"Sam."

"What's wrong?"

"Andy heard from an attorney in California that the twins' grandparents intend to file for custody."

Her heart stopped for a second, and her stomach turned. "*What?* We already took care of that."

"Apparently, they're basing their case on the fact that living with us, the kids are surrounded by Secret Service agents, and that's no way for two children who've tragically lost their parents to live."

"Oh my God. Do they have a case?"

"Andy doesn't think so, but he isn't a hundred percent sure."

"Come on. How can this be happening again?"

"I don't know, but Andy said we should take comfort in the fact that Jameson and Cleo's instructions were airtight. Elijah is their legal guardian, and it's very rare for a court to undo the wishes of the parents."

"Rare but not unprecedented?"

"He didn't say that, but it was implied, and this is certainly an unusual situation."

"Have you told Eli?"

"Not yet. You were my first call after I heard from Andy."

"I was thinking of you because they were so cute this morning, and I wanted to tell you…" Her voice caught on the huge lump in her throat.

"Try not to panic, Sam. We still have their parents' wishes on our side, and that counts for a lot."

"We could adopt them. All of them. Eli, too. If we did that, maybe then…"

"That's not a bad idea. Let me run it by Andy and see what he says. Don't forget that the twins are old enough to speak for themselves about what they want. That'll matter."

"God, I hope so. I feel like I've had the legs knocked right out from under me."

"Me, too. Tell me what happened this morning."

Sam smiled as she relayed the story about the chickens and the egg.

He laughed. "I love that, and good call about not telling them what goes on at a chicken processing factory. They'd never let us eat chicken again."

"That was my fear." Her heart contracted painfully. "We can't lose them, Nick. We just can't."

"We won't. I'll make sure of it."

She wanted so badly to believe he had the power to fix anything, but life didn't work that way, even for the president.

"Try not to worry, babe. We've got the best people on this, and I'll talk to Elijah about adoption and see what he thinks."

"Let me know."

"I will. I'm sorry to have to drop this on you with everything else you've got going on."

"I'm glad Andy is on it. He doesn't fuck around."

"No, he doesn't. I have to run to a meeting, but I'll keep you posted. Love you."

"Love you, too."

Sam felt hollow inside as she tucked the BlackBerry into her pocket.

"Everything okay?" Vernon asked.

"The twins' grandparents are making noise about custody again."

"Oh damn. No way."

"It's unbearable."

"Did I hear you say something about adoption?"

"I suggested to Nick that we should consider adopting all three of them and putting an end to this madness."

"That's a great idea. Will Elijah go for it?"

"I really hope so."

She couldn't bear to think of a world without Aubrey and Alden in their daily lives.

. . .

THE CALL to Eli was as difficult for Nick as the one to Sam had been.

"How can they do this? The will is airtight."

Nick heard panic in every word the young man said. "Yes, it is, and Andy says that'll matter more than just about anything."

"But you're worried. I can hear it in your voice."

"They have a point about the kids living with Secret Service, security concerns, high profiles..."

"They're living with people who love them! That should matter more than anything else."

"You and I agree on that, but who knows what the courts will say?"

Nick feared getting a judge who thought he was an illegitimate president and who might stick it to him, but he'd never say that out loud, even to Sam or Eli. They were upset enough.

"Sam had an interesting thought."

"What's that?"

"What if we adopted all three of you?"

"Can you adopt a legal adult?"

"I don't see why not. Would you be down for that?"

"We'd keep the Armstrong last name?"

"Whatever you want."

"That'd be important to me."

"Totally understood."

"What does Andy think?" Eli asked.

"I haven't asked him yet. I wanted to talk to you about it first."

"I'd be for it, if it would put an end to these people trying to take the twins from us."

"It would certainly do that, and not for nothing, it would make us a legal family. I like the idea of that."

"I do, too, since we're already a family."

"We love you all, Eli, and we're going to do whatever it takes to keep our family together. Try not to worry too much. Your parents' wishes will be heavily weighted, like they were before."

"Since they've barely checked on the kids in months, this makes me wonder if Cleo's family is having financial trouble and they want to get their hands on the kids' money." Jameson Armstrong had been worth billions, which his three children had inherited.

"I'll mention that possibility to Andy. He'll put someone on it. I'll be back to you as soon as I hear anything. In the meantime, try not to worry too much."

"Not sure how I'll think about anything else."

"I know. Hang in there. More to come."

After he ended that call, Nick asked Julie to get Andy on the line for him.

"Hey," he said to his longtime friend and lawyer. "I spoke to Sam and Eli, and we have an idea. What if Sam and I were to adopt all three of them?"

"You could certainly take those steps. I'm not sure if it would shut down this latest volley by the mother's family, though. You might still have to go through the motions of a hearing and whatnot."

"How can they do this when Elijah is their legal guardian?"

"They're claiming extraordinary circumstances, and the presidency certainly qualifies as extraordinary."

"Worst thing I ever did was become the VP."

"Don't look at it that way."

"How should I look at a decision that upended my life and the lives of my family and put a level of scrutiny on us that gives these people a case for custody?"

"It's a long-shot case. Remember that."

"All we need is one judge with an ax to grind against the president or his wife, and we've lost our kids."

"A lot of other things would have to happen for that to occur, so don't go there yet. Let me look into the adoption angle and see what we can do."

"Hurry, Andy. We need to get this locked and loaded before they can take those kids from us. It would ruin us."

"I understand. I'm on it."

"While you're at it, have someone look into the family's financial situation. Eli suspects they're more interested in the kids' money than they are in them."

"Will do. I'll be back to you soon."

Terry came into the Oval Office as Nick was concluding the call with Andy. The news about the twins' grandparents had sent his morning careening off the rails. "We're due to head to Baltimore, Mr. President."

"I'm ready."

"Is everything okay?"

"Nope. I'll tell you about it in the car."

Nick's lead agent, John Brantley Jr., led the way to the West Wing foyer and to The Beast outside. Once ensconced in the back seat of the presidential limousine with Terry, Nick updated his chief of staff and friend on what was happening with the twins' grandparents.

"Oh, jeez. I thought you'd seen the last of them."

"Me, too, but they're suing this time using the special circumstances of me being president to make a case that the kids would be better off with them. Eli suspects it's got more to do with the kids' money than with wanting them."

"Of course it does. Does Andy have someone looking into that angle?"

"Yeah, he's on it. Sam suggested we adopt the three of them to put an end to this once and for all."

"That's a great idea. What did Elijah say?"

"He's for it if they can keep Armstrong as their last name."

"They could also hyphenate."

"I guess."

"Are you okay?"

"It's exhausting, all this shit happening simply because of

the office I hold. If I'd had any idea it would be this crazy, I never would've become vice president."

"Lindsey and I were talking about Juan last night and everything that's happened since you took over for Nelson. She made a great point about the difference between internal conflict and external. You have some control over the internal stuff, but not the external. Going all the way back to Raskin and the bad decisions he made in Iran—that was on him, not you. The Fort Liberty shooting was on the shooter, not you. What the Joint Chiefs did and what happened to Juan is not on you."

"I get that, but it's all happened *because* of me holding this office."

"Sure, but other people's actions are no reflection on you."

"Aren't they, though? A soldier shoots up his colleagues because he'd rather do that than serve under me as his commander in chief. Take me out of the picture, and those people are alive today. Juan is alive today."

He experienced a twinge of guilt at keeping the news about Juan from Terry, but for now, discretion was important. That whole situation was beyond fucked up, and he dreaded the fallout that would occur when the truth came out. It would be more bad publicity, especially if the twins' grandparents went public with their efforts to gain custody. And why wouldn't they appeal to the public's sympathy for the poor grandparents denied access to their orphaned grandchildren?

"I wish there was something I could say to relieve you of this burden of responsibility for other people's actions, but I know how hard it is for you."

"I'll survive. Don't worry."

"The DNC is circling, wanting to hear you're running for reelection."

Nick laughed. "No fucking way. I'm three years and out. Make that two and a half now. Can't go by fast enough for me."

"Nick…"

"Terry. It's not happening."

"They'll be very disappointed."

"They'll survive."

Nick watched the world go by as they traveled north on the Baltimore-Washington Parkway, trying to shed the shit mood he was in so he could give his brothers a day they'd never forget. Brock and Brayden were more than thirty years younger than him, so they'd never be brothers in the traditional sense of the word, but Nick loved them and wanted to be there for them as they grew into men. As the younger brothers of the president, people would be interested in them, always watching them. He intended to do everything he could to make sure they succeeded in this world, despite the added scrutiny that came from being his brothers.

CHAPTER ELEVEN

The motorcade pulled up to the colorful façade of Cecil Elementary School on Cecil Avenue. The K-5 school had more than three hundred students, and it seemed most of them were outside waiting to greet him with WELCOME PRESIDENT CAPPUANO signs and balloons. The Secret Service had been there weeks ago to scout the location. Every person attending, even the children, had been fully vetted.

When he spotted his dark-haired brothers, wearing navy blue suits and matching ties, their hair slicked into submission, his bad mood immediately lifted. The rest of the kids wore yellow polo shirts with a logo on them with blue pants or skirts.

Smiling, he emerged from the back of the limo and received hugs from Brock and Brayden. "You guys look like future presidents."

"We do?" Brayden asked, his little face wild with excitement.

"Definitely."

While Nick's detail cleared a path through the crowd, his brothers took his hands and led him into their school. He spotted his dad and Stacy off to the side and smiled at them as they waved. Being the president sucked much of the time, but this was fun, and he intended to fully enjoy whatever they had planned for him.

He shook hands with the principal and met the mayor and several of the city's school committee members, all of whom told him how honored they were to have him visit.

The boys led him on a tour of the school, pointing out their second-grade classrooms as well as the cafeteria and library before they ended up in the gym, where a stage had been erected at the far end and covered in presidential bunting.

Nick recognized members of the White House Press Corps mixed in with local TV reporters standing next to cameras in the back of the room. Maybe the good publicity from this event would offset some of the Joint Chiefs madness.

"Do you like it?" Brock asked of the setup.

"It's awesome. Did you guys decorate the stage?"

"With some help from the teachers, Mom and Dad. We bought the… What's it called again, Brayden?"

"*Bunting*." Brayden giggled. "He can never remember that word."

Brock shrugged sheepishly. "We had to buy it online because it's only available in stores for the Fourth of July."

"We have to wait here," Brayden said. "The band is going to play a song for you."

Sure enough, the school band launched into a choppy version of "Hail to the Chief."

"That's your song!" Brock said.

"Sure is," Nick said, charmed by the effort put forth by the band.

"Let's go," Brayden said as each of them took him by the hand again to lead him down the center aisle between rows of chairs to the stage, where three chairs had been positioned. The student body, teachers, staff and guests clapped as they entered.

"You sit in the middle, Nick," Brock said.

"We're supposed to call him *Mr. President*," Brayden reminded his twin.

"Oh, sorry."

"You should call me Nick. Always."

Brock gave Brayden a smug smile.

The three of them were handed microphones by a man wearing a yellow school polo shirt.

"We flipped a coin to see who got to introduce you, and I won," Brock said.

"Let's get this party started," Nick said.

"Hello," Brock said into the microphone. When the crowd went silent, he said, "My name is Brock Cappuano, and this is my brother Brayden and our other brother Nick, who's the president of the United States. He says we're supposed to call him Nick, but you have to call him Mr. President."

It was all Nick could do to keep from laughing out loud.

"Mr. President," the principal, Mrs. Montrose, said into another microphone, "we're delighted to welcome you to Cecil Elementary. On behalf of the mayor, superintendent and school committee, as well as the entire staff and student body, we're honored to have you as our guest. Brayden and Brock are so excited to have their brother the president visit our school. They've requested questions from other students over the last week and they will be our moderators today. I turn it over to them."

The audience gave the principal a warm round of applause.

"Nick," Brock said, "thank you for coming to our school today. We're so excited to have you here."

"Thank you for inviting me."

"We have a bunch of questions that were submitted to us, so is it okay if we start asking them?" Brayden said.

"Ask away."

"The first one is from Henry, who's in fourth grade. He wants to know if it's fun to be president."

Nick wanted to laugh out loud and say, *No, it sucks balls,* but of course he couldn't say that. "Where's Henry?"

The boy stood and waved, grinning from ear to ear.

"Hey, Henry. Thanks for the question. It's a lot of fun in some ways. I get to ride on the *Marine One* helicopter and *Air Force One*, which is the president's own airplane, and in the limousine we call The Beast. My family and I get to live in the White House, where the amazing staff take very good care of us. There's a pool and bowling alley in the White House that my kids love, so yes, it can be fun. But it's also a lot of responsibility to keep our country safe and everything working the way it should be."

"Teegan, a first grader, wants to know if Skippy the dog likes the White House," Brock said.

"Where's Teegan? Hi, Teegan. Skippy loves the White House. She thinks she owns the place."

Lots of giggling followed that statement.

"She's made friends with the staff, and they keep her in dog treats. My son, Scotty, is supposed to keep track of her, but she doesn't like being supervised. She likes to visit the kitchen, where there's always something for her to snack on, and the flower shop. And did you know she has five million followers on Instagram? How many of you have seen her pictures there?"

Lots of hands went up.

"Kevin, a third grader, had another question about Skippy. Has she gotten into trouble or bitten anyone?"

"Where's Kevin? Hi there. Well, thankfully, Skippy hasn't bitten anyone except for us when we're playing with her, and the only trouble she gets into is wandering around the White House like she's the president."

He loved the sound of children laughing.

"Cali, a second grader, wants to know if it's hard being president."

"Hi, Cali." By now, the kids were standing up to wave at him when their names were mentioned. "Some days, it's hard being president. You have to make decisions that affect other people's lives, and sometimes, the best decision for the country makes people mad at the president. But I've learned that I'll never make everyone happy, so I have to do what I think is best for most of us."

For another hour, he answered questions about the White House, the Oval Office and what it was like to live in the most famous house in the world.

"We're going to have to wrap it up," Mrs. Montrose said. "The president has other commitments today, but what do we say to him for coming to see us today?"

A roar of applause and "thank yous" came from the children as Nick stood to hug his brothers and wave to the other kids. "Thank you for having me and for all the great questions."

In the back of the room, several of the parents gave him a thumbs-down as he made his way off the stage, which shouldn't have surprised him but did anyway. At least they hadn't made a scene in front of their kids. He'd learned to be thankful for small favors.

After posing for pictures with each class, he received hugs from his dad and Stacy.

"That was amazing," Leo Cappuano said. He was an older version of Nick, with gray hair at his temples. "The boys couldn't have been more excited."

"I don't think either of them slept last night," Stacy added.

"They looked so cute in their suits."

"Thank you for making the time," Stacy said. "They'll never forget this."

"Neither will I. It's the most fun I've had since the big promotion."

They laughed at how he described his ascension to the presidency.

"What've you got going on for the rest of the day?" Leo asked.

"Lunch with the governor and the Baltimore mayor, followed by a fundraiser later in the day."

"Sounds like fun."

"Does it, though?"

Leo laughed and then immediately sobered. "We were sorry to hear about your colleague Juan."

"Thank you. It's been tough. He was a great young man."

Brant appeared by his side. "Mr. President, we're ready for you outside."

"Duty calls." Nick hugged his dad and Stacy again. "We're going to Camp David for Easter weekend if you and the boys would like to join us."

"They'd love that," Leo said. "We'll make it happen."

"I'll be in touch with the details."

"Very proud of you, Nicky," Leo said gruffly. "My son, the president. It's unreal."

Nick gave his dad another quick hug. "To me as well, but thank you. That means a lot to me."

His father's words filled his heart as the agents hustled him out of the school and into The Beast. After a chaotic childhood in which his parents had played infrequent roles, having his dad in his life and hearing he was proud of him went a long way with Nick, especially after the recent uncomfortable encounter with his deadbeat mother.

Even though he'd told her to get lost, he was quite certain he hadn't heard the last of her.

THE CHIEF CALLED while Sam was on the way to HQ. "Morning."

"Morning. I received a call this morning from an Agent Truver with NCIS. I believe you've met her."

"That's right. What'd she want?"

"To ask us to stand down on our investigation into Juan Rodriguez's murder."

"Did she say why? Just yesterday, she wanted our help."

"She didn't say why, and when I asked, she said the investigation is now classified and under the auspices of the United States Navy."

"Huh. Well, that helps." Sam was careful what she said on a phone line that could be subpoenaed.

"My thought exactly."

"If only something about this didn't stink to high heaven."

"Also my thought."

"What do you want me to do?" Sam asked.

"Let's keep a low-level eye on what's happening with the investigation, but back off. We've got plenty to keep us busy."

"Agreed. We'll focus on the Myerson case we caught last night and wait to hear more from NCIS."

"Sounds good. Keep me posted on anything you hear about the Rodriguez case. We don't want to be caught flat-footed on that."

"Will do."

"What'd you decide about Nick?"

"I followed your advice, and he agreed."

"Had a feeling he would."

"Thank you, as always, for the advice and support."

"You got it."

As she closed her phone, Sam was relieved to be rid of the fake investigation. The chief was right. Nothing good would come from that for any of them. She hoped NCIS would quickly close their investigation and reunite Juan with his loved ones so she could come clean to her colleagues and friends.

She withdrew the secure BlackBerry from her coat pocket to text Nick. *How'd it go at the school?*

He replied a few minutes later. *Amazing. The boys were so cute in their suits and slicked-back hair, bouncing with excitement. Lots of fun.*

So glad it went well. Having a much better day today so far working on the case of a woman found dead in her house and nothing else.

She chose her wording carefully so there would be no way the text could be used against them in the future.

Good luck with the new case. Glad to hear you can focus just on that.

Which meant he understood what she was telling him. *See you when you get home. Love you.*

Love you, too. Be careful out there.

Always.

He would be relieved to know she wasn't working on the fake case anymore, but they still needed answers about who'd wanted Juan dead in the first place.

BTW, he texted, *I talked to Elijah, and he's down with your plan. Talking to Andy about it shortly. More to come.*

Trying not to get my hopes up.

Right there with you, babe. Remember, the law is on our side. I have to believe it'll be okay.

I really hope so.

The twins and Elijah had completed their family. Neither of them wanted to imagine life without the children they'd grown to love as if they'd been with them all their lives, even though it had been only six months. Sam couldn't consider the possibility of losing them without derailing her entire day.

Instead, she focused on the upcoming Easter holiday when she texted her eldest sister, Tracy. *Nick wants to go to Camp David for Easter. Angela won't want to do that—hell, I don't want to —so can you do something with them that day?*

Tracy wrote back a few minutes later. *I've got it covered. Go have some time with your fam. We're all looking forward to the egg roll on Monday.*

What did it say about Sam that she hadn't had a single thought about the egg roll, but her sisters and their children were looking forward to it? She sucked at being first lady. That's what it said.

Do the kids need clothes for Easter? Tracy asked.

And she sucked at being a mother. *I don't know. Do they?*

YES, SAM! LOL! I gotcha. I'll do Easter baskets, too.

What would I do without you?

You'll never have to find out. I get to go shopping with YOUR credit card. Best day ever!

LOL, have a blast.

Oh, I will. I might even get something nice for you to wear, too.

Thank you so much for everything. I love you.

LY2

What would she do without her sisters, mother and stepmother, friends, devoted White House staffers and coworkers? Thankfully, she was surrounded by the most incredibly supportive group of people in the world.

Speaking of being supportive, she texted Shelby to check on Avery and the new baby.

Avery is cranky and sick of being sidelined, and Ms. Maisie Rae is delightful. Noah is crazy about his baby sister. We're hoping to move into our new place as soon as next week.

There's no rush on that. Take your time. You've got enough going on. We're doing Easter at Camp David if you want to come.

We might do that. My parents are going to my sister's, and I wasn't up for a mob scene, so I told them we'd sit it out.

Can't promise peace and quiet at camp, but you'll have your own cabin and amazing staff to take care of you.

That sounds perfect to me! Count us in.

Nick is traveling this week. Let's do dinner one night.

Yes, please. We'll babysit you while he's gone.

Someone's gotta.

HAHAHAHAHA.

When she arrived at HQ, she waved to Lindsey on the way past the morgue. Normally, she'd stop for a quick chat, but the guilt of lying to her friend had her rushing by to get to the pit, where more friends who'd been lied to waited for her. It was funny to think about how often she'd lied effortlessly to her parents as a teenager and never felt an ounce of guilt. Most of the time, her dad had been on to her, but she'd still managed to get away with a lot as the daughter of a savvy police officer.

Lying wasn't as much fun as a responsible adult in charge of people who not only liked her but respected her—and vice versa. Respect was hard-earned in her world, and it pained her to do anything to jeopardize that among the people she worked closest with.

Her pit was hopping when she arrived. "Morning, people. Everyone in the conference room in five for updates."

She unlocked her office to drop off her jacket, and as she turned to head for the conference room, Dr. Anthony Trulo, the department psychiatrist, appeared in her doorway, startling her.

"Sorry," he said with a grin. "Didn't mean to scare you."

"No problem. What's up?"

"Checking in about grief group tomorrow night. Are you able to attend?"

"I should be able to stop in for a minute." With Nick leaving the next day, she wouldn't linger.

"It means a lot to the group to see you."

"I'll be there."

"Thank you. Everything good with you?"

"As good as it ever is these days."

"You're holding up?"

"Doing my best." She hesitated before she added, "The twins' grandparents are making noise about custody again. It's stressful, to say the least."

He winced. "I'm sure it is, but you've got the law on your side. The parents were very clear about what they wanted."

"Did they want those precious babies living in the White House with Secret Service agents surrounding them and the eyes of the world on them?"

"Maybe not, but their brother knows they're very well loved

in their home, and that's what is most important to him. I'm sure their parents would agree."

"I hope so."

"You know where I am if you need me."

"Always, and that's a source of great comfort to me."

He smiled. "I'll let you get to work. See you tomorrow night, if not before."

"See you then. Thanks for checking in and for the words of wisdom."

"Any time, my friend."

Sam took a second to get her emotions over the situation with the twins in check so she could focus on the task at hand —getting justice for Elaine Myerson.

She went to the conference room, where the rest of her team was gathered around two new murder boards—one for Juan and the other for Elaine. "Update on Rodriguez," she said after she took her place at the head of the table. "NCIS has called us off for now."

"Can they do that?" Gonzo asked. "We have jurisdiction."

"Understood, but they've made a case to the chief, and he's agreed with their position."

Lindsey came into the room, wearing a stormy expression. "Are you talking about the Rodriguez case?"

"Yes, I was telling the team that NCIS has asked us to back off, and the chief agreed."

"Maybe you can tell me why Juan Rodriguez's mother called to tell me that the photo she requested of the body in my morgue is *not* her son."

Oh shit. "Could we have the room, please?"

Sam waited until her team had left, closing the door behind them.

"What the *fuck*, Sam?"

She'd never seen Lindsey look so furious, and her anger made Sam feel sick. "The NCIS agent-in-charge came here yesterday and asked me to go with her. She made me swear to keep our meeting entirely confidential and to confirm that the body was that of Juan Rodriguez. They said it was a national security situation and they needed my assistance."

"You gave me a *false* ID?"

"I did. And I feel awful about it, but they were adamant that no one know that Juan is alive. They said their investigation hinges on their targets believing he's dead."

"You've got to be kidding me!"

"I wish I was. NCIS is deep into an investigation involving the former Joint Chiefs of Staff and their plot to overthrow Nick's administration. Juan was the one who tipped Nick off to the plan, and he apparently has been followed ever since, to the point that NCIS decided to stage his disappearance and murder to get their subjects pointing the finger at each other. Or something like that."

"His mother is devastated. How could he do this to her?"

"He certainly didn't want to, but they said it had to be believable. They asked us to run the investigation the way we always do, and after I consulted with the chief, we decided to give them some leeway."

"By lying to me and the rest of your team?"

"What was I supposed to do, Lindsey? They said it was an imperative national security situation."

"I want Mrs. Rodriguez told—*immediately*—that her son is alive, or I'll tell her. And P.S., who the hell is that in my morgue?"

"He's a service member who closely resembled Juan. He was killed in a motorcycle accident over the weekend."

"This is diabolical! I honestly can't believe you went along with it."

"Again, I'll ask you, what was I supposed to do? They brought me in because of my dual roles as the Homicide commander and first lady and because Juan said he wouldn't go through with it unless I knew the truth. I'd already agreed to keep their secret when they revealed to me that Juan is alive. They put me in a very difficult position."

"You could've told me the truth. I wouldn't have breathed a word of it to anyone."

Sam felt sick to her stomach. "I'm sorry. I should've trusted you."

"Yes, you really should have, because now I have to wonder if I can trust *you*. Mrs. Rodriguez will be told the truth within thirty minutes, or she'll hear it from me."

Lindsey stormed out of the room and slammed the door behind her, rattling Sam's nerves even further. She found the contact info for Agent Truver in her notebook, and as she dialed the number, she realized her hands were shaking.

"Truver."

"This is Sam Holland. We have a problem."

CHAPTER TWELVE

"What problem do we have?"

"Our medical examiner, Dr. Lindsey McNamara, sent a photo of the body to Juan's mother, who confirmed it's not of her son. Dr. McNamara has given us thirty minutes to tell Mrs. Rodriguez that her son is alive, or she'll do it."

"Son of a bitch."

"Will you have Juan call her?"

After a long pause, she said, "We'll take care of it."

The line went dead.

"Goodbye to you, too."

She texted Lindsey. *NCIS is handling the notification of Mrs. Rodriguez.*

Sam got up, went to the door and called her team back into the room.

"Is it true, Sam?" Gonzo asked when the team was seated around the table with the door closed. "Is Juan alive?"

She simply couldn't perpetuate this fraud for another second. "Yes."

"*Whoa,*" Freddie said on a long exhale. "What the hell?"

Sam explained what NCIS had asked of her before they'd revealed that Juan was alive. "When I returned to HQ, I went right to the chief, and we agreed to play it as if it was an actual investigation per their request. I'm sorry I lied to you. I never would've done that under ordinary circumstances. I hope you know that."

"Lindsey is pissed," Cameron said.

"With good reason. I provided the ID for the body in the morgue and confirmed it was Juan. His mother requested a photo, and that's how she found out the young man in the morgue isn't him."

"This is seriously fucked up," Gonzo said.

"Yes, it is. And I'm very sorry for the role I played in it. I was put in a difficult position."

"Why did they tell you the truth?" Freddie asked.

"Juan insisted I be told, but the chief also suspected they wanted Nick to know what was going on but couldn't involve him directly without causing him other problems. Or something like that."

"So they expected you to tell him?" Neveah asked.

"I think so."

"Did you?" Gonzo asked.

"I'm not going to answer that on the grounds that it could involve you all in situations you want nothing to do with. You can make your own assumptions about what I did or didn't do." After a pause, she added, "I want you to know that the trust we share is one of the most important things in my life, and it pained me deeply to violate that trust, even for national security reasons."

None of them looked at her, which only added to her considerable anxiety. "I'm sorry, guys."

They still didn't look at her.

"We need to move on to the Myerson case. Who wants to give me an update on where we are?"

Freddie stood slowly and moved to the murder board. "Elaine Myerson, age forty-six, found in the bathroom adjoining the main bedroom of her home on Webster Street

Northwest in the Crestwood neighborhood. She's the chief communications officer for a company that lobbies Congress on behalf of the oil industry. Her husband, Frank Myerson, is a well-regarded and very successful real estate broker."

That explained the fancy house, Sam thought, assuming Elaine's job would pay a more regular salary than his.

"Carlucci and Dominguez canvassed the neighbors, who reported seeing nothing out of the ordinary yesterday. The husband's alibi checked out. He was at a staff retreat in Bethesda, and his assistant confirmed he was with her from eight in the morning until they parted company after dinner at seven thirty."

"What do we know about the daughters?" Sam asked.

"Zoe is seventeen, and Jada is fifteen," Freddie said.

"Where were they yesterday?"

"Zoe was reportedly with her boyfriend all day, and Jada was on a day trip to Harpers Ferry and Antietam with a friend's family."

"I'd like to talk to them today. Do we have the address where they're staying? Frank said something about a sister in Bethesda?"

"Yes," Gonzo said. "We have the address."

"Freddie and I will head out there to interview the daughters while the rest of you work on financials and social media. Gonzo and Matt, if you could go to Elaine's office to interview her colleagues, that would help."

"Will do," Gonzo said. "Let's go, Matt."

Her sergeant and close friend got up and left the room without once making eye contact with her. Was she reading too much into that? She didn't think so. To Freddie, she said, "Let's get going to Bethesda."

He, too, got up and left the room without so much as a glance in her direction.

Awesome.

"Cameron, would you please write up any notes we have on

what was done on the Rodriguez investigation so I can forward it to NCIS?"

"Will do."

"Thank you."

Sam went to her office to grab her jacket and portable radio. Then she followed Freddie to the morgue entrance.

Lindsey came out of the morgue when she saw them there. "I'd like information about what to do with the body that was passed off as Juan's."

"I'll send you the point of contact for NCIS."

"Thank you." When she turned and went back through the automatic glass doors that led to her domain, Sam wanted to chase after her, to do whatever it took to make this right. But she couldn't do that now.

When she and Freddie were settled in the back of the SUV, she asked Vernon to raise the privacy screen.

She glanced at Freddie. "Say what's on your mind."

"I don't know what to say."

"Please tell me you know I'd never be involved in something like this voluntarily."

"I do know that, but I wish you'd trusted us with the truth."

"They were very adamant that no one know. I only told the chief so he could tell me how he wanted it handled. It was his decision to go along with their request. I was put in an impossible situation."

"Yes, I realize that."

"You're pissed. Everyone is pissed."

"I think we're more shocked than pissed."

"How do you think I felt when I walked into that room and saw Juan alive and well right after swearing to keep anything I learned there a secret for national security purposes?"

"I don't know. The whole thing is bonkers."

"Yes, it is, and I handled it the best way I could under the circumstances."

"By giving Lindsey a false ID?"

"Yes! That had to happen to make the rest of it work."

"The rest of what?"

"The details behind the plot to overthrow Nick's administration and get rid of the guy who blew the whistle on them."

"It's weird that they revealed Juan to you right after the body was found."

"I agree, but they had to get me onboard quickly before I got a good look at the body and realized it wasn't him. The chief thinks they wanted me to tell Nick."

"Tell me the truth. Did you tell him?"

"I can't tell you that. It would expose you if this comes out later."

"*If* it comes out? It'll come out like a scandal the likes of which you've never seen before."

"The scandal should be focused on the high-ranking military officials who tried to overthrow the president. Neither of us has done anything other than the jobs we were asked to do on behalf of the country—and the District of Columbia. That's a hill I'll die on."

Her phone rang with a call from Darren Tabor, a reporter at the *Washington Star*. Normally, she dodged his calls. Right now, she was thankful for something to take her attention off the disapproval she felt coming from her partner and best friend.

"Hey, Darren."

"Sam... People are saying that Lieutenant Commander Rodriguez isn't dead. What do you know about that?"

"We're referring all inquiries in that investigation to NCIS."

"Why? Don't you have jurisdiction? The body was found in DC."

"I'm following orders, Darren, and this situation is way above my pay grade."

"Do you know whether Juan Rodriguez is alive?"

"No comment."

"Come on, Sam. Give me something, will ya?"

"Gotta run." She closed the phone as a new level of apprehension overcame her after hearing that Darren had caught wind that Juan was alive and what Freddie said about the potential for a massive scandal. From her pocket, she withdrew the BlackBerry and texted Nick. *Call me when you can.*

When he called ten minutes later, she said, "I just got the oddest call from Darren Tabor from the *Star*. He said he heard Juan might be alive." It was the best way she could think of to tell him that Darren was sniffing around without disclosing to Freddie or anyone who might gain access to their phone records that he already knew. God, what a messed-up situation this was.

"What? Did he say anything else?"

"No, only that he'd caught wind of something being off about his murder."

"Wow, if it's true, that'd be the best news I ever got. I'll see what I can find out."

"Let me know."

"Will do. How's your day?"

"Strange." She was unaccustomed to being at odds with her colleagues. "Yours?"

"About to go into lunch with the governor and mayor."

"Have a good lunch. I'll talk to you later."

"Love you, babe."

"You, too."

"So you really didn't tell him?" Freddie asked.

"I'd rather not talk about that."

"Whatever."

They didn't exchange another word before arriving at the two-story colonial-style home of Frank Myerson's sister, Diane, who had a mini freak-out at finding the first lady on her doorstep.

"Oh my God! Frank told me you were working on the case, but now you're at my house and... *holy shit*."

Annoyed, Sam showed her badge. On a normal day, she'd

roll her eyes at Freddie, but today wasn't normal. "Lieutenant Holland and Detective Cruz. We'd like to speak with Mr. Myerson and his daughters, please."

"I, um, yes, of course. Come in." She led them into a lovely home full of restored antiques and paintings depicting events in U.S. history. Sam recognized the Gettysburg Address and a long-ago inauguration. They were shown to a sitting room where a painting of George Washington crossing the Potomac spanned the length of a sofa. "I'll get them."

"This place is like a museum," she said.

"Uh-huh."

Few things in her life had hurt more than knowing Freddie, of all people, was truly angry with her. Or maybe it was more accurate to say she'd disappointed him with her lack of trust and candor.

Frank Myerson had aged five years since the last time Sam had seen him, or at least that's how it seemed to her when he came into the room, wearing a T-shirt and sweats. His hair was a mess, and he hadn't shaved. His daughters followed him, similarly attired and looking exhausted.

"These are my girls, Jada and Zoe."

Both had light brown hair. Jada had green eyes, and Zoe's were blue.

"I'm very sorry for the loss of your mother," Sam said to the girls.

"Thank you," Zoe said for both of them while Jada burrowed into her dad's embrace.

"I hope you understand that there're certain routine questions we have to ask you."

"It's fine," Zoe said.

"Where were you yesterday during the day?"

"My boyfriend and I hung out at his house."

"Where's his house?"

"In Arlington."

"Was anyone else there?"

"No, just us. His parents and two sisters were at a horse show for the sisters."

"His name?"

For the first time, Zoe glanced at her dad, seeming apprehensive. "Why does that matter?"

"Answer the question, Zoe," Frank said.

"He has nothing to do with our family. Why do we have to drag him into this?"

"Because he was with you when your mother was murdered," Sam said, "and can provide an alibi for where you were when she was killed. Any other questions?" She was usually gentler with the children of murder victims, but something about this girl irked her.

Zoe's eyes had gone wide with shock. "N-no."

"His name?"

"Zeke Bellamy."

Sam handed over her notebook and pen. "Write down his name, address and phone number."

"Are you going to talk to him?"

"Yes, we are."

"Dad! Come on! Zeke has nothing to do with this. If I send cops to his house, he'll never speak to me again."

"Which is more important to you, Zoe?" Sam asked. "Finding out who killed your mother or keeping your boyfriend?"

That she hesitated, even for a second, was telling. "Of course I want to know who killed my mother, but why do we have to involve him?"

"I told you why."

"Knock it off, Zoe," Frank said, sounding as if he'd said those exact words a million times in the past.

"Mr. Myerson, are you acquainted with Mr. Bellamy?"

"I am."

"Did you or your wife have any issues or concerns with him?"

"We felt their relationship had gotten too serious too fast. We'd argued with Zoe about that."

"Dad! That's private."

Sam glanced at the girl. "Nothing is private in a murder investigation."

"What does my relationship have to do with my mother's murder?"

Sam didn't blink as she stared back at the girl. "I don't know."

"It has nothing to do with it! She barely knew Zeke."

"That's not true, Zoe," Jada said.

"Shut up. What do you know about anything? You've never had a boyfriend, and you never will because you're such a fucking weirdo."

Whoa.

"Girls, that's enough," Frank said.

"Jada, where were you yesterday?" Sam asked.

Zoe sat with her arms crossed, visibly seething.

"I was with my friend and her family for the day. We visited Harpers Ferry in West Virginia and Antietam in Maryland for a school project."

"Can you give me your friend's name and number? Also, her parents' names."

Jada recited the information and used her phone to give Sam the girl's phone number.

"Thank you," Sam said. "That's very helpful."

"That's our Jada," Zoe said. "A real Girl Scout."

"Shut up, Zoe, and quit being a bitch. Mom was *murdered.* We have to find out who did it."

Sam wanted to give Jada a high five. At least one of the girls seemed to be in touch with reality. Zoe's behavior had sparked a number of other questions that Sam might not have had otherwise.

"What was your relationship like with your mother, Jada?"

"We're super close," she said tearfully as Frank tightened

the arm he had around her. "Or I guess I should say we *were* super close. I can't believe she's really gone."

"I'm so sorry for your loss."

"Thank you." Jada used a tissue Frank handed her to wipe away tears.

"What about you, Zoe? What was your relationship with your mother like?"

"We fought about everything."

Sam's phone rang with a call from Faith Miller that she declined.

"What does 'everything' include?"

"My clothes, my attitude, my boyfriend, my grades, my driving. You name it, she didn't approve of how I did anything, and her only goal in life was to ruin mine."

Sam glanced at Frank.

"We've had the typical challenges that parents of teenagers experience," he said in a weary tone.

"None of my friends put up with the shit that I do," Zoe snapped.

"Sounds like you were pretty angry with your mother," Sam said.

Zoe shrugged. "She made my life a living hell."

"Were you angry enough to hurt her?"

"*What?*" Frank sat up straighter. "What're you insinuating?"

"I'm asking if your daughter was angry enough with her mother to want her out of the picture."

"This interview is over."

"We can continue it downtown if you'd prefer," Sam said.

"I want a lawyer."

"Detective Cruz, please call Patrol for transport to HQ. You can call your attorney after you're processed."

As Freddie got up and left the room, Frank said, "We're being *arrested*?"

"You're being taken in for further questioning."

"Why do I have to go?" Jada cried. "I haven't done anything!"

"We have more questions for all of you. Once you request an attorney, we're not allowed to ask you anything else, so you'll all need to come to the station."

Jada turned on her sister. "This is all your fault, Zoe! As usual, you ruin everything!"

Frank intervened before their conflict could turn physical. From the way he reacted, Sam wondered if he'd had to get between them before.

"If you don't want to be handcuffed for the ride," Sam said, "you'll keep your hands to yourselves."

"I can't believe the family members of a murder victim are being treated like criminals," Frank said.

"No one is treating you like a criminal. If you'd like criminal treatment, we can certainly arrange for that."

Frank gave her a hateful look and then told the girls to get their shoes on. "You can bet that I'll be filing a formal complaint with your supervisors."

"Please, feel free. They love to hear from the friends I make while I'm out here doing my job."

"My wife was *murdered*, and you have the audacity to be flippant."

"I would think you, more than anyone, would want to know who did this to your wife."

"I do!"

"Then you'll cooperate with our investigation, no matter where it leads."

"What does that mean? 'No matter where it leads'?"

"Just what I said."

Freddie came back into the room. "Patrol is here for transport."

CHAPTER THIRTEEN

After they'd turned over the Myersons to Patrol, Sam and Freddie returned to her SUV.

Vernon opened the door for her.

"Thanks, Vernon."

"You're more than welcome. How's it going?"

"Taking an interesting turn."

"Is it, though?" Freddie asked.

Sam turned to him. "Something you want to say?"

"I feel like you goaded that kid into acting like a suspect."

"*What?* I didn't have to do anything to make her look suspicious. She did that all on her own by fully sharing the animosity between her and her mother."

"That's your opinion."

"Sure is."

They didn't say another word on the ride back to HQ. Could this day get any better?

When she got back to the pit, Agent Truver was waiting in Sam's office. She closed the door behind Sam. "I need your help."

"I'm not inclined to do anything for you. Your secrets have

gotten me in deep shit with most of the people I associate with every day."

"This situation is so incredibly fraught, Lieutenant. I'm sure you can appreciate being part of a months-long investigation that's in danger of blowing up in our faces and letting a traitor get away with conspiracy to commit murder, among other things."

Sam sat behind her desk, thinking of the Johnson case that had, in fact, blown up in her face when a child was killed during a raid she'd overseen after months undercover. "I'm listening."

"We're *so* close. So, *so* close to charging the former chief of Naval Operations with multiple felonies, including conspiracy to commit murder and treason. We've built an airtight case that shows him to be the ringleader of the plot to overthrow the Cappuano administration."

Sam appreciated that Truver didn't say *your husband's administration*. It conveyed professional respect that could be hard to come by these days when her multiple hats blurred the lines between personal and professional.

Truver leaned forward, her expression earnest. "This person has been collecting a huge salary as a top military adviser to the president while plotting to disregard the Constitution of the United States and the oath they took to defend it."

"What do you want from me?"

"I need you and anyone who's discovered the truth to keep up the ruse for a few more days."

"A reporter I deal with at the *Star* called me earlier to say he's hearing rumblings that Juan might be alive."

Truver hadn't expected that. "What'd you tell him?"

"That I have no info on that. I think I held him off."

"I'll look into that separately."

"What about Juan's mother and family?"

"His mother has spoken to Juan and will be going forward

with planning a funeral and acting the part of the grieving mother."

"And the rest of his family?"

"They understand the assignment. It's critical to our investigation that the people closest to Juan act as if he's been murdered."

"You certainly don't expect my husband to speak at a fake funeral, I hope."

"The funeral will be delayed by bureaucratic wrangling and scheduling concerns with POTUS."

Sam sat back in her chair, relieved to hear that Nick wouldn't be asked to participate in a fake dog and pony show that could come back to bite him in the ass.

"Will you help me keep the lid on this, Lieutenant?"

"I'll ask my people to keep the information confidential. I can't and won't ask them to lie if it comes to that."

"Understood. Thank you. The whole story will be public before long, or so I hope. In the meantime, it's essential that the subject of our investigation believes Juan Rodriguez is dead and can't testify against him."

"We'll do what we can to assist you."

"Thank you very much. I know this is a highly unusual situation—"

"To say the least."

"Trust me, I never expected to be building a case for conspiracy to commit murder and treason against an admiral, but here we are."

"Good luck with the grand finale."

"Thank you. I'm going to need it."

After she left, Sam picked up the phone to call Lindsey.

"What's up?" Lindsey asked with none of the usual friendly warmth in her voice.

"Agent Truver from NCIS just stopped by to update me. She said they're close to an arrest of the former chief of Naval Operations, an admiral, for conspiracy to commit murder and treason, among other charges. She told me Juan has spoken to his mother and stressed the importance to her that she continue to appear to be a grieving mother planning a funeral. She asked that the rest of us maintain the ruse until an arrest is made imminently."

"Anything else?"

"Nope, that's it."

"Got it."

The line went dead.

Motherfucker. It'd been a while since she'd had multiple close friends pissed at her at the same time, and it totally sucked. She valued the relationships she'd built on and off the job with her colleagues and hated that she'd disappointed them.

She got up and went to the door. "Everyone in the conference room in five."

When they were gathered in the room with the door closed, Sam conveyed the update from Truver. "It's critical to the NCIS investigation that their target continues to believe Juan has been murdered."

"We won't say anything about it," Gonzo said, "and we wouldn't have if you'd told us the truth from the outset."

She held his gaze. "I'm sorry I didn't. I honestly didn't know what to do when they cited national security concerns. They were adamant that no one know."

"That shouldn't have included us," Freddie said.

"You're absolutely right, and I apologize."

"I think it's somewhat egregious that you were put in this position to begin with," Neveah said.

Sam wanted to thank her—and kiss her face. Finally, someone was seeing this situation from her point of view.

"They were using you due to your position as our commander and the first lady," Neveah added.

"I tend to agree," Sam said. "In addition to Juan insisting I be told the truth, I believe they were hoping I'd tell Nick about it—well, that and I was required to investigate Juan's murder, which could've messed up their case."

"Did you tell Nick?" Gonzo asked.

"I'm not going to answer that for many important reasons. There're some things I simply can't discuss with anyone, even my closest people, which you certainly are. And that's one of them."

"Fair enough," Cam said. "We're not entitled to know what goes on between you and your husband, even if you are POTUS and FLOTUS."

"We're walking a fine line all the time, but especially since this situation with the Joint Chiefs blew up. I hope you understand... In a perfect world, I'd share everything with you. Unfortunately, the world I live in is not perfect like that."

"I couldn't do what you're doing," Matt said. "No way. The scrutiny, the Secret Service, the nonstop demands... I give you both credit for holding it together."

"Thank you. We're trying. I blew it this time, guys, and I apologize again for lying to you. That won't happen again." She looked at each of them, seeking eye contact. "Are we good?"

"Yeah," Gonzo said. "We're good."

Sam stared at her partner. "Freddie?"

"All good," he said, but he didn't meet her gaze.

It would take a minute to get back on track with her best friend, which was fine. Whatever it took to fix things with him, she'd do it.

"Now, back to Myerson. Where are we with the family's lawyer?"

"He's in court until later this afternoon," Freddie said. "He'll be here as soon as they adjourn."

Sam nodded. "What else have we got?"

Cameron used a remote control to put documents on the screen at the front of the room. "Some interesting social media posts from the older daughter, talking about how parents ruin everything for their kids."

As she wondered how he'd managed to put the posts on the screen, Sam zeroed in on the content of the posts.

"Go back to the one before."

Cam clicked backward.

"Look at the comment from Zeke Bellamy, Zoe's boyfriend." It said, *Hang tough, babe. You haven't done anything wrong.* Acting on a hunch, she said, "Let's pick him up. I want to have a chat with him."

"We'll go," Cam said, including Matt.

Sam handed him the piece of paper with the kid's address that Zoe had given her earlier. "Thank you." After they left the room, she said, "Let's take a deep dive into Zeke and see who we're dealing with there."

"On it," Gonzo said as he led the others out of the room.

"Cruz," Sam said. "A minute, please?"

Freddie turned back.

"Close the door."

He did as she asked.

"Say what's on your mind."

He gave Sam a look full of hurt and betrayal. "I can't believe you lied about this. I really can't."

"I understand. I was very confused when I returned from my initial meeting with NCIS. Before I'd had time to fully process it, I was expected to step into the investigation. I did what I thought was right at the time, but I was wrong to lie to you and the others. I wish I hadn't done that."

"I admit they put you in a bad spot, but after everything we've been through, it's shocking to me that you would lie to me, of all people. Don't you know that I'd protect you with everything I have, right up to my life, if it came to that?"

Moved by the starting of tears in his warm brown eyes, she got up and went to him. "I do know that, and P.S., don't you *dare* ever endanger your life for me, since I wouldn't want to go on without you."

"Likewise."

She stepped closer to him, put her hand flat on his chest. "I'm not sure when you became my best friend, but I hope you know that you are, and I'm very sorry I didn't tell you the truth about this from the get-go. I should have. National security or not, I trust you with everything. More than anything, I hate that I hurt you. I won't let that happen again."

He hugged her.

She hugged him back. "Let's get to work."

"Sam."

"Yes?"

"You're my very best friend, too."

"I know. And I didn't bait that kid into acting guilty."

He grinned. "Yes, you did."

Sam followed him out of the room. "Didn't."

"Did."

"Children, are you fighting?" Captain Malone asked when he entered the pit.

"We're *debating*," Sam said with a smile for Freddie, relieved to have cleared the air with him. "What's up?"

"I come bearing warrants for the Myerson family electronics. Gonzales asked me to request one for the boyfriend, Zeke Bellamy, too."

"Excellent, thank you. Detective Cruz, will you please go relieve the family members of their phones and deliver them to Lieutenant Archelotta?"

Freddie took a copy of the printed warrant from Malone. "Will do."

"Assume Haggerty and the CSU team have the laptops and other devices covered?" Sam asked Malone.

"You assume correctly. They're still processing the scene."

"What's going on at Stahl's house?" Sam asked hesitantly. She tried to never think about the bodies that'd been found there or how those victims had been murdered by a man who'd taken the same oath to uphold the law that she had.

"The forensic team will be wrapping up their work this

week. Then we'll sit down and go over everything we've got and meet with the U.S. Attorney's team about additional charges."

"Any word on who the new USA will be?"

"I'm hearing the president plans to appoint Catherine McDermott. She'll have to be confirmed by the Senate."

Again, how bizarre was it to hear one of her colleagues refer to an action by the president, who happened to be Sam's husband? "What do we know about her?"

"She's the former Attorney General of Oregon, known for being extremely by the book with a take-no-prisoners approach."

"Charming." Sam glanced over her shoulder at her team hard at work on the Myerson case. "Do you have a minute?"

"Sure."

"Your place or mine?"

"Yours is closer."

They went into Sam's office, and she closed the door before taking the seat behind her desk.

"What's on your mind?"

"You're up to speed on what's gone down with Juan Rodriguez?"

"I am. It's unbelievable."

"It is, but I wanted to talk to you about something else." She tried to collect her thoughts.

"Yesterday, when I went to the church to observe the operation involving Judge Sawyer, I was in the Emergency Response trailer where Captain Ruiz holds court."

"Speaking of charming."

"Yes, she's a piece of work who doesn't think too much of me, apparently."

"Why do you say that?"

"She treated me like I was radioactive or something, and as I watched and listened to the operation go down outside the church, I felt incredibly impotent. While my team was out there putting themselves in danger, I was locked away in the trailer, unable to help them because my face would ruin everything if the perp got a good enough look at it."

"And yet, you were the one who ended up arresting him."

"That was a lucky break."

"A lucky break that led to the arrest of the man who murdered a U.S. Attorney, who happened to be our friend and colleague, and shot our friend and colleague Agent Hill."

"I'm glad we got him. Don't get me wrong."

"*You* got him. There was no *we* in the arrest."

"The whole team worked on that case, put themselves in danger to see it through. He was at the church and made us. He could've shot and killed Cori Sawyer or any member of our team, while I sat on the sidelines, out of harm's way, with my lead Secret Service agent by my side."

"What're you saying, Sam?"

"It doesn't sit right with me, being off the front lines while continuing to command my squad. Asking them to do things I can no longer do myself."

"Do you think they care?"

"No, they probably don't, but I do. How long will it be before they resent me for making all our jobs harder and much less safe than they used to be?"

"How are they less safe?"

"People recognize them because they're always with me. That's especially true for Cruz and Gonzales, but the others, too. If something ever happened to one of them because of their association with me... How would I live with that?"

"Have you talked to Trulo about this stuff?"

"Not yet."

"Maybe you should."

"I will, but what do *you* think? Am I crazy to keep doing this job while being first lady? Am I putting people I love in danger by showing up here every day?"

"I can't say whether you're crazy to try to do both, but I can assure you that you're not putting your team in danger by showing up to work. What you do here keeps people safer, Sam."

"But does it risk the people I do it with?"

"I don't think so."

"Is it wrong for me to be off the front lines in the safety of the comms trailer while they're wearing vests and risking their lives?"

"If you asked them, would they say they'd prefer to have you in the comms truck than not there at all?"

"I don't know."

"Maybe you should ask."

"I guess."

"I can't possibly know what it's like for you these days, but I can try to put myself in your position, and I'd feel the same way you do about having to sit out the dangerous stuff. But that doesn't mean you can't continue to make very valuable contributions, including arresting the man who murdered Tom Forrester."

"Ruiz has a beef with me."

"It's the same old thing, Sam. She wants to *be* you."

"I don't think that's true."

"Of course it is. Everyone wants a career like you've had, and very few will."

"Really? Because this career is not the one I set out to have. If I had my way, no one would know who I am."

"Then you should've married someone else."

"Which is unthinkable, of course." She leaned forward on the desk. "If I tell you something, do you promise to never repeat it?"

"Of course."

"You know how much I love Nick. If it's a choice between him and all the madness that comes with him and this place? I pick him every time."

"Understood."

"It's just that I had no idea what it would be like to try to do this job with a high-profile spouse who made me famous along with him."

"How would anyone know what that's like until it happens?"

"I'm not—in any way—expressing regret about who I chose to marry."

"I know that, Sam. Thanks to *SNL*, the whole world knows how devoted you are to each other."

Sam cringed. "Freaking *SNL*."

"I was in the car the other day when 'My Humps' came on. I had to pull over because I was laughing so hard."

Glaring at him, she said, "That's great. Thanks for sharing."

His laughter filled her small office. "Sorry," he said, wheezing. "It's so flipping funny."

"Sure it is."

He cleared his throat and made an obvious effort to get himself together.

"Will you do something for me, Cap?"

"Anything for you, kid."

"If the day comes when you think I'm more trouble than I'm worth around here, or that my presence is endangering the people I work with, will you tell me?"

"That's not going to—"

"Will you please just tell me if that day comes?"

"Yeah, I will, but today's not that day. I want you to consider the fact that the only reason you were in that comms truck to begin with is that you had the brilliant idea to lure Harlan Peckham out of hiding by using his next obvious victim. You put the whole thing together. You made the connection between Forrester, Hill and Judge Sawyer and the case that was made against his parents. Without you, we'd still be trying to figure out who had a reason to kill Tom. You make a difference here every single day. I know it's harder now, but you're figuring it out, and those people out there... They'd kill for you."

His kind words touched her deeply. "You'll tell me if it becomes untenable."

"I will. I promise."

"Thank you."

"Any time."

As he was leaving the office, Freddie came to the door. "Myerson's attorney is here."

"Let's go have a chat."

CHAPTER FOURTEEN

S am enjoyed how the Myersons startled as she and Freddie burst into the room. Good. She hoped they were a little nervous about how this might go. Not that she relished putting murder victims' families through the wringer, but she'd picked up a vibe from the eldest daughter, and she'd learned to trust her instincts on these things.

She recognized Roland Dunning, the same defense attorney representing former Deputy Chief Paul Conklin, the rat fink who'd sat on information about her father's shooting for four years before coming clean after her dad died. Sam hadn't expected that punch to the gut today, and it briefly threw her off her game.

"Roland Dunning for the Myersons." He placed a gold-embossed business card on the table as if they didn't know exactly who he was and who he represented.

Sam ignored him and his card, focusing on Frank and Zoe while Jada sat off to the side. "Are you ready to talk now?"

"We're ready," Frank said with a stern look for Zoe.

Freddie engaged the recording device on the table that would capture audio and video and recited a list of who was in the room and which case they were discussing.

"Zoe, were you angry enough with your mother to want her dead?" Sam asked.

"What the hell kind of question is that to ask the child of a murder victim?" Dunning asked.

Sam kept her gaze trained on Zoe. "It's the question I most want the answer to."

"You don't have to answer that, Zoe," Dunning said.

"Of course I didn't want her dead!" Zoe said. "She was my mother!"

"You said, and I quote, 'She made my life a living hell.' Was that true?"

Zoe glanced nervously at her father. "We fought a lot."

"Can you be more specific?"

"She didn't want to let me do anything! It didn't matter what it was, she said no."

"Why was that?"

"She didn't trust me."

"How come?"

"Because she lies as easily as she breathes," Jada said.

"Shut the fuck up, you stupid bitch. That's not true."

"Girls, stop," Frank said. "This isn't helping anything."

"Is that true, Zoe? Do you lie a lot?"

"A teenager lying to her parents doesn't make her a murderer, Lieutenant," Dunning said.

Sam never looked away from Zoe. "I'd like Zoe to answer the question."

Zoe shrugged, seeming exquisitely uncomfortable. "Sometimes."

"*All* the time," Jada said.

"Dad! Tell her to shut up!"

"That's enough, Jada."

"I'm just telling the truth."

Frank turned to Jada. "*Enough.*"

"Do you have a challenge with the truth, Zoe?" Sam asked.

"Sometimes it's the only way to get to do anything!"

"I'd like to speak to each of you individually."

"That's not happening," Dunning said. "These girls are minors."

Sam stared him down. "Who may have information pertaining to the murder of their mother."

"They don't know anything about it!" Frank said. "They're children, for God's sake."

Jada began to cry.

Frank looked to Dunning, his eyes wild. "I want to take my daughters home. They lost their mother yesterday! This is outrageous."

"I agree it's outrageous," Dunning said, "but the police have the right to question the people closest to the victim."

Sam wanted to thank him for pointing out the obvious.

"I will not have my girls alone in a room with this woman."

Sam loved when people referred to her by titles such as "this woman."

"They won't be alone," Dunning said. "I'll be with them. The sooner we get this done, the sooner you can take them home."

"And you really think this is necessary the day after they lost their mother?" Frank asked Sam.

"I do, or I'd never ask it of any of you."

"Fine," Frank said. "Let's get this over with."

"Detective Cruz, would you please take Jada and Frank to interview two while I have a word with Zoe?"

"Of course. Right this way."

Before he followed Freddie and Jada out of the room, Frank gave Zoe a look that would've had Sam curling into the fetal position if it had come from her father.

It didn't seem to faze Zoe, who seemed impervious to parental stare downs.

Dunning stayed seated next to Zoe, who'd slid into a slouch that conveyed her utter disdain for the entire process.

Sam decided on a different approach. "I feel like we've

gotten off on the wrong foot. I want you to understand that I'm asking you these questions because it's my job to find out what happened to your mother. You do want me to find out who killed her, don't you?"

"Of course."

"There might be something you can tell me, something you don't realize you know or something you think isn't important but is, that could help with my investigation. So I'd appreciate it if we could just start over and have a conversation like adults. I'm not trying to pin anything on you. I'm trying to solve a murder."

"Okay."

"So, Zoe... Do you know what happened to your mother?"

"I... uh... I heard she was in the bathroom upstairs?"

"Yes, and from the looks of things, she'd been bludgeoned by a heavy object. Do you know what that word means? Bludgeoned?"

"Like... hit over the head?"

"That's right." Sam was relieved to see the slightest cringe from Zoe at hearing how her mother had died. "She was found naked on the floor of her bathroom. It looked like she'd just gotten out of the shower and was taken by surprise."

Zoe looked down at the table.

"How would someone have gotten in the house?"

"I have no idea."

"Your family's house has keyless entry on all the doors. Who has the code?"

"Just the four of us."

"You haven't given it to any of your friends?"

"No. My dad is adamant that no one else have it."

"If we check the locations of your phone and your boyfriend's, will they show either of you anywhere near your house yesterday at the time your mother was killed?"

"No! I told you. We had his house to ourselves. We didn't leave there. We were... you know... taking advantage of the chance to be alone for once." She looked at Dunning and then back to Sam. "You don't have to tell my dad that, do you?"

"I can't promise he won't find out."

She shrugged. "He's not the one who'd flip out over it and act like I'm the only kid in the world having sex."

"Your mom would've done that?"

Zoe rolled her eyes to high heaven. "Oh God. I can't even think about her finding out about us having sex. She'd have lost her mind."

"Is it possible she knew?"

"No way. She would've locked me in my room and thrown away the key."

"That's an interesting saying." And it predated Zoe by decades. "Where did you hear it?"

"My mother threatened me with that daily. It was her favorite thing to say when she couldn't bend me to her will."

"Did your family seek out any therapy or counseling to help with the conflict you were experiencing?"

"We went to this woman my mom sees for a few months, but it didn't really help. Mom was unwilling to allow me to grow up and do all the things kids my age get to do as they get older. I've had my license for almost two years. She's let me take the car three times by myself. She wouldn't even let me get a job so I could make my own money."

"Did she say why?"

"She wanted me to focus on school."

"You couldn't have a job on the weekends?"

"That's what I said, but she wouldn't hear of it."

"Do you know why she was like that?"

"Her sister was murdered years ago, when they were teenagers. My dad told me it really messed my mom up and made her insanely overprotective."

Sam made a note to look into the aunt's murder. "Do you know anything more about what happened to her sister?"

"Just that she was walking home from her friend's house,

and someone snatched her. They found her body a couple of weeks later."

"Where did this happen?"

"She's from Manassas, so out there somewhere."

"Was the killer ever found?"

"I don't know. She never talked about it with us. I only heard about it because my dad told me. He wanted me to understand why she was over-the-top protective of us."

"Did it help to hear about that?"

"I mean... kind of? I felt bad about her sister, but what did that have to do with me? It's not like the same thing was going to happen to me or anything. I was just trying to live my life."

Sam felt incredibly sorry for Elaine Myerson and what she'd endured losing her sister to murder. "Can you see how a trauma like that would've made her extra worried about something happening to you?"

"I guess, but she took it way too far. Even my dad said so." She leaned in a bit. "To you, I sound like a seventeen-year-old brat who didn't appreciate what she had, but that's not true at all. I know how lucky I was to have a nice home, plenty to eat, the best of everything and parents that love me. I really do know that. But having a parent who refuses to allow you to grow up and spread your wings makes for a very difficult existence."

Sam was taken aback by the girl's sincerity.

"Did you love your mother?"

"I did—and I do. I always will. She was a great person who did so much for so many. She was always volunteering or fundraising for someone in need or taking an elderly friend to the doctor or whatever anyone needed. People knew they could call on her. Even as busy as she was with her work and our family, she'd help if she could. I admired her, but I didn't agree with the way she treated me as I got old enough to be more independent. I really love Zeke, but she said that was ridiculous. It hurt me, you know? Like, how could she possibly know how I feel?"

Sam agreed with her, which was interesting. She'd come into this interview convinced the girl had had something to do with her mother's murder. Now she wasn't so sure. "Stay here. I'll be back."

Dunning followed her out of the room and into the one next door where Frank and Jada waited.

"May I speak to Jada?" Sam asked Frank. "You can wait outside with Detective Cruz."

Freddie stood at the door and waited for Frank to come with him, which he did after giving his younger daughter a hesitant look.

Dunning sat next to Jada as Sam engaged the recording device.

"Lieutenant Holland with Jada Myerson and her attorney, Roland Dunning, in the Elaine Myerson case. Jada, when we were in the room with your sister, you mentioned that she often lied to your parents. Can you tell me more about that?"

"She lied to our mother mostly."

"She said your mom wasn't letting her do things that other kids were allowed to do. Is that true?"

"My mom had issues... Did Zoe tell you about her sister being murdered?"

"She did."

"That made her crazy overprotective with us, which she often admitted wasn't fair, but it was like she couldn't help it. I tried to be understanding, but I like being home, so it didn't bother me as much. Zoe wants to be out and about all the time, which messed with my mom's need to keep her close."

"It must've been tough for you to live with the fighting."

"I hate it. I spend a lot of time in my room with headphones on, so I won't have to hear them."

"Did you participate in the family therapy?"

"For a while, but it gave me anxiety, so I stopped going. I

was really hoping it would help them to figure out a way for everyone to get what they wanted, but that never happened. It was World War III every day in our house, which led Zoe to being sneaky."

"Were you angry with her for that?"

"Not really. I steer clear of her most of the time. We don't get along either."

"It seemed to me like she's kind of mean to you..."

"Sometimes. It's mostly that she has no use for me, which is fine. I don't like being around her either."

"Do you think Zoe could've had anything to do with your mom's murder?"

Jada thought about that for a long moment. "I want to say no way, but honestly? I don't know. Things between them were really bad and getting worse all the time. Zoe was counting down to her eighteenth birthday in July. She told my mom she'd never see her again after that."

"What did your mom say to that?"

"She said, 'Good luck with supporting yourself without our help.'"

"Do you think Zoe meant it?"

"I know she did. I heard her on the phone talking about getting an apartment with some friends and possibly Zeke to make it more affordable. She told our cousin that she couldn't wait to get a job and run her own life."

"What do you think of Zeke?"

"He seems okay. He really likes Zoe, which is the baffling part to me. She's so unlikable."

"Does she have friends?"

"A lot of them. I guess she saves all the ugly for her family. Lucky us."

"How was your relationship with your mom?"

"Fine. I didn't always agree with her, but after witnessing the battles with Zoe, I didn't want that for myself. I hated the fighting. It made me sick with anxiety."

"Where was your dad in all of this?"

"He tended to avoid the fighting by staying late at work or finding excuses to be somewhere else."

Sam took copious notes as Jada spoke.

"Can you think of anyone who might want to harm your mom?"

Jada's eyes filled with tears as she shook her head. "People loved her."

"You didn't know of any concerns she had with anyone?"

"I never heard anyone say a bad word about her, except for Zoe."

"Stay here. I'll be back."

Freddie had positioned Frank in Gonzo's empty cubicle with a bottle of Coke and a bag of pretzels.

"How's it going?" Freddie asked her.

"Some interesting revelations. How do we get playback of the recordings in the interrogation rooms?"

Freddie gave her a curious look.

"What? I usually write down everything they say so I don't need them."

Smiling, Freddie said, "Which one do you want?"

"The last five minutes of Zoe's."

"I'll get that for you."

"Put Patrol officers outside the rooms where the girls are. Bring the recording, Frank and the lawyer into the conference room when you're ready."

"Got it."

Sam went into her office and took a sip of water from an abandoned bottle on her desk and then sat to think about her next move. Earlier, she'd picked up a vibe about Zoe that had changed after she talked to the girl one-on-one. That didn't happen very often, so it had thrown her. People usually were exactly as they initially seemed, and few of them surprised her the way Zoe had with what she'd said at the end of their conversation.

She took the rest of the water with her to the conference room.

Freddie came in with Frank and Dunning a few minutes later. They sat in the chairs across the table from her.

"Mr. Myerson, I've spoken to both your daughters and learned that the conflict between your wife and Zoe was quite significant and impacted every member of the family. Would you agree with that assessment?"

"Yes. They were constantly at odds. It was a very difficult situation."

"How did you feel about the way your wife parented Zoe?"

"I thought she went too far in trying to control her. Zoe will be a legal adult this summer, but Elaine treated her like she was still a little kid. My wife and I fought over that for years, but after a while, I gave up trying to change her mind. She lost her sister to murder years ago. It messed her up."

"Zoe mentioned that. What can you tell us about what happened to her sister?"

"Elaine and her family didn't often talk about what happened to Sarah."

"What was Elaine's maiden name?"

"Corrigan."

"How long ago was her sister murdered?"

"Um, more than twenty-five years ago, I'd say."

Sam wrote a note to Freddie. *Ask someone to get everything they can find on the murder of Sarah Corrigan in Manassas about 25 years ago.* She tore the page out of her notebook and handed it to him.

He got up and left the room.

"Zoe wasn't sure if the murderer was caught."

"No one was ever arrested."

"Your girls believe that played a big part in why your wife was overprotective with them."

"It did. Elaine was traumatized by what happened to Sarah. She told me that when we first met and had a lot of anxiety about her own safety, my safety and that of the girls. It was a bone of contention between us as a family. While we certainly understood where it was coming from, it didn't make it easy to live with the constant surveillance and high-level fear. I worried that our girls would turn out to be afraid to live their lives."

Freddie came back into the room and returned to his seat. "Cam and Matt are back."

Sam nodded. "I'd like to play you the last few minutes of Zoe's interview."

Freddie cued up the recording on his phone and pressed Play.

CHAPTER FIFTEEN

They listened to Zoe talk about how she knew how lucky she was to have all the things she did but how difficult it was to have a parent who refused to allow her to become more independent as she got older. She went on to say that she admired her mother for the way she led her life and how much her mother's dismissal of her feelings for Zeke hurt her.

Sam watched Frank battle his emotions as his daughter spoke. "What do you think of what she said?"

"It's all true. Elaine made Zoe's life very difficult and was dismissive of how she felt about Zeke, which I didn't think was fair. I mean, Zoe is old enough to know her own heart and how she feels about someone. I told Elaine it was a mistake to diminish her feelings. While this was a problem for all of us, my wife was a good person who did a lot for others."

"What was your marriage like?"

"We had our ups and downs, like any couple. The teenage years with the girls have been rough, but I was hopeful it would get better as they got older and left home. Although I feared Elaine would get worse about trying to control them after they moved out."

"Was your wife under the care of a physician for her anxiety?"

"She took anxiety meds and saw a psychiatrist every week for years and twice a week recently."

"Do you know the doctor's name?"

"Colleen Barker in Woodley Park. Elaine liked her a lot and said she'd been a big help to her, but I was frustrated that the therapy hadn't relieved the pressure in our home."

"Would you be willing to sign a release that would allow us to talk to her?"

"Yes, I suppose so, if you think it would help."

"We'd appreciate it."

"Okay."

"I hope you understand that I have to ask whether you think either of your daughters could've harmed their mother."

"Absolutely not. They didn't get along, but Zoe would never have hurt her, and Jada tended to avoid the conflict rather than engage."

"What about you?"

"What about me?"

"Were you angry enough to want your wife out of the picture?"

Frank's mouth fell open in shock as he shook his head. "I loved her. I could never hurt her. She's been the center of my life for more than twenty years."

"Can you think of anyone else who might've wanted to kill her?"

"I was awake all night trying to figure out who could've done something like this, and I drew a blank. It's possible someone broke in and took her by surprise..."

Sure, Sam thought, that was possible, but with no signs of forced entry, her gut was telling her this act hadn't been random. Not with the level of anger these people had been living with for years. That sort of thing tended to metastasize and boil over at some point. If she had to guess, that's what'd happened in this case. She just needed to prove it.

"What can you tell me about her coworkers?"

"They adored her. She worked countless hours writing and editing position pieces and white papers for them."

"What organization was it?"

"CVX. They've done work for most of the major oil companies, which was another bone of contention with Zoe, who's a card-carrying environmentalist and was appalled at her mother's involvement in a business that she claims is harming our climate and our planet."

This family had been tearing one another apart with endless conflict, Sam thought, wondering how they'd withstood the nonstop arguing.

"I'm going to release you and your daughters to return to your sister's home. We'll arrange a ride for you." She glanced at Freddie, and he nodded as he got up to take care of it. "I'd like the three of you to stay local, as we might have additional questions for you."

"We don't have anywhere else to go, and we have a funeral to plan."

"If you know what funeral home you'd like to use, I'll ask Dr. McNamara to call them for you after she completes her work."

"I guess Green's over on Arkansas Ave would be fine."

"I'll pass that on and be in touch."

"Tell me the truth, Lieutenant. Are you looking at one of my daughters for this?"

"Our investigation hasn't yet identified a suspect." It was interesting to her that he included both daughters in his question when only one of them had had obvious animosity with Elaine.

"But are they in the mix?"

"Everyone is until they aren't."

"They're children who just lost their mother. You can't believe for a second that they'd have anything to do with this."

"We just don't have enough information yet to rule out anyone."

Freddie poked his head back in. "Haggerty wants prints for the family."

"Have someone come over here to do that," Sam said, not wanting to subject them to Central Booking.

"They have to be fingerprinted?" Frank asked, incredulous.

"Yes, so the Crime Scene detectives can tell which prints belong to the family and which ones don't."

"Oh, I see. I think."

"It helps us to eliminate prints that belong there from those that don't. Unless you have other questions, we'll get that done and then get you back to your sister's."

"How long will our home be a crime scene?"

"Probably a few more days."

"I don't understand how any of this is happening. Elaine is such a wonderful wife and mother. She's never harmed anyone."

"I'm so sorry for your loss. We'll do everything we can to get you some answers."

She left him with Freddie to be fingerprinted and went to speak to Cameron Green. "How'd it go with Zeke Bellamy?"

"He was a bit hostile about being asked to come in for a chat, but he calmed down when we threatened to cuff him. We put him in interview two."

"Do you want to come in with me?" she asked Cam.

"Sure."

Sam and Cameron walked into the room where Zeke was being minded by Officer Keeney.

Sam nodded to the officer, who left the room. They sat across from Zeke, who had a lanky build, short, spiky hair dyed white-blond, brown eyes, sleeve tattoos on both arms and small hoop earrings in both ears. She wondered if Zoe had been attracted to the bad-boy vibes he put out.

Sam engaged the recording device on the table.

"I'm Lieutenant Holland. This is Detective Green."

"Why'd they take my phone? They can't just do that."

"We have warrants to examine it."

"Examine it for what?"

"We won't know until we complete our investigation."

"I'm not sure what me or my phone has to do with anything."

"You're Zoe Myerson's boyfriend, right?"

He shrugged. "So?"

"Her mother was murdered, Zeke."

"Yes, I know. I still don't understand what that's got to do with me."

"Where were you yesterday?"

His eyes bugged out of his head. "You think *I* killed her?"

"I asked where you were."

"I was at my house with Zoe for most of the day. My family was out at something with my sisters, and we had some time to ourselves."

"What time did you meet up with Zoe?"

"Around noon? We met at Union Station, got some food and then took the Metro back to my house around two. We were still there when her dad called to ask her to come home."

"Was it unusual for her to have that much time to spend with you?"

"Very. Her mom was a hard-ass about letting her do anything. She kept waiting to get a call or text demanding she come home, but that never happened."

Because her mother was dead, Sam wanted to say but didn't.

"Zoe must've talked to you about the situation with her mom."

"She did. It was batshit crazy, if you ask me. Who doesn't let a seventeen-year-old have a job or a boyfriend or a life? Zoe couldn't wait to turn eighteen and get out from under her mother's control."

"Was she eager to speed that process along?"

He looked confused for a second, until her meaning registered with him. "What? No. She had a countdown on her phone to her eighteenth birthday. She was making plans for July to move in with some friends and figure out a life free of her mother. We talked about how she could suck it up for a few more months to have the rest of her life to do what she wanted."

Sam had learned to trust her gut first and foremost, and nothing about this kid was sending a tingle down her spine, especially since he told the same story Zoe had about where they'd been yesterday. "Is there anything else you can tell us about Zoe's mom or anything you know about their family that might be relevant?"

"Not that I can think of. I mostly stayed away from her mother. She acted like she hated me simply for existing."

Sam pushed her notebook across the table. "Write down your name, address, phone number and list any social media accounts you have."

When he was finished, he pushed the pad back across the table with info about Instagram, Snapchat and TikTok accounts. "When can I get my phone back?"

"Let me check on that. I'll be right back." She signaled to Keeney, who was leaning against Matt O'Brien's cubicle. He straightened up when he saw her. "Hang with him for another minute, will you?"

"Yes, ma'am."

She went into her office to call Lieutenant Archelotta.

"What's up?"

"Where are we with Zeke Bellamy's phone?"

"I'm almost done with the dump. Give me ten more minutes?"

"Sounds good. I'm ready to send him home, and he wants

the phone."

"He doesn't have as much junk on there as you'd expect from kids his age. Much smaller download than usual."

"What do you make of that?"

"He has other interests besides those on his phone?"

"Yeah, that's possible. I'm very interested in his texts and other communications with Zoe Myerson as well as getting a location on where he was yesterday."

"I'll have it for you shortly."

"Thanks, Archie."

She took a seat at her desk and checked the BlackBerry to see if there was word from Nick about the situation with the twins' grandparents.

Nothing new.

If she allowed herself to think too much about what might happen there, she'd fall into a full-blown panic. She loved Alden, Aubrey and Eli so much. What would they do if the grandparents succeeded in taking the twins away from them?

"Sam?" Freddie was in the doorway and had apparently been there for a few seconds already. "Are you okay?"

"A new thing with the twins' grandparents has thrown me for a loop."

"What new thing?"

"They're coming for them again."

"It won't go anywhere. Eli is in charge, and he wants them with you."

"I know. I'm trying to cling to that. Thanks for the reminder." She took a deep breath and blew it out slowly, trying to move on from the terrible worry so she could stay focused on work. "What's up?"

"I've sent the Myersons home with Patrol. Cam said you spoke to Zeke. How'd that go?"

"I don't catch a buzz with him, but I'm waiting for Archie to bring me the dump on his phone."

"Here I am," Archie said.

Freddie stepped aside to admit the IT lieutenant.

"The texts with Zoe are on top, followed by the GPS location that puts him at a residence in Arlington from about two p.m. on yesterday. Her phone also supports that timing, and Jada's phone shows she was in West Virginia and Maryland for most of the day yesterday."

All that info matched what Zoe, Jada and Zeke had reported to her.

"Thanks for the quick work, Archie." To Freddie, she said, "Send Zeke home with Officer Keeney."

Archie handed Freddie an evidence bag that contained Zeke's phone.

"You got a second?" Archie asked after Freddie walked away.

Sam waved him in.

As he closed the door and took a seat, Sam noticed he seemed tense. "What's up?"

"I've been seeing someone."

"Okay..." Sam was surprised he'd mention that to her since they had hookup history from before she'd reconnected with Nick.

"I really like her."

"That's great, Archie. I'm happy for you." His odd expression confused her. "This is a good thing, right?"

"I'm not sure. She's secretive."

"How so?"

"I feel like she only gives me bits and pieces, enough to keep me on the hook but not the full story."

"Do I need to remind you that you're a detective?"

"I'm resisting that avenue. It feels sneaky to me."

Sam sat back in her chair as she studied him closely. "But you know something's not right."

"Yeah, I guess. The thing is, when we're together, everything is just right. It's the rest of the time that concerns me."

"And you won't investigate her."

"I don't think I should." He gave her a tentative look. "But you could."

Sam wondered if she'd heard him correctly. "Um... *what*?"

"I think it's different if a friend casually looks into the woman I'm seeing as a way to protect me versus me doing it, which could be seen as an act of aggression."

"Archie... Are you listening to yourself? You don't trust her."

"It's not that..."

"Isn't it, though? We joke about our Spidey senses as cops, but we've learned to take them seriously. Your gut is telling you something is wrong. Why don't you ask her what you want to know rather than investigating her or having me do it?"

The face he made told her what he thought of that idea.

"Let me tell you something, pal. You know what makes Nick Cappuano different from every other guy I ever dated? Present company excluded, of course."

"Of course. We didn't technically date."

Sam snorted out a laugh. "True. What makes him different is that I don't ever, ever, *ever* have to wonder what he's thinking, what he's doing, who he's doing it with, where he is—especially now. There's no bullshit, Archie. Do you see what I'm saying?"

"I do. I don't like it, but I get it."

"I had *so* much bullshit before him that the lack thereof is the single best thing about being with him. Well, that and his—"

"Stop! I get it."

Sam laughed. "I was going to say his sweetness, his kindness, the way he worships the ground I walk on... among other things."

"You make good points."

"Call her out on the bullshit or cut her loose. Don't have me or anyone else investigate her. What if there's nothing to find? And *when* she finds out—not if—that'll ruin everything."

"Thank you for the advice."

"Free of charge to you at any time."

He laughed.

"Keep me posted?"

"I will."

After he left, Sam marveled at how they'd managed to carve out a nice friendship after their friends-with-benefits arrangement had ended years ago. He was one of her favorite colleagues, as he could always be counted on to get the job done quickly and efficiently, which was hard to come by at times. Not with Archie. He was as reliable as it got.

"Everything okay with Archie?" Freddie asked when he appeared in the doorway.

"Believe it or not, he was looking for girlfriend advice."

Freddie's brows arched with surprise.

"What? I'm good for romance advice. You should know. You frequently benefit from my wisdom."

It was a wonder he didn't sprain his eyes from the force of the roll. "What. *Ever*."

Sam snorted with laughter.

"Sometimes I think you actually believe your own PR."

"I know my strengths, and romance is one of them. Just ask Nick."

"I'll pass on that, but thanks anyhow. Are we still working on the case, or are you off in la-la land somewhere?"

"I'm right here, ready to work. I want to dig into Elaine's murdered sister and get the details on that."

"Have you ruled out the daughter and her boyfriend?"

"For now. Their phones put them at the boyfriend's house for hours yesterday afternoon. I still need a time of death from Lindsey—"

Lindsey appeared behind Freddie.

"Speak of the devil."

CHAPTER SIXTEEN

Lindsey handed Sam several pages stapled together.
"Elaine Myerson died from blunt force trauma to the head that cracked her skull. She died almost instantly at approximately three thirty yesterday afternoon. The tox screen has been submitted, and I'll get you results when I have them."

"Thank you. That's just what we needed."

"No problem."

When Lindsey turned to leave, Sam called her back. "Give us a second, will you, Freddie?"

"Sure."

Lindsey stepped into the office reluctantly, or so it seemed to Sam.

"Do you mind closing the door?"

She shut the door.

"What do I have to do to make this right with you?"

"You can't. You gave me a fake ID, Sam. How the fuck do I ever trust you again?"

Her sharp words were like knives to Sam's heart. "I told you why I did that."

"I don't care why. If you'd asked me to bet my life if you'd ever do something like that, I'd be laid out in my own morgue right now."

"I'm very sorry, and I swear to you it'll never happen again."

Lindsey leaned back against the closed door, folded her arms and looked down at the floor.

"Linds." Sam waited until her friend finally looked at her. "I'm really sorry. I shouldn't have promised to keep secrets from my closest friends and colleagues, even under the guise of national security. I'll never do that again. You have my word."

Sam hoped her word still meant something to Lindsey.

"I want you to know... I understand the position you were in, and I empathize with that. I mean, this whole thing is unbelievable. But..."

Sam got up and went around the desk, stopping a foot from one of her closest friends. "It'll never happen again."

"I accept your apology."

"Thank you."

A knock sounded at the door. "Sam! Come quick."

What now?

Filled with apprehension, she walked into the pit with Lindsey.

"They've arrested the former CNO," Gonzo said as he led the way to the conference room, where the rest of her team were gathered around the television.

Agent Truver stood at a podium as she announced the arrest of Nathan Goldstein, the former chief of Naval Operations, on attempted murder and treason charges. Acting Attorney General Conrad stood behind Truver, along with several high-ranking naval officers and other officials.

Gonzo let out a low whistle. "A freaking admiral."

"Since the plot to overthrow the Cappuano administration came to light, we've been working diligently with the Justice Department and numerous other agencies and law enforcement personnel to piece together what took place. Through interviews with other former members of the Joint

Chiefs, we've learned that former Admiral Goldstein was the mastermind behind the plan to enact, for all intents and purposes, a military coup to wrest control of the United States government away from President Cappuano and his administration.

"Goldstein believed the president lacked, and I'm quoting others who spoke on the record, 'the experience, gravitas and skill to command the United States Armed Forces and to protect the country from hostile actors who would see those failings as an opportunity to attack, invade or otherwise threaten the sovereignty of the United States.' Goldstein believed the potential for terrorism or other violence could not and should not be ignored."

Sam ached at the thought of Nick hearing these things said about him and his presidency.

"The plan, as outlined by Goldstein and detailed by people in the know, was for the military advisers to notify the president that they were taking command of the government, the United States Armed Forces and all associated properties and holdings. The former Joint Chiefs had intended to give the president the opportunity to resign and peacefully vacate the White House."

"*Holy shit*," Cameron whispered.

"What if he hadn't done what they wanted?" Freddie asked.

"If necessary," Truver continued, "the former Joint Chiefs were prepared to declare martial law to remove the president from office."

Since she no longer trusted her knees not to buckle, Sam took the first available seat at the table.

"The plan, which was intended to be held strictly between the principals and their top aides, leaked, the way these things do. Staff members, appalled by the plan, began to talk amongst themselves, and a decision was made at the staff level to inform Lieutenant Commander Juan Rodriguez, one of the president's military attachés who'd become friendly with the president.

Lieutenant Commander Rodriguez was not explicitly asked to inform the president, but it was understood that he would. And he did.

"Upon learning of the plot, the president acted quickly and decisively to foil it, confronting the now-former Joint Chiefs, and when they refused to acknowledge their involvement, he instructed now-former Attorney General Cox to take them into custody.

"After being charged with numerous federal crimes and dishonorably discharged from the military, Goldstein wasn't satisfied. He wanted revenge against the man who'd tipped off the president. He arranged for the murder of Juan Rodriguez, whose body was found in a clothing donation bin on New York Avenue earlier this week. Since Mr. Goldstein has been in custody, he's unaware that Lieutenant Commander Rodriguez has been murdered by the man he hired to do the job."

"Goldstein doesn't know that Juan isn't dead," Gonzo said, incredulous.

"They're going to get him to flip on the guy he hired to do the deed, who didn't actually do the deed—but he doesn't know that—before they charge him with conspiracy to commit murder," Sam said. "That's why they need Juan to stay 'dead' awhile longer."

"This whole thing is unbelievable," Neveah said. "My grandfather was a Marine. He was always saying how military members take an oath in which they swear allegiance to the president, no matter who it is. The specific words are 'I will obey the orders of the president of the United States.'"

"It's hard to believe they'd risk huge pensions and their stellar reputations for something like this," Freddie said.

"Why did they?" Sam asked. "When they had so much to lose, why would they do such a thing?"

"They let power go to their heads," Cameron said. "They thought an inexperienced president would be easy to mess with. They found out otherwise."

"If Juan hadn't heard about it and tipped him off, they might've gotten away with it." Hearing Agent Truver's recitation of the details, Sam was reminded of just how close they'd come to disaster. "Nick would've been caught off guard, unprepared to fight back when they came in with the military behind them, or so they would say."

"We expect additional charges to be forthcoming against Mr. Goldstein," Truver concluded. It was satisfying to hear her deny him the use of his former title. "The others involved in the plot have taken plea deals that require them to testify against Goldstein in exchange for lesser prison sentences. We'll update you as future developments transpire."

As she left the podium, reporters shouted questions that she and the others ignored.

Sam reached for the BlackBerry and typed a text to Nick. *I saw the press conference. I'm so sorry they tried to do this to you, love. I know you're busy, but are you okay? What can I do?*

She ought to go home to him, but he was probably sealed away with his team, figuring out how to deal with the news that would resurrect the pontificating of pundits about the incident. It had gone on for weeks when the initial news of the plot had broken.

Sam hated that he'd have to deal with this nightmare all over again, along with talking heads questioning whether the Joint Chiefs might've been right to want to depose him.

"It's complete bullshit, Sam," Freddie said, tuning in to what she was thinking. "He's going to show everyone how lucky they are to have him as their president. He already is."

"All he did was step up when he was asked to," she said.

"Like you always say, no good deed goes unpunished," Gonzo said.

"It's so true. He would've been so much better off remaining a senator and doing what he could in the Senate to make a difference."

"I don't agree with that," Neveah said hesitantly, as if she wasn't sure she should be so blunt. She'd joined Sam's team recently and didn't have the history with her and Nick that the others did.

"How come?" Sam asked her.

"I think he's amazing—and not just because I work with his equally amazing wife."

Sam gave her a playful scowl over the compliment, even though she was touched by the kind words.

"People my age can relate to him—to both of you. We feel like he understands our generation and the struggles we've faced. He doesn't come from a big, fancy family that raised him with every advantage. He's a regular guy who ended up in the Oval Office through hard work and dedication to his country. All my friends agree with me that he's *our* president, and we're with him for the long haul. What the Joint Chiefs did was appalling. So many people think so." She seemed to catch herself when she realized she was going on a bit. "Anyway... That's what I think, and I'm not alone."

"Thank you, Neveah. That means a lot to me, and it will to him, too, when I pass it on to him."

"We all feel that way, Sam," Gonzo said. "And again, not because we know him or because you guys are our friends, but because he leads with his heart and genuinely wants to do what's best for everyone—not just what's best for him. He doesn't give a shit about being reelected, which gives him the freedom to do the right thing over the politically expedient thing. You watch. He'll go down in history as one of our best presidents. I know it."

"Agreed," Cam said. "I'd rather have him in that office than ninety-nine percent of the political animals that populate this city. He cares about people. He wants to make things better. His efforts on gun control alone make him a star in my book. Our jobs were always dangerous, but with the whole world armed these days, it's worse than it's ever been before. Responsible gun control should be a no-brainer, and Nick gets that."

"I appreciate the support, you guys. And he will, too. I just wish more people knew him the way you all do. The way I do."

"I thought he was thinking about doing a big interview," Freddie said. "This might be a good time to do that."

"Yeah, probably. I'll ask him where that stands. In the meantime, let's get back to work on the Myerson case."

Freddie shut off the TV and took a seat across from Sam. "I keep going back to the way Elaine controlled her kids with an iron fist. I don't know anything about being a mother to teens, but listening to Zoe describe her life under Elaine's regime made me really uncomfortable."

"Me, too," Sam said. "There was something seriously unhealthy about it. That she wouldn't even let Zoe have a job is so bizarre. My parents were kicking my ass out to go to work from the time I was old enough to babysit for the neighbors."

"Same," Gonzo said. "I had a paper route at ten, which is kind of bonkers when you think about it now. I'd never let Alex run around by himself at ten."

"Different times," Cameron said. "I worked in the funeral homes from the time I was thirteen and old enough to print memorial cards and programs and stuff."

"I was twelve the first time I made babysitting money," Neveah said. "I got hooked on having my own money after that. I worked as much as I could."

"We need to take a closer look at the sister's murder," Sam said.

"I have the lowdown on that," Cam said. "Sarah Corrigan, age seventeen, was kidnapped off a residential street in Manassas twenty-six years ago this June. She'd been at a friend's home to study and was walking the six blocks home. Her backpack was found on the sidewalk, but despite a massive manhunt, no other sign of her was found until about six weeks later when her naked body was located in a ravine. The murderer was never caught, and the case remains open. I spoke with a Lieutenant Kirkland at the City of Manassas Police

Department, and he told me the detective who originally caught the case is still working on it. He asked us to share our info on the Myerson case with them.

"Are we thinking there's a connection?" Freddie asked.

"I don't know," Cam said. "Two sisters murdered twenty-six years apart would be a stretch to pin on the same person. Wouldn't it?"

"I think so," Sam said. "Are the parents still around?"

"The mother died ten years ago and the father six years ago."

"Those poor people died without ever knowing who did that to their child," Sam said.

"I can't even imagine that," Gonzo said.

"Any other siblings, Cam?"

"There's an older brother, Charles, goes by Chuck, who still lives in Manassas."

"I'd like to see him," Sam said. "Let's find out where he is today."

CHAPTER SEVENTEEN

Goldstein's arrest unleashed an all-new nightmare for Nick and his team. Having the story of the Joint Chiefs' treachery resurrected was the last thing he needed, even if he was glad to see charges filed against the officers who'd plotted to overthrow his administration. Nick's team had been briefed by the acting AG minutes before the news conference, which was the only heads-up they'd received that a new shitstorm was headed their way.

They'd learned that Michael Wilson, disgraced Army general and former chair of the Joint Chiefs, had accepted a plea deal that would lead to lesser prison time in exchange for his testimony against the ringleader, Goldstein. The briefing revealed that the former chief of staff for the Army was also involved in the plot, as was the now-former commandant of the Marine Corps. Both had also accepted plea deals in exchange for testimony against Goldstein. The former chief of staff of the Air Force, the former chief of the National Guard Bureau and the former chief of Space Operations had been cleared of criminal involvement.

Nick had inherited the former Joint Chiefs from President Nelson and had kept them in place after he assumed office, believing they would remain faithful to their oaths of office and the Constitution. Like several other now-former members of Nelson's team, they'd shocked and disappointed him profoundly.

He'd watched Agent Truver's press conference in the personal sitting room that adjoined the Oval Office. It still took his breath away to consider how close he'd come to being removed from office in a military coup, the likes of which normally occurred in unsettled countries known for violent uprisings, not the United States of America.

Thank God for Juan Rodriguez and the enormous risk he'd taken to inform Nick of the plot. Otherwise, he'd have been caught unprepared, possibly giving the traitors the opening they would've needed to see their plan through to fruition. Honestly, he had no idea how it would've gone down. Would the Secret Service have drawn weapons against the military officials? Or would they have ceded to the demands of Goldstein, Wilson and the others who'd been involved?

Nick wasn't sure. He'd never imagined asking such questions when he became president, but he'd really like to know. He got up and went to the door that separated the sitting room from the Oval Office and asked Brant to come in. His lead agent was always close by.

"Close the door, will you?"

"Yes, sir, Mr. President."

"Have you heard the news about charges being filed against Goldstein, Wilson and two other former members of the Joint Chiefs?"

"I have, sir."

"I want to ask you something, and I'd like you to be honest with me, even if it's not the official Secret Service party line. Do you understand?"

"Yes, sir."

"If Juan Rodriguez hadn't warned me about the plot and the Joint Chiefs had gone forward with their effort to remove me from office, what would the Secret Service's response to that have been?"

"We would've removed them from the White House, forcibly if necessary."

"What about the agents who might've agreed with them that I needed to go?"

"I don't know of any agents who hold that belief, sir."

"Would you, as my lead agent, hear about that if there were agents who aren't loyal to me?"

"I believe the word would eventually reach me, sir, and there's been no undercurrent that I'm aware of."

"Would you tell me if there was?"

Brant hesitated, but only for a second. "Would you want me to, sir?"

"Yes, Brant, I'd want to know if there're agents working in the White House who don't think I should be here."

"Very well, sir. If I hear any such rumblings, I'll let you know."

"Could you get into trouble for doing that?"

"Only if you were to mention where you heard of the rumblings, sir."

"You don't have to call me sir when we're alone, Brant, and I'd never tell anyone where I heard such information."

"That's good to know."

Nick smiled. "You did it. You didn't call me sir."

"It's not an easy habit to break, sir. I mean..."

Laughing, Nick said, "I understand. Thank you for your candor."

"Of course."

"Could I ask you something else?"

"Anything you'd like, sir."

He couldn't help himself with the sir business. "What's your life like away from this place?"

"What is this life you speak of, sir?"

"Seriously, Brant? No family, friends, girlfriends, boyfriends?"

"My family is in Arizona, where I grew up. I get home once a year, and they come here to visit. I have three siblings, all of them married with kids, which keeps the pressure off me to produce grandkids. I don't have a girlfriend. Wouldn't be fair with the hours I keep."

That was more than the young man had ever revealed to Nick in all their time together. "I want you to take more time off. There's more to life than protecting the president."

Brant cracked the smallest of grins, which felt like a win to Nick.

"Please don't run yourself into the ground or give up the best years of your life for a job."

"This is not your average, ordinary job, sir. It's a tremendous honor to work with and for you."

"The best thing in my life is my family. Don't miss out on that by thinking work is the most important thing. It isn't."

"Thank you for your concern, sir. It's appreciated."

"Go get a girlfriend, Brant. And hurry up about it."

Brant's left eyebrow lifted ever so subtly. "Is that an order, sir?"

"Take it any way you wish. Life is short. Don't wake up twenty years from now and realize you missed the good stuff."

"Thank you, sir."

After Brant left the room, Nick settled back into the upholstered chair and attempted to eat part of the turkey club he'd requested for lunch. However, his stomach wasn't interested in food after he'd heard more about the coup that was barely thwarted. He tried to imagine what it would be like to be the first U.S. president to be deposed by the military. The action would've sent the entire world into a spiral from which it might've never recovered. Had the Joint Chiefs considered that kind of fallout while they made their plans?

As seasoned military leaders, they surely knew that the

ripple effect would've resulted in worldwide instability. As the United States went, so went the rest of the world. It was unfathomable to him that people who'd served more than thirty years in the military and achieved the highest ranks preferred that kind of instability to working with Nick to ensure a successful presidency.

He picked up the phone and asked Terry to come in.

His chief of staff knocked on the door a few minutes later and entered the sitting room.

"Want some turkey club?" Nick pushed the plate toward his friend.

"I won't say no to that. Haven't had time to eat yet."

"Don't skip meals on my behalf."

"I rarely miss a meal." He patted his flat stomach. "Gotta work out like a fiend to offset my intake."

Nick handed him the ketchup, knowing he liked his fries smothered in it.

"I take it you saw the press conference," Terry said as he dipped a fry.

"I did."

"I know it's hard not to take these things personally..."

"How else should I take it?"

"It's ridiculous. Goldstein will spend the rest of his life in prison rather than living large on his fat pension. The other three will lose their pensions and do some time. A lifetime of honorable service and sterling reputations gone in an instant. I don't get why they'd take such a risk."

"I guess they felt the situation was dire enough that extreme measures were warranted."

"The situation isn't dire, and you know that. They knew it wasn't. This was a craven power grab and nothing more."

"This makes six members of the Nelson administration who've either betrayed me or disgraced themselves and their offices on my watch."

Former Secretary of State Martin Ruskin had cavorted with

prostitutes in Iran, and after Nick had demanded his resignation, he'd become a vocal opponent of all things Cappuano. He was a frequent guest on cable news, deriding every move Nick made.

During the investigation into Tom Forrester's murder, Sam had learned that Attorney General Cox was up to his neck in gambling debt, which made him a blackmail risk. And now four former members of the Joint Chiefs of Staff were facing charges or had accepted plea deals to testify against the ringmaster.

"What're you thinking?"

Nick glanced at Terry. "We need to clean house. Bring in our own people. We should've done that from the start, but the shock of Nelson's sudden death and my ascension made it easier to keep the existing team in place."

"Are you talking about *everyone*?"

"I think it has to be, don't you?"

"Um, well… It'll take a minute to replace them with our own people, which will hamper our ability to get things done in the meantime. Do we even have enough people to replace them all?"

Terry's reminder that Nick's political career thus far had been somewhat brief wasn't lost on him. He didn't have the deep stable of allies and supporters that most people had by the time they landed in the Oval Office. "Probably not, but how do I go forward with the current team when I have no idea who I can trust and who I can't?"

"It's a problem, for sure. We could bring Dad in to oversee this project. You might not have a deep bench, but he sure does." Retired Senator Graham O'Connor had one of the deepest benches in town, with more contacts, friends and associates than anyone in politics.

"That's a good idea. We could have him prepare the new team and then clean house all at once when we're ready to introduce the new people."

"I'll ask him to come in tomorrow to get the ball rolling before you leave for the West Coast."

Nick grimaced at having to deal with the trip in the midst of the news about charges being filed against the former Joint Chiefs. Everyone he encountered would be thinking about how the admirals and generals who'd worked closely with him had wanted him gone so badly, they'd risked criminal charges as well as financial and personal ruin.

"How will anyone take me seriously after this?"

"Don't go there. If you keep showing up every day, doing the best job you can for the American people, I have to believe that, over time, we'll move on from this. And if we can't, well, you're out of here in two and a half years."

"That's a long-ass time to have the whole world think you're incompetent."

"The whole world doesn't think that."

"Right... They have no reason to believe that admirals and generals might know better than I do about what it takes to run this country."

"And yet, David Nelson didn't ask any of them to replace his ailing vice president. He asked *you*, because he had faith in *you*."

"Did he, though? Or did he just want the political bump that came from elevating a senator everyone was talking about, mostly because of his romance with a homicide detective."

"That wasn't the only reason they were talking about you, Nick. Look at the way you stepped up when John was killed. Your eulogy was so heartfelt and genuine. People responded to that and the story about your humble beginnings. They saw hope in you. They saw a new generation of leader. You and your beautiful young family have captivated the world. I firmly believe that, in time, you'll win over most of the detractors. The ones who don't see how lucky they are to have you in this office never would've supported you anyway. They aren't your people. Focus on opportunities to engage, like what you did at your brothers' school. Keep showing people who you really are, and things will turn around."

"You really think so?"

"I really do." Terry used his phone to call up a news site that was featuring the photo of Nick with his brothers at the school event. "We're getting really nice coverage of the school visit and the events in Baltimore."

"They didn't get drowned out by the NCIS press conference?"

"Maybe a little, but it's making for a positive counterbalance to that madness. 'Look, here's your president, out doing the job.'"

"I guess."

"There's one headline that might annoy you."

"What's that?"

"Cappuano's Much Younger Brothers a Symbol of the Complicated Life He's Led."

"What the actual fuck does that even mean?"

"It's a rehash of how your dad was in high school when he fathered you and how he has a second family with Stacy and the boys."

"With all the problems and challenges facing this country, *that's* what they're writing about?"

"Only because of the school visit. Most of the coverage has been positive. People thought it was adorable the way they interviewed you."

"I'm sure my dad is enjoying having his high school indiscretion broadcast to the world."

"He doesn't think of you that way, Nick."

"What I hate most about this is the impact it has on the people I love. Sam doesn't say much, but her job is a thousand times harder than it was when I was the VP, and now this shit with the twins' grandparents has come up again." He shook his head. "Sometimes I wish the Joint Chiefs had gotten their way."

"That would've been much worse, and you know it. Don't

think that way. Your wife and kids are getting an incredible experience that they'll remember for the rest of their lives."

"As they're surrounded by Secret Service."

"They don't care about that. They care about *you*, and they're happy to support you this way. I get that the Joint Chiefs situation continues to be a gut punch, but don't let it become a distraction we can't afford right now. You gotta keep your head in the game, Nick."

"You're right. Thanks for the kick in the ass."

"Thanks for the turkey club."

He'd polished off the whole plate of food in ten minutes.

"Anything for you."

"Same goes. I'll call Dad and get him here in the morning. He'll love being needed, especially by you."

Nick smiled. "Yeah, he will. It's a great idea to bring him in, Terry. Thanks for always having my back."

"My pleasure, Mr. President."

After Terry left, Nick thought about what his friend had said. Terry was right. He needed to keep his eye on the ball lest things get worse than they already were. Graham liked to say, "They hate us cuz they ain't us," and sometimes Nick believed that was true more than anything lacking in him.

He got up, used his private bathroom to freshen up and then went back to work. As long as he held this office, he'd do whatever he could to make things better for the American people.

CHAPTER EIGHTEEN

S am and Freddie were in the Secret Service SUV on the way to see Elaine's brother when Faith Miller called again. Shit. Sam had forgotten to return her earlier call.

"Hey, Faith. Sorry I missed you before. Crazy day."

"No worries. I told Leslie Forrester I'd check in with you about the funeral on Wednesday."

Shit. Fuck. Damn. Hell. She was scheduled to speak at Tom's funeral and hadn't given it a thought. "Yes, it's on the calendar."

"It's at ten a.m. at the National Cathedral."

"I'll be there."

At the thought of speaking in front of much of official Washington at the esteemed cathedral, her anxiety kicked into high gear.

"How're you all holding up?" she asked Faith.

"Minute to minute. It's still so hard to believe he's really gone. He was such a life-force."

"I know. I'm so sorry for everyone who worked so closely with him and loved him."

"He was one of the good guys. He'll definitely be missed."

"I heard they're already moving forward with a new USA," Sam said.

"Yeah, and about that... Not sure how you feel about getting involved in an official act of your husband's, but her reputation precedes her."

For a second, Sam didn't compute what Faith was saying—until she realized Faith was referring to Catherine McDermott, Tom's potential replacement. Anxiety was replaced by surprise and disappointment. "I wouldn't feel right talking to him about that, Faith."

"I had a feeling you might say that. Read up on her so you'll know what we're in for if she's approved by the Senate."

"I'll do that."

"I'm sorry to be inappropriate or to take advantage of our friendship. Grief is making me stupid."

"Don't think anything of it."

"How're you making out with the Myerson case?"

"Slow going so far, but we're doing what we do. Pulling the threads. I'll keep you posted."

"Sounds good. I'll see you Wednesday, if not before."

"See you then."

Sam slapped the phone closed and immediately opened it again to call Roni Connolly, her communications director at the White House.

"Hey," Roni said. "How's it going?"

"It's going. I was just reminded that I have to deliver a eulogy for U.S. Attorney Tom Forrester on Wednesday morning, and I could use some help with that."

"I heard you were speaking and started some notes in case you asked for help."

"I don't deserve you."

Roni laughed. "Likewise."

"Oh, I'm a real treat. A gift that keeps on giving."

Roni and Freddie both laughed at that while Sam gave her partner the side-eye. He wasn't allowed to agree with her.

"I'll put something together for you. I assume you want the

focus on your professional relationship with him as well as his accomplishments as the USA."

"You assume correctly. We had a close working relationship that was full of respect and admiration—at least from me to him. Sometimes, I think he wanted to smack me."

"We'll leave that part out."

"Probably for the best."

"I'll be in touch shortly."

"Thank you again for this."

"My pleasure."

She closed the phone. "Thank God for qualified people who know what they're doing."

"And who make you look good," Freddie said.

"That, too. I feel kind of guilty outsourcing such a personal thing."

"I have no doubt you'll put your own personal spin on whatever she comes up with."

"I will for sure."

"Don't feel guilty, Sam. You can only do so much."

"I've been having a bit of an existential crisis since Sunday."

"What? Why?"

"Me, sitting in the comms truck while the rest of you were on the front lines. Doesn't sit well."

"You came up with the idea, put the whole thing together and ended up making the arrest. We'd still be looking for him without you leading our team."

"That's nice of you to say, but asking you guys to take risks I can no longer take myself gives me a pit in the stomach."

"Don't let it. No one is thinking a thing of it."

"I am. Ruiz had plenty to say about it, too."

"Who cares what she thinks? The team that surrounds you doesn't give a rat's ass about her opinion."

She gave him a scandalized look. "Are you *swearing*, young Freddie?"

"You drive me to it."

Vernon grunted with laughter. "You should listen to your grasshopper, Sam. He's wiser than you give him credit for being."

"Thank you, Vernon," Freddie said.

"I appreciate your support, as always, but can you guys understand why it feels wrong, as a commander, to be behind the front lines, safely locked away while the people you supervise are putting their lives on the line?"

"I'd feel the same way," Vernon said, "but I also agree with Freddie that the only people whose opinions matter are the ones under your command. If you ask me, they'd rather have you in the trailer than anyone else leading them."

Freddie pointed to Vernon. "What he said."

"That's nice of you to say, Vernon."

"I'm not trying to be nice. It's the truth."

"Yes, it is," Freddie said. "We have an amazing team, led by an inspirational commander who we're all honored to work with and for. You're looking for problems where there are none."

"Inspirational, huh?"

"I said what I said."

"Excellent sucking up."

"Are you trying to piss me off?"

"Nope. I appreciate what you said, and I'll take it to heart. When we first got the call about Nelson passing away, one of my first thoughts was about how I'd manage to keep my job while Nick was president. I figured not much would change for me between him being VP and POTUS. I was wrong about that, and it weighs on me that my higher profile could put you guys in danger."

"That's fair, but we all know who and what you are on and off the job, and we have a choice about whether we want to continue to work with you. No one is heading for the door."

Sam hadn't really considered the fact that they had a choice about whether to stay or go. Any one of them could request reassignment at any time. Those requests were often taken seriously by the department. "That's true."

"Our eyes are wide open. Don't worry about us."

That was like telling her not to breathe, but she kept that thought to herself. "It helped me to talk about this, so thanks."

"Any time," Freddie said. "You might want to also consider how cool our friends and family think we are because we get to work with you."

"I am a treat."

He snorted. "You sure are."

"So Faith was kind of weird just now."

"How so?"

"She asked me to mention to Nick that the woman he's planning to nominate as the new USA could be a nightmare for us."

"Oh damn. Will you do that?"

"I think I should probably stay out of that, don't you?"

"Yeah, for sure."

"Except I keep thinking that if she does turn out to be a nightmare, I might've been able to prevent that. If I asked him to, he might reconsider the nomination."

"That's a very slippery slope. What if it got out that you were involved in picking the new USA?"

Everything in her recoiled from that potential scandal. "Yeah, that'd be a disaster."

"Then you've answered your own question."

They pulled up to a raised-ranch-style home in Manassas a few minutes later. As there were several cars in the driveway, Sam was hopeful they'd find Chuck Corrigan at home.

The woman who came to the door seemed to go stupid in the head when she saw Sam standing on the doorstep. "Oh my God," she said. "Is the first lady working on Elaine's case?" Her eyes got even bigger when she spotted the Secret Service SUV at the curb.

Sam wanted to bitch-slap her, but instead she showed her

badge. "I'm Lieutenant Holland, and this is my partner, Detective Cruz. We're looking for Chuck Corrigan. Is he at home?"

"Uh... He's here, but this isn't a great time."

"We're sorry for the intrusion, but every minute matters in a homicide investigation. We'd like to see him, please."

"Um, come in. I'll see if he's available."

Sam didn't respond to the "available" comment. When cops came to your door, you were always available. This woman would find that out soon enough if she didn't produce Chuck.

They were shown to a small living room.

"I'll be right back."

"You showed nice restraint there. Our little girl is growing up."

Sam snorted. "Easy, grasshopper."

"The first lady reaction is always entertaining to those of us who get the pleasure of witnessing it."

"Glad you're entertained. That's what really matters here."

"We see eye-to-eye on that."

Smiling, she looked over at him, next to her on a floral sofa. "Thanks for this, for what you said before, for all of it."

"I do what I can for you."

"That's trademarked."

"No, you doing what you can for the *people* is trademarked. My comment is not."

She scowled at him. "Semantics."

The sound of footsteps approaching had them snapping out of the banter and back into professional mode. Sam was relieved to see a heavyset middle-aged man with gray hair accompanying the woman who'd met them at the door. She so didn't want to have to fight with grieving people today.

Sam stood. "Chuck Corrigan?"

"That's me."

"Lieutenant Holland with the Metro PD. This is my partner, Detective Cruz."

"This is about Elaine," Chuck said.

"Yes, sir," Sam said as she returned to her seat.

He sat across from them in an upholstered chair.

The woman hovered nervously.

Sam gave her a look as if to say, *Get lost*, hoping she could read between the lines.

"Give us a minute, Jane."

She scurried from the room.

"She's my girlfriend."

Sam was glad she'd left without her having to ask. "We're very sorry about your sister."

"Thank you. It's hard to believe this could happen again."

"We heard about your sister Sarah being murdered and were wondering if you could tell us more about that case."

"It was a long time ago," he said with a sigh. "A lifetime ago."

"Whatever you can tell us about what happened then might help us to solve Elaine's case."

He gasped in shock. "You're not suggesting they're related, are you?"

"We're not suggesting anything. We're looking for information from someone with ties to both cases. Can you tell us what happened to Sarah?"

He leaned forward, elbows on knees. "I can't believe how hard it is to talk about her, even after all this time. She was the sweetest girl. We all adored her."

"You were older?"

Nodding, he said, "Five years older than Elaine and eight years older than Sarah. She'd gone to hang out at a friend's house down the street. She was only, like, six blocks from home. It was spring, and the sun was setting later. My mom told her to be home by eight, before it got dark. Eight came and went. Sarah was known for being a bit absent-minded at times, so we didn't think anything of it. Mom sent me to get her at her friend's house. I was about halfway there when I saw her backpack on the sidewalk. I'm not sure how I knew not to touch it, but I backed away from it and started screaming for help. One of the neighbors came out, and I think she's the one who called the police."

"You would've been twenty-five then?"

"Yes, I'd gotten home a few days earlier after getting my master's degree in Ohio."

"What happened after the police arrived?"

"I told them what I knew, which wasn't much except for where she'd been and how I'd found her backpack on the sidewalk. I ran home to get my parents, and we searched for her all night while the police went to the friend's house. The friend's mother reported that Sarah had left about half an hour before I spotted the backpack."

"Did the police ever suspect the friend and her family of involvement?"

"God, no, never. They were as distraught as we were."

"Were there any suspects?"

"Not that we ever heard. The police worked the case hard from the beginning and are still on it. The detective in charge refuses to retire as long as Sarah's case is active."

"His name?"

"William Truehart. The name says it all. He's remained faithful to Sarah and our family for all these years. Since my parents passed away, he still checks in with me and with Elaine monthly to keep us abreast of any developments, not that there have been many. But he's never forgotten us or her."

"She was later found, correct?"

"Yes," he said with another sigh. "About six weeks later, naked in a ravine out by Clifton, about ten miles from our house. The autopsy showed that she'd only been dead a short time when she was found."

The implications of the kidnapper abusing her for six weeks were horrific to imagine.

"I'm very sorry for the terrible ordeal your family has endured and that you've now lost Elaine, too."

"I can't believe it. I've been in complete shock since Frank called yesterday."

"Were you close to her?"

"I mean... We had our own lives, but we stayed in touch. Talked every couple of weeks. Had dinner a few times a year. Even though we didn't see each other often, it was a comfort to me to know she was there, and I think she felt the same about me. When you go through something like we did with Sarah... It forms a bond, but it's also painful to be together when there's always someone missing."

"Did you know of any problems she was having?"

"Her daughters were driving her crazy, but it was the usual teenager stuff."

"Both daughters?"

"Yeah, she had challenges with both of them."

Sam found it interesting that nothing had been said before about Jada being at odds with her mother. "Frank and the girls told us Elaine was extremely strict with them because of what happened to Sarah. Were you aware of that?"

"Yes, I've heard that from Frank and the girls over the years, and I understood her position better than most."

"Do you have children?"

"No."

"Did she share her concerns about her girls in relation to what'd happened to Sarah?"

"Not specifically, but there was no doubt Elaine was traumatized by the experience, as we all were. If I'd had kids, I probably would've been the same way. When someone you love is snatched from your life in broad daylight... It changes your perceptions of safety and security and... well... everything."

"Is there anything else you can tell us that might be relevant to Elaine's case?"

"Not that I can think of. I've been away on vacation the last few weeks, so I hadn't spoken to her in a while. I feel bad about that now. I can't believe I'll never again pick up the phone to call her. It's so strange. My entire immediate family is gone now. There's just me left."

"We're very sorry for your loss."

Sam couldn't conceive of a life without her sisters. It was bad enough moving on without her dad, but losing them... Nope. Not going there.

"Thank you again for taking the time to talk to us."

"I wish there was more I could do to help."

Sam left him with her card and the usual instructions to call if he thought of anything else that might be relevant.

"I don't know about you," Sam said to Freddie when they were outside, "but I want to see Detective William Truehart."

"You read my mind."

CHAPTER NINETEEN

W hen the young officer manning the desk realized who'd strolled into the reception area of the Manassas Police Department, he nearly had a stroke. He still had acne and couldn't be more than twenty or twenty-one.

"I, uh... May I help you?"

Sam flashed her badge and made the usual introductions. "I'd like to see Detective Truehart, please."

"I... um... Let me see if he's in."

Freddie chuckled as the young man took off like his pants were on fire. "You've just given him a story to tell for the rest of his life."

"Whatever."

The officer returned a few minutes later. "Right this way, ma'am."

"You can call me lieutenant."

"Yes, ma'am. Lieutenant, ma'am."

"For fuck's sake," Sam muttered as Freddie rocked with silent laughter.

Every cop in the place was on their feet, stretching their necks for a look at the celebrity in their midst as Sam and Freddie were led to the far back corner of the detectives' area where Truehart had a small desk tucked away from the others.

He bore the grizzled, weary look of a seasoned officer, with snow-white hair, a red, ruddy complexion, tired hazel eyes and a build that might've once been muscular but was now ceding to age. Sam guessed him to be in his late sixties.

To his credit, he was the only one in the big, open room who didn't act a fool over her.

He stood to shake her hand and Freddie's as she introduced them. "Have a seat in my office."

She appreciated his decorum as much as his wry humor. "Sorry to bomb in unannounced."

"No problem at all. What can I do for you?"

"Have you heard that Elaine Myerson was murdered in her home yesterday?"

His amiable expression went slack with shock. "*What?* No, I hadn't heard that. What happened?"

"She was felled by a single blow to the head from an object that remains missing."

"Oh God, poor Elaine. And Chuck. What that family has endured..." He shook his head as his shoulders sagged. "I can't believe this."

"We understand you're still working on their sister Sarah's case," Sam said.

"That's right. Technically, I'm retired and collecting a pension, not because that's what I wanted, but because there're rules, don't you know? I come in every day and go over the case file from beginning to end, hoping to see something I've missed."

"Have you ever had suspects?"

He shook his head. "Nothing that ever panned out. There were fingerprints on the body, but we've never been able to match them to anyone. I run them monthly, just in case, and I've checked the DNA found on her body against the family DNA sites and come up empty there, too."

"Chuck told us how much the family appreciates your dedication to the case," Freddie said.

"People tell me I'm obsessed, that I should let it go. My own daughter was sixteen when Sarah went missing. She's gotten to grow up, go to college, get married, have children. Sarah was cheated of all that, while the person who tortured and killed her is still out there living his life. Personally, I can't live with *that*. I can't let it go."

"I've had a few cases like that," Sam said. "Not as long-standing as yours, but no less frustrating. I admire your dedication, Detective." She realized he'd probably also missed out on some deserved promotions due to his obsession with one cold case.

"How can I help you?" he asked.

"We're not sure, but after hearing about your work, we wanted to meet you, to let you know we're on Elaine's case and to ask if you have any thoughts to share that might help."

"I wish I did. I haven't spoken to Elaine in a couple of months because I had nothing new to tell her. Last we spoke, she was working a lot and dealing with teenagers. We laughed about that. My grandchildren are around the same ages as her girls and giving their mothers fits."

"Did Elaine talk to you about how she was a highly overprotective mother?"

"She did. She struggled with letting the girls spread their wings, but I told her I didn't blame her. I had the same struggles with my kids after working Sarah's case. That someone could go missing like that, without a trace, only to be found weeks later after having been held captive somewhere. It haunted me. Continues to."

Sam had never been more thankful for Secret Service protection for her kids than she was while hearing about Sarah Corrigan's case. She would never have to worry about where they were because they had eyes on them at all times.

"I can certainly understand why," she said. "Some victims just stay with you."

"Yeah, they do. They become ours, if you know what I mean."

"I do."

"A lot of these guys," he said, waving his hand toward the other detectives, "they come in, do their tour and punch out. Never give the place another thought until they're back on duty. That's never been me. They make fun of me for still working after I'm technically retired, but it was never just a job for me."

"I feel that so deeply." Sam glanced at Freddie and then back at Truehart. "We both do. It's never been just a job for us either."

"That why you're still doing it when your old man is in the Oval?"

Sam laughed at the phrasing. "That's exactly why."

Truehart nodded. "I figured that when I heard you were gonna keep the job. I decided you were like me. Nothing could make you want to give it up, not old age or even the White House."

"No matter what happens with our case, I want to help with yours if you'll have us. If you want to make a copy of the case files for me, I'll put some people on it as time permits. I can make a case for the possibility of it being linked to ours."

"Do you think it could be?"

"I mean... Anything's possible, but I'm not leaning in that direction. Not yet, anyway. But with the connection to the sister, I can justify spending some time on her case. Not that I think we'd do anything you haven't already covered. It's just that sometimes a fresh set of eyes—or two—can see something new."

"You'd have no objection from me. I'll make a copy of everything and get it over to your shop tomorrow. Thank you for the offer. It's much appreciated."

"You know what's another hallmark of an outstanding police officer?" Freddie asked.

"What's that, young man?"

"All you care about is justice for your victim, not glory for yourself."

Truehart was visibly moved by Freddie's comment. "She's mine. If I could put away her killer, she and I could both rest in peace when my time comes."

Sam stood and offered him her hand. "We'll do everything we can to help you, Detective."

He took her hand between both of his. "It was an honor to meet you."

"No, sir," Sam said. "The honor was all ours."

THEY WERE quiet on the ride back to town. Sam had been ridiculously moved by Truehart and his dedication to Sarah's case. It reminded her of Calvin Worthington, the teenager gunned down in his own driveway fifteen years earlier, and how the case had been solved in an afternoon because someone had finally decided to give a shit.

"Truehart makes me extra ashamed of what happened with Worthington," Sam said.

"That wasn't the same thing at all. It wasn't your case from the get-go."

"I was the responding officer."

"You were in Patrol. No one was going to let you investigate it. No comparison, Sam."

"Still... there was more I could've done much sooner than I did."

"What matters is that his family has answers now. It never should've taken as long as it did, but that failing was on the department collectively."

"You can't solve them all, as much as you might want to."

Vernon met her gaze in the mirror. "'Most' is a pretty good track record."

"I suppose so." Sam ceded to their insistence but would never forget the massive failing that the Worthington case represented. By remembering it, she could hopefully ensure nothing like that ever happened again.

Back at HQ, Sam stopped at the morgue to check in with Lindsey.

"I haven't had a chance to review the Myerson autopsy report, so give me the gist."

"One blow to the back of the head fractured her skull and caused a brain bleed that killed her pretty quickly. It was straightforward, as these things go. The tox screen will tell us more, but I don't expect any smoking guns there. She was in good health overall."

"Any thoughts about what kind of object we're looking for?"

"I'd say it was something smooth, like a baseball bat perhaps. There were no grooves or indentations in the wound that would indicate something pronged."

"I'll pass that on to Haggerty. Thanks for the input."

"No problem. I wanted to tell you…"

Sam tipped her head, surprised to see Lindsey look so uncomfortable, and hoped her friend wasn't still upset about Sam lying to her. "What's up?"

"You're going to hear from my sister, Margo, about a bridal shower."

"Okay…"

"I made her promise there won't be any stupid games or other such bullshit and that she won't go dumb in the head about talking to you."

Sam laughed. "Appreciate that." She shuddered. "I hate shower games. Why do we wrap our friends in toilet paper just because they're getting married?"

Lindsey laughed. "Couldn't agree more. I told Margo I want

something classy and elegant. No nonsense. I think she understands, but I'm counting on you to keep her on track."

"I'll do my best for you, Doc. Who else is in the wedding party?"

"A cousin, who's local, two college friends and a med school friend. The three of them live on the West Coast."

"I'm looking forward to meeting them."

"You'll be glad to know I've spared you the wedding party group chat."

Smiling, Sam said, "You really do know me, but don't leave me out of anything I need to know. I assume there'll be a bachelorette party?"

Lindsey recoiled. "Absolutely not. I'm not a twenty-two-year-old nitwit."

"Aw, come on! I already bought the dildos and handcuffs."

"If you were ever quoted saying that, the scandal would be enormous."

"Let's make sure that doesn't get out."

Lindsey pretended to lock her lips and throw away the key. "Thank you for being in my wedding party, even though you don't have time to breathe."

"Anything for you, kid. Happy to be included. Back to work I go. Thanks again for the autopsy summary."

"No problem."

As she returned to the pit, Sam was glad to be back on track with Lindsey, even as she cringed at the many ways bridal showers could be ridiculous. For Lindsey, however, she'd step up to the bridesmaid plate with a smile on her face.

"Everyone in the conference room for updates."

Sam went into her office to take a closer look at Lindsey's full report before she joined the others in the conference room to convey the ME's findings to her team. "Cruz, please let Lieutenant Haggerty know we're looking for a smooth object as the murder weapon, possibly something like a baseball bat."

Freddie texted the info to Haggerty.

"Lindsey confirmed that Elaine died after a single blow from this smooth object. There were no puncture wounds or anything to indicate texture on the murder weapon. We spoke with Elaine's brother, Chuck, in Manassas. He confirmed that Elaine talked to him about problems with her daughters, and we learned more about their sister Sarah's abduction and murder."

"That poor guy," Neveah said. "To lose both his sisters to murder."

"Indeed." Sam worried about Neveah being close to murder all the time when her own mother's killing from years ago remained unsolved.

"Did anything about him stand out as suspicious?" Cameron asked.

"Not to me," Sam said, glancing at Freddie.

He shook his head. "Not at all. He was genuinely grief-stricken, in my opinion."

"One thing he said stood out to me," Sam said. "He mentioned Elaine had trouble with her *daughters*, plural, while the family led us to believe Zoe, the older one, was the problem."

"You want to take a closer look at Jada?" Freddie asked, sounding surprised.

"I want to know more about where she was yesterday and speak to the people she was with. Call Frank and get the info on the family who took her to the Civil War sites."

Freddie left the room to make the call.

"What else have we got?"

"I did a deep dive on the family's social media," Cameron said. "Elaine posted often, usually funny memes or pictures of sunsets and flowers. Not much about the family."

"Did she have social media for work?"

"Yes, I was going to add that. As the chief communications officer for CVX, she was actively advocating in Congress for member countries, especially the three biggest petroleum-producing countries—the U.S., Russia and Saudi Arabia."

"That's an interesting angle," Sam said. "You don't often hear of those three countries working together."

"In this case, and I'm quoting their website here, they collaborate on a number of issues of common concern and promote best practices in the industry while working with Congress to balance economic, environmental and climate concerns related to the petroleum industry."

"Does that mean they work with Congress to keep the oil coming no matter what drilling does to the environment?" O'Brien asked.

"That's not how I read it," Sam said. "What did the colleagues have to say?"

"We talked to a few of her work colleagues, who were beside themselves over her death." Neveah listed the names of the coworkers and their titles within the organization. "They reported that she was well liked, well respected in the office and within the industry, and a hardworking employee who could be counted on to deliver on time and with no drama. The executive director mentioned they've had a lot of staff turnover, so someone like Elaine, who'd been with them for years, was very much appreciated."

"Did the ED give you any insight into their personnel issues?" Sam asked.

"Not specifically. I deduced that it was the usual problem organizations have attracting and retaining quality help."

"I'd like to dig deeper into that angle. Go back to the ED and get some specifics about people who might've worked directly with Elaine and then left the organization, especially anyone who left under less-than-ideal circumstances."

"Will do," Neveah said.

"How about friends?" Sam asked. "What did Frank say about who she was close to?"

"He didn't," Gonzo said. "He said something to the effect

that she was so busy at home and at work, she didn't have much time for extras."

"Are friends considered extras?" Sam was busier than anyone she knew, but made time for her loved ones—those who were related and those who weren't. "The girls said she had a lot of friends. It would be odd to me if she didn't spend time with some of them. Let's talk to Frank some more about that."

"We're not looking at him at all?" Cam asked.

"Carlucci and Dominguez confirmed he was at the work thing all day yesterday."

"Doesn't mean he couldn't hire it done," Gonzo said.

"Where are we with the financials?" Sam asked.

"Still reviewing," Cam said, "but nothing stands out. The usual bills, groceries, money moving in and out. The largest transaction in the last thirty days was paid to the mortgage company. They have about three thousand in credit card debt, close to twenty thousand in savings and a credit score over eight hundred."

"I'd like to have those stats," Gonzo said.

"Right?" Freddie asked with a laugh.

"So nothing in the financials to show any big withdrawals that might indicate hiring it done," Sam said.

"Not that I've seen so far," Cam said.

"I'd like to speak to some of the girls' friends. What are you seeing on social media about who they were close to?"

"I'll get you a list," Cameron said.

"Divide up the friends and knock them out tomorrow after school."

"Will do," Cam said.

"I'll be in late tomorrow. I'm meeting with Roni about my eulogy for Tom."

"We'll see you when you get here, LT," Neveah said for all of them.

CHAPTER TWENTY

On the way home, Sam took a call from an unknown number. "Holland."

"This is Collins Worthy."

Her stomach turned at the sound of the smooth, cultured voice belonging to her mother-in-law's attorney, or lover, or whatever he was. "How'd you get my number?"

"Does that matter?"

"Yeah, it kind of does."

"When Nicoletta was in the hospital some time ago, Nick gave her both your numbers in case of emergency. His doesn't work anymore, so I called yours."

"Oh right, you mean the time she threw herself down a flight of stairs so she could call her kindhearted son to Cleveland to shake him down for money?"

His silence spoke volumes.

"Did she tell you about how she crashed his wedding, knowing full well that the sight of her would ruin the biggest day of his life? Or did she tell you how I got in her face and kicked her out, which would be her version of what took place? I'm sure she's made me out to be the source of all her problems where her son is concerned. The fact of the matter is that *she's* the reason her son wants nothing to do with her, not me."

"I understand that you're not the problem."

"Does she?"

"We're working on that."

"Let me ask you something, Mr. Worthy. You seem like a decent enough kind of guy—at least on the surface. What's your game plan with her? You must realize that she's probably using you the way she uses everyone to advance her own agenda."

"Do you believe in love at first sight, Lieutenant?"

Sam rolled her eyes so hard, it was a wonder she could still see. "Didn't you meet her when she was incarcerated?"

"I did, but from the first second I laid eyes on her, I was captivated."

"Do you have a family?"

"I have three adult children."

"What do they think of their dad cavorting with a criminal?"

"They're not too happy about it."

"Take my advice. *Run.* Run for your life as far from her as you can get. She's a grifter, a taker, a loser. She has no idea what really matters in this life, and she doesn't care about anyone but herself. She's done nothing but hurt her son from the day he was born."

"She regrets that very much."

"Of course she does," Sam said with a harsh laugh. "Her beautiful, brilliant, handsome, loving son grew up to be president of the United States through absolutely no thanks to her, and she wants a piece of that action. If you're seeing any other motivation for this renewed interest in him and us, then you're missing the lead story."

"While it may seem that way, I'm the one who's encouraged her to make amends with her son and with you."

"Why?"

"Because I'm a softie that way. My children are the most important people in my life. I wouldn't have survived losing their mother to cancer without their love and support. I want Nicoletta to have a relationship with her son, to have a chance to repair the hurt and to go forward together as a family."

It was all Sam could do not to laugh out loud at the idea of Nicoletta suddenly figuring out how to be a mother at fiftysomething.

"I'm not sure what you expect me to say. My number one priority is protecting my husband and family from things that can hurt them. Your girlfriend, or whatever you want to call her, lives at the top of the things-that-can-hurt-my-family list."

"She wants the chance to know her son and grandchildren. And you, too, of course."

Sam laughed. "Of course. She can't wait to get to know me. I'm not sure if you two are watching the news from your love nest, but Nick and I both have much greater concerns right now than whether or not he has a relationship with his deadbeat mother."

"We're aware of what you're both dealing with. We were very sorry to hear that his young aide was murdered."

"If you want to know who Nicoletta's son is... He's the kind of man who would weep for a junior officer who'd become his friend over the last few months when friends have been few and far between. That's the man into whose already very complicated life you want to bring a woman who's never once cared about anything but her next mark. It seems as if she's found a good one in you. I hope you've locked up the family silver and valuables. I wouldn't put it past her to cut and run as soon as you've used up your usefulness to her."

"Long before I met Nicoletta, I admired your husband and how he handles himself."

"That's nice to hear, but it doesn't change anything. I have no issue with you except to question your judgment in who you choose to associate with."

"I've stepped out of character with this relationship, but I can't seem to help myself. I see something in her, something beyond the grift and the hustle and the con. I see a woman who's never had anyone truly love her or care about her. Did you know her mother disowned her when she became pregnant with her son?"

"Did she tell you that?"

"No, I learned that when I contacted a childhood friend of hers when I was considering whether to take her on as a client."

"How did you find this friend?"

"I asked her for three personal references. Dorinda was one of them. She told me how Nicoletta's mother was so outraged and embarrassed that her teenage daughter was pregnant that she put her out on the street to figure it out for herself. She never again had anything to do with Nicoletta. She was sixteen, Lieutenant."

Sam would never admit to feeling a tiny bit sorry for teenage Nicoletta.

"Luckily, a school counselor took mercy and helped get her placed in a home for young mothers until the baby was born. Hours after the birth, the paternal grandmother showed up at the hospital, took the baby and left Nicoletta to fend for herself. She did the only thing she could and figured out how to survive on her own. Did she make some unfortunate choices? Absolutely. Did she fail her son during those years? She certainly did. She has many, many regrets, most of them centered on him. What she doesn't regret is doing what it took to keep a roof over her head and food on her table."

"People have their struggles, Mr. Worthy. No doubt about that. But that doesn't justify going on live TV to tell horrible lies about her son for money. It doesn't justify shaking *him* down for money or taking advantage of his caring heart time and time again. Do you know what it does to him when she swoops in, acting like she finally wants to be his mother, only to realize it's just another con?"

"No, I can't imagine what that must be like."

"Do you know that the scent of Chanel No. 5 triggers trauma for him? On the rare occasions when she visited him as a child, he'd refuse to shower for days to retain the scent of his mother. If he encounters that scent anywhere at any time, it sends him spiraling, regardless of where he is or what he's doing. *That* is her legacy with him."

"I can understand how upsetting that must be for him— and for you."

"And for everyone who loves him, which is a lot of people, and not one of those people yearns for him to have his mother in his life. If anything, we yearn for her to go away and leave him alone."

"Nicoletta is trying to change. She desperately wants to make things right with him and you and to know her grandchildren."

"Again, I keep coming back to the same question. *Why?*"

"She's witnessed the close bond I have with my children, and she wants that with her son, and his family.

"And it has nothing at all to do with the fact that he's the president of the United States, and a close bond with him would be good for whatever scam she's running next?"

"She's out of business, Lieutenant. As a condition of her release, she's not allowed to do business in the state of Ohio."

"I'm sure she'll relocate to one of the other forty-nine states when she tires of trying to please you."

"I hope that doesn't happen. I've made it clear to her that I want us to be together, and I believe in her ability to change her life."

"I wish I shared in your belief. I need to get going to be with my family. Thank you for calling."

"Will you consider talking to her? We're both well aware

that you're the gateway to making things right with her son, and she's very interested in speaking to you one-on-one."

"I'll have to think about it. Unlike you, I don't believe a tiger changes her stripes. You'll understand my reluctance to let her anywhere near my husband or children, knowing what she's capable of."

"I do understand. I'm asking you to give her a chance. That's all. Just a chance."

"I'll think about it. No promises. You'll either hear from me, or you won't. Please don't call me again."

"Thank you for your time, Lieutenant."

"Have a nice evening."

"You do the same."

For fuck's sake, Sam thought as Vernon held the door for her.

"Everything all right?"

"Never better. Just another day in paradise."

Vernon smiled. "Try to have a nice evening with the family."

"Oh, I will. Don't worry. Best part of the day."

"Are we bright and early tomorrow?"

"You get to sleep in, my friend. I have an early meeting here, so let's plan to leave around eight thirty."

"See you then."

"Thanks for everything."

"A pleasure, ma'am."

Sam shot him a scowl over her shoulder that made him laugh. *Ma'am.* Worst title ever.

"Evening, ma'am," Harold the usher said. "Hope you had a nice day."

Sam held back a laugh at yet another *ma'am.* "My day was busy and often not so nice, but it sure is good to be home."

"The president and the children are upstairs in the residence. I believe they just sat down to dinner."

"Hope they made enough for me."

"I'm sure they did."

As Sam took the stairs two at a time, she was relieved to note that her hip was now fully recovered from the break she'd suffered after a fall on the ice over the winter. It'd been a while since she'd raced up the stairs, and it felt good to be strong again. She had no time or patience for the injuries that seemed to strike her far more often than they did most people.

Upon reaching the residence, she followed the voices to the family dining room, stopping short when she heard Aubrey saying that Scotty ate too many eggs, and if he wasn't careful, he was going to have a chicken.

Scotty's laughter was the best thing she'd heard since breakfast.

The twins let out a shriek of excitement when Sam walked into the room. They got up from their chairs to come hug her. "Hello, my loves. How was your day?"

"Collin ate paste at school and threw up in the cafeteria!" Alden reported.

"Gross. Why did he eat paste?"

"He said it tastes good."

"It doesn't."

"I think he figured that out."

Laughing, she scooted them back to their seats and dropped a kiss on Scotty's head as she made her way to Nick for a different kind of kiss.

"Children are watching," Scotty said.

"Mind your business," Sam said as she smiled at her husband.

"Your business is happening right in front of me."

"When is he going to get a girlfriend?" Sam asked Nick.

"Any day now, and I can't wait."

"Me either. Where's my mom?" Her mom, Brenda, had been filling in with the kids after school while Celia was on her trip.

"Out for dinner with her girlfriends," Nick said.

"Ah, okay." She leaned in to see what they were eating. "What's for dinner?"

"Chicken," Scotty said with a grin.

Sam sputtered with laughter. "Oh damn." She took a seat next to Nick and helped herself to roasted chicken, mashed potatoes, stuffing, green beans and a bit of gravy while trying not to think about carbs or calories. "How was everyone's day besides the paste incident?"

"I got an eighty-two on my algebra quiz," Scotty said.

"Holy crap," Sam said. "That's amazing!"

"I thought so, too. I was kinda shocked, actually."

"I would be, too. I think a sixty-five was my high score in algebra."

"Sam."

"What? It's true."

Nick's expression conveyed disapproval even as a smile tugged at his lips.

"He doesn't want you telling me how mediocre you were in school," Scotty said.

Nick pointed to Scotty. "That. Exactly that."

"Why? It's the truth, and it wasn't my fault. I was battling dyslexia, and no one knew that. I was thrilled to get a sixty-five under those conditions."

"What's dys... dys... lexa?" Aubrey asked.

"Dyslexia. It's a learning disorder that makes reading difficult."

"Do I have that?" she asked.

"No, my love, you do not have it. You're an awesome reader."

Aubrey beamed with pleasure at the compliment. "Do you still have dys... dys... What is it again?"

"Dyslexia. Yes, I'll always have it. Reading is a struggle for me, especially when I'm tired. That's why I prefer audiobooks and let you guys read to me."

"I prefer audiobooks, too," Scotty said. "Especially for things like *The Canterbury Tales*." He shuddered. "Horrendous."

"You were supposed to *read* that, Scotty," Nick said. "Not listen."

"I did both at the same time. It helped me survive it, as did the CliffsNotes thingies Mom got me."

"I suppose that's okay, then."

"It's all about survival in the eighth grade, Dad."

Nick, who'd been a rock-star student, laughed at the face Scotty made. "Oh, the drama."

After dinner, Sam and Nick supervised the kids clearing the table and loading the dishwasher. The White House staff had told them they'd clean up, but they wanted the kids to know how to take care of themselves and to have some responsibility for chores. More than anything, they didn't want them spoiled by the staff. When their time in the White House ended, they'd go back to normal life and would have to fend for themselves.

"Anyone who quickly takes a shower and puts on pj's can watch a little TV before bed," Nick said.

The twins took off running. They'd recently begun taking showers rather than baths and preferred to do so privately. Their Littles were growing up quickly.

"Is your homework done?" he asked Scotty.

"Yep. Gonna go shower so I can watch TV with the twins." With a cheeky grin, he added, "Gotta follow the rules set by POTUS."

"That's right."

After Scotty left the room, Nick reached for Sam and gave her a proper kiss. "Hi there."

"How's it going?"

"Best thirty minutes of my day, hands down."

She smiled. "The bar is set pretty low these days."

"True," he said with a chuckle. "I can never wait to get back upstairs to real life."

"How was the rest of your day?"

"Terrible, but who cares about that now that my best girl is in my arms?"

Sam couldn't tell him about Worthy's call. Not now, anyway. Not when he was finally getting a break from a day of nonstop bullshit. "Any word from Andy about the situation?"

"Not yet, but he told me not to lose any sleep over it. The Armstrongs' will is crystal clear in its directions for custody of the twins."

"Have you talked to Eli?"

"Not since this morning, but we texted a bit. He's trying to stay calm."

"How's that going?"

"Not so great, as you can imagine. I'm glad Candace is there with him." Eli and his now-wife were thrilled to be back together after her parents had gone to extreme lengths to keep them apart for years.

"Yeah, me, too." Sam couldn't bear to think about any threat to their family, let alone another volley from Cleo's parents. They'd shown little interest in the kids since their daughter's murder and resurfaced only when they needed money, or so it seemed to her.

"How was the rest of your day?" Nick asked.

"Not terrible. We're working the new case, making some progress."

"Any suspects?"

"Not yet, but it's early days. Speaking of early days, I have a seven o'clock meeting with Roni to figure out my eulogy for Tom."

"That's on Wednesday, right?"

"Yes, at the National Cathedral."

"I'm hoping to attend before I leave for the West Coast."

"Stop reminding me that you're leaving."

"It's only for a couple of days."

Sam shook her head. "Lalalala, I can't hear you."

CHAPTER TWENTY-ONE

Aubrey picked *Descendants 3* for TV time, much to Alden's dismay. He was into all things *Star Wars* these days and wanted to watch it on repeat. He cuddled up to Nick while Aubrey snuggled with Sam, and Skippy landed on Scotty.

Sam glanced over at Nick, who smiled at her. She loved seeing him happily ensconced in the family he'd wanted his whole life. No one deserved a happy family more than he did. The thought of anything threatening his hard-earned happiness put her into fight mode.

Hearing more about Nicoletta's past had been enlightening, but it didn't change anything for Sam. She was still the same grifter she'd been before Sam knew about how she'd been treated by her mother when she'd gotten pregnant as a teenager. Having witnessed Nick's devastation more than once as his mother had breezed in and out of his life, she couldn't bear to see him leveled by her again.

She recalled him rushing to Cleveland after a doctor had called him, at Nicoletta's request, to say she'd fallen down a flight of stairs. He'd been so full of hope that his mother wanted her only child with her, but that hadn't been her ultimate goal. Nick had come home believing she'd thrown herself down the stairs as a ploy to get him there so she could hit him up for money.

The outrage of that incident and many others was a reminder of why they needed to keep their distance from Nicoletta and her madness. Sam picked over the conversation with Worthy, looking for deeper motivations on his part. Was he hoping for access to Nicoletta's famous son? She wouldn't put anything past Nicoletta or anyone who associated with her.

Tomorrow, she'd take a deeper look at Worthy. She wanted to know who he was and what he was about.

The twins fell asleep watching the movie, as they usually did after a long, busy day. Nick and Scotty carried them to bed, and Sam helped to tuck them in before going to spend a few minutes with Scotty.

"I'm so proud of your algebra quiz grade."

"Thanks. I was shocked but pleased."

"Hard work pays off."

He raised an eyebrow. "Does it, though?"

Sam laughed. "Don't get me in trouble with Dad."

"You do that all on your own. You don't need my help."

"That's true."

His face lost all hint of amusement. "This thing with the Joint Chiefs getting arrested. How bad will it be for him?"

"I don't know. I'm hoping it'll be a distraction more than anything."

"We talked about it in school today."

That shocked her. "They talked about it right in front of you?"

"We do current events in social studies every day. Mr. Estes and I have talked about how Dad and his administration might come up from time to time and that I'm allowed to excuse myself and go to the library if the conversation makes me uncomfortable."

"Oh. Wow. I didn't know that."

He shrugged. "It's usually no big deal. But today... That was the first time I wanted to go to the library."

"Did you?"

"Nah, I stuck it out, but it was hard to hear that some people think the Joint Chiefs were heroes for sacrificing themselves and their careers to try to do something for the good of the country."

"They're not heroes. They're criminals."

"That's what you and I believe, but other people, who don't know Dad the way we do... it's given them doubts about him."

"I hate that you had to sit there and listen to that."

"I could've left if I wanted to."

"Which would only draw more attention to you."

"Yeah, that was a concern."

"Scotty..."

"It's okay, Mom. Don't give me that I'm-gonna-cry face. I'm fine. There are far more perks of being the first son than there are negatives."

"You have to let me hug you."

"If you must."

"I must." She put her arms around him and held him close. "I'm sorry you had to deal with that."

"I'm sorry *he's* dealing with it."

"Yeah, me, too."

"Don't tell him about this, okay? He's got enough on his mind without worrying about me."

"He'd want to know."

"He doesn't *need* to know. It happened, I'm fine, we're moving on."

Sam pulled back so she could see his face and brushed the hair back from his forehead. "Will you promise to tell me if it becomes untenable?"

"I assume that means intolerable?"

"Roughly translated."

"I'll tell you."

"Promise?"

"I promise."

"Please don't suffer in silence over what goes on with us. Neither of us would ever want that."

"I know."

Sam kissed his cheek. "We love you more than anything."

"Love you just as much."

"Don't stay up too late."

"I won't."

Sam gave Skippy a scratch between the ears that earned her a loving gaze from the dog. "Night."

"Night."

Sam walked to their suite at the end of the hall, feeling weighted down by what Scotty had told her. How had it not occurred to her—or Nick—that they'd be discussed in his classes from time to time? Should she speak to the teacher about that? Could she ask him not to talk about the current president while the man's son was in the room? Would that even be appropriate? She had no idea, and who could she ask? Who else did she know who was in this situation?

Only Nick could relate, and Scotty didn't want to upset him when he had enough things on his mind. But Scotty wasn't just another *thing*. He was their beloved son, and it was up to them to make sure he was well cared for.

He would absolutely hate having her make anything of it with the teacher. She was sure of that. He didn't want to be treated differently because of who his parents were. It was bad enough that he went to school surrounded by Secret Service agents.

Ugh, what to do?

She would mention it to Vernon tomorrow and get his take. Depending on what he said, she'd take it to Nick—or not. Scotty was right. Nick had enough on his mind without worry about being the cause of angst for their son in his social studies class.

Wearing gym shorts and the "I love you more" T-shirt Sam had given him for their anniversary, Nick was seated in front of the TV, watching the latest discussions about the charges pending against the former Joint Chiefs of Staff.

"Goldstein must've had his reasons to risk everything," one white-haired pundit said. "He worked closely with the president and had seen him in action. Clearly, he didn't like what he saw and took the courageous step of trying to do something about it. We should all be thankful to him."

"Right," Nick said. "He tried to cause a constitutional crisis, but let's show him our gratitude."

Sam sat next to him and reached for his hand.

"I don't agree," a younger woman with red hair said. "What Goldstein did was treasonous. When President Nelson died, the Constitution worked the way the founders intended with the elevation of the vice president to the presidency. The number one role of the VP is to be ready to assume command should the president die in office. Where were all the doubts about Cappuano when he was the VP, sitting a heartbeat from the Oval Office?"

"That's a good question," the middle-aged male host said. "The Senate confirmed him as VP, and that was the time for people to raise their concerns. Mike, what kind of time is Goldstein looking at on these charges, especially with his coconspirators accepting plea deals to testify against him?"

"It could be as much as life in prison, but the government will have a difficult path to get a jury to convict. Goldstein and the others were careful not to leave paper trails of their discussions. A lot of this case is he-said, she-said testimony from people with knowledge of conversations that fall under the hearsay rules."

"Awesome," Nick said. "So all this and they're going to have trouble proving he did what we all know he did."

Sam reached for the remote and shut off the TV. "That's enough of that."

He sat back against the sofa, glass of bourbon in hand.

Sam had noticed that the bourbon had become an every-night thing lately, rather than the occasional indulgence it used to be. "What can I do for you?"

He wrapped his hand around hers. "I'm okay."

"This whole thing is an outrage, and lots of people see it that way. More so than approve of what they did."

"It's hard to know for sure which way the wind is blowing." He glanced at her. "Trevor wants us to do that big interview, like, yesterday. Do you think we could squeeze it into Wednesday before I leave on the trip?"

"As in the day after tomorrow?"

"I know it's ridiculous to even ask, but we have to get me out there to fight back, and I fight best when my own personal Wonder Woman is next to me."

She leaned her head on his sturdy shoulder. "Well, when you butter me up that way... I'll make it work. Whatever you need, whenever you need it."

"Trevor is talking to several big names to see who can make it happen fast."

"Let me know when and where, and I'll be there."

"It'll probably happen here, since that's easier logistically."

"Okay." Sam yawned. "Are we ready to be done with this day?"

"So ready."

He stood and offered her a hand up.

Sam wrapped her arms around him and held on tight, sensing he needed all the love and comfort he could get.

He dropped his head to her shoulder and held her just as tightly.

She pressed her lips to his neck. "Remember what we always say. They can't touch us unless we let them."

"Keep reminding me, will you?"

"Any time you need to hear it."

"That could be a lot."

"I'm here for it. All of it. Anything for you."

"How lucky am I to have the amazing Samantha Holland Cappuano as my wife?"

"Soooo lucky."

His huff of laughter made her smile. Whatever she could do to give him some relief from the stress.

Sam changed into a tank and pajama pants and joined him to brush her teeth at side-by-side sinks, thankful that she got to begin and end every day with him. No matter what those days brought—and it was always something crazy for both of them —having this time together when the day was done made it all bearable.

She crawled into bed and straight into his warm embrace. With her head on his bare chest and his arms tight around her, she exhaled, letting go of the stress, aggravation and anxiety that accompanied her days.

"Are you really okay or are you just saying it?" she asked him after a long period of silence.

"I really am. I keep telling myself that none of this is my fault. I just need to keep showing up, doing the job and powering through while the circus swirls around me. Any time it gets to be too much, I picture you and the kids and our life together, and that calms me. All I have to do to feel better is think of you and us."

"I love that, and it's the same for me. When my day is going sideways, I take a little mental side trip to visit you and instantly feel better. I used to do that during the years after we first met. I'd think about one perfect night with the most amazing man and wish for everything I have now."

"Ugh, all those years we missed out on infuriate me."

"We've got the rest of our lives to make up for lost time."

She needed to tell him about the call from Worthy and Scotty's problems in social studies class, but that stuff would keep for now.

He'd had more than enough for one day—and so had she.

CHAPTER TWENTY-TWO

W hen she strolled into her first lady office suite in the East Wing at seven the next morning, both Roni and Lilia were waiting for her. Every strand of Lilia's dark hair was perfectly in place, along with her trademark pearls. She wore a sharp lavender suit with a matching silk blouse. Roni wore a navy maternity suit with a patterned silk blouse. Her dark hair was in a ponytail, and Sam noticed her cheeks had gotten fuller as her pregnancy progressed.

"How do you two pull off the pressed-and-polished look at seven a.m. when I look like roadkill?"

Both women laughed.

"You do not look like roadkill," Lilia said.

"Next to you, I always do."

"Not true."

"We all look like roadkill next to Lilia," Roni said, earning a playful scowl from her boss as Lilia led them into the conference room.

"I took the liberty of ordering breakfast for us," Lilia said.

Sam saw omelets, fresh fruit and coffee waiting for them. "My God, I love you and don't deserve you."

"Stop," Lilia said, laughing. "Just doing my job."

"You're the best at it. Both of you... I so appreciate everything you do to make me look good. Freddie shows me the Instagram and Facebook posts. They're brilliant and make me sound like the perfect first lady when I'm anything but."

"We hear every day how much people admire you for holding down a job outside the White House," Lilia said, "when most people would've stepped away from that to be a full-time first lady."

"That's what I probably should've done."

"Nah, it's all good," Roni said. "You're making it work. I did a bunch of research yesterday and took a first cut on your speech for Tom, figuring you could add some personal anecdotes." She handed over a clipped pile of pages. "It's very rough."

As she sipped her coffee, Sam read through the draft. "How can you say this is rough? It's outstanding and just the tone I was hoping to strike. I was so worried about getting it right, but I can see now I shouldn't have been."

"Oh good," Roni said. "I'm so glad it works for you."

"It's perfect."

"Great, then I'll send it to your work email so you can make any tweaks. When you're done, send it back to me, and I'll print it out for you and make sure it gets put on the teleprompter at the cathedral tomorrow."

"Thank you. I've got some things I can add from my years of working with Tom that'll personalize it. And I can add in his devotion to Leslie and their girls. I learned a lot about that during the investigation."

"It's so sad," Roni said. "I feel for his wife and daughters."

"I'm sure their story struck close to home for you." Her husband, Patrick, a DEA agent, had been murdered by a stray bullet on 12th Street last October when he'd gone out for lunch. Roni was expecting their baby in June.

"It did for sure, but it was okay. I'm getting used to the grief showing up at the oddest of times. In other news, we've been overrun with media requests after your takedown of Harlan Peckham went live online."

"Crap, I never did get to see it before they released it. I hope I don't look like a water buffalo tackling a rat."

Both women cackled with laughter.

"You crack me up," Lilia said. "You looked ferocious. We can show you, if you want to see it."

"I guess that'd be okay as long as it's not horrible."

"Definitely not." Lilia called the video up on her iPad and turned it so Sam could see herself jumping out of the SUV and tackling Peckham from behind on the sidewalk. "Look at our first lady in action."

Sam cringed to herself over what people would say about the president's wife tackling murderers as part of her daily routine. "I had the full advantage because he didn't see me coming."

"We've had more than a hundred requests for interviews," Roni said.

Sam curled up her lip. "Isn't there real news to report?"

"The first lady taking down a U.S. Attorney's murderer is real news," Lilia said.

"Politely decline the interview requests. Tell them Lieutenant Holland is already hard at work on another homicide case and doesn't have time for interviews. Although Nick and I are going to do one together, possibly as soon as tomorrow, about this Joint Chiefs situation."

"I'm working with Trevor to set that up," Roni said. "He's close to nailing down the particulars."

"I can't even hear the words 'Joint Chiefs' without seeing red," Lilia said. "Everyone I know feels the same way. It's such a betrayal."

"I agree," Roni said, "and Derek is beside himself over it. He worked closely with Goldstein and the others during the Nelson administration. He's in shock over their audacity."

"I'm glad we're not the only ones feeling the outrage," Sam said.

"Definitely not," Lilia said. "From what I hear, much of official Washington is disgusted by the whole sorry situation."

"As Derek said last night," Roni added, "nothing makes our enemies happier than to see us fighting amongst ourselves."

"That's so true," Sam said. "But enough about that." She checked her watch. "I have thirty minutes until I have to meet Vernon and Jimmy for a ride to work. Tell me what's new in your lives."

"This guy is already keeping me hopping." Roni put her hand on her belly, which was much bigger than it had been even a few weeks ago. "He—or she—is very busy."

"I've heard busy is a good thing," Sam said.

"That's what they say."

"And you might've casually mentioned what Derek said last night, so does that mean things are moving ahead there, too?"

Roni looked almost pained as she thought about how to answer that. "It's the strangest thing... that Patrick is gone, and six months later, Derek is here, and he's become my best friend through the worst year of my life. We're not romantic, but I'm pretty sure we will be at some point. When I'm ready for that. Unfortunately, he knows all too well what I'm going through, but he always says the right thing at the right time. He's been such a blessing to me, but still... It's weird. It's too soon and right on time. It's all the things." She shrugged. "That's probably more information than you wanted."

Sam placed her hand on top of Roni's. "I'm so proud of you for soldiering onward, for finding the support you need to get through this and for thinking about what's next. I give you tons of credit for surviving the unimaginable."

"What choice did I have?"

The simple poignancy of Roni's question brought tears to Sam's eyes and Lilia's.

"We love Derek and Maeve so much," Sam said. "We're thrilled that you two have found comfort in each other."

"And you didn't even have to set us up."

"There is that, although I'll probably take credit for it because that's what I do."

Roni laughed as she dabbed at tears. "Tell Sam about your wedding plans, Lilia."

"We wanted something quintessential DC, so we've booked the National Press Club."

"Oh, that's amazing, Lilia. I've been to a few things there. It's a perfect venue."

"Our photos will capture the White House and the Capitol in the background, and it's such a gorgeous space steeped in history. We're thrilled."

"I'm so happy for you and Harry—and that one I *can* take credit for."

"Yes, you can. We're happy for us, too. It's like a fairy tale." Lilia seemed instantly sorry she'd said that. "I apologize, Roni. I don't mean to be insensitive."

"Oh please, don't do that! You're so excited, and I'm excited for you. I'd never want you to feel bad about your wedding or your happiness."

"That's very kind of you to say."

"I mean it. Life is for the living. As sad as I am every day that Patrick isn't here anymore, joy still creeps in, little by little. Your joy makes me happy. Please don't hold back on my account."

"I'll try not to."

"You and Harry have waited a long time for this," Sam added. "Enjoy every minute of it."

"We're trying to be present and absorb it all."

Sam glanced at the clock on the wall. "Welp, I'd better get to my other job."

"Before you run off," Lilia said, "I wanted to let you know that I've coordinated with the new White House photographer,

Adrian Fenty, for a Saturday next month to do the photographs we discussed with you and hopefully the children, too. Does that work?"

"Should be fine." Sam said of the date Lilia suggested. They wanted a collection of photos with various outfits and hair styles that they could use to accompany social media posts. More smoke and mirrors, Sam thought, to make her look like a working first lady.

"You've met Adrian, right?"

"I've seen him a few times, but he was always busy, so I haven't had the chance to get to know him." Sam did notice he was exceptionally handsome, with longer hair than she normally preferred and an interesting, artistic look to him that had caught her attention. Not that she was looking or anything. However, she wasn't so married that she couldn't notice a good-looking man when she saw one.

"You and the kids will be at the Easter egg event on Monday, correct?"

"Yes, we're keeping them home for it."

"Excellent. That'll give us some wonderful images."

"Nick told Derek about the twins' grandparents resurfacing," Roni said. "What are you hearing about that?"

"Andy's on it, and we're hopeful it won't be a problem because their parents' will is very clear about their wishes. But it's just another thing to worry about."

"I'm so sorry to hear that's happening," Lilia said.

"We are, too."

"Please keep us posted," Roni said, "and let us know if we can do anything to help."

"I will. Thank you for all you do for me, the yummy breakfast and this much-needed girlfriend time." She hugged them both. "Let's do this more often."

"Any time you want," Lilia said.

.   .   .

"I NEED YOUR ADVICE," Sam said to Vernon and Jimmy when they were on the way to HQ.

"The doctors are in, and no charge for you," Vernon said with a grin for her in the mirror.

"Y'all are too good to me. So last night, Scotty told me that in his social studies class they do current events discussions that're sometimes critical of his father, and he's not sure how he feels about that. The teacher has told him he's free to go to the library if he's not comfortable, but he hates the idea of making that kind of statement in front of his classmates. He doesn't want Nick to know about this, because he feels like his dad has enough to worry about, but Nick would want to know if Scotty is upset about something. So... I find myself in a parenting quandary with no clue what to do."

"I defer to Vernon on this one," Jimmy said, "as my first baby is on the way, and I wouldn't know what to do either."

"Oh, my young grasshoppers," Vernon said indulgently.

"That term is trademarked," Sam said.

They laughed.

"All your best lines are."

"Exactly."

"Young Scotty is in a tough spot," Vernon said. "If there's anything more complicated than the social lives of eighth graders, I've yet to encounter it."

"Iranian relations are less complicated," Jimmy added.

"That's probably true," Sam said, amused. "I feel for him because he wants to come out swinging in defense of his father, but he doesn't want to be fighting with his classmates, many of whom are woefully uninformed about the true situation."

"He shows a commendable amount of maturity in realizing there's nothing to be gained by arguing with people who don't know any better," Vernon said. "I wonder if headphones are an option if he chooses to remove himself from the conversation without physically leaving the room."

"That is a great idea. Wow, why didn't I think of that?"

"You're still new to this parenthood gig. You'll pick up the tricks along the way. By the time the twins are in eighth grade, you'll be an old pro."

"I hope they still live with us then," Sam said with a sinking feeling as she contemplated having to turn them over to grandparents who probably wanted them only for their money.

"Of course they will," Vernon said. "There's no way those people are going to prevail against you two. They have no idea who they're dealing with."

"Thank you for the vote of confidence. All this fighting wears me down. Every day brings a new battle. It's exhausting."

"I'm sure it is, but you two have what it takes to power through and take care of business. My money is always on you and your husband."

"Thank you, Vernon. That means a lot coming from you."

"You got this. Don't let the haters get you down. You're Sam freaking Holland Cappuano."

Sam smiled at him in the mirror. "Yeah, and she kicks ass and takes names."

"That's right, and don't you forget it."

"I won't."

They pulled up to the morgue entrance a short time later.

Vernon held the door for her.

Sam turned to face him. "No one can ever take his place, but you..." Her throat tightened, and tears stung her eyes, making her thankful for sunglasses. She squeezed his arm. "Thank you."

"My pleasure, Sam. Your dad would be so very proud."

"Don't make me cry."

"Sorry. Not sorry."

Sam laughed as she headed inside where she removed the sunglasses and wiped away tears while saying a silent thank-you to her precious father for sending Vernon to stand in his place. She liked to think such things were possible.

CHAPTER TWENTY-THREE

S am's phone rang with a local number she didn't recognize. "Holland."

"It's Cori Sawyer."

"Judge Sawyer. How nice to hear from you."

"If I can call you Sam, you should call me Cori."

Sam had liked the federal judge from the first time she met her. "Deal."

"I wanted to thank you for catching Harlan Peckham and allowing me to breathe deeply again for the first time in days."

She wanted to say that she did what she could for the people, but she wouldn't be flippant with a federal judge, even if Cori had begun to feel like a friend. "I'm glad we got him, but I wish we could've done it before we lost Tom and nearly lost Avery."

"Tom's death is a terrible tragedy, but I'm deeply grateful to hear that Agent Hill is on the mend, especially after he just became a daddy again."

"Yes, for sure. He and his wife are close friends of ours. We're very relieved."

"Of course I knew you were friendly with him and his wife. In addition to my relief at hearing Harlan is in jail where he belongs, I have a second reason for my call. I wanted to invite you and your husband to a dinner party next month. I'm known for my parties, and I think you'd enjoy it. I promise a friendly group who'll be thrilled to meet you both."

Sam wanted to say no. She had no desire to spend a Saturday night with people she didn't know when she didn't get enough time with the people she *did* want to see.

"I bet that sounds like hell to you," Cori said with a laugh.

Sam laughed at the blunt statement. "Not at all."

"Sure it does, but I think you'll enjoy it, and if you don't, you can feel free to leave whenever you'd like."

"It's nice of you to ask us. We'd love to come, if we're free."

"I'll plan it for a night that works for your schedule."

"There'll be Secret Service nonsense."

"That's no problem at all. Who should I talk to about coordinating things?"

"Lilia Von Nostrand at the White House. I'll send you her contact info."

"Excellent, and I'll look forward to seeing you soon. Thank you again for what you do, Sam. I'm sure the cases blur together after a while, but there're real people who are safer because of you."

"That's nice of you to say. I don't get to hear from the people we save very often."

"Well, now you have, and I'm deeply grateful. I'll see you soon."

"Thanks for calling, Cori."

"Of course."

Sam closed the phone and glanced into the morgue, where Lindsey was at her desk, coffee cup in hand as she stared at her computer screen.

Sam experienced a rare feeling of anxiety as she stopped in to see her friend. "Morning."

"Morning," Lindsey said without looking away from the

computer. "I was going to hit you up to let you know that the sailor's body has been returned to his family."

"Thank you for handling that."

"What's the plan for Juan now?"

"I need to check in with Agent Truver to see how the investigation is unfolding. I assume they need Juan to stay 'dead' for a while longer so they can use his 'murder' against Goldstein as they interrogate him."

"What do you think their strategy is?"

"To make Goldstein believe that someone killed Juan on his behalf because he told the truth about their dirty little plan."

"What do they get from doing that?" Lindsey asked.

"Maybe he points the finger at one of the others, claiming that's who wanted Juan dead."

"Ah, I see. Well, his mother must've been relieved to hear from him."

"That poor woman. I feel so bad for what they put her through."

"She probably doesn't care as long as he's okay."

"True. Well, I'd better get to it. Hoping to make some progress in the Myerson case today."

"How's that going?"

"Slower than I'd like and more complicated than it appeared at first glance. Her sister was abducted and murdered twenty-six years ago. The case is still open."

"Oh Lord, that poor family. Two sisters murdered."

"There's only a brother left, and he's in shock that it could happen again."

"I can't even imagine, and I don't want to."

Sam's phone rang with a call from Max Haggerty. "Gotta take this. Have a good day, Doc."

"You, too."

"Hey, Max. What's up?"

"We found your murder weapon in an apartment complex dumpster about six blocks from the Myersons' home. The killer didn't bother to clean the blood and hair off the barrel of the bat, so we're hoping they didn't think about fingerprints either. We've got it in the lab now, and I should have more for you soon."

"Great job to you and your team, Max. Thank you so much."

"You got it."

Sam walked into the pit, where her team was hard at work in their cubicles. "Good news, citizens. CSU found our murder weapon in a dumpster six blocks from the Myersons', complete with blood and hair and hopefully prints. It's at the lab now."

"Wow," Gonzo said. "That's a lucky break."

"Sure is. Today, I want to talk to the people who took Jada on the outing on Sunday."

"Her friend Alison Gauthier's parents, Cole and Trina." Neveah handed Sam a printout with info about the family and their address.

"Thank you, Neveah. Anything jump out about them?"

"Not at first glance. Both are government employees. He's with HHS, and she's at the USDA. They have three kids. Alison is the oldest at sixteen. They also have eleven-year-old twin boys who were not on the outing on Sunday."

"Where'd they go again?"

"The girls are studying the Civil War in school, so the parents took them to see two of the sites—Harpers Ferry and Antietam."

"And Jada was with them all day without interruption?"

"That's what Trina Gauthier told me."

Despite the apparent dead end, Sam wasn't satisfied for some reason. "I think I'll still pay her a visit just to dot the I's. Can you track down the mom's location during the day?"

"Yes, ma'am."

There was that word again. "What else do we have on the Myersons?"

"Not much," Cameron said. "We went back a year on the

socials, and nothing stood out. If there was dirty laundry, they kept it in the house. We're going through texts now and finding a lot of animosity between Elaine and her daughters."

Even though she knew about the animosity, she wanted details. "Like what?"

Cameron sifted through some pages. "Last Friday, for example, Zoe wanted to go to the movies with her friend, who drives. Elaine replied, 'Not in her car. You can go on the Metro.' To which Zoe said, 'Fuck the Metro. I'm going with my friends.' Elaine threatened to shut off her debit card. Zoe said, 'Go ahead. My friends will pay for me because they love me.'"

"Jesus," Sam said. "It was nonstop with them."

"Seemed that way."

"How is it possible the girls aren't involved in this somehow?"

"They both have alibis," Gonzo said, "and just because they're assholes doesn't make them murderers."

"That's true. I'm spoiled by my teen, who isn't an asshole— not yet, anyway." Sam was convinced he never would be. "Were there contentious texts with Jada, too?"

"Yeah, she was less aggressive with her mother than Zoe, but Zoe was older and sick of the restrictions."

"What kind of stuff did she fight with Jada about?"

"Two weeks ago, Jada texted her that she was going to walk home from school, and Elaine freaked out."

"Because of what happened to her sister," Sam said. "That points right back to the greatest trauma of her life."

"We got the files from Manassas about that," Cam said. "I'll dig in after this."

"Thanks."

"Elaine's teenage daughter probably didn't care about the aunt she never knew who was abducted, tortured and then murdered," Cam said. "Jada said, 'I'm already halfway home, so chill.' Elaine told her to not use that word with her—or 'relax'—which was another word they used frequently that Elaine didn't care for."

"Were there texts between the dad and daughters?"

"Those were about rides to practice or pickups from various things. The mom supervised their comings and goings. He seemed almost like a bystander. Every so often, one of the girls would plead with him to talk to Elaine, but those texts went unanswered."

"How could they stand the nonstop fighting and tension?" Sam asked.

"Gigi and I were talking about that last night," Cam said. "It would drive us crazy to live in a war zone like that."

"Me, too. I hope I never have those kinds of issues with my kids."

"Oh, you'll probably run up against a little tug-of-war from time to time, but I suspect you'll be more reasonable than Elaine was."

"Easy for me to be reasonable when my kids have Secret Service protection."

"True."

Neveah handed Sam a piece of paper. "Address for Trina Gauthier's office at the USDA. She said she's there all day."

"All right everyone, let's get to it. Neveah, could I have a minute, please?"

Neveah followed Sam into her office and closed the door. "What's up?"

"Two things. One, I'm checking in to make sure this case isn't triggering for you."

Neveah's apprehensive expression immediately softened. "It's so nice of you to think of that, but I'm okay."

"Let me know if that changes?"

"I will. Thank you for caring."

"I do."

"What's the second thing?"

"I need a personal favor in between work on the case."

"Whatever I can do for you."

"You should say, 'No, ma'am, I don't do side jobs while I'm on the clock.'"

"Except you don't want me to call you ma'am, ma'am."

Sam laughed. "You're coming along very nicely, young Neveah."

"Really? You think so?"

"If you cry, I'll throat-punch you and then deny it."

Neveah sputtered out a laugh. "What do you need?"

"You really are coming along very nicely, and I'm thrilled to have you on my team. Do not cry."

"Not crying."

"My husband's dirtbag mother has resurfaced after her recent troubles, represented by a smooth-operator lawyer named Collins Worthy from Cleveland, Ohio. He told me he has three grown children and lost his wife to cancer some time ago. Otherwise, I don't know anything about him, and I'd like to get the deets."

"I'm on it."

"Don't tell anyone what you're doing. I shouldn't be asking this of you."

"I'll do it on my own time later, if you'd feel better about it."

"Sneak in what you can today and finish up at home. I'll spot you some comp time for whatever time you spend on it."

"Please don't worry about that. It's my pleasure to help you with anything you need."

"Don't be like that around here. People will chew you up and spit you out if you're too nice."

Her left brow lifted ever so slightly. "Do I need to be worried about that with you?"

"Of course not. I'm just saying that, as a rule, being too nice isn't the way to be in this place."

"Got it, but I'm allowed to be nice to you?"

"Honest to God..."

Neveah laughed—a full-throated, whole-body laugh that

took Sam by surprise because it was the first time she'd heard it.

Sam smiled. "I like you."

"I like you, too."

"Get back to work, and don't get in any trouble because of me, or I won't like you anymore."

"Got it."

"Thank you, Neveah."

"You're welcome, Sam."

Sam laughed to herself after Neveah left the office.

Freddie came to the door. "Are we going to see Jada's friend's mom at the USDA?"

"Yes, let's do it."

TRINA GAUTHIER WORKED for the USDA's Food Safety and Inspection Service in the office of the administrator, located in the Jamie L. Whitten Federal Building on Independence Avenue.

When they arrived, a security officer showed them to a first-floor conference room and said Trina would be right with them. Unlike the usual security rodeo performed at federal buildings, this one had been quite simple to access, with no scanners or requests to turn over their weapons.

"They must not get many visitors here," Freddie said.

"You read my mind."

"Ew."

Sam laughed. "It's not my fault that I've got you so well trained that you think the same thoughts I do."

"I do *not* think the same thoughts you do, and if you tell anyone I do, I'll quit you so fast."

"Haha, you will not. You love me too much to quit me."

"Ew."

The sound of footsteps approaching had them straightening up and slipping back into professional mode.

"They told me the first lady was here to see me, but I didn't believe it," Trina said when she came into the room, wearing a gray suit with a pink blouse. She was pretty, with short, curly blonde hair and blue eyes framed by extravagant lashes.

Sam showed her badge while Freddie did the same. "Lieutenant Holland and Detective Cruz. We understand Jada Myerson spent Sunday with you and your husband."

"She did. We left around eight in the morning and got home shortly after eight that evening. It was a long day, but the girls appreciated seeing the sites they're writing about for their Civil War project. Jada was still with us when she got the call from Frank about Elaine."

"Do you know Jada well?"

"We do. She and our Ali have been friends since third grade. She regularly sleeps at our house, and Ali sleeps at hers. We love Jada like one of our own."

"Was she her usual self on Sunday?"

"Yes, the girls were laughing and talking the way they always do, in their own special language. My husband and I were saying afterward that they never took a breath all day, or so it seemed to us."

"Has she said anything to you about the tension at home?"

"Yes," Trina said, deflating ever so slightly. "And I'd talked to Elaine about it at one point. She struggled terribly with letting the girls out of her sight, which I totally understood after what happened to her sister."

"How long ago did she tell you about her sister?"

"Long time. When the girls were very young. I think that it was the defining event of her life."

Of course it was, Sam thought. "Did Jada ever express frustration about her mother to you?"

"Often," Trina said. "While she tried to be understanding of why her mother was the way she was, in reality, Jada and Zoe never knew their aunt and didn't have an emotional connection to what happened to her before they were born. In the way that kids can be, they were focused on their own lives and didn't have clear perspective on what their mother had endured in losing her sister so traumatically."

Sam, who was taking notes, thought that was an excellent summary of the way teenagers seemed to think.

"That's not to say they weren't empathetic to their mother's terrible loss, because they were," Trina added. "At least I know Jada was. We talked about it once. She said that even though she couldn't stand Zoe most of the time, she couldn't imagine something like that happening to her or what it must've done to her mother to go through that kind of ordeal."

"The girls said Elaine had a lot of friends, but Frank said she didn't spend much time with them. Was that your observation as well?"

"I didn't know a lot about her other friends. She never talked about others."

"Would you say you considered her a friend?"

"Yes, but it took a long time for me to feel like I knew her at all. She was very guarded for the first few years and seemed to keep our interactions focused on the girls, while I was trying to get to know her. She didn't seem to want that, so I backed off. Over time, though, as we spent more time together, she started to open up a bit more. She told me once, years after we first met, that she'd debated having kids at all because she knew it would be so hard for her when they got older, but she loved Frank, and he wanted kids, so she'd gone along with it for his sake."

That was an interesting piece of information they hadn't had before, which made the interview worth the bother.

"Is there anything else you can tell us about Jada, Elaine or their family that might shed some light on our investigation?"

After thinking on that for a minute, Trina said, "There is one more thing, and I debated whether I should mention it or not."

"I'd urge you to tell us anything you know. Every detail is critical in a homicide investigation."

Trina crossed her hands on the table and then focused on them when she said, "About a year ago, Jada asked if she could come to live at our house for the rest of high school."

Holy bombshell!

"What did you say?"

"We told her we'd have to discuss it with her parents."

"Did that conversation ever happen?"

"It did."

"When?"

"Shortly after Jada asked us. Things with Elaine and Zoe were bad and getting worse all the time around then, and Jada wanted out of there."

"Tell us about the meeting with Frank and Elaine."

"We asked to meet them for dinner, figuring it would be better to have that conversation in public so it couldn't get heated. That was a mistake."

"How come?"

"Elaine totally flipped out and didn't care who was listening. She said we had some nerve interfering in her family this way and that if we wanted Ali and Jada to remain friends, we needed to butt out of their business."

"What did Frank say?"

"He tried to get Elaine to calm down. He said that we were just the messengers delivering Jada's request, and it wasn't our fault, but Elaine took the whole thing as us being disloyal to them as fellow parents. I tried to reason with her and make her see how difficult it was for Jada to be in the middle of Elaine's war zone with Zoe. That was the wrong thing to say. She told me to fuck off with my judgment, got up and walked out."

Judging by the tingling in her spine, this felt like a breakthrough of some sort to Sam.

"What did Frank say?"

"He told us he appreciated our concern and that he was

sorry for the way Elaine had reacted. Then he went after his wife."

"Did you eventually patch things up with her?"

Trina shook her head. "She never spoke to me again, not directly anyway. If we invited Jada to do something with us, that was all done through the girls."

"I need to ask you something that may seem obscene to you, but I have to ask it anyway."

"Okay..."

"Do you think there's any chance that Jada killed her mother?"

Trina's mouth fell open in shock. "God, no. Jada is the sweetest girl you'll ever meet, and besides, wasn't her mother killed while Jada was with us?"

"That doesn't mean she couldn't have arranged it."

"She's fifteen years old, Lieutenant! Where in the world would a fifteen-year-old girl find someone to commit murder for her?"

"I don't know, but kids are savvier than we give them credit for being. Anything is possible."

"*That* is not possible. Jada would never be part of something like that."

"How about Zoe?"

"I don't know her very well, but I can't see it with her either. Both girls were just trying to live their lives, which was the cause of the nonstop fighting with Elaine."

"Had you heard of a particular escalation in recent days or weeks?"

"It was always bad, but from what Jada said, it was much, much worse since Zoe started dating her boyfriend."

"This has been very helpful." Sam pushed her card across the table. "If you think of anything else, even something that might seem like a minor detail to you, please call me."

Trina picked up the card and examined it. "You give out your cell number to people you don't even know?"

"It's part of my job."

"It's cool that you're still doing this when you don't have to."

Sam never knew what to say to that. To her, she *did* have to. Police work was in her DNA. "Thank you again for your help."

"I hope you find the person who killed Elaine. She was a complicated person, but she didn't deserve to die that way. No one does."

Trina walked them to the reception area, where they said their goodbyes.

"Impressions?" Sam asked Freddie as they walked out to meet Vernon and Jimmy.

"I got a buzz off the confrontation between the two couples in the restaurant and how Elaine never spoke to Trina again, as if it was her fault Jada had wanted to move out."

"I got the same buzz."

"Where to next?"

"I want to see Elaine's therapist. See if she can see us between appointments."

CHAPTER TWENTY-FOUR

D r. Colleen Barker's office was in Woodley Park, about two miles from Freddie and Elin's apartment. When Freddie called her, she said to come now because she was on a two-hour break.

She had short red hair, green eyes and pale skin that looked like it would burn like crazy in the sun. She wore a dark green tunic with black leggings and invited them into a warm, cozy space with plush chairs, a sofa and a coffee table that made it look like a random living room rather than a psychiatrist's office.

After gesturing for Sam and Freddie to have a seat on the sofa, she sat in a deep purple chair and crossed her legs.

There was something so soothing about the office and the woman who worked there that made Sam want to settle in and share her troubles with the good doctor.

"Did Frank sign the release allowing us to speak with you?"

"He did, and let me say... I was so very sorry—and truly shocked—to hear about Elaine's murder. Are you getting any closer to figuring out who did it?"

"We're making some progress. We've heard a lot about the difficulties she was having with her daughters."

"Yes," Colleen said. "Elaine was having an awful time handling the usual rites of passage with her girls as they approach adulthood. We spent a lot of time working on that. As you can imagine, her sister's violent death cast a long shadow over her life and made her afraid of history repeating itself, especially since her sister's killer was never found."

Sam took notes and made an asterisk next to the part about her sister's killer still being at large. "Everything in me is thinking Elaine's murder involved her kids in some way."

Colleen shook her head. "I can't see that. I've met her girls. We had some group therapy sessions with the whole family, and the girls loved Elaine very much. They just hated her rigidity when it came to rules and safety."

"Did they hate the rigidity enough to want to eliminate the person who was causing so much grief for them?"

"I didn't know them as well as I knew Elaine, but I can't see either of them being involved in something like that."

"Zoe indicated that the therapy wasn't productive."

"No, it wasn't. Elaine refused to budge on the things the girls identified as important to them, such as being able to walk home from school or friends' houses or riding in cars driven by peers. These were hard limits for Elaine, and we tried to find a compromise, but she wasn't having it."

"What role did Frank play in these discussions?"

"He mostly stayed on the sidelines. The dispute was between Elaine and the girls."

"Both girls?"

"Primarily Zoe because she was older, but as Jada matured, things were heating up with her, too. In addition, Jada had a visceral dislike of the constant fighting and begged her entire family to make it stop."

"How did her parents react to that request?"

"They both wept. I think they very much wanted peace in their family, but with Elaine dead set on protecting her daughters from anything that could harm them, they were at a stalemate."

Sam had an itchy feeling working its way down her backbone, and the tingling intensified any time Jada's name was mentioned. How was it even possible to suspect her when she'd been in West Virginia and Maryland the day her mother was murdered?

"Sam?"

Freddie's voice dragged her out of her thoughts.

"I'm sorry."

"Did you have more questions?" Colleen asked.

"Was there anything else happening in Elaine's life that might have led to murder?"

"Not that I can think of. She had the usual stressors of work and kids and juggling all the responsibility, but she wasn't experiencing conflict with anyone else, at least not that she told me."

"What did she say about friends?"

"She had friends, but preferred to keep to herself and spend her free time with her family."

"In your experience, was that unusual?"

"Not as unusual as you'd might expect. More and more, I'm hearing from women who prefer to have smaller friend groups due to the drama and bickering that can come with larger groups."

"I get that," Freddie said. "My wife has distanced herself from some high-maintenance friends lately."

"Everyone is busy," Colleen said. "People want to be with friends who build them up, not bring them down."

"That's my wife's feeling as well."

"Trina Gauthier, Jada's friend Ali's mother, told us about a falling-out she and her husband had with Frank and Elaine."

Colleen nodded. "When they told them Jada wanted to live with them. Elaine was very upset about that and how the

Gauthiers handled it. She felt they should've said no and shut it down right away."

"Did you agree with that?"

"Not really. I could see it from Jada's point of view, but Elaine was resolute in her anger over it."

"Can you think of anything else that might be relevant?"

"I've gone through all my notes since I got the news, and there was nothing that stands out to me that would lead to murder."

"Thank you for taking the time to do that review and to meet with us."

"I really hope you find the person who did this to Elaine. Despite how it might seem to you after hearing about the difficulties with the girls, she was a sweet lady who had a difficult life. She didn't deserve this."

"No, she didn't."

Sam left her card, with the usual request to call if anything else came to mind that might help. "What do you think?" she asked Freddie when they were back outside.

"I want to look closer at the daughters. The situation inside their house was combustible for years. I can't see how it doesn't involve them in some way."

"I agree, but how? They both have airtight alibis, the phone data and witnesses put them where they said they were, and there was nothing unusual in the financial reports."

"We pulled them for the parents, not the daughters."

Sam looked at him. "No, we didn't."

"We never pull financials for minors."

"Maybe we should in this case."

"We definitely should. I'll call Cameron and get that moving."

FRANK MYERSON vociferously objected to the request to access the girls' financial records. "That's outrageous," he said on a call to Sam after receiving Cameron's request for permission to access the data, which was required since the girls were minors. "They're *children*."

"We can get a warrant," Sam told him.

"What in the world could you possibly want with the bank accounts of two teenage girls?"

"We're trying to rule them out as suspects, Mr. Myerson. I would think you'd have the same goal we do."

"There's no need to rule them out of anything! They had nothing to do with this!"

"That's what we're trying to prove."

"If you want that information, you're going to have to get a warrant. There's no way I'm betraying my daughters this way."

"Fine, then that's what we'll do."

The line went dead.

"Did he hang up on you?" Freddie asked as Vernon drove them back to HQ.

"Yep. Call Malone to get a warrant going for all three kids. We may as well include Zeke in the warrant, but we don't need to notify his parents because he's a legal adult."

Freddie made the call and put it on speaker.

"That's going to be a tough ask," Malone said. "Judges tend to require a higher burden of proof when minors are involved."

"You can say that our investigation has yielded extreme tension between Elaine and her daughters," Sam said. "And not with anyone else."

"I'll do what I can, but just know it's not a certainty."

"Would it help to have an affidavit of all the reasons we think the daughters could be involved in this murder?"

"Yep."

"We'll get on that. Hold off on the request until we get back to the house."

"Will do."

"I'll write it up," Freddie said after she ended the call.

"I'd like to take a stab at it, and then you can spruce it up, if you don't mind."

"Fine by me." He glanced over at her. "Are we really thinking teenage girls plotted their mother's murder and then went about their days like nothing of any importance was happening?"

"I don't want to think that's possible, but we've looked at every other aspect of her life and have found no real trouble anywhere but right in her own home. There's no sign of forced entry, which means whoever did this had the code to the house. Where would that person have gotten the code except from someone who lived there?"

"Good points. It's just hard to fathom."

"It is, but maybe they'd reached a breaking point with her and thought it would make everything easier to have her out of the way." The statement added to the buzz working its way down her back.

"And you think these two sisters, who had not a nice thing to say to each other, worked together on this?"

"Roll with me... What if the nastiness was part of the plan? 'If we act like we hate each other, no one will believe we're capable of doing something like this together.'"

"The hatred was very convincing."

"There's probably enough actual hatred to make it easy to act that way. Just because they worked together on this doesn't mean they're suddenly BFFs."

"You're really digging this angle."

"It's the only thing so far that's given me a buzz."

"Accusing minors of murder, if that's where we end up, will be dicey."

"For sure."

When they returned to HQ, Sam went directly to the captain's office and knocked.

"Enter." Malone sat behind his desk, his attention on a stack of folders in front of him.

"What's all that?"

"Forensic reports from Stahl's house. Just some light reading to keep me awake all night."

"Jeez, better you than me."

When the captain looked up at her, she saw anguish in his eyes. "It's still so unbelievable... That he was a *serial murderer* while showing up here every day and pretending to be one of us."

"He was never one of us. Not for one day of his entire miserable career."

"No, he wasn't." Malone sighed and made a visible attempt to shake off the horror that would stay with them all forever. "What's up?"

"As I mentioned on the phone, the Myerson investigation is pointing toward the daughters at this point."

"What've you got on them?"

"At this moment? A ton of animosity between the vic and her daughters, as well as a really big hunch. We're hoping the financials will show some money moving around that might lead us to the person they hired to take care of their most pressing concern."

"How old are these girls?"

"Fifteen and seventeen."

"It's a bit of a stretch to picture teenage girls arranging their mother's murder."

"They were at war with her. Full-blown, bloody war. They couldn't move without her approval, which they hardly ever got. They'd learned to be sneaky to get around her unyielding rules. I don't think anything about them is 'normal teenager' by any definition of that term."

"What does the dad say?"

"What you'd expect: 'They're children, and it's obscene to even consider they had anything to do with this.' But he was kind of punched out of the whole situation with the mom. Both girls pleaded with him to intervene on their behalf, and those pleas went unanswered as far as we could tell."

"I'd like to get him back here and dig a little deeper into what he knows before we go full-on in that direction."

Sam didn't think that would help, but she wasn't about to question him. "Will do."

Back in the pit, she asked Freddie to call Frank and ask him to come back in.

"What's the plan?"

"Malone wants us to talk to him some more and get a feel for whether there's any *there* there."

"Ah... Okay..."

"I agree, but he's the boss."

"Making the call."

"I'll write up the affidavit for the warrant on the girls' financials." Sam went into the office, shut the door and sat before the computer to collect her thoughts. Anything to do with writing or reading was challenging for her due to her dyslexia, but she was determined to put their case, such as it was, on paper to persuade a judge to grant the warrants.

She put her fingers on the keys and began to type, having learned to just let the thoughts and words flow and not worry if they were correct until the story was on the page. Freddie would check her work for any mistakes.

This past Sunday, Elaine Myerson was found dead in the bathroom that adjoined her bedroom in her home on Webster Street Northwest in the Crestwood neighborhood. The medical examiner has determined that she died as the result of a single blow to the back of her head, we believe from a baseball bat that was recovered by CSU from a dumpster six blocks from the home. The bat, which had blood and hair stuck to it, is being processed by the lab. We have fully investigated Mrs. Myerson's life, spoken to her husband, daughters, brother, coworkers, therapist and neighbors. Throughout our investigation, we learned of significant strife...

"Is 'strife' the right word to describe what was going on in that house?" she asked herself. "Not really."

...we discovered that Elaine was essentially at war with her daughters, Zoe, 17, and Jada, 15. To give some context, when Elaine was twenty, her sister Sarah, age 17, was abducted in the family's Manassas neighborhood while she was walking home from a friend's house. Sarah's naked body was found six weeks later. The autopsy showed she had been sexually assaulted while held captive and had died recently. The killer was never found, but the case remains open, with the original detective still actively pursuing new information. Needless to say, the trauma of this incident stayed with Elaine. We were told that she wasn't sure she wanted children because she feared being overprotective to the point of absurdity. However, her husband, Frank, very much wanted children, so they had two daughters. As the girls matured toward young adulthood, Elaine resisted their desire to be independent, to have jobs, boyfriends, ride in cars with peers, etc. By all accounts, the situation in their home had escalated to "warfare," especially since Zoe now had a boyfriend. At the time of the murder, Mr. Myerson was at an all-day work event. His alibi has been confirmed. Zoe was at the Arlington home of her boyfriend, Zeke Bellamy, and their phones confirm their locations at the Bellamy house for the entire afternoon.

Like a bolt of lightning from above, an idea hit her that had Sam standing and heading for the door. "Freddie."

When he stood to see what she needed, she tipped her head to bring him into the office.

"What's up? Do you need help with the narrative?"

"No, but something just occurred to me that I should've thought of before now."

"What's that?"

"What if Zoe and Zeke left their phones at Zeke's house and went to Zoe's to deal with her mother?"

"I suppose that's possible, but would kids think of doing that?"

"Go ask Archie to look at the history on their phones and

see if there was an unusual lack of activity. Also see if there are any true-crime fans among the three of them."

"On it."

Every cell in Sam's body buzzed as this theory took hold. It *had* to have been the daughters. No one else would've wanted Elaine dead. If the surviving family members were to be believed, no one else had access to the house. No one else was at "war" with Elaine. No one else was motivated to do whatever it took to get the person causing them nonstop grief out of the way.

Sam was seated at her desk when Freddie came to the door. "Frank said the girls took the car to visit friends, so he doesn't have a ride. I told him I'd send Patrol to pick him up. He wasn't thrilled about that, but I let him know it wasn't optional."

"Good job. So the girls are out and about?" Sam asked herself where she would've been shortly after her mother was murdered. It would depend on when in her lifetime it happened, but she probably wouldn't have been out with friends right after, even if it had occurred during their long estrangement.

"He said Zoe was taking Jada to Ali's before she went to see Zeke."

"Is it weird to you that they're already going out?"

"I don't know. I mean, there's only so much they can say and do with their dad and aunt. Maybe they need the support of their friends."

"Does that mean you're not fully on board with them being involved?"

"Despite the buzz I was getting before, I honestly don't know what to think. I'm keeping an open mind."

"I'll have this ready for you in a few minutes."

"Okay."

Turning back to her computer, she changed the last line to accommodate the possibility that only the phones were at the Bellamy house. *Zoe was at the Arlington home of her boyfriend,*

Zeke Bellamy, and data shows their phones remained at the Bellamy house for the entire afternoon.

Sam picked up the desk phone and dialed Archie's extension.

"Hey," he said.

"I'm wondering where we are with camera activity near the Myerson home."

"There was nothing useful."

"Do you have a contact with Arlington IT?"

"Yep. What do you need?"

Sam gave him Zeke Bellamy's address. "Can you find out if they have anything from Sunday near their house?"

"What're we looking for?"

"Male and female teenager leaving the house together at any point from two o'clock on, and anything from the surrounding area."

"That's a big chunk of time. Might take a minute to go through all that."

"We can send someone over to help if they need it."

"I'll make the offer."

"Cruz is on his way up with a couple of other things."

"He just walked in."

"How's your girlfriend?"

"Eh, not sure. Haven't talked to her."

"Keep me posted?"

"I will if there's anything to report. Might be a dead end."

"I hope it works out the way you want it to. Thanks for the help."

"Sure thing."

CHAPTER TWENTY-FIVE

As Sam put down the phone, her mind continued to race with ways to prove that Zeke and Zoe hadn't been holed up at his house all afternoon like they'd claimed.

She called Max Haggerty.

"What's up?"

"Is it possible to determine whether a car was used during a certain time frame?"

"If there're any tolls, you can get a warrant for the E-ZPass."

"Are there tolls leaving Arlington?"

"Some, but that's based on which direction they went. Depending on what kind of car it is, you may be able to detect acceleration, braking, idle time, driving patterns, Bluetooth activity and navigation use."

"If we seize the car, will we be able to tell if it was driven at a certain time?"

"Again, depends on what kind of car it is and how old it is."

"Thank you for the help, Max."

"No problem. I was going to call you to say that while we found no outside fingerprints in the house—yet—there were fingerprints on the bat, which means the killer must've removed the gloves to dispose of it. The prints aren't in the system, but the blood was a match for Elaine Myerson."

"That's confirmation of our murder weapon. Send over the full report when the lab is finished with it."

"Will do."

Sam put down the phone and went to consult with Cameron. "Are there pictures of Zeke's car on his social media?"

"I think I saw something. Let me check."

While he did that, Sam went back to the office to finish typing up the affidavit.

We're further investigating both daughters and need access to their financial data to detect whether there were any significant withdrawals in the last few weeks. We believe the warrant is fully justified in light of the information we've been given about the state of their relationship with their murdered mother.

Cameron came to the door. "He's got a two-year-old Mustang convertible."

Sam picked up the phone to call Archie again. "I also need every piece of data from Zeke's phone and Zoe's after two p.m. Sunday."

"That's easy enough. I'll send a report to your email."

"Thanks."

"What're you thinking?" Cam asked.

"I want to know if there was any activity in Zeke's vehicle or on their phones during the time he and Zoe were supposedly hunkered down at his house."

"Why don't we consult with Arlington Police and do a canvass of the neighbors around his house to see if they saw anything?"

"That was going to be my next thought, but you beat me to it. Can you arrange that?"

"Yep. I know people there."

"That's handy."

After Cameron went to see to that, she called Malone. "I want to seize Zeke Bellamy's Mustang."

"For what reason?"

"I want to see if we can prove that it was used during the time that Zeke and Zoe say they remained at his house. We've got the phones showing them there for the entire six hours, but phones can be left behind when people leave to commit murder."

"I'll request a warrant to seize the car."

"Thank you. I'll have the affidavit for financials on the Myerson daughters and the boyfriend momentarily."

"I'll get it to a judge."

"Thanks, Cap."

Sam returned to her office, reread what she'd written and sent it to Freddie for proofing. Once he made the needed corrections, he would forward it to the captain, so he could work his magic with a judge. Hopefully, it wouldn't take long to get the warrant and the data.

As she went to notify him that it was on the way, a Patrol officer arrived with Frank Myerson, who was rumpled and visibly annoyed.

"Thanks for coming in, Mr. Myerson."

"Like I had a choice."

"Officer Smith, please escort Mr. Myerson to interview one and stay with him until we're ready to talk."

"How long are you going to make me wait?"

"Not long."

Smith gestured for Mr. Myerson to head toward the interview rooms.

"What's that about?" Malone asked.

Sam hadn't seen him approaching. She turned to him. "He's pissed about being brought back in for another conversation."

"If, God forbid, my wife had been murdered, I'd be camped out in the lobby waiting for updates. I'd want to help in any way I could."

Sam considered what he'd said. "I'll mention that to him when we're in the room."

"You're not liking him for being part of this?"

"I wasn't until you said what you did about his attitude. I'm trying to imagine being annoyed with the people trying to figure out who killed my husband. And, my God, I hope I never have to say that sentence for real."

"I felt the same way with my rhetorical example. It's unthinkable."

"Yes, it certainly is, unless you knew it was going to happen, and now you just want to get on with your new life without your wife causing so much strife."

"It's an angle."

"Which means I need to advise him that he should request that his lawyer join us ahead of our chat."

"Go to it, Lieutenant."

"Can I just say… I love the way we all work together here, how we come up with new angles on a case through a passing conversation. It's pretty cool, and to be honest, it's the number one thing that keeps me here when I guess I don't technically have to be anymore."

"You do have to be. I don't want to do this job without you doing yours. Besides, I'm only sticking around for you as it is, so don't you dare quit on me."

He and the chief had recently brought her to tears by telling her they intended to put off retirement until Nick left office so they could be there to run interference for her as needed. Because that's what her dad, their best friend, would've wanted them to do.

"Haha, I won't. Off to make Frank Myerson's day by suggesting his attorney be present for our next discussion."

"Keep up the good work, Miss Congeniality."

Laughing, she said, "Will do." She went to the interview room, nodded to Officer Smith and entered.

Myerson sat up a little straighter when she came in.

"I'd like to advise you that you have the right to an attorney being present for our discussion. Would you like me to call Mr. Dunning for you?"

"I thought you just wanted some more details about Elaine's life. Why do I need him here for that?'

"I believe it would be prudent. Shall I call him?"

He shook his head, as if in disbelief that any of this was happening. "Go ahead."

"I'll be back when he arrives."

In the pit, she stopped at Freddie's cubical. "Will you please ask Roland Dunning to come in?"

"Did he request him?"

"Nope. I did. Malone just made a great point. He said if it was his wife in our morgue, he'd be camped out in the lobby, asking for updates and offering to help. This guy is pissed off that we requested more of his time to assist with the case."

"That is an interesting take. I'll call Dunning."

"Thank you."

As Sam was heading back to her office, a female Patrol officer came into the pit. "Lieutenant, there's an Isaac Erickson here to see you."

It took her a second to recall that he was Juan Rodriguez's roommate. "Go ahead and bring him to my office, if you would."

"Of course."

"Thanks."

Sam went into her office and sat, wondering what had brought Isaac to HQ.

The young man who came in looked as if he hadn't slept for a minute since the last time she'd seen him. His hair was messy, and he hadn't shaved. Wearing a NAVY T-shirt and jeans, he was the picture of grief. She immediately felt sick with guilt for what he was going through.

"Come in, Isaac."

"Thank you for seeing me."

"Of course. What can I do for you?"

"I've been hoping to hear something about the investigation, but no one is telling me anything, and I didn't know what else to do, so I came here."

"Oh, um, well, we're not working on that case anymore. NCIS has taken it over since Goldstein's arrest."

"Was he the one who killed Juan?"

Sam ached for the guy. "I don't know anything about that. Have you spoken to NCIS?"

"They won't return my calls."

"How about I reach out to them and ask them to get in touch with an update?"

"That'd be good. I've been thinking about calling Juan's mom, but I don't want to bother her at such a difficult time."

"Let me make some calls and see if I can get you some info, okay?" She flipped through her notebook to make sure she still had his number from the other day. "I'll have someone call you."

"I'd really appreciate that."

"No problem."

"Something about all of this feels so weird to me. I can't explain it. But it doesn't feel right."

Sam had no idea what to say to that. She wanted to tell him his instincts were spot-on, but it wasn't her place to tell him the truth. "I'll see what I can do."

"Thanks again for seeing me."

"No problem."

Sam was waiting for Agent Truver to answer her call when Freddie came to the door.

"What was that about?"

"A heartbroken best friend looking for info about his buddy's murder."

"Oh my God."

"My thought exactly."

Truver's voice mail picked up.

"This is Sam Holland. Issac Erickson was just here looking for information about his dead roommate. Someone needs to tell him what's going on. Call me to discuss." She closed the phone. "I hope I hear from her soon. Isaac needs to be brought into the loop. It's unfair that they're doing this to him."

"Agreed. I figured they would've told him by now."

"I'm ashamed to say I never gave him a thought after we spoke to him the other day."

"We've been a little busy."

"Still… I should've demanded that Truver tell him the truth, too."

"Not your circus, not your monkeys."

"What the hell did you just say?"

"You've heard that saying before."

"No, I haven't. Say it again. Slowly this time."

First, he rolled his eyes, then he said it again.

"I really like that. How could you sit on a gem like that for all this time?"

"You're mad at me for not saying that to you sooner?"

"Yes, I believe I am. I count on you to keep me hip and relevant."

"Where is that in my job description?"

"Under other duties as assigned."

"What're you two fighting about?" Gonzo asked when he joined Freddie in the doorway.

"She's making up new rules as she goes along."

"It's called leadership, young grasshopper," Sam said.

"Except your rules have nothing to do with the job, old owl."

Gonzo snorted out a laugh.

"That name is *not* going to be a thing," Sam said.

"I really like it," Gonzo said.

"I expect better from you."

"Why?"

Sam laughed at how the two of them cackled like little boys

pulling one over on Mom. "Did you need something, Sergeant?"

"Yes, in fact, I wanted to talk to you about Ninth Street. We've got to move out of our place by the thirtieth of this month, so I wondered if we can start to move some crap into Ninth."

"Absolutely. I'll get you the keys, and Nick and I will find some time to get over there to move our stuff to the third floor so it's out of your way."

"We really appreciate this."

"Glad to have someone using the place. No sense in it sitting empty. Speaking of sitting empty, I talked to Celia about my dad's house for you, Frederico."

"*What?* Seriously?"

"Yes, seriously. When is your lease up?"

"Not until June."

"Well, by then, Celia might be ready to turn her place over to you. She said she doesn't want to be there without my dad, so it's probably time since she's living with us full time anyway."

"Wow, this is incredible. Elin and I were talking about trying to find a bigger, safer place in the next few weeks, but the thought of the search exhausted us before it even began."

"Now you don't have to."

He gave her a tentative look. "Do you know what the rent would be?"

"Whatever you're paying now." Sam was fairly confident Celia wouldn't mind if Sam worked out the details. "She owns the house outright, so anything you pay her will be a nice extra income after she pays taxes and insurance."

"I can't believe this. Elin will flip. A whole house *in* the District! We thought we were years away from being able to swing that."

"Same, brother," Gonzo said. "Thanks for making this possible, Sam. We sure do appreciate it."

"We're thrilled that you guys can use the houses while we don't need them."

"And Skip's house..." Freddie said. "That means so much to me."

"It'll mean a lot to us to have someone who loved him living there."

"What happens after Nick leaves office?" Gonzo asked hesitantly.

Sam shrugged. "We'll cross that bridge when we come to it. Celia will stay with us wherever we end up. No one will get evicted, so don't worry about that."

"We're not worried, but if you want your house back, all you gotta do is say so."

"Understood. We'll probably have to go somewhere with better security than what we had on Ninth. We'll see what happens."

"You know how you're always worried about how you're asking too much of us since everything changed for you?" Freddie asked.

"Yeah, that weighs heavy on me."

"Look at everything you do for us, and don't give that another thought, you hear?"

"What he said," Gonzo added.

"My two best friends."

"Likewise," Freddie said.

"Same," Gonzo said.

"Let's get back to work and close this case. My husband's going on the road for a few days. There's sex to be had."

"For the love of God," Freddie muttered as he walked away while Gonzo laughed.

CHAPTER TWENTY-SIX

Roland Dunning arrived ten minutes before Sam was planning to leave for the day, so she sent a text to Nick to go ahead with dinner and she'd catch up when she got home.

She showed Dunning into the room where Frank Myerson had been pacing.

"Took you long enough," he said to Dunning.

"I have other clients. I was in court."

Myerson didn't care for that response as he took a seat at the table. "Can we get on with it? This is starting to feel a lot like harassment after my wife was murdered."

Sam started the recording, noting who was in the room before she sat across from the two men. "My captain made an interesting point earlier."

"Care to share it?" Dunning asked.

"In fact, I do care to share it. He said if, God forbid, his wife had been murdered, he'd be camped out in our lobby, wanting every update he could get and offering to help us in any way he could. Frank, on the other hand, is annoyed by our requests for more information. I find that interesting, don't you, Mr. Dunning?"

"Are you accusing my client of something, Lieutenant?"

"I'm merely stating that his annoyance with our investigation leads me to wonder if he's not relieved that his wife is dead."

Frank's mouth fell open as his expression registered shock. "You think I'm *relieved* that Elaine was *murdered*? What kind of monster do you think I am? I've loved that woman since I was twenty-three years old. She's been the center of my life for more than twenty years. I am *not* relieved that she is gone."

"You're not relieved that the fighting in your house is over, that you and your girls can coexist peacefully now that Elaine is no longer setting the rules for them?"

Frank looked at Dunning, as if he expected his lawyer to do something.

Dunning remained silent.

"I'm not relieved. I'm heartbroken. Is that all you dragged me in here to ask? Because if so, you've wasted my time, yours and Mr. Dunning's."

"There's no such thing as wasted time in a homicide investigation, Mr. Myerson. Every detail matters, such as the one in which your daughter Zoe told us she was at Zeke's house all afternoon, which was confirmed by cell phone data. If we dig deeper, will we find that she and Zeke left their phones behind when they returned to the District to deal with her mother once and for all?"

"Are you going to sit there and let her say these things about my daughter?" Frank asked Dunning.

"Answer the question, Frank. The sooner you tell them what they want to know, the sooner you can get out of here."

"Zoe did not kill her mother. Any other questions?"

"What about Jada? Was she fed up enough with what was happening in her home to do something drastic, like hire someone to take care of things for her while everyone else was out of the house for the day?"

"No," he said through gritted teeth. "She didn't. Are you

going to tell me that almost two days later, you're so focused on my children that you haven't got a single other lead as to who did this to Elaine?"

"Do you know what the major element is in a homicide investigation, Mr. Myerson?"

"No, I don't, because I've never been involved in one before."

"*Motive* is the key to everything. Who would want this person dead? And the only people we can find in your wife's entire life who wanted her out of the way are your daughters."

"How can you accuse *children* of such a thing? That would make them psychopaths." He looked frantically to Dunning, as if hoping he would back him up. "My daughters are difficult at times. Show me a teenage girl who isn't. But they're not psychopaths. They're not murderers."

"I'd like you to call them and ask them to stop by to talk some more."

"Why? So you can entrap them into admitting something they didn't do?"

"No, so we can dig deeper into who else might've done this."

"They've told you everything they know."

"Have they?"

Freddie came into the room, handed Sam a sheet of paper and then sat next to her at the table.

Her backbone buzzed with sensation when she saw several highlighted rows of data that showed multiple thousand-dollar withdrawals from bank accounts belonging to Zoe and Jada.

Sam turned the page toward Frank and pointed to the highlighted rows. "What did your daughters need with thousands of dollars?"

"I... I don't know. Those are their college funds. They aren't allowed to access them."

"Looks like they broke the rules. Where'd all that money go, Frank?"

He gave Dunning another frantic look. "Do something, will you?"

Dunning looked as if he had an itch he couldn't scratch in polite company. "The lieutenant has asked you to call your daughters. I think you should do that now."

"Look," Myerson said, "I didn't want to bring this up, but Zoe has had some trouble with drugs. She's been sober for six months now, but it's possible she's relapsed. That would explain what she did with the money."

"Where did she attend rehab?" Freddie asked.

Myerson looked like the proverbial deer in headlights. "We handled it as a family."

Freddie looked at Sam. "You ever heard of anyone getting sober with only the help of their immediate family?"

"Nope."

"We didn't want it to ruin her life! We handled it."

"Funny that none of you mentioned a drug problem before now," Sam said.

"Because it's personal and has no bearing on this case."

"Well, now it does. What was she addicted to, and who supplied the drugs to her?"

"I... uh, you want specific drugs?"

"That'd be good."

"I don't recall."

"Your seventeen-year-old daughter was an addict, and you don't remember what she was taking? Can you understand how preposterous that sounds?"

Once again, Frank looked to Dunning for help.

"Tell her what you know, Frank. This is no time for evasiveness."

"I'm trying to protect my daughter's privacy. Doesn't that count for anything?"

"I'm trying to figure out who murdered the wife you claimed to love with all your heart," Sam said. "Doesn't *that* count for anything? Doesn't *she* count for anything?"

"Of course she does! But she's not here anymore, and Zoe is. What good will it do anyone if it becomes public that Zoe had a drug problem?"

"Call your daughters, Mr. Myerson. Tell them to come here right away."

"You're not going to do anything to stop this madness?" Frank asked Dunning.

"There's nothing I can do. This isn't an unreasonable request."

"Then get out of here. You're fired. I don't need your kind of 'help.'"

Dunning got up and left the room.

"Can you please confirm for the record that you've fired your counsel, Roland Dunning?" Sam asked.

"I fired Roland Dunning."

"Are you planning to retain new counsel?"

"Yes."

"While you arrange that, please call your daughters." Sam engaged him in a stare-down that she won when he reached for his phone. "Put it on speaker."

He called Zoe first. The call went right to voice mail.

"This is Zoe. You know what to do."

"It's Dad. I need you to come to the police station right away. They have more questions for you. Call me."

Next, he called Jada, got her voice mail and left the same message.

"Why would their phones be off?" Freddie asked.

"I... I don't know. They're chained to those phones."

"Are you able to track their locations?"

He shook his head. "Elaine did that."

She turned to Freddie. "Can their locations be tracked if the phones are off?"

"We can see where they were most recently."

"Go get Elaine's phone from Archie, please." After he left

the room, Sam said, "We were told that Jada was going to her friend Ali's house. Is that correct?"

"Yes, she wanted to spend some time with her best friend."

"Do you have the number for Ali's parents?"

Again, he shook his head.

"Good thing I do."

That shocked the shit out of him, but he tried to hide that from her. He failed.

She sifted through the pages of her notebook until she found the number for Trina Gauthier and made the call on her phone, with the speaker on, staring down Frank as she waited for Trina to pick up.

"Hello?"

"Hi, Trina, this is Sam Holland."

"Oh, hi. Have you found the person who killed Elaine?"

"We're working on that. I wondered if I could speak to Jada."

"To Jada? She's not here. Did you call her phone?"

"I did, and it went straight to voice mail. But she was supposed to be visiting Ali."

"Ali has been at cheerleading practice since school let out. She's not due home until after nine."

"Thank you for letting me know. If you or Ali hear from her, will you give me a call?"

"Yes, of course. Jada isn't in trouble, is she?"

Sam never blinked as she continued to stare at Frank. "I'm not sure yet. Thank you for your help."

"Whatever we can do."

"I'll be in touch if we need anything further."

After she ended the call, Sam said, "Did you hear that? 'Whatever we can do.' That's called cooperation with a homicide investigation. Also, did you hear the part where Ali has been at cheerleading practice all afternoon and not available for a visit from Jada, who told you that's where she was going?"

"I heard it."

"So where's Jada, Mr. Myerson?"

"I have no idea."

"TRACK DOWN ZEKE BELLAMY'S parents, will you?" Sam said to Freddie when she met him outside the interview room where she'd left Frank working to acquire a new attorney. She'd tried to call Zeke and had gotten his voice mail, too.

"I think Cam has the dirt on them. I'll ask him."

"I'm going back in there to make sure Frank is only shopping for a new lawyer."

It was unusual for them to allow a potential suspect to keep his cell phone, but he wasn't technically in custody, and they didn't have enough evidence to charge him or anyone in the case. She was giving him some latitude while the pieces fell into place, or so she hoped. After learning that Jada had lied about where she was going and that large sums of money had been withdrawn from both accounts, Sam was more convinced than ever that the girls were involved. What she didn't know yet was whether Frank was, too.

Sam sent another text to Nick on the secure BlackBerry. *Might have a break in the case. Will be later than expected. Tell the kids I love them and I'm sorry to miss dinner.*

She hated missing dinner with her kids and hearing about a day they'd never experience again. As she was about to step back into the room with Frank, Dr. Trulo came around the corner from the pit.

"Ah, there you are."

Oh shit. The grief group. She'd totally forgotten. "Not sure I can make it tonight, Doc. Got a case heating up fast."

"No worries. I was just coming to give you the reminder you requested."

"Thank you, because I did forget."

"I'm shocked."

"Haha, no, you're not."

"Is there any word from the lawyers about the twins?"

"Not yet."

"That's got to be weighing on you."

"It is, but I'm keeping busy, which helps. And everyone keeps telling me we've got the parents' will on our side, not to mention what the kids themselves want."

"Those are all strong points in your column. Keep me posted?"

"I will, and I'll run upstairs if I get the chance tonight. Please give everyone my regards if I can't get there."

"You got it, kiddo. Hang in there."

"Thanks."

Freddie greeted Dr. Trulo as he returned from the pit. "Fired up Elaine's phone and couldn't get current locations on either kid." He handed her a sheet of paper. "Here's a number for Zeke's mother."

"I'm getting a buzz. Are you?"

"Oh yeah. Big-time."

CHAPTER TWENTY-SEVEN

S am called the number for Zeke's mother.
She answered on the third ring.

"Mrs. Bellamy, this is Lieutenant Sam Holland with the DC Metro Police."

Silence.

"Hello?"

"Is this the first lady? Oh my God!"

"I told you who I am in this context. I'm trying to reach your son Zeke, and he's not answering his phone. Is he home?"

"No, he isn't. I just got home myself, so I'm not sure where he is."

"Do you know where he was earlier today?"

"He was at school earlier and then baseball practice. Why?"

"We're trying to reach him and Zoe, and both their phones are going straight to voice mail. Is his car gone?"

"Yes."

"Is Zoe's car at your house?"

"No, it's not."

"Are you able to track him?"

"Goodness no. He'd never go for that."

Who's in charge? Sam had to bite her tongue so she wouldn't actually ask the question. "What's the plate number for his car?"

"Why do you want to know that?"

Sam rolled her eyes at Freddie. "Because we're looking for him and Zoe. Please give me the information, or I'll send an officer there to get it." They could get the info on their own, but getting it from his parents would save time and paperwork.

"I... Um... Hold on for a second."

Sam took a deep breath and let it out while she waited for the woman to return.

"It's a black Mustang that we bought for him two years ago. It's registered in Virginia." She recited the plate number, which Freddie wrote down.

"Have you ever heard Zeke talk about anything to do with Zoe's mother?"

"Only that she was difficult and gave Zoe a hard time about everything. Once, he thanked me for not being like her."

"If you hear from him, I'd like you to have him call me at this number. Tell him it's urgent."

"Is he in trouble?"

"I'm not sure."

"What does that mean?"

"Just what I said. Have him call me."

"I... I will. What should I do in the meantime?"

"Figure out where your son is. That'd help."

"Oh... Okay. I will. I'll do that."

"Thank you." Sam slapped the phone closed. "*Is this the first lady?*' For fuck's sake. A cop is calling you right after your son's girlfriend's pain-in-the-ass mother was murdered, and that's your first question?"

"If I didn't work with you every day, it might be."

"You'd never act a fool like that."

"I might."

"Don't you dare! I've raised you better than that."

"Whatever you say. What's next?"

Sam thought about that for a second. "We need to put out a BOLO for the car Zoe is driving, as well as Zeke's And get the plates out to Flock," she said of the company that monitored license plate cameras. Doing that would make it more official that they were considered suspects, but they'd hit a wall in trying to locate them. She led the way back into the interrogation room, where Frank was on the phone asking when he might hear back from whomever he had called.

"I need someone immediately. I'm at the police station now, and she's going after my kids. This is an emergency."

Maybe you shouldn't have fired Dunning, Sam wanted to say in her best smug tone.

Frank muttered a curse as he ended the call.

"I'd ask how the lawyer shopping is going, but apparently not well."

"People don't understand the word 'emergency' these days."

"They understand the saying 'your lack of planning isn't my emergency.'"

"How could I have *planned* to need a defense attorney?"

Sam shrugged. "Seems to me that you had one of the better ones before you ran him off."

"One of the better ones wouldn't allow you to abuse the family of a murder victim."

"He's an officer of the court. He's not going to risk his license or reputation for you. He was giving you his best advice to cooperate with us so you could be done with this. Your lack of cooperation is a huge red flag, which he could see as well as we can."

"We *are* cooperating! What more do you want from us?"

"I want to know where your daughters are."

"I told you I don't know!"

"Are you willing to continue this conversation without having an attorney present?"

He was obviously torn.

"We can charge you with obstruction and make you

comfortable downstairs until your new attorney arrives. It's up to you."

"Downstairs?"

"The city jail is in the basement."

"Yeah, hard pass on that."

"Are you waiving your right to an attorney in this matter?"

"For now. Yes."

"Please let the record show that Mr. Frank Myerson has waived his right to legal representation in the homicide case of his wife, Elaine Myerson."

"Let the record show that I did not kill my wife."

"As their only living parent, shouldn't you know where your minor children are?"

"They're not babies! I don't have to know where they are every second of every day."

"Elaine would be so disappointed in you."

His eyes flashed with barely concealed rage. "Don't you speak of her as if you knew her."

"I know her pretty well after the last few days, and it seems to me that she knew exactly where her kids were at all times."

"That was our biggest problem! She never gave them an ounce of independence or freedom."

"Is that why they decided to kill her?"

"They did not kill her!"

"What's the plate number on the car Zoe is driving?"

His face went blank for a second. "The plate number?"

"Yes, the number on the license plate."

"I... I don't know that off the top of my head."

"What make, model and year is it?"

"It's a silver BMW SUV. I think it's two years old."

"Registered in the District?"

"Yes."

"Detective Cruz, can you please get the plate number and put out a BOLO alert to all local departments?"

"Yep."

"What's a BOLO alert?" Frank said as Freddie left the room.

"Be on the lookout."

"For what?"

"For the car and the people in it."

"Is this what you do when your investigation is going nowhere fast? You focus on the family of the victim?"

"In many homicide cases, someone close to the victim is directly involved."

"Not this time."

"So you say, but you can't tell me where your daughters are after they took thousands of dollars out of their bank accounts and checked out to be in specific places that it seems they never intended to go."

"Weren't you a teenager once, Lieutenant? Did you ever sneak around?"

"Of course I did, but if my mother had been murdered, I wouldn't have fallen off the grid. I would've stayed close to home and spent time with my family."

"That's you. Not everyone reacts the same way to trauma. My kids wanted their friends."

"Mr. Myerson, your kids lied to you. Is that the first time they've done that?"

He hesitated, only for a second, but long enough to answer the question without saying a word.

"So it happens a lot, does it?"

"You have to understand. It was the only way they could do anything with Elaine tracking their every move."

"How did they pull off lies if she was watching them?"

He seemed to be deciding whether to tell the truth or not.

"I feel that I need to warn you that you're perilously close to being charged with obstruction, sir."

He sighed deeply. "They have other phones that Elaine didn't know about."

"*What. The. Fuck?*"

"I'm sorry! I know I should've told you before now."

"Do you think?"

Sam pushed her notebook and pen across the table. "Write down the numbers."

Frank pulled out his phone and scrolled through his contacts to find the numbers, which he then wrote down.

Sam took the page from the notebook and went to the door, calling for Freddie.

He came around the corner.

"The girls had other phones that Elaine didn't know about."

"Holy crap."

She handed the page to him. "Let's get warrants moving for these numbers and see if their location, or locations, can be determined."

"I'll run this right up to Archie."

"Tell him it's 911."

"Yep."

Sam went back in the room. "Call Zoe on this number."

Frank eyed her with trepidation. "I'm not sure I should do that."

"I'm very sure you should, unless you're looking to spend the rest of your natural life in prison."

"I didn't kill my wife. How can you pin that on me?"

"You've obstructed the investigation into her murder by withholding relevant information. That's a slam-dunk conviction that comes with years in prison."

Nothing was ever a slam dunk, but he didn't need to know that.

"Call your daughter and put it on speaker."

He placed the call and set the phone on the table.

Zoe's voice mail picked up with the same message that was on her other phone.

"Try Jada."

Same thing. Straight to voice mail.

"So they've shut off all their phones and gone off the grid. Why would they do that if they have nothing to hide?"

"Maybe they got scared because you seem to be looking only at them for this."

"Or maybe you told them to shut off their phones, get in the car, go as far away as they could get and don't come back."

"I did not!"

"Did you know they wanted Elaine dead?"

"*Elaine* knew they wanted her dead, but that doesn't mean they did it."

"No one else in her life wanted her dead. According to you and the girls, no one else had access to your house. There was no sign of forced entry. Elaine was killed coming out of the shower, which means she most likely didn't admit the person who killed her." Sam leaned in closer to him. "Who else could it be?"

"I don't know! Someone could've gotten in somehow and killed her."

"For what reason? You said nothing was missing, right?"

"At first glance. Who knows if they took things that belonged to her? I don't know every piece of her jewelry. She inherited some valuable things from her mother. Maybe they were after those."

"How would they know she had them?"

"Isn't it your job to answer these questions?"

"Yes, it is, and usually the family members of murder victims are helpful because they want answers, too. For instance, they don't wait days to tell me their daughters have second cell phones that their mother didn't know about. They come clean with details like that the first time we ask so we won't waste valuable time chasing our tails."

"I should've told you that. I'm sorry that I didn't."

"Why didn't you?"

He took a second, seeming to collect his thoughts. "My first thought was protecting Elaine."

"From what?"

"From the whole world finding out that the three people

closest to her lied to her about everything. I hope you can try to understand... She was intractable when it came to guarding the safety of her loved ones. Her brother wouldn't tell you that he put distance between them because he couldn't handle having to report in to her every day and flatly refused to let her track his phone. She was *obsessed*, Lieutenant."

"You said before that you understood why she was obsessed, after the way her sister was murdered."

"I did, but understanding doesn't make it easy to live under that kind of regime. If I was ten minutes later than planned getting home, she'd grill me about where I'd been. If an open house ran late, she'd start texting, fearing that some rando had killed me in the house. It was all day, every day. I used to wonder sometimes how she held on to her job with all the time she spent spying on us."

"Were you faithful to your wife, Mr. Myerson?"

His expression hardened. "Yes, I was."

"Always?"

"Yes. I told you. I loved her."

"Even when she was spying on you all the time?"

"She did that because she was concerned about my safety. Not because she didn't trust me. I never gave her any reason not to trust me."

"I think you gave her a very good reason not to trust you— she just didn't know that you betrayed her by providing her children with secret phones so they could defy her."

"You don't understand how it was."

"To me, it seems like life with Elaine was torturous for you and your daughters."

"It could be. At times. Other times, it was wonderful. She went all out for birthdays, holidays, anniversaries. She was an amazing cook who loved nothing more than having all four of us at the table for dinner after a long day. She loved gardening and reading and binge-watching her favorite shows. There was a lot more to her than the traumatized sister of a murder victim."

"That murder was never solved. Do you think Elaine feared the murderer might come for someone else she loved?"

"I don't think she was lying awake at night, worrying about that particular scenario, but of course it was a possibility as long as the person who killed her sister remained at large."

"Try calling your daughters again."

He tried both numbers and got voice mail for both. "They're supposed to answer those phones. That's the deal we made when I agreed to get them."

"What else did you negotiate with them on the side?"

"Sometimes I would put their phones where they were supposed to be so that when Elaine tracked them, she wouldn't panic about where they were."

"That's diabolical."

"We did what we had to, Lieutenant. It was a very difficult situation, and we were full of empathy for the cause of it, but that didn't make it easy to live with."

"What was your plan if Elaine found out about the second phones and the planting of the ones she knew about?"

"How was she going to find out? Only the three of us knew, and we weren't going to tell her."

"What if, say, Jada was supposed to be at Ali's and Elaine went there, but Jada wasn't there?"

"Thankfully, that never happened, but we were careful. We made sure to mostly tell her the truth. Like, for example, if Zoe was going somewhere in a friend's car, we would tell Elaine that she was at the friend's house and would be home at whatever time. The plan worked well, and it gave us all some breathing room. The fighting was less intense than it had been before."

"How long ago did you get the second phones?"

"Two months or so. Zoe came to me with the idea and begged me for help. I agreed to it only if they both promised to always tell me where they really were—and always answer those phones if I called. Today is the first time they haven't done that."

"Tell me the truth. Do you think it's possible they harmed your wife?"

"No way. They couldn't have."

"Look at it from my point of view for a second. Remember all the things I've mentioned about no forced entry and no sign that Elaine let someone in and then went to take a shower. Why would she do that? Recall how Zoe's main cell phone was at Zeke's house all afternoon, but if we dig deeper, will we find that they weren't there at all? If we seize his car, will we see movement during the hours in question on Sunday? If it was them, we'll prove it eventually."

His eyes filled with tears. "These last few years... It's been a lot. There were times when I wanted to kill all of them. I remember thinking this is the kind of shit that causes people to snap and kill their whole family and then themselves. But it never once occurred to me to actually do that, and I can't imagine for the life of me those two girls planning something like this. I just can't."

"What about Zeke?"

"What about him?"

"Could he have planned it for them?"

"I... I don't know him well enough to say that."

"Was he frustrated by the restrictions placed on Zoe by her mother?"

"Everyone who knows Zoe was frustrated by it. She's lost friends over it. I mean, who wants to be friends with someone who isn't allowed to do anything?"

"One thing keeps nagging at me."

"What?"

"Elaine must've known that Zoe was at Zeke's on Sunday afternoon. Zoe told me herself that her mother would freak out if she knew they were having sex, and yet, Elaine had nothing to say about her being there alone with him for six hours?"

"She didn't know they were alone. Zoe told Elaine that his parents and sisters would be home."

"And Elaine wouldn't have checked that to be sure?"

"She was trying to be more trusting of her."

Sam felt for Elaine, who'd been deceived by her family, but she also had empathy for Frank and the girls, who'd struggled to live under Elaine's unreasonable rules. Her empathy ended when it came to murder, however. If the girls had killed their mother, or arranged to have someone else do it, Sam would make sure they paid for their crime.

CHAPTER TWENTY-EIGHT

When it became clear they were moving in circles with Frank and that the girls had made a run for it, Sam decided to make Frank their guest for the evening.

"You've got to be kidding me! I haven't done anything. My wife has been murdered, and you want to lock me up in jail?"

"Here's the deal, Frank. I don't trust you. You lied to me. You held back vital information, and you may or may not know where your daughters are. Since we don't need another person attached to this case running from us, you'll be our guest for the next little while until we sort this out."

"Can you do that without charging me?"

"Do you want me to charge you with obstruction or being a flight risk since your daughters already took off? I can easily make a case for both those things."

"No, I don't want that."

"So go with Detective Cruz, and we'll talk to you in the morning. In the meantime, if you happen to think of where your daughters might be, I'd recommend coming clean on that. If I find out you've known all along, you *will* be charged with obstruction. Do we understand each other?"

"Yeah."

"Right this way," Freddie said.

Frank got up and followed him from the room.

Sam went to find Carlucci and Dominguez. "Evening, ladies."

"Hey, LT. What's up?"

She briefed them on the day's events and filled them in on the BOLO for the Myerson girls and Zeke Bellamy.

"So we're thinking they did it, and now they're on the run?"

"Possibly, or they didn't do it and are scared they're going to be charged."

"What's your gut saying?"

"They did it, they thought they were in the clear because they had alibis, and now they're running scared. We'll continue to look for them tonight, and if we don't get anywhere, I'll bring in the marshals in the morning. Keep me posted on any developments overnight."

"Will do, LT," Carlucci said.

Freddie came to join them. "Bellamy's Mustang was found at a mall in West Virginia with no sign of him or the girls anywhere near it. It's being seized and brought in for analysis."

"Well, that's something, anyway," Sam said. "Now we know they're heading west."

"Or they want us to think they are," Freddie said.

"True. I'm punching out. You know where to find me if you need me."

"We got this," Dominguez said.

"Thanks, ladies. Freddie, go home."

"I'm gone."

Sam collected her belongings and locked her office. She was headed for the morgue and a quick getaway when she remembered the grief group meeting.

"Son of a bitch," she muttered as she took a hard right and went upstairs to poke her head in for a few minutes. At the door to the meeting room, she stopped short when she saw her sister Angela being comforted by Lenore Worthington and several other people.

Angela hadn't told Sam she planned to attend tonight, and while she was glad to see her there, she wasn't sure Ang would want Sam to witness her grief. So she stayed in the doorway and out of view.

"Thank you, guys," Angela said after a full minute of silence. "It helps to be able to air it out with people who understand."

"We understand, honey," Lenore said as she tucked a strand of Angela's reddish-brown hair behind her ear.

Angela rested her head on Lenore's shoulder. "I'm just not sure what to do with the anger I feel toward him. It's eclipsed all the good to the point that I can barely recall why I loved him. Before this happened, I had no trouble listing the many reasons I loved him. But this…"

"Being angry with someone who was fighting a disease is a difficult space to be in," Dr. Trulo said gently. "On the one hand, you know intellectually that he couldn't help it. Emotionally, however, you wonder how he could've chosen the drugs over you and your children."

"That's it exactly."

Dr. Trulo leaned in a bit. "But you know he didn't actually make that choice, right?"

"Yes, I know he didn't, that in his right mind, he never would've chosen anything over us, but when he bought those drugs on the street, he had to know how dangerous that was."

Sam's entire body ached for her sweet sister.

"He couldn't have known they were lethal," Sam said as she stepped into the room.

The woman sitting on the other side of Angela got up to make her seat available to Sam, who sat and reached for her sister.

"He couldn't have known he was taking poison," Sam said softly as she held her beloved sister. "He was murdered."

"How c-could he have let this happen?" Angela asked on a sob.

"One thing I know for certain about your Spencer was that he loved you more than anything in this world. He was besotted with you from the very beginning. He would look at you like you hung the moon. There's no way he would've left you unless he had no choice."

"I'm angry, too, Angela," a man said.

Sam glanced his way and recognized Brad Albright, who'd lost his wife, Mary Alice, to the same poisoned drugs that had killed Spencer.

"Sometimes I'm so angry, I scare myself," Brad said. "But then I try to rein it in because I don't want my kids to see me that way. I don't want them to know I'm angry with their mother for being an addict or buying drugs on the street or dying because of that choice. I want them to remember how much she loved them. So I'm trying to control the anger. It won't bring Mary Alice back, and it certainly won't make anything easier in this new normal."

"You're right," Angela said. "Thank you for that reminder, Brad."

He nodded and used a tissue to wipe away a tear.

"The anger is normal," Trey Marchand said. His young daughter, Vanessa, was shot during a sniper siege. "For months after my Nessie was killed, I wanted to kill someone. I thought it would make me feel better. Luckily, I figured out that wouldn't help before I acted on it. But, oh, that urge was hot and wild in me for a *long* time."

"If any of you feels the need to kill someone, please give me a call," Dr. Trulo said, sparking laughter that broke the tension in the room.

The meeting ended a short time later, and Sam walked out with Roni and Angela, who stopped in the hallway.

"I'd like to talk to Brad," Angela said. "Don't wait on me. I'll be fine." She hugged them both. "Thank you for being there for me and for the support."

"Call me if there's anything I can do—any time," Roni said.

"Thanks for being such a great friend to me. I'm inching closer to joining your Wild Widows. I'm not quite there yet, but soon."

"There's no rush. We're not going anywhere."

"Let me know you got home okay," Sam said with another hug for her sister.

"Okay, Mom."

"Just do it."

"I will."

Angela walked over to speak to Brad, who was talking to Trey and Lenore.

"You and the good doctor have created something very special and important with this group," Roni said as she and Sam walked downstairs. "I hope you know that."

"I'm sorry there's so much need for it."

"Me, too."

"Where'd you park?"

"I took the Metro."

"I'll give you a ride."

"Really?"

"Yes, silly. You're not walking to the Metro alone at this hour."

"I do it all the time."

"Cut that out. It's not safe." They stepped into cool darkness outside the morgue entrance. Vernon jumped out of the SUV when he saw them coming. "Sorry to keep you so late, Vernon. Can we drop my pal in Capitol Hill?"

"We sure can."

"Thank you, Vernon," Roni said.

"My pleasure, ma'am."

"Good. Call her that instead of me."

"You're ma'am, too, when we have company, ma'am."

"One step forward, three steps back."

"We're a work in progress." He shut the door and got in the driver's seat. "What's the address, second ma'am?"

Roni laughed and recited her address. "He's funny."

Sam lowered her voice. "He's amazing. They both are. A pleasure to be with all day."

"Correct me if I'm wrong, but don't you have a bit of a reputation for—how shall I say this diplomatically—hating people?"

Sam snorted out a laugh. "You're not supposed to know that."

"It's my job to know stuff about you, ma'am."

"Call me that and you won't have a job for long, *ma'am*."

"I stand corrected."

"I'm teasing, and you're not wrong about me and people. These two—especially Vernon—they're special. He reminds me of my dad."

"Oh wow. I love that for you."

"I love it for me, too. Funny how that comes along right when there's a void to be filled."

"I know all about that."

"Yes, I guess you do. I hope you know how happy we all are for you and Derek. And for little Maeve."

"She's my buddy. I adore her."

"I love to hear that. He suffered so much after he lost Vic, and I know you did, too, after Patrick. I hear stories like yours and his and Angela's, and I just wonder how people survive that kind of loss. I'm not sure I would."

"Yes, you would. You'd find a way for your kids. But let's not talk about things that aren't going to happen."

"Didn't mean to make it about me. We were talking about you and Derek, and I'm so proud of you for continuing to move forward and for all of it."

"That means a lot to me. Your friendship and the job have

been such special gifts to me on this journey I never expected to be on."

"I hate how we met, but I'm so glad to have you in my life. I can't wait to meet your little one."

"It's a boy," Roni whispered. "I haven't told anyone except Derek. Even my parents don't know."

"Congratulations, Roni. He's a lucky boy to have you as a mom."

"We'll see about that."

"I already know it."

When Vernon brought the SUV to a stop outside Roni's building, she leaned over to hug Sam. "Thanks for the lift."

When Roni reached for the passenger door handle, Sam said, "Wait for him, or he gets cranky."

"I heard that," Vernon said.

"Heard what?"

Roni laughed as Jimmy helped her out and walked her to the door.

"Thanks for the detour, guys," Sam said when they drove past the turn that would've taken her to Ninth Street once upon a time.

"No problem," Vernon said.

Sam's phone buzzed with a text from Neveah. *Did the deep dive on Worthy and found him to be a well-respected attorney and an upstanding citizen of Cleveland who's the ultimate family man. He's known for being close to his children and grandchildren. Lost his wife to cancer fifteen years ago and has been active in cancer-related charities ever since. He's also on the board of the Rock & Roll Hall of Fame. I couldn't find anything negative about him.*

"Then what the hell is he doing with my dirtbag mother-in-law?" Sam said out loud.

"What's that?" Vernon asked.

"Talking to myself." She responded to Neveah to thank her for the assist.

No problem!

Ten minutes later, they pulled through the gates to the White House.

"What time are we out of here in the morning?" Vernon asked as he held the door for her.

"Around seven thirty?"

"Is that for the funeral?"

"Shit. Don't tell anyone I forgot about that."

"They won't hear it from us."

"It's at nine at the National Cathedral. What time should we leave?"

"Eight thirty should be good."

That gave her another hour of sleep. "Thanks for everything today, guys."

"An honor and a privilege," Vernon said as Jimmy nodded. "See you in the morning."

THOUGH SHE WAS eager to get home to her own family, Sam continued up the stairs to the third floor to check on Shelby, Avery, Noah and baby Maisie. As she went, she texted Freddie, Gonzo and Malone to remind them she'd be in after Tom's funeral in the morning.

See you there, Malone replied.

She gave a soft knock on the door, hoping she wouldn't wake a sleeping baby or toddler.

Shelby came to the door, wearing a pink silk bathrobe and a big smile. Her blonde hair was pulled back into a ponytail. "This is a nice surprise."

"Sorry to come by so late."

"It's only eight. Noah's down for the count, but the rest of us are up. Come in."

"I thought it was later for some reason. I lose track of time during days like this."

"Was it a long one?"

"I'm just getting home. How are things here?"

"Pretty good. Avery's recovery is to the point of itching and bitching."

Sam laughed as she took in her FBI agent friend, holding his little girl with one arm while his other was in a sling, healing from a bullet wound inflicted by Harlan Peckham. He'd set out to avenge his imprisoned parents by killing the law enforcement officers who'd prosecuted their case. He'd succeeded in killing Tom Forrester, but had thankfully only injured Avery.

"Don't listen to my lovely wife. There's been no bitching."

Shelby gave her husband a withering look.

"Okay, maybe a little bitching, but I hate being sidelined."

"You'll be back to the rat race before long, so try to enjoy this downtime with your family."

"That's what I've been saying, too," Shelby added. "He's on a forced paternity leave."

Avery kissed the top of Maisie's head. "I'm trying to decompress and enjoy the time off, especially since you caught that son of a bitch Peckham."

"Avery! Language. Not in front of the baby."

"She's not even two weeks old, darlin'."

"She's already learning."

"Is that true, Sam?"

"How the hell would I know?"

"Sam! Language."

"That counts as a swear?"

"I've been asking for a list," Avery said, grinning at his wife, "but so far, it seems the rules are being made up as we go."

When Maisie started to fuss, Shelby took her from her daddy. "Thanks for popping in, Sam. We'll miss having ya'll right downstairs. I'm going to put this little girl down for the night. Talk to you tomorrow."

"Sleep tight, little one," Sam said.

"We're moving out next week," Avery added when they were alone. "Thank you again for having us for all this time."

"I wish you could stay. We like having you here."

"I'd stay forever if I wasn't getting flak at work about being too cozy with POTUS and FLOTUS."

"To hell with them. They're just jealous."

He got up to walk her out. "Probably, but the flak is a distraction."

"It's good to see you up and about," Sam said. "I didn't care for you getting shot, so please don't let that happen again."

"I'll try not to. Hey, before you go... Heard an interesting rumor through the grapevine."

"What's that?"

"Juan Rodriguez might not be dead after all."

Having learned her lesson with her colleagues, she quickly decided to tell Avery the truth. "He's not."

"How long have you known?"

"Almost from the start."

"Hmmm."

"Hmmm what?"

"Apparently, his best friend and roommate is making some noise about you interviewing him as part of a homicide investigation when you might've known he was alive."

Sam hadn't seen that coming, even though she was glad to know Isaac had been told the truth. "I was doing what NCIS asked me to do as a matter of national security."

"You really interviewed the roommate, knowing the guy was alive?"

"Yes! They asked me to conduct the investigation the way I normally would, so that's what I did."

"Huh."

Exasperated now, Sam said, "What else is on your mind, Avery?"

"I think you should expect some trouble over this, Sam. People are a bit... incredulous... that you'd put the guy through it, knowing his friend is alive."

"Anything else?"

"That's it."

She reached for the doorknob to leave. "Thanks for the heads-up."

"Don't be pissed at the messenger. I wanted you to be prepared."

"And now I am. Sleep well, friend. Glad to see you on the mend."

"Are you going to the funeral in the morning?"

"I'm speaking."

"Can I hitch a ride with you? They're not letting me drive yet."

"Of course. Leaving at eight thirty."

"See you then, and don't be pissed at me. I wanted you to know what was being said."

"Good night, Avery."

As she went down one flight of stairs to the residence, she processed what Avery had told her. People were talking about Juan and her role in perpetrating the deception. Should she get out ahead of any reporting on the matter, or would it be better to keep her mouth shut when, or if, it became public?

She had no idea, so she planned to ask the savviest media strategist she knew—the guy she slept with.

CHAPTER TWENTY-NINE

Before heading into their suite, Sam wanted to check on the kids. She stood outside Alden and Aubrey's room, smiling when she heard whispering. She went in to sit on the edge of their bed. "Why are you guys still awake?"

"We were waiting for you, Sam," Alden said with a cheeky grin.

"Are you trying to charm me, mister? If so, it's working."

He giggled madly when she bent to kiss his sweet face.

"I'm charming, too, Sam," Aubrey said.

"Yes, you are, my love. How was your day? Did anyone puke at lunch?"

"Not today," Alden said.

The joyful sound of their giggles filled her soul and brought tears to her eyes as she thought of their selfish grandparents trying to upset their lives once again. She couldn't entertain the possibility that they might succeed, or she'd be sobbing in no time.

"You need to go to sleep." She adjusted their covers and kissed them both again. "I'll see you in the morning, okay?"

"Okay, Sam," Aubrey said.

"I love you."

"Love you, too," they both said.

Sam took their sweet love with her when she went to check on Scotty, who was out cold with Skippy by his side, the two of them snuggled up to each other, snoring like two old men. Smiling, she bent to kiss Scotty's forehead and gave Skippy a pat on her soft head. She wondered if the dog had been outside recently, but she'd wake up Scotty if she needed to go, so she let sleeping dogs—and boys—lie.

After she shut off Scotty's TV and the lights in his room, she crossed the hall to their suite where Nick was in his office, poring over the correspondence and briefing books he brought "home" with him every night.

Sam stood in the doorway for a few seconds, just watching him, before she cleared her throat to let him know she was there.

As he spun around to face her, his smile made her whole damned day. "There's my lovely wife, home late from running the streets and causing trouble."

"That's me, your little degenerate."

He reached up to take off his glasses.

Sam stepped forward to stop him. "Leave them on. They do something to me."

"What is this *something* you speak of?"

She fanned her face as she straddled his lap and curled her arms around his neck. Leaning her forehead against his, she said, "I missed you today."

He grasped her ass to pull her in tighter against his instant erection. "I missed you, too." He nuzzled her neck and sent shivers down her spine.

"We might have a teeny, tiny problem."

He pressed his cock against her. "Nothing teeny or tiny about it."

She huffed out a laugh. "I'm not talking about *that*."

"Well, you caused *that*, so maybe you ought to deal with *that* before we discuss this problem you speak of."

"Like, right now?"

"Are you busy?"

"I wasn't, but it seems like I am now."

"You've very busy." He tightened his hold on her and stood as she wrapped her legs around him and held on for the ride to wherever they were going. Right to the sofa, apparently, as he came down on top of her, capturing her lips in a deep, desperate kiss.

Sam's mind was full of a million things—Tom's funeral and the speech she needed to give, her sister's unbearable grief, the twins' grandparents' latest volley, three missing teenagers who might or might not be murderers and concerns over the rumors circulating about Juan and her role in perpetrating a lie.

But with one kiss after another, Nick wiped away all those thoughts, forcing her to focus on him and them and the magical connection they shared.

His hands were under her top, pushing it up and over her head before he resumed the kiss.

Then her breasts were free of her bra, and his shirt was off.

How did he do all that without seeming to miss a beat in the kiss of all kisses?

"Smooth moves, Mr. President. Very smooth."

"You like that?"

"Uh-huh."

"Can I take off the glasses now?"

"Not quite yet." She gave his shoulder a gentle push to let him know she wanted to move.

While they were standing, they helped each other out of the rest of their clothes.

Then Sam directed him to sit on the sofa, grabbed a pillow and used it to cushion her knees as she knelt before him.

"What is happening?" he asked, smiling as he twisted a length of her hair around his finger.

"It's the glasses." She wrapped her hand around his cock,

smiled at him and then bent to run her tongue over the crown, making him gasp from the pleasure. "How lucky are we?" she asked between strokes of her hand and tongue.

"Luckiest people on earth because we have this."

"Mmm." She made sure her lips were well positioned for the vibrations the sound made.

"*Fuck*. Samantha."

"Yes, dear?"

"Don't stop."

She continued to tease him with her tongue and lips while he buried his hands in her hair and tried to move things along. "Don't get bossy with me. I'm busy."

The sound he made was a cross between laughter and agony.

God, she loved him, and she set out to show him how much, working him until he was a quivering, pleading shell of his usual commanding self. Then she backed off and started all over again, making him groan and gasp, and finally, when she was good and ready, she finished him off with a grand finale for the ages.

For a long time afterward, he kept his eyes closed behind those sexy-as-fuck glasses while he breathed deeply.

Moving up, she straddled his lap, kissing him until his eyes popped open.

"A man ought to be warned before something like that happens."

She flashed her most satisfied grin. "How much warning does a man require?"

"At least twenty-four to forty-eight hours so he can take his heart medication."

She laughed. "He's not on heart medication. Is he?"

"No, but he might need to be after that."

"Should I give Harry a call?" she asked of their friend, the White House physician.

"Do you want to have to tell him what put me in this condition?"

"Um, well…"

Nick laughed and ran his hands over her back, making her squirm. "If you keep that up, things are going to happen."

"Things? Like, what kind of things?"

"Oh, some of this." He moved against her, ready for round two, as he squeezed her bottom. "And some of that."

"I love when you threaten me this way."

"I love you all the time, every minute of every day of every week and month and year. I love you more than anything in the whole wide world."

It was all she could do not to swoon like a teenager in the throes of first love when he said things like that. "Okay, I'll have more of the good sex with you."

"That's all it takes? Some sweet nothings?"

"Those weren't nothings. They were everythings, and as you know, I'm exceptionally easy where you're concerned."

"Easy. Huh. Well…"

"Don't ruin my good mood." She raised herself up and took him in, coming down slowly, going for maximum effect.

Nick watched her with those amazing hazel eyes gone hot with desire. "Sexiest wife I ever had."

"I better be the only wife you ever have."

"Only one I'll ever want." He gathered her in close to him and held on tightly as they moved together in the kind of perfect harmony she'd only ever had with him. He moved just right, gazing up at her with love and desire and all the things. He knew just what to do to get them both to the finish line, straining and gasping from the power of their releases.

His head fell back against the sofa, breathing like he did after a good workout. "That should hold us over for a couple of days."

Sam deflated at the reminder that he'd be gone for two nights.

"Whoops. Had you forgotten?"

"Not entirely, but I wasn't actively thinking about it."

"Sorry."

"I feel pathetic for wanting to wail about you leaving for two nights, which is insane. What the hell is wrong with me?"

He tightened his hold on her. "There's absolutely nothing wrong with how much you love me."

"It's making me into a lunatic."

"Um, I hate to point out that you were a lunatic long before you met me."

Sam raised her head, planning to object, but laughed when she saw his amused expression. "I can't really argue with that."

"I love that you're a lunatic."

"Said no president to any first lady until now."

"There's never been a first lady quite like mine."

She held herself up with her hands on his shoulders while he cupped her breasts and ran his thumbs over her nipples. "Speaking of your wife, the political liability, we might have a problem brewing."

"I have my naked wife draped over me. I haven't got a problem in the world."

"I'm not 'draped.'"

"What would you call it?"

"I'm sprawled at best, and we need to talk about this, so I'm going to get up."

"Not yet."

Sam gave him five more minutes, because she needed it as much as he did, and then she kissed him and got up to take a shower. She turned on the water and put her hair up in a clip to keep it dry since it would be done by a professional in the morning in preparation for the very public Forrester funeral.

Nick followed her into the shower, wrapping his arms around her from behind and kissing her shoulder as they stood under the warm water. "What's on your mind, love?"

"Avery told me people are finding out Juan is alive, and his roommate, who we interviewed that first day, is telling people I knew he was alive when I came to their place."

Sam felt him go still behind her, which did nothing to soothe her nerves. "How would he know what you knew and when you knew it?"

"I'm not sure, but that's what he's saying." Sam turned to him. "What're you thinking?"

"You went to his apartment after you saw Juan?"

"I did because they asked me to work the case the way I always do, and my first stop was his apartment. We talked to Juan's roommate, Isaac, who's been his friend since the Naval Academy. He'd reported Juan missing and was distraught over the news of his murder. As you know, I felt sick about the whole thing, but I did as NCIS asked and worked the case. I was led to believe it was possible we might uncover more information that'd be useful to the overall investigation into the Joint Chiefs."

Nick reached for the body wash and filled his hands with soap to wash them both.

After they'd rinsed, he grabbed towels, wrapped hers around her and then tucked his around his waist.

"You're freaking me out with this quiet efficiency."

"I'm thinking."

"Let me know when you're done."

"You'll be the first to know."

"Guess what else?"

"What?"

"We got invited to a dinner party at my new friend Cori's—aka federal Judge Corrinne Sawyer. She promised a friendly crowd who'll be thrilled to meet us."

"You made a new friend and want to go to a dinner party with strangers? Are you feeling all right?"

"Haha. I saved her life by capturing Harlan Peckham before he could try to kill her, too, so she's feeling grateful. But I like her. She's cool."

"Wow, does she know how rare it is that you actually like someone?"

"It's been pointed out to me that I'm liking a lot more people lately. I may be mellowing."

"Don't you dare do that. I like you nice and feral."

Smiling, she said, "Speaking of dinner parties, I'm starving. Did you eat?"

"Ah, yeah, hours ago."

"I totally forgot about dinner."

"What do you feel like?"

"Maybe a turkey sandwich and some chips?"

"I'll place the order."

"We're getting so ridiculously spoiled here."

"It's temporary, and besides, we may as well enjoy a few perks to go with the massive downside."

Sometimes she could forget, for a second or two, that he was the freaking president of the United States. Her husband. The president. Like... *what?* It was still surreal all these months later, as were the room service, the butlers, the ushers, the deluxe accommodations and the other trappings of White House life.

The downside, though, lurked on the edges, always waiting to remind them that the whole world was watching their every move.

Nick returned to the bathroom, where she hadn't moved from where he'd left her, standing at the vanity, staring into space.

"They said they'll be up in a few minutes."

"Thanks. Now tell me what we're gonna do about Juan."

"After the funeral tomorrow, we'll do that interview before I leave for the West Coast. We'll say you were told Juan was alive and asked by NCIS to conduct the investigation the way you normally would. We'll add that you were told it was a national security matter and that you could be most helpful by working the case and reporting any new information you uncovered."

Sam leaned back against the vanity and crossed her arms over the towel. "Doesn't that throw NCIS under the bus?"

"I'll speak to Secretary Jennings first thing and let him know that we plan to go public with what took place."

"What if he asks you not to?"

"He works for me, not the other way around."

Sam smiled and fanned her face. "Power is sexy on you."

He scowled. "I'm being serious."

"So am I. But back to business... What if NCIS feels that us going public with this would jeopardize their case against Goldstein?"

"How could it? Juan had nothing to do with the coup attempt that Goldstein orchestrated. Whatever involvement Goldstein had in plotting Juan's demise would be separate from the treason case."

Sam considered that. "I guess that's true. Okay, talk to Jennings first thing and set up the interview for after the funeral. I'll see Joe at the funeral and will give him a heads-up that this might get ugly."

"I'll text Trevor now to make it happen right after the funeral. We'll come back here for that, and then I'll head to Andrews."

"We're not talking about you going away."

He stepped toward her, put his arms around her and held her close. "Will you be able to sleep now that we have a plan?"

"Yeah, thanks for that."

"Are we really going to the judge's dinner party?"

"I think I might like to, if you don't mind too much."

"Anything for you, love."

CHAPTER THIRTY

I n the morning, Nick got the kids up and ready for school while Sam went to the in-house salon for hair and makeup, which made her feel ridiculous when other women would feel pampered. To her, it felt like a waste of valuable time that could be spent more productively—having breakfast with her kids, for instance. But since the eyes of the world would be on her at the funeral and at the interview afterward, she forced herself to sit still as Ginger and Davida made her shine.

"You ladies are magicians," she said when she saw the results of their efforts. "And you're quick and efficient, which is greatly appreciated."

"Our pleasure, ma'am," Davida said.

"Thank you for coming in early for me."

"No problem," Ginger said.

Sam returned to the residence to change into the black dress she'd wear to the funeral and interview, which Trevor had confirmed for eleven thirty in the Map Room. That meant she wouldn't get to work until close to one. She texted Freddie and Gonzo to let them know her plan for the day.

Gonzo replied right away. *The roommate is on the morning*

shows, and people are taking to social media to express outrage that you interviewed him while knowing Juan was alive. This could get ugly fast.

Sounds like it's already ugly. We'll put out a statement from my office here and clarify in the interview.

I'd move fast on that statement. You're already losing control of the story.

Will do. Thanks.

Sam called Lilia.

"Morning," her chief of staff said. "Are you ready for the funeral?"

"That's become the least of my concerns."

"So you've heard about Isaac Erickson's comments this morning."

"I have, and I'd like to put out a statement that says that Lieutenant Holland is aware of Lieutenant Commander Erickson's claims and will address them further in an interview she's doing with the president later this morning."

"We'll get that out for you right away."

Sam went up the stairs to the residence. "Thanks, Lilia."

"Is it true that Juan is alive?"

"Yes."

"Oh, thank heavens. That's the best news I've heard in a while."

"It was for me, too, but it's since caused me a ton of heartburn, and I suspect that's not over yet."

"The story is catching wind, for sure. Let me get that statement posted for you. Trevor notified me of the interview. I'll see you in the Map Room at eleven thirty. Good luck with the eulogy this morning."

"Thanks."

Sam was closing her phone as the twins came running out of the family kitchen, nearly crashing into her in the hallway. She hugged them both, thankful she hadn't changed into her dress before going to the salon as the scent of maple syrup overtook her. "What's the good word, my loves?"

"Nick said we gotta hurry up and brush our teeth or we're gonna be late," Alden said. "If we're late, no recess."

"Oh snap. Get going, then." She kissed the top of two blond heads. "Love you to the moon."

"And back?" Aubrey asked.

"Always."

They ran off to finish getting ready for school.

Sam continued to the kitchen, where Scotty was scrolling on his phone while sipping from his coffee cup.

Nick used his chin to gesture to their son. "He says you okayed the coffee?"

"I did *not* okay it. I was passively aggressively backed into a corner that led to him *believing* I agreed to it."

Without looking up from his phone, Scotty said, "There was nothing passive about it."

His parents tried, and failed, to stop the laughter that burst from them simultaneously.

"That's not funny," Nick said, attempting a stern tone.

"Yes, it is," Scotty replied with a grin. "And P.S., you suck at not laughing when the kid is being fresh."

"We're working on that," Nick said.

"Don't work too hard. It cracks me up how you try to be all parental, but you're like a couple of fourteen-year-olds on the inside."

Sam glanced at Nick. "I'm offended by that."

"Truth hurts," Scotty said.

"Don't let it get out that Dad is like a fourteen-year-old on the inside. He's got enough troubles being the youngest president in history."

"The secret is safe with me if I still get my morning coffee. Do we have a deal?"

"See how he does that?" Sam asked Nick.

"I see, and it's terrifying."

Scotty got up, rinsed his cup and plate and put them in the dishwasher. "No need to be terrified, parentals. I promise to use my negotiation skills for good rather than evil. Most of the time, anyway."

"Gee, that's super comforting, son," Nick said. "Thanks for clarifying."

"No problem. Mom, you need to do something about Juan's roommate who's all over the interwebs spouting off about you lying to him about his best friend being dead."

"We're on it, but thank you for the advice."

"Any time. Y'all have a good day."

"What is happening?" Sam asked Nick after Scotty left the room.

"I believe our son is growing up and is now officially smarter than me and more diabolical than you. That's some scary stuff."

"Why do you get to be the smart one, while I'm the diabolical one?"

"Um, do you want examples?"

"Don't you dare throw that Harvard degree in my face."

That smile of his was devastatingly sexy, even when she was pretend-arguing with him. "Okay, I won't."

"And I'll remind you that I have a *master's* degree, and you do *not*, so maybe you should be the diabolical one."

"It just comes so much more naturally to you."

She headed for their room to change. "Oh, those are fighting words, mister."

"Are they untrue?"

"I refuse to dignify that with a response."

"You're very sexy when you're refusing to dignify me."

"Not as sexy as you are in those glasses, or when you flex your power muscles. Did you talk to Jennings?"

"I did, and he told me to do what I felt was necessary, that the NCIS case is solid against Goldstein on the coup scheme, and they're still piecing together the secondary plot to murder Juan."

"I need to talk to Joe before we say anything publicly. He'll be on the hook for this, too."

"You said he's attending the funeral?"

Sam went into the walk-in closet to get dressed. "As far as I know."

"Well, you can talk to him there, or maybe call from the car?"

"Yeah, I'll do that. The funeral will be packed. I may not get to talk to him there."

Sam put on her engagement ring, the key necklace he'd given her for their wedding as well as the bracelet and other jewelry he'd given her. "Will you zip me?"

"I'd love to, but for the record, I much prefer *un*zipping you."

"How did I know you would say that?"

He nudged her hair aside and kissed the back of her neck. "Because you know me." When she was zipped, he gave her a soft pat on the bum and went back to finish packing for his trip.

"We had a dog when we were kids who'd literally moan when the suitcases came out," Sam said. "I feel like that right now."

"It's two nights. I'll be back so fast, you won't have time to miss me."

"That's true."

"Really?"

Sam laughed. "Got you."

"Yes, you did," he said with a chuckle.

"You know I'll miss you every second you're gone and be counting down until you get back. Nothing is the same when you're not here."

"There's nowhere else I want to be but wherever you and our kiddos are."

"Speaking of the kiddos, any word from Andy?"

"Not yet, but I'm going to call him from the car. Let's get going."

They went down the stairs hand in hand to where Brant, Vernon, Jimmy and the rest of their details awaited them.

"Agent Hill said to tell you he'll meet you at the cathedral," Vernon said to Sam. "He had a stop to make on the way."

"Got it, thanks." To Nick, she said, "I hate that we're going to a funeral for a good man who died far too young, but I like that we get to spend a rare weekday morning together."

"That's my girl, always seeing the bright side."

"Morning," Brant said. "Are you ready to go?"

"We are," Nick said. To Harold, the usher, he said, "My suitcase is packed in the residence if someone can grab it for me."

"We'll take care of that for you, sir."

"Thank you, Harold."

"You got the word that I'm riding with POTUS?" Sam asked Vernon.

"I did. All good."

Their coats were produced from some secret closet, and they were loaded into the back of The Beast for the ride to the National Cathedral.

As they drove through the White House gates, Sam called Chief Farnsworth.

"Morning."

"Hi there. Wondering if you're seeing the news with Isaac Erickson this morning?"

"Unfortunately, yes. What're we doing about it?"

"We're putting out a statement from the White House that I'm aware of his concerns and will address them more fully in an interview the president and I are giving later today."

"Is the plan to come clean?"

"Yes, which is why I wanted to check in with you. I believe I'll need to say I was working with the approval of my commanders."

"I think you should say with the approval of your chief—and only your chief—since no one else in the command structure was aware of this."

"That's going to cause us secondary issues, isn't it?"

"Probably, but we've dealt with that before, and I'm sure we will again."

"Okay, then, that's what I'll say. Be ready for the blowback."

"I'm wearing my metal suit today."

Sam laughed. "See you shortly."

"I'll be there."

"All good with him?" Nick asked.

"Yep. We've got a plan."

"Andy texted to say he doesn't have anything to report yet, but he hopes to know more by later today."

"I can't even think about that without wanting to howl."

"Same, but I think it'll all work out."

Sam nodded. "I'm clinging to that."

She used the rest of the ride to review her speech and prepare herself to speak in front of a crowd, which would never come easily to her due to her dyslexia.

When they arrived at the cathedral, they were driven to the main door.

"Remember coming for John's funeral and how we had to take the Metro because we wouldn't be able to park?"

"I do remember that, and how nervous I was to speak."

"Now we're dropped off at the main door."

"One of the perks. How're you feeling?"

"As okay as I ever am when I have to do stuff like this."

"You'll be fine. You're an old pro by now."

"Sure I am."

Her stomach was on fire with nerves as she took in the huge crowd that'd turned out for the funeral. Many faces were familiar to her, but far more were not. Did the strangers in the audience wish her well, or were they among the many who wanted to see her and Nick fail as the first couple?

She couldn't think about that, or she might need to vomit.

As they made their way down the center aisle of the soaring cathedral, everyone wanted to shake their hands and have a word with them. Sam wondered how many of the people, currently kissing up to them, would've backed Goldstein's efforts to overthrow Nick's administration. Probably more than half of them.

It took more than fifteen minutes to reach their assigned seats in the row behind Tom's family. She noted that the now-disgraced former Attorney General Cox was in attendance, along with Congressman Damien Bryant, who was out on bail on numerous felonies, including kidnapping Forrester's family. She couldn't believe he'd had the audacity to show his face at Tom's funeral.

The two men glared at Sam as if they'd rather have her in the casket. She was always amused at how people looked for someone else to blame when they'd ruined their lives all on their own.

Sam hugged Leslie Forrester and her daughters, Aurora and Naomi, as well as the Miller triplets, Faith, Hope and Charity, who'd served as Assistant U.S. Attorneys under Tom's leadership. Conlon Young, Tom's chief administrative assistant in the USA's office, and his wife greeted Sam, who introduced them to Nick.

"I never got a chance to personally thank you for arresting the man who killed Tom," Conlon said to Sam. "We're forever in your debt."

"I was just doing my job."

"It means everything to us that the person who took him from us will be brought to justice."

Sam, who'd never met Conlon before Tom was murdered, had found him to be a bit smarmy during the investigation. That impression hadn't changed in the aftermath of Peckham's arrest.

"Thank you for being here, Sam," Leslie said. "And you, too, Mr. President. Tom would be honored by your presence."

"Sam thought of him as a friend," Nick said. "We appreciate his service to the Justice Department."

They were asked to take their seats when the service got underway with a stirring hymn as the pallbearers rolled Tom's casket down the center aisle. Moving through the motions of the service, Sam was reminded that Nick had been raised in church, while she'd grown up without religion.

After the opening prayers and readings by the Forrester daughters, an usher escorted Sam to the lectern. She laid the printed pages of her speech on the dais in case the teleprompter failed her. At times like this, she most feared her dyslexia kicking in and making a fool of her in front of the crowd gathered before her as well as those watching the live stream.

"On behalf of Leslie, Naomi and Aurora Forrester, as well as Tom's dedicated staff at the U.S. Attorney's Office, thank you for being here today to honor the life and service of a man who gave most of his career to public safety and the pursuit of justice. Many people are unaware of how involved U.S. Attorneys are in keeping our communities safe from all kinds of crime. Tom was an inspirational leader, a law enforcement officer of the highest order and a friend to many of the people gathered here today, including me. I've worked closely with Tom and his team for years, especially since assuming command of the Metropolitan Police Department's Homicide division.

"He was the kind of public servant we all aspire to be—honest, ethical, loyal, hardworking and true to the rule of law. He gave his life in service to his country and should be remembered as the hero he was. As a U.S. Attorney, Tom was part of a tradition that dates back to the Judiciary Act of 1789, which directed the president to appoint in each federal district 'a meet person learned in the law to act as an attorney for the United States.' President Washington nominated the first U.S. Attorneys on September 24, 1789. The United States Attorney was 'to prosecute in (each) district all delinquents for crimes and offenses cognizable under the authority of the United States, and all civil actions in which the United States shall be concerned.'

"I'd like to share with you a statement made by Mr. Justice Sutherland in Berger v. United States in 1935 that aptly summarizes the role Tom fulfilled so admirably.

"*The United States Attorney is the representative not of an ordinary party to a controversy, but of a sovereignty whose obligation to govern impartially is as compelling as its obligation to govern at all; and whose interest, therefore, in a criminal prosecution is not that it shall win a case, but that justice shall be done. As such, he is, in a peculiar and very definite sense, the servant of the law, the twofold aim of which is that guilt shall not escape or innocence suffer. He may prosecute with earnestness and vigor—indeed, he should do so. But, while he may strike hard blows, he is not at liberty to strike foul ones. It is as much his duty to refrain from improper methods calculated to produce a wrongful conviction as it is to use every legitimate means to bring about a just one.'*

"Tom was indeed a 'servant of the law,' who strove every day to be impartial, to prosecute with earnestness and vigor and to enforce the law with an eye always on justice, fairness and equality for all. Tom gave his life in service to the law, his country and our city. We are lesser for having lost him to this most senseless of crimes.

"To Leslie, Naomi and Aurora, he was a husband and a father. I had the honor of getting to know Tom's family during the investigation and learned more about who he was off the job. Leslie noted how Tom's work was busy and intense, but he always tried to leave the job at the office when he came home to her and their girls. His daughters reported how much he enjoyed driving them to school, practices and games and how he made a point to be present with them during their time together, ignoring his phone and the relentless demands of his job for the few minutes a day that he had with them. I know I speak for everyone who had the pleasure of working closely with him when I say he was almost as beloved on the job as he was at home."

She looked up and caught Faith Miller dabbing at her eyes with a tissue.

"Tom, we thank you for your service to our country and the District. Those of us who are left behind will endeavor to live up to your legacy as we continue the important work of keeping our community safe. May you rest in eternal peace."

"Why don't you tell them how he cut you a deal to avoid being prosecuted for assault, *you fucking bitch*?"

Everyone turned as one to see former Sergeant Ramsey, looking disheveled and possibly drunk, standing in the center aisle, his fist directed at Sam, who ignored him as she made her way back to her seat next to Nick. At the same time, several police officers and Secret Service agents swiftly escorted the former SVU detective out of the church and hopefully into custody.

"What the hell?" Nick whispered.

"Ramsey is still mad that Tom didn't charge me with assault after I pushed him down the stairs." Tom had saved her career by convening a grand jury that had, after hearing about how Ramsey had told Sam she'd deserved to be wrapped in razor wire by Stahl and threatened with fire, chosen not to indict her on assault charges.

"So he disrupts the man's funeral?"

"That's the least of what he's done."

With Ramsey removed from the cathedral, the service continued with several other speakers, including Conlon Young, who spoke from the heart about his close friend and mentor.

When the service concluded, Leslie turned to them.

"Thank you again for your beautiful words and for being here today."

Sam hugged her. "I'll be thinking of you and your girls."

"We appreciate everything you did for us—and for Tom."

She nodded. "We'll be with you through the long haul in getting justice for Tom—and for your family."

"That brings me comfort."

Sam hugged the Miller sisters and then took Nick's hand as they were escorted to a side door by Brant, Vernon, Jimmy and several other agents. She climbed into The Beast first and immediately called Freddie.

"Did you hear what Ramsey pulled at the funeral?"

"Everyone's talking about it. He's being booked on numerous charges, including creating a public nuisance."

"Cox and Bryant were there, looking at me as if they wanted me dead. All examples of men who screwed up their own lives and need someone to blame."

"I can't believe Bryant had the stones to show up after orchestrating the kidnapping of Forrester's family."

"I can't believe he made bond."

"Apparently, it was set at three million, and he put up one of his houses to secure it."

"Disgusting. What else is happening? Any sign of the Myerson girls or Zeke?"

"Nothing new."

"I guess it's safe to assume at this point that they're on the run. Let's bring in Jesse Best and the marshals to find these kids before they hurt themselves or someone else."

"I'll call him."

"What's happening with Frank?"

"We brought him upstairs, got him a hot breakfast, a shower and a change of clothes. He tried to call the girls again, but didn't get through."

"Thanks for handling that. I've got the TV interview at eleven thirty. I'll be in right after."

"See you then."

Sam hated days like this in which it seemed everything else took priority over her victim of the moment, but Tom's funeral and the interview were both important. She'd take care of business and then get back to securing justice for Elaine Myerson.

CHAPTER THIRTY-ONE

"Why'd you take us out the side?" Nick asked Brant when they were standing next to The Beast. Sam had gotten in ahead of him to call Freddie.

"A massive gathering of press materialized while you were inside, and from what we heard, they were planning to ambush the first lady about the Juan Rodriguez situation. Over the last hour, every major media outlet has reported on the story."

"What're they saying?"

"That she interviewed his grief-stricken roommate while knowing that Juan wasn't dead."

"Shit."

"From what I can see, it's blowing up into a big story."

"Just what we needed."

"Yes, sir, that was my thought as well. We're still going back to the White House?"

"Yes, thank you."

Brant held the door for Nick until he was settled inside the car, next to Sam, who was still on the phone.

"What is?" she asked. "Seriously? Okay, well, we're going to address it in the interview. Yes, I hear you. I'll be there soon."

She slapped the phone closed. "The shit storm with Juan's roommate has gone nuclear."

"I heard. Brant said every major outlet has published or aired something on it while we were at the funeral."

"So I heard. I'm sorry if this causes a problem for you."

"Don't worry about me. This doesn't even count as a problem in the grand scheme of things."

"It'll make me look like an asshole."

He reached for her hand. "You'll explain why you did it in the interview, and we'll ask them to release that portion of it ASAP. It'll be fine."

"I wish I shared your optimism. Between this and Ramsey's outburst, it's going to be an I-hate-Sam-Holland kinda day."

"Not for me. Every day is an I-*love*-Sam-Holland kind of day."

"Thank goodness for that." She released a deep sigh that was part agony for the loss of Tom and part relief that her speech hadn't been a disaster. "My heart aches for Leslie and her girls and what they're going through. I can't imagine it."

"You did a beautiful job speaking about Tom. I'm sure it meant a lot to them."

"I hope so."

"I know so. Don't let the haters get you down. Remember our mantra—they can't touch us unless we let them. You did what you thought was right, what you'd been asked to do by NCIS in the interest of national security. You'll say that as much as you disliked having to go through the motions with the roommate and others, you'd do it again for the same reasons if it came to that, which you hope it never does."

"You're good at this. You ought to run for office."

Snorting with laughter, he said, "No fucking way am I ever doing that again."

"Never say never."

"I'm saying it, and you should be, too. Three years of this madness will be more than enough for me."

"If you wake up one day and decide you want more, I'd support you. I hope you know that."

He felt her forehead as if checking for a fever.

She swatted his hand away. "I'm serious."

"I know. It's terrifying. Are you sure you're not feverish or under the influence of something that would explain this insanity?"

"It's not insanity to predict that my gorgeous, sexy, intelligent husband is going to have a very successful presidency, and if he decides he wants to continue being president for four more years, his wife would support him."

"When is this 'successful' portion of the program going to begin?"

"It already has."

He gave her a skeptical look. "Doesn't seem that way."

"It does to me. Other people's opinions are none of our business."

"Even admirals and generals with thirty-plus years of experience?"

"Especially them. They're envious of your meteoric rise to power and your popularity with regular people. They thought you'd be weak and easy to manipulate because you're young. They found out otherwise."

"Only because Juan warned me. I can't imagine how it would've gone down if they'd caught me by surprise."

"They wouldn't have succeeded."

"Brant said the Secret Service would've taken them into custody and escorted them from the premises."

"They were never going to succeed at that mission, which was fueled by their own hubris and sense of importance."

"It shook me. I can't deny that."

"Of course it did, but remember, they were Nelson's people, not yours. Put your own people in these important positions and get to work."

"Terry and I are working on that now, with Graham's help. I don't have enough people on my bench, but he does." Nick slid across the seat, put an arm around her and snuggled her in close. "Enough about me. I want to talk about how amazing my sexy wife was this morning, talking about the history of the U.S. Attorneys. I had no idea they went so far back that George Washington chose the first ones."

"Wait, I know something you don't about the government?"

"Yep."

"True confession. Roni wrote that part."

Nick laughed and kissed the top of her head. "You knew it before I did."

"There is that."

"You did a great job. You were warm, compassionate, sincere, and your affection for Tom was very apparent."

"He saved my ass once upon a time, as Ramsey so eloquently noted."

"I hope they lock that guy up. He's a ticking time bomb waiting for a place to detonate."

When Sam's phone rang, she fished it out of her pocket and took the call from Gonzo. "Hey, what's up?"

"Ohio State Police called to tell us they found Jada Myerson, bound and gagged in a motel room off Interstate 70 outside of Columbus."

"Oh my God," Sam said.

"I'm going to send some of our people to pick her up and bring her home. Just wanted to run that by you first."

"Do it. We need her to tell us where Bonnie and Clyde are headed."

"Bellamy's mother has been calling every thirty minutes, asking if we've found her son. We've told her that if she hears from him to tell him to turn himself in and to let us know. She refuses to believe it's possible he's involved in anything criminal."

"Her baby would never do something like this. I'm feeling the buzz. These two planned the whole thing, brought Jada in as a coconspirator and then turned on her when things got hot. They're too stupid to realize she has all the dirt on them."

"I wonder why they didn't kill her, too," Gonzo said.

"They're panicking, which is good news and bad. Did you guys reach Jesse Best?"

"We did, and he's deploying a team in Ohio as we speak. We're also working on getting Bellamy's car from the West Virginia State Police."

"Great job. I'll be in this afternoon to catch up."

"See you then."

"Sounds like you're getting some breaks in the case," Nick said.

"Yeah, which are leading to a seventeen-year-old and her boyfriend murdering the girl's mother to get her out of their way."

"Jeez."

"I didn't want to believe it, but nothing else pointed to murder other than her draconian rules with her girls. I feel sorry for Elaine, the mother. Her sister was kidnapped, tortured and murdered when Elaine was twenty and the sister seventeen. As a result, she's been incredibly overprotective of her kids."

"As anyone would be."

"But try explaining the rationale for that to two kids who never knew the aunt who was killed years before they were born. How can you possibly make that kind of trauma relevant to kids who just want to live their lives and spread their wings?"

"You can't, but that doesn't give them the right to end her life over it."

"No, it sure doesn't. They left the younger sister gagged and bound in a motel room on I-70 outside of Columbus. She'll be the key to this whole thing." Sam's backbone was on fire with the tingles that came from getting closer to solving a case. She wanted more than anything to go right to HQ and dive into the home stretch.

But Nick needed her, and she needed his big platform to set the record straight about what'd transpired after Juan Rodriguez's alleged murder.

Her phone rang again with a local number she didn't recognize. "Holland."

"It's Claire Truver."

"What can I do for you, Agent Truver?" Sam asked as she glanced at Nick.

"I understand you plan to go public with what transpired after you learned Lieutenant Commander Rodriguez had reportedly been murdered."

"You understand correctly, as my reputation is taking a public flogging thanks to the roommate I interviewed after you asked me to conduct my usual investigation."

"I'm aware of Lieutenant Commander Erickson's statements, and his command is encouraging him to shut his mouth about things he knows nothing about."

Truver's sharp tone indicated an all-new level of tension.

"The word is out that Juan is alive. It might be time to end the ruse and come clean on what you were hoping to achieve by faking his death."

"If I do that, part of our case against Goldstein disappears."

"How so?"

"He's being held in isolation and still doesn't know Juan is alive. We're hammering him hard on what the plan was to get rid of the guy who blew up their plot by telling the president. We're close to a breakthrough, but if Goldstein finds out that Juan isn't dead, we're never going to get him to break on that."

"Can you keep him isolated in lockup?"

"We have been, but you know how these things go. The more people who know the truth, the more likely he is to find out."

"Not if you keep a tight control over who has access to him."

"He's got a lawyer, Lieutenant, and as you know, we can't control what his lawyer tells him."

"You've caused me tremendous grief with my closest colleagues and friends by asking me to lie to them and others. Erickson is justified in his outrage. What I—and you—did to him and others who love Juan is unforgivable in their eyes."

"It was done in the interest of national security."

"So you say, but as far as I can tell, our nation is secure with Goldstein in lockup and the others who participated in this plot dishonorably discharged from the military and facing charges that will send them to prison. What more needs to happen to protect the national interest?"

"I want justice for Juan Rodriguez, who was stalked and pursued by senior officers intent on doing harm to the man who exposed their dirty secrets."

"You'll have to make your case another way against those who wanted to harm Juan, because I'm going to publicly own the role I played in this in an interview I'm doing with my husband shortly."

"I urge you not to do that."

"Your objection is duly noted, Agent Truver. I have to go now." Sam slapped her phone closed. "What are you hearing from her bosses?" she asked Nick.

"We've notified Jennings and the Navy secretary of our plans to go public with what was asked of you under the guise of national security. They were notifying the NCIS director, which is probably why you heard from Agent Truver."

"You're not hearing anything about us endangering investigations by going public, then?"

"Nothing specific. I asked for an update during the security briefing this morning but haven't heard anything new yet."

"When did you do a security briefing?"

"Zero six hundred, baby."

"Where the hell was I?"

"Out cold."

"This is what I mean when I say people have no idea how dedicated you are."

"I'm just doing the job the best way I know how. I knew it would be a busy day, so I scheduled an early briefing to get that out of the way before the funeral."

"Thanks for coming to that with me."

"I'm always glad to accompany my beautiful wife, but I'm sorry it was to a funeral for a friend."

"Me, too. He was one of the good guys." Sam hesitated for a second before she shared another thought. "I'm hearing the prospective new USA is a ballbuster."

"Catherine McDermott?"

"Yeah, her."

"Do you guys not want her?"

"I absolutely should not be discussing this with you. It crosses all the lines."

"Tell me what you're hearing. This is a major nomination. I want to get it right."

"I heard she's super by the book and takes no prisoners."

"I'm not sure what to make of that."

"Me either, but you should do what you think is best."

"She comes highly recommended by people at all levels of the system—judges, prosecutors, defense attorneys, law enforcement."

"Then it sounds like she's a good choice. I can't believe it's up to my husband to nominate the next U.S. Attorney. That's kind of bonkers to me. In most cases, it would have no impact on me as a municipal police officer. But in DC, the USA is our prosecutor, so the appointment of Tom's replacement is hugely consequential to us."

"If we get it wrong, then your already complicated life becomes more so."

"I'm sure you're fully vetting her. I have faith in you and your team."

"That's nice to hear, but I sure as hell hope my choice for the new USA doesn't cause problems for you and your team."

"Don't worry about me. Do what you think is right."

He kissed her softly. "I'll always worry about you."

CHAPTER THIRTY-TWO

Peter Wagner had been chosen to conduct the interview. Sam had met him once before, during the whirlwind days that followed Nelson's sudden death and Nick's ascension to the presidency. He'd handled their inaugural interview as the first couple with kindness and compassion, and she was relieved to see his familiar, friendly face. Wagner was a TV personality known for big interviews with the most important people in the news. Apparently, they met that criterion, which would never *not* be preposterous to her.

Like the last time, Wagner was done up in pancake makeup that looked ridiculous to the naked eye but gave him the look he wanted on camera. He shook their hands, thanked them for doing the interview and invited them to be seated across from him.

The Map Room was a maze of lights, cables and cords that Sam stepped over to take her seat.

A young woman dressed all in black clipped a microphone to her lapel and tucked the other end of it into Sam's pocket. This was all done with the kind of efficiency Sam appreciated in others. "Thank you."

"My pleasure, ma'am."

Ginger and Davida suddenly appeared to refresh her hair and makeup. "Thank you, ladies."

"No problem."

Sam noticed Lilia standing off to the side and gave her a thumbs-up to thank her for making sure Ginger and Davida were there to ensure Sam looked her best on TV.

Nick reached for her hand. "Ready?"

"As I'll ever be."

Peter launched into his introduction. "I'm delighted to sit down today for my second visit with President Nick Cappuano and First Lady Samantha Holland Cappuano for a wide-ranging interview as they approach their six-month anniversary in the White House. Can you believe it's already been almost six months?"

"Not at all," Nick said. "It's gone by fast."

"And hasn't been without its difficulties. You've faced enormous backlash as the youngest president in U.S. history, as well as for the fact that you were never elected to this office. What do you say to the detractors who won't let either of those things go?"

"I understand the concern with having the youngest president, and I can see why people worry that I wasn't elected. But the thing is, President Nelson was resoundingly elected—twice. He chose me to take the place of Vice President Gooding. The Senate confirmed me. All the proper steps were followed, and our Constitution worked as the founders intended when the former vice president fell ill while in office and then again when President Nelson died suddenly. I'm not sure what else I can say about how I became president other than all the traditional steps were followed."

"How much do you feel these issues have dogged your first six months in office?"

"They haven't stopped me from doing the job I was asked to do when President Nelson died. Every day, I'm doing what's necessary to keep our country safe, prosperous and moving toward a sustainable future with a focus on economic growth, national security, strengthening partnerships with our allies around the world, undertaking measures to address our changing climate and an all-new focus on sensible gun control. These are the issues that everyday Americans have told me matter most to them, so that's where my focus shall remain."

Sam was so proud of him that the buttons on her blouse would've popped right off if she'd been wearing one. The silly thought nearly made her laugh at the worst possible moment.

"Mrs. Cappuano, you've had your own challenges during the transition while you make history as the first first lady to work outside the White House. Can you tell us how that's been going for you?"

"It's been an interesting and exciting time for our family." She glanced at Nick and took comfort from the warmth in his eyes as he looked at her. "I think we've made a smooth transition. Our children are doing remarkably well and have adjusted to their new home and circumstances with tremendous resilience. As for me, the job unfortunately continues at the same pace it did before."

"You recently closed the investigation into the murder of U.S. Attorney Tom Forrester with a takedown of the suspect on a city street. That video has been viewed more than fifteen million times. What do you say to that?"

"It boggles my mind that so many people are interested in me or my work. I'm thankful that we arrested the man who murdered an outstanding public servant, a husband and father and a friend to so many."

"Including you?"

"Yes. I considered Tom a friend."

"He once did a rather spectacular favor for you, did he not?"

Blindsided, Sam glanced at Nick and noticed a tick in his cheek that hadn't been there before. "If you're referring to what I think you're referring to, it wasn't a favor at all. Whether to file charges against me after an unfortunate accident in which a colleague was injured was decided by an impartial grand jury. Tom did his job by presenting the case to the grand jury. There were no favors."

"Fair enough. What do you have to say to Lieutenant Commander Isaac Erickson, who's accusing you of lying to him as part of the investigation into the alleged death of his closest friend and roommate, Lieutenant Commander Rodriguez?"

"Lieutenant Commander Erickson is not aware of all the facts of that case, and once he is, I'm sure he'll have a better understanding of what transpired."

"Did you lie to him?"

"I did what was necessary as part of a very complex investigation that involves multiple agencies and jurisdictions."

"Is Lieutenant Commander Rodriguez alive?"

"I defer that question to NCIS, which is overseeing that investigation."

"It's a simple yes-or-no question, ma'am."

"It's not my question to answer."

He didn't like that. Too bad. She was doing her best to honor Truver's wishes while not getting herself into deeper shit than she was already in.

"Mr. President, I understand you were close to Lieutenant Commander Rodriguez."

"Yes."

"His death must've been a terrible shock to you."

"It was."

"Do you know if he's alive, sir?"

"As my wife said, NCIS is running that investigation, and we're eager to get all the facts before we comment." After a beat, Nick added, "Let's move on to other topics, Peter."

Sam released a silent deep breath full of relief when Peter began a series of questions about Nick's thoughts on pressing domestic and foreign relations matters that demonstrated his command of the issues facing the country. She hoped people would see how smart and capable he was and would stop questioning his ability to do the job.

He dazzled her with his deep understanding of complex issues overseas and with common sense solutions to a wide variety of domestic concerns. She had to school her expression to not come across like a teenager in love with the football team captain, but she was truly and deeply in love—and wildly impressed.

"Thank you for taking time out of your busy schedules to sit down with us," Peter said as he wrapped things up.

"Thanks for having us," Nick said.

They turned over their microphones and gave each other a relieved look as they greeted their staffers.

"Well done, you two," Lilia said. "As always."

"What Lilia said," Terry added. "Spot-on."

"Let's hope it helps to take some of the pressure off," Nick said.

"Can you make sure the part about Juan gets released ASAP?" Sam asked them.

"Trevor is on that," Terry said.

"Thank you so much."

"I need a moment with my first lady before we leave. Meet you in the foyer in ten?"

"I'll see you there," Terry said.

"Thanks for everything, Lilia," Sam said.

"Happy to help."

Nick took Sam by the hand and led her into the room next door, closing the door behind them.

"You're going to get everyone talking about the first couple hooking up in the China Room."

Smiling, he put his arms around her. "We won't be here long enough for a proper hookup."

"Damn. You had me all excited."

He looked around before bringing his gaze back to hers. "We could be quick."

"As good as that sounds, I have to go to work."

"I hate when you're responsible that way."

"I hate when you go away and make me sleep alone."

"I'll be right back. I promise."

"It's *two nights*, Nicholas."

"I'll miss you every second of both those nights and all the daytime, too, Samantha."

"Swoon," she whispered. "Hurry back. Nothing is fun without you."

"You know there's nowhere else I want to be but right here with you and our kids. Well… maybe not right *here*, but you get what I mean."

Sam laughed. "You just told the people how much you love being their president, so you'd better not let anyone else hear you say that."

"When did I say that?"

"Everything you said was full of enthusiasm for the task before you. I was wildly impressed."

He kissed her neck. "Wildly?"

"Mmm. Extremely wildly."

"Don't talk dirty to me when you don't have time to follow through."

She curled her hand around his neck and combed her fingers through his hair, breathing in the rich, clean scent of home while she could. "Go before I make a scene about you leaving."

"Don't want to."

"Love you more than ice cream," she said.

"Love you more than anything."

Sam laughed. "Leave it to you to find a way to top ice cream."

"I only speak the truth."

They held on tightly for another few minutes before reluctantly separating and returning to reality, where Terry waited to accompany him to California.

In the foyer, Sam kissed Nick once more and waved him off as he walked out to board *Marine One* for the trip to Joint Base Andrews.

"Ready to go?" Vernon asked her after the chopper had lifted off, taking her whole heart with it.

She felt unsettled, off her game and despondent after saying goodbye to him for a few days, but she had work to do and a team waiting for her to join them. When Nick got back, she needed to talk to him about the call from Collins Worthy and Scotty having to sit in a classroom and listen to others criticize the job his father was doing running the country. But those things would keep for now.

"I'm going to run upstairs to change," she said to Vernon, "and then we can go."

"Ready when you are."

SAM ARRIVED to a screaming match in the pit between Gonzo and Frank Myerson, who was demanding to be released from custody.

"What's going on here, gentlemen?"

Frank spun around to her, his face red and his eyes wide. "I demand to know why I'm being treated like a criminal when you don't have one scrap of evidence that I had anything to do with my wife's murder!"

"One of your minor children is our prime suspect, and as such, we need your help and cooperation."

"You want me to help you nail my kid? That's not going to happen."

Sam gave him an assessing look. "We found Jada."

That stopped him short. "Where?"

"Bound and gagged in a motel room in Columbus."

"What?"

"Apparently left there by Zoe and Zeke."

"Why would they do that to her?"

"Maybe she was getting in the way of their plan?"

"Zoe didn't kill her mother."

"Then why is she on the run? Why would she ditch Jada in a strange place?"

"I don't know! But she's not a killer, and I'm not about to help you make her out to be one."

"Sergeant Gonzales, please escort Mr. Myerson back to lockup until he's willing to help us find the person or people who killed his wife."

"I didn't do it, and neither did my kid! You can't hold me unless you're going to charge me!"

"Sergeant, please charge Mr. Myerson with obstructing a homicide investigation. Perhaps by the time he's arraigned, we'll know more about where his daughter is."

"This is complete bullshit. I want my lawyer. Get Dunning over here."

"We'll get right on that," Sam said. "In the meantime, Sergeant Gonzales will get you processed and settled downstairs."

"That place is a hellhole. I'll be filing a lawsuit against you and this department for harassment of a grieving family."

"Knock yourself out."

He ranted all the way to Central Booking as Gonzo half dragged him away.

"He's unhinged," Freddie said.

"I suppose I would be, too, if it was becoming clear to me that my own kid was capable of murder."

"Probably."

"Will you call Dunning and get him over here?"

"Yep. Does this mean he's un-fired?"

"I guess so. Where are we with Jada?"

"She's dehydrated and traumatized. She's receiving care at a local hospital, and then she'll be brought back here by the marshals. Since they were already on the job in Ohio, we decided not to send anyone out there."

"Do we have an ETA on her arrival?"

"Around four o'clock this afternoon."

"Okay. What else did I miss?"

"Archie was here looking for you. He seemed stressed about something."

"I'll run up and check in with him." Sam unlocked her office door and draped her coat over a chair. Her cell phone rang with a call from Darren Tabor that she took, feeling exasperated, the way she always did when he called. "Yes, Darren?"

"The whole world is on fire about you lying in the Rodriguez case. Are you going to address that or let it fester?"

"I'm gonna let it fester."

"Seriously?"

Sam left her office and headed for the stairs. "We did a sit-down with Peter Wagner earlier. It'll be dealt with there."

"You gave *him* an exclusive? What the hell, Sam? I thought we were friends."

"We're not friends. We know each other through work."

"Wow, that hurts. I think of you as a friend."

"Stop being sensitive, Darren. You know we're not friends in the traditional sense of the word. We have an adversarial relationship that involves you wanting me to tell you things I can't or won't."

"What can you say on the record about the Rodriguez case?"

"I'll tell you this... It's a very complicated situation that involves multiple agencies and jurisdictions. We're not the lead on that case, so there's not much I'm able to say about it."

"Did you lie to Juan's roommate?"

"No comment."

"Sam, come on! People want to know!"

"It's not my story to tell. You should contact Agent Truver with NCIS."

"They're not talking."

"So what makes you think I will? It's their case, not mine. I have to go, Darren."

She closed the phone before he could try to continue the conversation that was going nowhere fast. On the second floor, she walked into the IT department, where Archie's team was hard at work. Sam would be bored stiff being chained to a computer all day. She preferred being out and about, talking to people and hunting down leads the old-fashioned way, even if that was much more complicated these days when everyone recognized her as the president's wife.

"Hey," she said in the doorway to Archie's office. "Heard you were looking for me."

He waved her in. "Close the door."

Sam shut the door and sat in the chair in front of his desk. "What's up?"

"The girlfriend has gone silent."

"I hear that happens these days. It's called ghosting."

"Except I don't think she'd do that. She mentioned how it'd been done to her and how she'd never do that to someone else."

"Huh. What're you thinking?"

"I'm not sure what to think, but my gut's telling me she's in some kind of trouble."

"What does she do for work?"

"She's a sales rep for a food company."

"That's not usually considered dangerous."

"No, it isn't, but something isn't right. I know it."

"What can I do?"

"Would it be wrong for me to ask you to put one of your people on looking into it and figuring out where she is?"

Sam thought about that for a second. Technically, the answer was yes, it would be wrong, but Archie was always there for her and her team, and she wanted to help him out if she could. "Give me everything you have on her, and I'll take it from there."

"Yourself?"

"Probably not."

"Who will you put on it?"

"Does that matter?"

"No, I guess it doesn't."

"I promise it'll be handled with the utmost discretion."

"Thank you." He ripped a sheet of paper out of a notebook and handed it to her. "No digital paper trail, right?"

"Right."

"Thanks, Sam."

"You're welcome. Try to chill. I'm sure there's a perfectly good explanation for whatever's going on."

"I hope you're right."

"I usually am."

He grunted out a laugh. "Walked right into that one."

"Yes, you did."

"I heard Ramsey disrupted the funeral this morning."

"Yep."

"What the hell could he be thinking?"

"He quit thinking a long time ago."

"Malone told me they're pushing to keep him in lockup until he stands trial on the other charges he's facing. Enough is enough."

"Glad to hear it. I agree on the enough part."

"Thought you would. What's the latest with the Myerson case?"

"The younger daughter was found bound and gagged in a motel room in Ohio, which leads me to believe that things between her and her sister went south on the road. She's being treated in the hospital now and will be delivered back here by the marshals later today. They're still looking for the other sister and her boyfriend."

"You think they killed the mother?"

"There's not a single scrap of evidence leading in any other direction than right back to them. The fact that they ran—and abandoned the sister—doesn't help their case either."

"No, it doesn't. Hopefully, the sister can shed some light."

"That's the goal. I'll get back to you with anything we learn about your friend."

"This is way outside the bounds of friendship."

"No, it isn't. Try to breathe. I'm on it."

As she was going down the stairs, SVU Detective Erica Lucas was on the way up.

"Heard about what Ramsey did this morning," Erica said. "Disgraceful."

"Truly."

"I also heard you gave an awesome eulogy. I'm sorry I missed it. I caught a new case late yesterday and was on it all night."

"Sounds like a tough one."

"They all are, but this was especially so. A Jane Doe found by the river. She was raped and beaten, but has no memory of what happened."

A tingle worked its way down Sam's spine. What were the odds? "Come with me." She went back up the stairs and straight to Archie's office.

"What's up?" he asked when they appeared in his doorway.

"What does your missing friend look like?"

"Pretty, with long dark hair, brown eyes."

Sam glanced at Erica.

"The description matches."

"Matches what?" Archie asked.

"The vic in a new case I caught last night," Erica said. "A Jane Doe at GW. I can take you there."

Archie had launched out of his seat and was already around the desk. "Let's go."

"Let me know," Sam said.

"I will," he said over his shoulder as he rushed out with Erica.

CHAPTER THIRTY-THREE

Archie's heart was in his throat as Erica drove him to the hospital. If Erica and SVU were involved, whatever had happened was bad.

"What's her name?" Erica asked.

"Harlowe St. John."

"That sounds like a fake name."

"I thought so, too, but she said she was named after her maternal grandmother. She said my name sounded fake, too, because I go by my last name exclusively."

Erica chuckled. "I don't even know your first name."

"No one does. It's Francis. I was named after my grandfather. He called me Franny, which wasn't my favorite name as a kid. In school, I only answered to Archie, and I've stuck with that ever since."

"Can't say I blame you. How do you know her?"

"We met at a party at the home of mutual friends."

"What do you know about her?"

"Not much. She's in sales for one of the big food companies. Grew up in the Pittsburgh area, came to DC for college and never left." He glanced over at Erica. "What happened to her?"

"We don't know the details yet, but she was beaten, raped

and left for dead by the river. A fisherman found her and called it in."

Archie groaned.

"We don't know for sure it's your friend."

"You said the physical description matches."

"It does. She seems to have amnesia and couldn't tell us the most basic facts, including her name. The memory loss could be the result of trauma. I've seen that before."

His mind was racing as he learned more details. He wasn't sure whether to hope the woman in the hospital was Harlowe or not.

As he followed Erica through the hospital's main entrance, his legs felt rubbery, as if they wouldn't support his weight for much longer. It was a feeling he'd never experienced before, and it did nothing to help his unsettled state.

They took the elevator.

He couldn't have said later what floor they landed on, what room she was in, or which Patrol officer was positioned outside her door, things he'd normally take note of and remember as a trained detective. His years of experience went out the window when he saw the woman he'd begun to care about in a hospital bed, her face bruised, her lip swollen and cut and her eyes wild as she seemed to shrink into the bed at the sight of him and Erica.

"It's her," he said quietly so only Erica would hear him.

Erica approached the bed. "This is Archie. He's a friend of yours. He said your name is Harlowe."

"I... I don't know him, or anyone with that name."

Her distress touched him deeply, making him wish he could put his arms around her and assure her that she was safe now. But he kept his distance out of respect for what she'd endured.

Erica spoke to her gently for a few more minutes and then ushered him out of the room.

"What do I do, Erica? Tell me what to do."

"Give her some space to recover. Hopefully, her memory will come back."

"What if it doesn't?"

"Let's just wait and see."

"They did a rape kit, right?"

"Yes, and it's with the lab. I asked for a rush."

He leaned back against the wall and exhaled a deep breath.

"Is there anyone you could call for her?"

"I don't know her people. We hadn't gotten that far yet."

"What about the company where she works?"

Archie tried to clear the noise in his brain so he could think about what she'd told him about her job. "I can't remember the name of the company, but she said it was sales for a food company that stocks restaurants and grocery stores."

"That helps. I'll do some digging. Why don't you come back to HQ with me?"

"I'd rather stay close here since she doesn't have anyone else."

"She's not comfortable having you in her room."

"I'll stay out here. Just in case."

"Of what, Archie?"

"I'm not sure. Whatever she needs."

"Stay out of there. I mean it. She's very fragile, and she didn't recognize you. I'd feel better if you came back to HQ with me."

"I care about her, Erica. I mean... I've only known her a short time, but there was a connection. I've been out of my mind with worry about her since she went silent on me a few days ago. The Harlowe I know would want me here."

"The Harlowe you know isn't in there right now, and she needs you to keep your distance. Come with me so you don't get yourself in trouble."

"I won't get in trouble. I promise. I'll stay right here with Officer... Smyth and stay out of the way."

Erica looked to the tall, muscular officer. "Keep him out here."

"Yes, ma'am."

Archie didn't remind them that he outranked them both. That wouldn't serve his purpose of being allowed to stay close to Harlowe.

"I'll check in in a bit," Erica said.

"I'll be here."

After she left, he slid down the wall, withdrew his phone and got busy. Hearing what she'd endured, he was determined to do what he could to help her, starting with the thing he'd hesitated to do before now—a deep dive online.

SAM WAS in the conference room with her team, going over each piece of evidence in the Myerson case, when she received a text from Erica Lucas.

My vic is Archie's friend. She doesn't recognize him and is nervous about having him in the room. He's undone in a way I've never seen before and insisted on staying outside the room. Officer Smyth is under orders to keep him out of the room.

I'll check on him in a little while.

He gave me some good info I can use to track down her family. I'm on that when I get back to the house.

Let me know if we can help.

Will do.

Captain Malone came into the conference room and handed Sam two printed pages. "Warrants for the Myerson girls' second cell phones. Judge McHenry said he wants solid proof they're involved before he'll issue any more warrants."

"Does he realize that's what we're trying to do?"

"I believe he does, but since they're minors, he's treading carefully."

"What's the latest from CSU about the processing of the house?"

"They've done the basement and are finishing up on the first floor. They haven't found anything they would deem helpful."

"I'd like to look through the girls' rooms myself. Let's head over there, Freddie."

"I'm with you, boss."

"Let me run these warrants up to IT first. I'll be right back." Sam went up the stairs and into the IT cave. "Who's Archie when Archie isn't here?"

A young man with brown skin and close-cropped dark hair stood. "I'm Sergeant Walters, Lieutenant. How can I help you?"

Sam went to him and handed him the warrants. "Can you get me a dump on these two lines ASAP?"

"Do you have the phones?"

"No, just the numbers."

"That'll take longer because we have to go through the carrier to get the data. They tend to resist giving out that info about their customers."

"Even when we have a warrant?"

"Even then."

"How about when lives might be at risk?"

"I can pass along that info, but in my experience, using the word 'critical' doesn't help to expedite things."

"What word would help to move it along?"

"I've yet to discover that word, ma'am."

Sam wanted to scream with frustration, but she couldn't do that there. "We've got two young people suspected of murder on the run. We need to find them."

"I'll get right on it and do what I can."

"Thank you, Sergeant."

"Is everything all right with Lieutenant Archelotta? It's not like him to run out of here without a word to any of us."

"He found out a friend has been injured. I'm sure you'll hear from him soon."

"I'll text him to let him know not to worry about things here."

"I'm sure he'd appreciate that." Sam handed him her card. "Call me if you have any luck with the phone company."

"Will do."

"Thank you, Sergeant Walters."

"My pleasure, Lieutenant."

Sam went back downstairs, collected Freddie and hurried toward the morgue exit, hoping to get to the Myerson home, do what needed to be done and then get home for dinner with her kids since Nick wouldn't be there.

Those words, *Nick wouldn't be there*, were enough to send her mood plummeting as Vernon drove them to Crestwood.

Her phone rang with yet another call from a number she didn't recognize. "Holland."

"This is Jillian Danvers. I'm a, um, friend of Juan Rodriguez's. Your, um, partner gave me your card."

"You're the friend from the coffee shop?"

"Yes, that's me. No one will tell me anything about what happened to him, and now people are saying he's alive, and... I haven't known him that long, but..." Her voice broke. "I don't know what to do."

"Let me make a few calls. I'll have someone get in touch with you."

"Do you promise someone will call? Juan always said you and your husband were good people..."

"I promise someone will call you."

"Thank you very much."

Sam slapped her phone closed. "This goddamned situation with NCIS is making me crazy."

As always, Freddie frowned at her using the Lord's name in vain. "What now?"

"That was Juan's girlfriend, or whatever she is, upset that no one will tell her anything." Sam found Truver's name in her contacts and made the call.

"Truver."

"I just got off the phone with yet another friend of Juan's who's heartbroken and concerned and can't get anyone to tell her what's going on."

"Who?"

"Jillian Danvers."

"I'll take care of it."

Before Sam could say anything else, the line went dead. "Charming." She closed her phone. "Remind me later to check with Juan's girlfriend to make sure she heard from NCIS."

"I got a text from the marshals that the doctors are keeping Jada for one more night. They'll have her back to DC tomorrow."

"Damn. She must be pretty banged up."

Her phone rang again, this time with a call from Cameron Green. "What's up?"

"I found something interesting with the twins' grandparents."

"What's that?"

"They're completely broke. They have less than a hundred dollars in all their accounts. I took the liberty of checking into Cleo's sister and brother-in-law, and they're down to their last thousand."

Sam's heart began to beat rapidly. "Do we know what caused this financial disaster?"

"They were sued by two former employees, who prevailed to the tune of six million dollars, which was ordered paid two weeks ago."

"Well, well, well. Isn't that interesting?"

"I thought you'd think so. I'm sorry it took so long. It took some serious digging to put the full picture together. They've gone to some considerable effort to keep the situation private."

"This is fantastic news, Cam. Thank you so much."

"I hope it helps to make this go away."

"I'm pretty sure it will. I'll let you know." She closed the phone and dug the secure BlackBerry out of her coat pocket to call Nick.

"Hey, babe," he said. "How's it going?"

"It's going extremely well. I asked Cam to look into the financial situation of the twins' grandparents, and what he found is very, *very* interesting." She filled him in on the details.

"Holy shit. You were right. It's a cash grab."

"What was that second thing you said? Could you say that again?"

He chuckled. "This is huge news, Sam."

"Trust me, I know. Should I call Andy?"

"Absolutely."

"I'll let you know what he says. Where are you?"

"Somewhere over Nebraska."

It gave her the willies to think of him thirty thousand feet in the air. "Text me when you land."

"You'll be the first to know. Love you."

"Love you, too." Sam ended that call and used her flip phone to call Andy. When his assistant answered, Sam said, "This is Sam Cappuano. May I please speak to Andy?"

"Are you able to hold for a minute, ma'am? He's finishing up a meeting."

"I can hold."

"Did they put the first lady on hold?" Freddie asked, amused.

"It's fine. He's finishing a meeting."

"Hey, Sam," Andy said when he came on the line two minutes later. "Sorry to keep you waiting. What's up?"

Sam told him what Cameron had uncovered about the financials.

Andy let out a low whistle. "Our people had gotten nowhere on cracking the firewall around their financial situation."

Sam felt a surge of pride for Cameron—and her entire team. She worked with the best of the best, and this was just another example of their skill. "Will this help to make the case go away?"

"It should. I'm going to call their attorney and let them know if they don't drop their custody demands, we'll file a countersuit that'll make public their precarious financial status and call this the money grab from their orphaned grandchildren that it is."

"Excellent. Let me know how that goes."

"I'll be back to you."

"Thanks, Andy." Sam closed the phone and texted Nick on the BlackBerry to update him.

He wrote right back. *I'll let Eli know what's going on. He'll be happy to hear this. He's been very upset.*

"This is great news, Sam," Freddie said. "You must be relieved."

"I am, but I still want to do whatever it takes to make them go away for good, up to and including adopting the three of them. I can't go through this every few months. My nerves can't handle it."

The BlackBerry buzzed with a text from Eli to her and Nick. He, too, had a BlackBerry so he could talk to Nick securely.

I'm so glad to hear this news, but we have to do something to make it so they can't do this again. I can't function when they're coming after us. Do you think it might be worth a one-time payment to Cleo's family that would come with some sort of signed agreement to go away and leave us alone?

Nick replied, *While I understand the thinking behind that, I'd hate to see you reward them for what's basically blackmail, especially since they haven't reached out to any of us to see or talk to the kids for all these months. It would be one thing if they'd stepped up for the kids, but they haven't. At all.*

I agree, Sam said. *We offered the opportunity for them to see the kids, and they never made a single overture. They've shown us who they really are, following the MURDER of their daughter and son-*

in-law/sister/brother-in-law. They don't deserve a dime of your father's hard-earned money.

I want them to go away, Eli wrote. *Whatever it takes.*

Let's leave it to Andy for now, Nick said. *We'll discuss again after he's had the chance to speak to their attorney. Try not to worry. Our position is solid, and this is an obvious attempt to get at the money. There's not a judge alive who wouldn't see it that way. Hang in there, and we'll keep you posted.*

Thanks for everything, guys. Not sure what we'd do without you.

You'll never have to find out, Sam said. *We love you.*

What my lovely wife said!

"Everything okay?" Freddie asked.

"Yeah, it's good. We're talking to Eli about what Cam found about the grandparents' financial position, or lack thereof."

"I can't believe they'd be shameless enough to come after their orphaned grandchildren's money."

"I can. They've been disgusting from the start. Imagine not showing a scrap of compassion for your daughter's devastated children."

"I can't. I would've been on the first plane to take them home and love them forever."

"I think a lot about what would've become of them that night in the hospital if Nick and I hadn't already been licensed foster parents."

"Thank God you were and that you stepped up for them when they needed you most."

"We love them so much. They've only been with us for a short time, but it's like they've always been part of us. I can't imagine life without them."

"You won't have to. The minute Andy tells their lawyer you're on to their scheme, they'll run away with their tails between their legs. And then you and Nick will adopt the three of them, and no one will ever be able to threaten your family again."

As if Eli had heard what Freddie said, the BlackBerry

buzzed with a new text from him. *I've also been thinking a lot about the adoption idea, and the more I consider it, the more I think it makes sense to shut the door on this bullshit forever. I talked to Candace, and she agrees that it would protect all of us, and she knows how much you guys mean to me and the twins. What do you think of Armstrong-Cappuano?*

Sam's eyes instantly filled with tears.

"What?" Freddie asked. "What's wrong?"

"Nothing," she said softly as she handed the phone to him so he could read Eli's text. "Nothing is wrong. Everything is just right."

SAM AND FREDDIE spent three hours sifting through the contents of Zoe's and Jada's bedrooms. What stood out to Sam after the first hour was how neat both rooms were, which was in sharp contrast to the mess in Scotty's room most of the time.

"Is the neatness a little weird?" she asked Freddie as they were finishing up.

"I think it's intentional. They knew we'd end up here and were ready for us. Or Elaine cleaned their rooms when she was home alone on Sunday."

Sam peeled off the latex gloves she'd worn to search the rooms. "Possibly. I hate that we wasted our time."

"Nothing is a waste of time if it checks a box."

"That's true, I guess." She checked her watch, saw it was nearly six and decided to call it a day. "Let's go home and regroup at eight tomorrow. I'll hand off to Carlucci."

"Sounds good."

They checked in with the CSU detectives still on-site before they left the house.

"Find anything interesting?" Lieutenant Max Haggerty asked.

"Not a single thing."

"Us either. We're thinking someone did a sweep in anticipation of our investigation."

"We picked up the same vibe upstairs."

"What're you thinking?" Max asked as he rubbed the back of his neck. He and his team had been working nonstop lately because of the scene at Stahl's house.

"I'm almost positive the older daughter and her boyfriend took out the mother. They're on the run, so they've more or less confirmed my hunch by running. The marshals are working on finding them."

"How old are they?"

"Seventeen and eighteen."

"Damn."

Sam's phone rang with yet another number she didn't recognize. "Holland."

"This is Sergeant Walters. I wanted to let you know that I've requested the data from the second cell phones and emphasized the urgency. I'll keep you posted."

"Thank you."

"Also, Lieutenant Archelotta had asked me to look into whether either of the daughters were true-crime fans, and on the original phones, I learned that Zoe listened to numerous true-crime podcasts and followed about a hundred true-crime accounts on TikTok."

"There it is." Sam's entire body lit up with the buzz that came from closing in on a killer. "That's how she planned this whole thing. One how-to podcast at a time. This is very helpful, Sergeant. Thank you."

"Happy to help."

Sam closed the phone and relayed the update to Freddie as they headed outside.

"What're you thinking about Jada's involvement?"

"She wasn't part of it," Sam said, feeling certain now. "This was all Zoe and possibly Zeke."

"Why'd they take her with them when they ran?"

"Maybe to make it look like she was in on it, too?"

"Our interview with her will be key to the whole thing."

"Yep. Drop you at the Metro?"

"Sure. Columbia Heights is nearby."

When they pulled up to the Metro station a few minutes later, Sam said, "I'll see you in the morning."

"Call me if anything breaks in the meantime. I can come back if need be."

"Hopefully, we can get a night at home before we wrap this one up tomorrow."

"That'd be good. Later."

CHAPTER THIRTY-FOUR

After Freddie had jogged off toward the station, Sam sat back in her seat, trying to decompress before she switched into mom mode. She felt ridiculous for being depressed that Nick wouldn't be there when she got home. It was two freaking nights, for crying out loud.

Thinking of Angela and how she had to spend all the nights remaining in her life without Spencer made Sam feel even worse for lamenting a two-night absence. She sent her sister a text. *Checking in to see how you're doing. Thinking of you all the time.*

Angela didn't respond immediately, probably because she was in the thick of dinner and bath time with her kids and doing it all on her own while eight months pregnant.

Sam texted Tracy. *Hey, just checking in. Angela came to grief group the other night and was upset about being angry with Spence for putting her through this. I think the group was helpful, but it was a tough one.*

Tracy wrote right back. *She told me, and she said it did help to talk it out. She was glad you were there. I think she's doing as well as can be expected. Not sure how she's going to deal with two little kids AND a baby, but she'll figure it out, and we'll help her.*

Yes, we will. I hate this for her. I'm over here moping bc Nick is away for two nights, and then I think of her, and it's just unbearable.

Sure is. She posted this on Instagram today: "I miss your smile. I miss the feel of your hand in mine. I miss the way you loved our babies and the way you loved me. I miss you more every day. When I think it isn't possible to miss you any more than I already do, I discover there's more. A deep well of ache for you. Sometimes I'm angry that you left, but I know you didn't leave because you wanted to. I love you forever, and I can't wait to see you again."

Oh God... I can't bear it for her.

I know. It's heartbreaking. I wish there was something we could do to make it easier for her, but there just isn't.

No, there isn't. I'm hoping the weekend at CD won't suck. I almost can't bear to go back there, but Nick needs the time away from the WH so badly.

Go and make new memories there. You can do it.

Hope so.

Mom brought the Easter outfits for the kids over today, and there're bags in your closet for Easter baskets.

What would I ever do without you?

Happy to help! It's fun to spend your money! HAHA

Thank you, Trace. SO, SO MUCH.

Love you, kid.

Love you, too.

It pained her to have to bring in help for basic mothering tasks like Easter baskets, but she'd learned to lean into her strengths and ask for help in the areas where she needed it. Tracy loved shopping and excelled at crafty things like creating memorable Easter baskets for the kids. Sam told herself it was about the love she gave to her kids, not who did the shopping for the baskets.

"Can I ask you something?" she said to Vernon and Jimmy.

"Anything," Vernon said with a warm smile in the mirror.

"Is it awful that my sister took care of Easter clothes and baskets for my kids?"

"I think it would be worse if no one did it," Jimmy said.

"Yes," Vernon said, "that's true. The base is covered, and that's what matters. The kids won't know your sister did it."

"Scotty will."

"Do you think he'll care when he wakes up to candy and treats and probably a few cool things in a basket with his name on it? And probably one for Skippy, too."

Sam never would've thought of Skippy on her own, but was sure Tracy had. "Probably not."

"Don't beat yourself up for asking for help. If it was up to me, my kids never would've had an Easter basket, a birthday cake or a Christmas stocking. I had someone at home taking care of that for our family so I could focus on work. You made sure it got done, and that's what matters."

"I might not have even thought of it unless Tracy asked me."

"You would've," Jimmy said.

"If it'd been left to me, the three of us would've been at a convenience store near Camp David on Saturday night."

The two men laughed.

"We're actually off this weekend, so you'll have the B team."

"It wouldn't have been as much fun to go to a convenience store with them."

"Aw, thanks," Vernon said. "That's nice to hear."

"I hope you guys are doing something fun with your families this weekend."

"We're going to my wife's parents' house in Annapolis," Jimmy said. "The whole family is coming, and they're having a baby shower for us, too."

"That'll be fun," Sam said, making a mental note to arrange a gift for them.

"We're doing dinner at the house with the girls and their families," Vernon said. "Note that I'm not lifting a finger for any of this while my wife runs around all week getting ready."

"That's because you're busy keeping me safe."

Vernon made eye contact in the mirror. "We all have our lanes."

"Yes, we do. I'm not sure when this SUV became my confessional and therapist office combined, but thank you both for always being willing to talk it out with me."

"We're honored to be part of your daily life," Vernon said.

"Indeed," Jimmy added. "Coolest job ever."

"I'm glad you think so."

"Our colleagues envy us this assignment," Jimmy said.

"They do? Really?"

"Oh hell yeah," Vernon said. "Protecting the first working first lady while she hunts down murderers and sometimes captures them single-handedly? Although we did get a talking-to from HQ about that."

"You did? Really?"

"Well, yes, Sam," Vernon said with exasperation. "When you run out of the back of our SUV and tackle a guy on the sidewalk, there's gonna be some questions about where your detail was when that was happening."

"Oh shit." She bit her lip so she wouldn't laugh. "Sorry."

He gave her a stern look in the mirror that played such a big part in their relationship. "I can *hear* you trying not to laugh."

"I'm not laughing!"

"But you want to."

"You can't prove that."

Cameron Green called as they pulled through the White House gates. "What's up?"

"Frank Myerson wants to talk."

"About what?"

"About Sunday and what happened to his wife."

In a past life, she would've turned right around—or asked Vernon to turn right around, except he hadn't been there in her past life—and gone back to work. In this life, where she had three children waiting to have dinner with her while their dad was away, she said, "Tell him we'll be happy to talk to him in the morning."

"I get the feeling he wants it to be tonight."

"He's going to have to wait. I'll be there at eight, and we'll take it from there."

"I'll let him know."

"By the way, it's not that I think you guys couldn't handle it, but I'd like to be there to hear what he has to say, and I've got plans tonight. Besides, we don't jump to the beat of his drummer. He had all day to talk to us, and I don't believe for a second he's looking to help us."

"I agree. I'll take care of it."

"Thanks. See you in the morning."

"Have a good night."

"You, too."

The BlackBerry vibrated with a text. *Landed at LAX.*

Are you seeing Hollywood people?

Maybe?

No way! WHO?

I don't remember.

I can't believe this. I need to quit my job and travel with you.

I won't ever say no to that.

I'll have Scotty find out who you're with.

HAHA, he'll have the dirt.

Just getting home and no Nick. That makes me very sad.

Love you. Miss you. Will call you later.

Love you, too.

But you don't miss me?

Did you see what I said above??

Vernon opened the back door as she sent that text, shaking her head at her husband's foolishness and wanting to wail over how much she missed him. Ridiculous. She wasn't a woman who *wailed* over a man. But that man... That man was worth wailing over.

"What time tomorrow?" Vernon asked.

"Seven thirty?"

"We'll be ready."

"I have a dress fitting thing in Georgetown at six."

"It's on the schedule."

"There's a schedule?"

Vernon rolled his eyes. "Good night, Sam."

"Good night, Vernon."

CHAPTER THIRTY-FIVE

After being greeted by George, the usher, she rushed upstairs, eager to see her kids after the long day apart. Skippy ran full-tilt to greet her, nearly knocking Sam over with her enthusiasm. A quick twinge in her healing hip had her gasping with surprise, as it had been feeling pretty good lately.

Scotty came running after the dog. "Skippy! Don't knock Mom over. We need her since Dad is away."

"I see how it is. If Dad was here, it'd be like, 'Knock Mom over. Who needs her anyway?'"

"I've never said that out loud."

Laughing, Sam bopped him on the head and then snuck in a kiss to the cheek. "How was your day?"

"Same old boring thing. But I got an eighty-six on another algebra quiz."

"Stop it! Are you in line for a B this quarter?"

"Don't say it out loud, or you'll jinx it."

"You remind me so much of me when I was your age."

He stopped short and looked back at her over his shoulder, his expression madly vulnerable. "I do? Really?"

She put an arm around him. "So, so much. If things were

going well in school, I was always afraid to say so because I never expected it to last."

"Yes, that. Exactly that."

"You're doing great. All that matters is you're trying your best."

"Dad would say all that matters are A's."

"He doesn't think that."

"I want to be smart like him."

"You are! You're the smartest fourteen-year-old I've ever met."

He raised an eyebrow, his expression full of skepticism. "How many fourteen-year-olds do you even know?"

"I've known my share. I was one once, don't forget."

"Yeah, like a hundred years ago."

"Watch it, mister. Where are the twins?"

"They're washing up for dinner, if they know what's good for them."

"Listen to you, acting like the big daddy."

"Someone's gotta when Big Daddy is away."

"What's for dinner?"

"Enchiladas. I'm so excited."

"Yum. Go round up the Littles and meet me in the dining room. I've got to put my stuff away."

"Mom."

"What's up?"

"Are you going to tell me what's going on with the grandparents?"

The question stopped her heart for a second. "How do you know about that?"

"You just mentioned how smart I am. I hear things."

"I think we've got it handled, so try not to worry."

"Handled how?"

"Andy is taking information to their lawyer that should make it go away."

"'Should' isn't definite."

"No, but you know what is? Adoption."

His gorgeous brown eyes went wide. "Really?"

"Yeah, we're talking about adopting all three of them so this can never happen again."

"What does Eli say about that?"

"He's all for it."

"So, like, it would be legal and locked down forever?"

"That's the idea."

"That'd be *sick*."

"We didn't want to say anything about it until we were sure it's going to happen, so don't say anything to the Littles yet, okay?"

"When will we be sure?"

"Soon."

"I love this so hard. We'd be real siblings then."

"You already are, Scotty. That'll never change."

"I'm tired of people trying to take them away from us. They're ours."

"Yes, they are, and we're doing everything we can to make it happen. I don't want you to worry. Dad and I will move heaven and earth to keep those babies with us."

"Thanks for telling me."

"I'm sorry you were worried."

"I wasn't too worried. I knew you guys would go to war to keep them with us."

"Yes, we would."

"I'll go see what's taking them so long. Oh, and I invited the third-floor tenants to dinner."

"Excellent," Sam said with a laugh.

As Sam watched Scotty and Skippy run off, filled with pride for a son that any mother would be proud to call her own. That he was hers, *her* son… He was one of the greatest blessings in her life, and she couldn't wait to watch him become a man, but she hoped that took a while to happen. She loved him at this stage, even when he was passive-aggressive about getting to drink coffee.

She went into their suite to lock up her service weapon and change into a T-shirt and pajama pants before she joined the kids and her mom, Brenda, in the family dining room.

"How was your day, dear?" Brenda asked as she handed Sam a glass of wine.

"Not too bad, but it got a whole lot better about fifteen minutes ago. How'd everything go here today?"

"Just fine. I love spending this time with them. Thank you for asking me to help out."

"Oh please, I should be thanking you. We could never do what we do without you and Celia."

"I know I speak for her when I say we love every minute of it."

For a lot of years, Sam had thought her mother was out of her life for good. She was glad those years were in the past now and that they were forging a whole new relationship.

Scotty and the twins came into the room, with Skippy hot on their heels.

Sam hugged Alden and Aubrey, who were so happy to see her that her heart nearly burst with love for them. Her babies. No matter how they'd come into her life, they were hers now, and she would do anything for them.

They were just settling into their chairs when Noah came charging in ahead of Avery and Shelby, who was carrying Maisie.

"Sorry we're late," Shelby said.

"You're not," Sam said. "We just got organized." She took the enchiladas provided by the White House chef out of the oven and put them on the table, along with a huge bowl of yellow rice and a salad.

"That smells amazing," Avery said. "We're going to miss the White House cuisine."

"Nick and I say that all the time. We fear we're going to be hopelessly spoiled by the time we leave."

"I plan to fully enjoy every second of it while I can," Scotty said as he took a huge mouthful of enchilada.

Aubrey, Alden and Noah laughed at the faces he made as he enjoyed his meal.

If only Nick were there, everything would be perfect, but this was pretty close to it.

"Dad is FaceTiming," Scotty said as he took the call.

Sam wondered how that worked outside the secure phone, but Nick would've found a way to make it happen.

Scotty held up his phone so everyone could say hi. "Have you met Chris Hemsworth yet?"

"No way," Sam said. "*That's* who he's seeing? This is so unfair."

"Right?" Shelby said. "We got robbed."

"I was afraid to tell you ladies that Thor was in the mix," Nick said with a chuckle.

"It's like we're not even in the room," Avery said.

"It's *Thor*, love," Shelby said. "No one can compete with him."

"Awesome," Avery said, making everyone laugh.

"What goes on there?" Nick asked.

"Enchiladas!" Aubrey said.

"Did we run out of napkins?" Nick asked with a laugh.

Scotty used his to wipe the sauce from Aubrey's face.

"Wish I was there with you guys."

"We miss you!" Alden said. "When are you coming home?"

"Friday."

"We have no school on Friday!" Scotty said.

"And then it's Easter," Alden said.

"And no school on Monday either," Nick said.

"Wait, *what*?" Scotty asked.

"You're staying home for the Easter Egg Roll," Sam reminded him.

"A four-day weekend. This is the best day of my life."

The adults laughed at his dramatic statement.

"I've got to run to a fundraiser with Thor," Nick said. "You guys have a nice rest of the evening. Love you all."

"We love you, too," Aubrey said. "Tell Thor we said hi."

"I'll do that."

"Really?" Alden asked, wide-eyed.

"Of course."

"That's so cool. Thank you."

"Anything for you, my loves. I'll talk to you all tomorrow. Love you."

Everyone shouted love to him before Scotty pushed the red button to end the call.

After dinner, Sam helped the twins finish math homework —with Scotty's help.

"How can I already need help with first-grade math?" she asked him after they'd tucked the twins into bed.

"Because you didn't pay attention the first time around."

"You're very sassy tonight."

"I'm sassy every night."

"Thanks for the help, pal."

"It takes a village to get first-grade homework done."

"Indeed it does." She gave him a hug outside his room. "Don't stay up too late."

"I won't. Are you gonna talk to your boyfriend later and make kissy faces at him? Oh wait, you can't because you don't have a smartphone."

"No, but I have a smart aleck for a son."

He grinned as he turned back at the doorway to his room. "Love ya, Mama."

"Love you, too, brat."

His laughter rang out and sent her into her room with a smile on her face. She glanced toward Nick's small office and felt an ache at his absence until she remembered Angela's words about missing Spencer and told herself to get over it already. Her husband would be home in two days, whereas Angela would never see hers again.

She hoped and prayed she would never know the kind of pain her sister was experiencing.

After she showered, she snuggled into bed and texted Vernon. *How can I send a gift to the weekend festivities for Jimmy and his wife?*

That's very nice of you, he replied. *I'll text you the info.*

Thank you! See you in the morning.

After he sent the link, she used Nick's laptop to access the registry and chose a fancy baby carriage that was the most expensive item on the list. Since Jimmy spent his days keeping her alive, it was the least she could do for him.

She signed the card, *With love and best wishes, from Sam and Nick.*

It felt good to do something nice for the young agent who'd become big part of her daily life in recent months.

With that done, she turned on the TV, hoping to find something to distract her until Nick called and cringed when she saw her own face on the screen. Shit. She'd forgotten that Peter's interview was airing that night. She forced herself to watch it with one hand over her eyes, so she saw only bits and pieces. It would never be "normal" to see herself on TV. Did she really look like that? Ugh. Horrible.

Her phone buzzed with a text from Angela. *Thanks for checking on me. I'm hanging in there. Eating popcorn and watching my sis and BIL on TV.*

It's horrible.

No, it isn't!

I hate my face on TV.

Shut up. You look great. Both of you do, and everything you said is spot-on.

She got another text, this one from Darren. *I still can't believe you went with Peter Wagner. What's he got that I don't?*

Forty million TV fans?

That's rude, Sam.

She laughed out loud.

Another text came in from Scotty. *MY PARENTS ARE ON TV! Everyone I know is texting me. Why wasn't I told about this?*

We told you.

DID NOT!

Blame Dad.

I'm blaming you!

Good night, son.

Quiet. I'm watching my parents. They're pretty awesome even when they don't tell me things.

The BlackBerry vibrated with a text from her favorite guy. *Not sure if you realize we're on TV at the moment.*

The whole world is texting me.

Hahaha. The whole world is watching.

SHUT UP with that!

Just saying...

This is all your fault.

Entirely. He sent a photo of himself with Thor. *Chris says hi.*

He's bummed because you're hotter than him.

OMG, you shut up. No one is hotter than Thor.

You are. Ask anyone.

Are you going to be up for a bit?

Depends on what I'm staying up for.

A call with your husband?

I might be able to fit that in. How much longer?

Thirty minutes, tops. I'm tired.

It must be exhausting hobnobbing with celebrities.

You said nob.

Grow up, Nicholas. You're the POTUS.

LOL. Talk soon.

Can't wait.

Sam was asleep when he called forty-five minutes later.

"Damn it, I woke you up."

"It's fine. I wanted to talk to you if you still had time for me after Thor."

"I've always got time for my best girl. How was the rest of your day?"

"Not too bad. We're close to closing the Myerson case and hoping to get a big break when we speak to the younger daughter tomorrow."

"Is the older one still in the wind?"

She loved when he used her lingo. "Yeah, the marshals are after her and the boyfriend, and we're waiting for the opportunity to talk to her younger sister."

"I can't imagine murdering someone at seventeen or eighteen."

"Or ever."

"Well, that, too, but especially then."

"I know. It's hard to fathom. Anyway, your son got an eighty-six on another algebra quiz. You might want to text him about that."

"I will for sure. That's awesome. He's going to get a B this quarter. I know it."

"We're not allowed to say that out loud. There's apparently some superstition."

"He's too funny."

"He really is. He's annoyed that he wasn't told we'd be on TV tonight."

"We told him that."

"I'm not sure we did."

"Whoops."

"Are you back at the hotel?"

"Yep, tucked in for the night all by my lonesome."

"No starlets to keep you company?"

"There were a few who wanted to, but I told them my wife would stab them with her rusty steak knife, and it'd be tough to explain the mess to housekeeping."

Sam grunted out a laugh. "You're damned right she would."

"Believe me, I know. She's scary with that rusty steak knife."

"I miss you so much it's stupid."

"I miss you more."

"No way."

"Yes way."

"Any word from Andy?"

"Not yet, but he knows we're anxious. I'm sure we'll hear from him tomorrow."

"I hope so. Scotty has caught wind of that situation and was asking me about it."

"What'd you tell him?"

"The truth. He's very pleased by the possibility of adoption."

"As am I."

"Same. I want that done yesterday so we can move on without having to worry about any of this crap again."

"I agree," Nick said. "It made me so sad to learn they're after the kids' money. How can anyone be so callous about those two perfect angels?"

"I don't know. It's definitely their loss."

"And our gain. Thank God you were there that night in the hospital and stepped up for them before they could become a meal ticket for relatives who don't give a shit about them."

"I was thinking about that earlier. If we hadn't brought Scotty into our lives, we wouldn't have been licensed foster parents, and it would've been a whole lot more complicated to bring them home."

"Everything happens for a reason."

Sam yawned loudly. "Sorry."

"Am I boring you?"

She laughed. "Not at all. I'm just out of gas."

"Go to sleep and have sweet dreams."

"You, too."

"I'm gonna dream about my sexy wife and a weekend at Camp David together."

"Hurry home. We love you and miss you."

"Love you and miss you, too. Night."

"Night."

Sam didn't want to hang up, but she could barely keep her eyes open. She fell asleep with the BlackBerry pressed to her chest, over the heart that beat only for him.

CHAPTER THIRTY-SIX

S am was up early to get the kids fed and off to school before she headed to work. Her first order of business was to see what Frank Myerson wanted.

When he and Dunning were settled in interview two, she and Freddie went to meet with them. While Freddie engaged the recording device, she sat across from Frank and stared him down.

He looked away.

"You asked for this meeting, Mr. Myerson. What can we do for you?"

"I... I want to confess to the murder of my wife."

Sam hadn't expected that. She sat back in her chair, noting that Dunning didn't seem surprised by Frank's confession. "Where's this coming from all of a sudden? What happened to 'I didn't kill my wife? I loved her more than anything'?"

"I do love her more than anything," he said tearfully, "but our lives had become untenable. She was so inflexible with the girls. All we did was fight because she refused to listen to anyone else's point of view. We were governed by a murder that happened more than twenty-five years ago, before any of us knew her."

"So you thought it would make everything better to commit another murder?"

"I didn't want to hurt Elaine! I loved her with my whole heart. But we couldn't go on that way."

"If it was so bad, why didn't you leave her and take the girls?" Freddie asked.

"I... I couldn't do that to her. Her children were her life."

"So you took her life?" Sam asked. "How does that make any sense?"

"You don't understand."

"You're right. I don't. What I think is happening here is that you're deciding to fall on your sword to protect your daughter, who's on the run with the boyfriend who probably helped her kill her mother."

"That's not true! Zoe had nothing to do with this."

"I don't believe you. I think she had everything to do with it, and you've decided to sacrifice yourself to save her because you failed to do that when Elaine was still alive."

"I did everything I could for those girls!"

"Except get them out of a toxic situation with their mother," Sam said. "My kids are everything to me. If they were being emotionally abused in their home, I'd take them and leave."

"Sure you would. As if your husband would let you take his kids."

"Let me? I do what I want, Mr. Myerson. I'm a full-grown adult with a mind and a bank account of my own. If my kids were in danger, you can bet your ass I'd take them and never look back. A lot of people don't have the luxury of being able to leave. I do. You did. Yet you chose to stay, so in many ways, this *is* on you. But you weren't the one to kill Elaine."

"Zoe didn't do this. She couldn't have. Someone broke in and killed Elaine."

"There's no sign of forced entry, and there was no one else who wanted Elaine dead besides the people in her own home."

"We didn't do this. Why won't you look beyond us for other suspects?"

"We have. There are no other suspects."

"There has to be! Zoe is a *child*! She couldn't have done this."

"So are you saying now that you didn't?"

"I'm saying you should charge me and forget about her."

"That's not how this works, Mr. Myerson. Surely Mr. Dunning told you that."

"I did," Dunning said.

"You'll be arraigned later today for obstructing our investigation. If you're released, I'd recommend you do what you can to get your daughter back here as soon as possible."

"Why would I do that? So you can throw her in jail for the rest of her life?"

"Stop talking, Frank," Dunning said.

"That's the plan, isn't it?"

"Detective Cruz, please let the U.S. Attorney's Office know that we recommend Mr. Myerson be held without bail so he can't assist his daughter in fleeing from justice."

Freddie stood. "I'll take care of that right away."

Frank's eyes narrowed as his face twisted into a nasty sneer. "You're all drunk off your own power, aren't you?"

"Not at all. You know what gets me drunk? Justice for murder victims who didn't deserve to be murdered by the people they loved the most." She stood. "This interview is over." After clicking off the recorder, she left the room and asked the Patrol officer outside to please escort Mr. Myerson back to lockup.

"Yes, ma'am."

Captain Malone was coming into the pit as she returned. "What did Myerson want?"

"To confess."

"Really?"

"Yes, but it was bullshit and I called him on it. We're asking that he be held without bail at his arraignment since he implied that he'd help Zoe stay in the wind if he was released."

"Got it."

"Any word from the marshals?"

"They found the silver SUV abandoned outside of Chicago."

"Shit. So now they have no clue what they're looking for."

"They're reviewing cars stolen in the area as well as bus and train stations and airports."

"I hope something pops soon."

"How's it possible that two teenagers can lead us on a multiday, multistate chase?"

"They planned every step of this. That's how. The sister should be here later today. I really want to talk to her."

"Jesse said she's not saying anything to anyone."

"How can she be protecting them when they left her bound and gagged when they took off?"

"I don't know what she's thinking."

"Maybe we can use Frank to get her to talk in exchange for dropping the charges against him."

"That's an idea."

"We'll float it when she's back here. Can you get me an ETA on that?"

"Yep."

While Malone headed to his office, she went into hers, planning to review the reports filed on the case thus far. Before she did that, though, she reached out to Archie to see how his friend was doing.

Thanks for checking in. She's doing okay. Today she asked for me to come into her room. She said she remembers my face and that I was kind to her.

That's great news. What's SVU saying about the investigation?

Nothing yet, but Erica is on it.

Let me know if there's anything I can do.

Thanks. Sorry to leave you hanging in the middle of a case.

Sergeant Walters has been great.
Glad to hear it.
Keep me posted on how she's doing.
I will.

Sam hoped they caught a break in the case that could explain what'd happened to Archie's friend and that he wasn't setting himself up for heartbreak.

ARCHIE WAS full of heartache as he stood by Harlowe's bedside, holding her hand while she sobbed through another examination of her injuries. He couldn't bear to see her traumatized or in pain, and he couldn't understand why she mattered so much to him when he'd seen her twice in his life before yesterday.

The doctor said she was much improved over the day before, and if she continued to make good progress, she could be released in a day or two.

"Where will I go?" she asked Archie tearfully.

"You'll come home with me, and I'll take care of you."

"Why would you do that for me?"

"Because I want to."

"I... I don't remember you."

He used a tissue to wipe the tears from her face. "You remember my face and that I was kind to you."

"Who are you?"

He'd already told her who he was, but he'd keep telling her until she retained the info. "My name is Archie, which is a nickname for my last name, which is Archelotta. Everyone calls me Archie. I'm a detective with the DC police, specializing in information technology."

"You... you're a police officer."

He'd also told her that—repeatedly. "Yes. You're safe with me. I promise."

"Tell me again how you know me."

"We met at a friend's party in Georgetown a couple of weeks ago. Remember Deb and Joe? You know her from yoga."

Her lovely brown eyes were frantic as she shook her head. "Why can't I remember anything?"

"Shhh. It's okay. You will eventually."

"What if I never remember?"

"I'm sure you will when you're ready to."

"Maybe it would be better if I didn't."

He ached to think of her recalling being assaulted, but he wanted her to remember her life and loved ones.

"Everything is going to be okay," he told her, even though he couldn't promise any such thing.

"Thank you for being kind to me."

"Of course."

"You... You must have somewhere to be."

"I'm right where I want to be."

He couldn't say why that was true. All he knew was that he wasn't going anywhere as long as she needed him.

SAM RECEIVED a call from a Detective Jones from the crime lab at three o'clock that afternoon.

"We've got the Mustang tied to your case and are able to show that it traveled thirty miles on Sunday afternoon, between the hours of three and five p.m."

Bingo, Sam thought. "Anything else?"

"The Bluetooth was used from 3:12 p.m. to 3:32 p.m. and then again from 3:40 to just after four o'clock."

That put Zoe and Zeke in the vicinity of the house around the time of the murder.

"Can you shoot this over to my email?"

"Yes, ma'am."

"Thank you very much."

She went out to the pit to share the news with the others.

"Now we can prove that Zeke's Mustang was used within the time-of-death window."

"That's huge," Cameron said.

"Yep." Sam loved the feeling that came with putting the pieces together to tie perps to murder.

Freddie came into the pit. "Uh, Sam, Mr. and Mrs. Bellamy are here."

She had to think for a second about who that was. Zeke's parents. "What do they want?"

"To talk to you and only you."

"All right," she said with a sigh. "Show them into interview one."

Sam wanted to be able to record the conversation, and she couldn't do that in her office or the conference room. She grabbed a bottle of water and her notebook from her office before she went to see what the Bellamys wanted. The were holding hands and looking terrified.

"I'm Lieutenant Holland."

"I'm Greg Bellamy, and this is my wife, Lillian."

"I'd like to record our conversation."

"Oh. Okay."

"Do you both agree?"

They glanced at each other before nodding.

Sam engaged the recording device, noted who was in the room and that they'd given their permission to be recorded. "You asked to see me?"

"Our son, Zeke, is missing," Greg said, "and no one will tell us where he is or what's going on."

"We believe he's on the run with Zoe Myerson after they killed her mother."

Lillian gasped. "*What?* He didn't kill anyone! He'd never do something like that."

"We're not sure which one of them took a baseball bat to the back of Mrs. Myerson's head, but we're fairly confident they were both there."

"There's no way," Greg said. "He has a scholarship to play baseball at Villanova next year. He'd never endanger that by being involved in something like this."

"We can prove that his car was used during the time of Mrs. Myerson's murder and that his Bluetooth was engaged for two twenty-minute rides, which is how long it would take to drive from Arlington to Crestwood."

"You're trying to pin this on my son when it was that girl who did this," Lillian said. "She *hated* her mother!"

"How do you know that?" Sam asked.

She looked down, seeming embarrassed maybe. "Zeke told me. Ever since he met her, Zeke has been obsessed. She's all he talks about. He's let his grades slide, and he's missed a couple of practices, which is unthinkable. This is his *senior year*, Lieutenant. Every game counts. If he misses practice, he's not allowed to play in the next game. Villanova made it clear that the scholarship is contingent upon him having a successful senior season. He has to get back to practice."

Sam didn't want to have to be the one to tell her that her son's baseball career was likely over. Even if he hadn't participated in the murder of Elaine Myerson, he'd helped Zoe run from the law and would be charged accordingly.

Unless, of course, he was willing to testify against her. Then they might be able to work something out.

"Has your son ever been out of touch with you like this before?"

"No!" Lillian said. "Never. He's a very good boy. He'd never do something like this to upset us under normal circumstances. It's that girl. She's got his head turned around so hard that he can't see anything but her."

"How would you feel about issuing a public appeal for him to contact you?" Sam asked.

"We've been able to keep this situation a private family matter," Greg said. "His coach has been told he's down with the flu, too sick to even go to the doctor. If it gets out that he's on the run with a murder suspect... His whole life will be ruined."

As a parent, Sam empathized with them. How could she not? But she also owed them the truth. "I'm sorry to be blunt, but I'm fairly certain that Zeke ruined his life when he chose to support Zoe in killing her mother and then running from the law."

Lillian's eyes filled with tears. "That can't be true! Tell her, Greg. He's an honor student and athlete with a *scholarship*. He made a mistake! That's all this is."

Greg put his hand on top of Lillian's. "The lieutenant is right."

"No! He'll come back and straighten this out. I know my son. He couldn't hurt anyone! Remember how he used to save the baby bunnies from the dogs? He wouldn't kill someone or help anyone commit murder! That's not who he is. Tell her, Greg."

He put an arm around his distraught wife. "He's always been a very good boy. Never gave us any trouble until he met Zoe. After she came on the scene, he was very different. He became almost unmanageable."

"But he still did what we told him to," Lillian added.

"When he wasn't sneaking around with her. She had a hold on him. We tried to help him see that his relationship with her wasn't healthy, but he wouldn't listen."

"I overheard her telling him how her mother abused her and her sister," Lillian said. "That she locked them in their rooms and wouldn't let them do anything."

"Neither of the girls told us anything about being locked in their rooms," Sam said.

"Do you think she told him that to make him sympathetic to her?" Lillian asked as Greg looked down at the table.

He was putting the pieces together faster than his wife, who was still in denial.

"Is there anywhere out west he would go to hide out?" Sam asked.

"No," Greg said. "There's nowhere... Wait. What was the name of the camp he attended in Colorado Springs that one summer? Remember how much he loved it?"

"Herron Creek?" Lillian asked.

"Yes, that's the one. He talked about it for years afterward, but he could never go back because of baseball commitments in the summer."

"This is helpful. I'll pass that information along to the marshals."

"What do we do in the meantime?" Lillian asked.

Sam pushed her notebook and pen across the table to them. "Give me your contact info, and I'll keep you apprised of any developments."

Greg wrote down the requested info. "I know you have no reason to believe us, Lieutenant, but our son is a good boy. If there was a plot to kill Zoe's mother, it certainly wasn't his idea, and in my wildest dreams, I can't picture him harming anyone."

"Thank you for sharing that with me. I'll keep you posted, okay?"

"Should we go there?" Lillian asked. "To Colorado Springs?"

"Absolutely not. Go home and wait to hear from me. Please don't make this worse by getting in the way of law enforcement."

"We won't," Greg said. "Thank you for your time, Lieutenant."

"No problem."

She walked them out and then returned to the pit.

"What was that about?" Freddie asked.

"They told me how Zeke is an honor student with a baseball scholarship to Villanova, and there's no way he'd ever have anything to do with killing someone."

"Do you believe them?"

"Strangely enough, I do. They said he was under Zoe's thrall and had changed a lot since she came into his life. He'd stopped caring about school and baseball and the things that'd been important to him. They told me about a summer camp called Herron Creek that he once attended in Colorado Springs that he loved. I want to pass that info on to Jesse. They said they didn't know of anywhere else out west that he might go."

"I'll give Jesse a call," Freddie said.

"Before you do that," Sam said, acting on a hunch, "what social media does Zeke have?"

"Instagram, Snapchat and TikTok."

"If I wanted to message him on those platforms, how would I go about that?"

"I can do it on your behalf." He sat in his cubicle and booted up his computer. "What do you want to say?"

Sam thought about it for a minute. "'Zeke, this is Lieutenant Holland with the DC police. Your parents just came to see me, and they're very upset and worried about you. They told me you're an honor student with a baseball scholarship to Villanova. You must've worked very hard for all of that. If you reach out to me, I can bring you home without any publicity. Your parents want you home to finish your senior year and move forward with your life. Running from law enforcement will result in charges. I don't want that for you. Please give me a call so I can help you.'"

"Got it," Freddie said. "I'll message him on all three platforms with your number."

"Thanks. Let me know what Jesse says."

"I will."

CHAPTER THIRTY-SEVEN

While he did that, Sam went to check in with Malone.
"Any word on an ETA for Jada?"

"She and one of the marshals are on a flight to DCA that lands in thirty minutes. I have Patrol officers meeting them."

"Excellent."

"They said she's in rough shape and very fragile. We need to proceed carefully."

"I can do that."

"I'd like to ask Lucas to be involved, too. She's good with managing trauma."

"And I'm not?"

"You're good at inflicting it."

"Wow. Ouch."

Malone laughed. "You know what I mean. Let's bring Erica in for the conversation with Jada."

"I'll see if she's available."

"I was joking," Malone said.

"I know you were. It's a totally different set of skills, and you're right that she's good with the vics."

"I heard the boyfriend's parents were here. What did they want?"

"To tell me what a great kid he is and how he'd never be part of murdering anyone. I tend to believe them. It'd be nice to try to salvage his future if he's a victim in this."

"How do we stretch to make him a victim?"

"Zoe told him Elaine locked her and Jada in their rooms, for one thing. There was no evidence of that or any mention of it from the family, and I think they would've mentioned it if it were true."

"Yeah, for sure. They would've."

"I think she played up Elaine's rigid rules with Zeke, made him think she was in danger and asked him to help her out. She was probably the first sex he ever had, so she used that as a weapon to get him to do her bidding."

"Who killed the mother?" Malone asked.

"Zoe did, but Zeke drove her there and maybe waited outside, possibly not knowing what was happening."

"That's a stretch, Sam. How do you know he wasn't the mastermind, trying to get Zoe out of a difficult situation?"

"I don't know that for sure, but I believed his parents when they said he'd never be part of something like this. On the other hand, I can see her doing it without having to stretch my imagination."

Sam felt a presence behind her and turned to find Sergeant Walters lurking. "May I help you with something, Sarge?"

"I was looking for you, ma'am, and your team said you were in the captain's office. I found something interesting on your victim's laptop."

"What did you find?"

"A very significant investigative effort into her sister's murder that'd recently yielded new results."

Sam perked up. "What kind of results?"

"A suspect."

"Come to the conference room so you can brief all of us at the same time." She glanced at Malone, who was already on his feet to follow them. Back in the pit, she said, "Everyone in the conference room for an update."

When her team was seated around the table, Sam gestured to Walters to give him the floor.

"Upon a thorough examination of Elaine Myerson's laptop, I found a file that'd been buried on an iCloud drive and given a name related to recipes, which is why it didn't stand out on our initial review. The file contained hundreds of items pertaining to the murder of the victim's sister, Sarah."

"She was conducting her own investigation?" Cameron asked.

"That's my conclusion after reviewing each of the documents. She'd closed in on a suspect, a man named Darryl Robinson." He gestured to the computer located in the front of the room. "May I?"

"Of course," Sam said.

He plugged a thumb drive into the computer and brought up an image of a white man, who Sam guessed was around sixty. He had gray hair and a goatee.

"The photo is from the Facebook profile of Darryl Robinson, age sixty-one, a resident of Springfield, Virginia. According to Elaine's notes, he was known locally as weird, but wasn't ever charged with anything and was never the focus of the original case. Elaine had done significant research on his whereabouts during the time of Sarah's disappearance and learned that he worked at a fast-food restaurant half a mile from where Sarah was taken."

Every cell in Sam's body began to buzz as Walters detailed his findings. If this panned out, would she ever be able to trust her buzz again?

"After trying to reach him by phone and email for months, Elaine paid him a visit three weeks ago."

"What?" Freddie said softly.

"Needless to say, it didn't go well, and Elaine noted that he ordered her off his property. He requested and was granted a restraining order that prohibited her from contacting him or being within five hundred feet of him." Walters clicked on the remote to bring up a copy of the order. "She had that in the file. Her notes are meticulous and detailed, indicating that she believed he's the man who kidnapped, tortured and murdered her sister."

"Is any of this in the file we received from Detective Truehart?" she asked Cameron, who'd been reviewing the files as time permitted.

"Not that I've seen."

"Let's get Truehart on the phone." She thumbed through her notebook and found his number for Freddie, who dialed the landline on the table and put it on speaker.

"Truehart."

"This is Sam Holland with the MPD."

"Oh, hello. How's your investigation unfolding?"

"Slow but sure. I'm here with my team, and we have a question for you. Had you heard from Elaine about a potential suspect in Sarah's case?"

"Many times over the years. She worked the case as hard as I did and had come up with several possibilities that I thoroughly investigated. None of them panned out, usually because they could prove they were somewhere else when Sarah was taken. I should've mentioned that the day we met, but I haven't thought about her leads in years."

"Had she mentioned anyone recently?"

"Not in the last three years or so."

"Does the name Darryl Robinson mean anything to you?"

"Can't say that it does."

"This is very helpful. Thank you."

"Of course. Please let me know if there's anything else I can do."

Sam disconnected the call. "So Elaine had brought him clues that went nowhere over the years. This time, she decided to take matters into her own hands." Sam thought about it for a second. "Wouldn't Truehart be told about a restraining order against his murder victim's sister?"

"Manassas is Prince William County," Cameron said. "Springfield is Fairfax."

"Ah, I see. That would explain why he didn't know about it. Detective Charles, please bring Frank Myerson up to interview one. Let's see what he knows about his wife's shadow investigation."

Neveah got up and left the room.

"What're you thinking?" Gonzo asked.

"That Elaine stirred up a hornet's nest, and maybe the hornet struck back at her."

"How does that explain the daughter and her boyfriend running from us?" Freddie asked.

"Maybe they felt like they were about to take the fall for something they didn't do and ran scared." Sam had a sick feeling in her stomach over how certain she'd been that Zoe had killed Elaine. Was it now possible she'd been totally wrong about that?

"That's possible, I suppose," Gonzo said.

Sam turned to Malone. "How would we approach this Robinson guy?"

"Carefully. You have no proof that ties him to either case, so there's no way you're getting a warrant for his devices or DNA."

"Unless..." She glanced at Walters. "If we could put him anywhere near Crestwood on Sunday, that'd give us probable cause for warrants."

"I'll review the film." He took his thumb drive when he left the room.

"Cameron, get me everything you can find on this guy ASAP."

"On it."

Neveah returned. "Mr. Myerson is in interview one."

"Thank you." Sam glanced at Freddie to tell him to come

with her. They stepped into the interview room, closing the door behind them.

"Talk to me about Elaine's involvement with Sarah's case."

His expression conveyed confusion. "She wasn't involved with it, other than living with the trauma of it."

"Did you know she was investigating the case the way a police detective would?"

"What? No, she wasn't."

"She was, and she had been almost from the beginning. Detective Truehart told us she regularly called him with suspects he should take a look at."

"Where did you find proof of this?"

"In an iCloud folder on her laptop that was labeled as a recipe folder."

"I know nothing about that."

"Did she speak to you about her sister?"

"Not much lately." He sat back in his chair, seeming to give it more thought. "When we were together about a year, I told her I couldn't bear to hear about her sister's murder every day for the rest of my life. I said I empathized tremendously with what she and her family had been through, but it was just too difficult to make that part of our daily life going forward. I wanted her to move on from it. I guess she never really did."

Who would? Sam wanted to ask him. "Thank you for the insight. This helps."

"When can I get out of here?"

"Perhaps later today. Jada will be brought here within the hour. We'd appreciate you being there when we speak to her."

"Whatever I can do to help."

"Your cooperation will go a long way toward seeing any pending charges against you dropped if we're able to identify another suspect."

"Understood."

"We'll keep you up here until Jada gets here. Is there anything we can get for you?"

"A coffee would be good."

"I'll grab that," Freddie said.

Outside the room, Sam said, "Put a Patrol officer outside the door."

He nodded and took off to get the coffee and the officer.

While she waited for someone to come mind the door, she leaned against the wall, closed her eyes and thought the case through from all angles. She'd been so certain that Zoe—and possibly Zeke—were involved. Now she wasn't sure of anything.

Her phone rang with a call from a Virginia number.

"Holland."

"This is, um... Zeke Bellamy. I got your message on Snapchat."

Sam stood up straighter. "Zeke, I'm so happy you called."

"You said my parents are upset."

"They're very upset and terrified you're ruining your very promising future by doing something stupid."

"Zoe... she said we had to run, that you were blaming us for her mother's murder, and we couldn't stand by and take the fall for something we didn't do."

Sam closed her eyes and exhaled. "Where are you, Zeke?"

"Are we in trouble?"

"Not if you do the right thing and come home. I can send someone to bring you back, but you have to tell me where you are."

"Will we be arrested?"

"No, you'll be escorted back to DC by the U.S. Marshals. We just want to get you both home safe. Can you help us do that?"

"I want to, but Zoe... She says if we go back, we'll get charged with murder because... We went to her house that day. She snuck in to get something, but no one knew she was there. I waited for her outside while she went in."

"What did she get?"

"Her birth control device. We were so afraid of her getting

pregnant that we wanted to double up on protection. She had a ring thing, but she forgot it at home, so we went back to get it. She was in and out in a minute and didn't see anyone, but she's freaking out that we were there at all and that we lied about it."

Sam felt weak in the knees at the role she'd played in sending two teenagers on the run. She'd been so certain they were involved. "You're not in trouble. Could I speak to Zoe? I'll tell her that myself."

"Sure. Hang on."

Sam heard him talking and a female voice responding, sounding annoyed. Then she heard a pleading edge to his voice.

More noise as the phone changed hands.

"Hello."

"Zoe, this is Lieutenant Holland. Zeke told me about why you returned home on Sunday and how you were only there for a minute."

"I told you I had nothing to do with this, but you wouldn't believe me."

"What happened to Jada in Ohio?"

"She wouldn't shut up about me killing our mother, which *I did not do*! I kept telling her it wasn't me, but she didn't believe me. We got into a fight over it, and I tied her up and left her in the room so I could get away from her. If the whole world is blaming me, I wasn't about to make it easy for you guys to find me."

"I'm sending the U.S. Marshals to meet you and Zeke to bring you home. They'll be told you're not suspects and shouldn't be treated as such. Will you come home with them?"

"Do you swear this isn't a trick?"

"I swear on the lives of my family."

"I told you I didn't do it," she said tearfully.

"I know you did. I'm sorry I didn't believe you."

Zoe sniffled repeatedly.

"Tell me where you are."

"What's the name of this place again, Zeke?"

"Herron Creek in Colorado Springs."

"Hang tight. Someone will be there soon."

Sam closed the phone and called Jesse.

"Best."

"Our fugitives have made contact. They're at a camp called Herron Creek in Colorado Springs. They're no longer considered suspects in our case and shouldn't be treated as such."

"Got it."

"Jesse... these are kids. Please don't let anyone get hurt."

"Understood."

The line went dead.

Malone came down the hallway. "What's wrong?"

"I fucked up."

"How so?"

"I was all set to pin this on Zoe and her boyfriend. It's very possible it wasn't them. I posted a message to Zeke's social media, and he called me like I asked him to. I mean... Would he do that if he was involved in a murder?"

"You're liking this Robinson guy for it?"

"That depends on whether we can put him in the area on Sunday."

"We can." Walters approached with printouts of grainy images. "That's him getting out of an Uber four blocks from the Myerson home at two o'clock on Sunday."

"Let's pick him up," Malone said. "I'll notify Fairfax County and submit warrant requests for DNA, electronics and his house."

Officer Clare came down the hallway. "Detective Cruz asked me to keep an eye on interview one."

"Thank you."

"How's the Myerson case coming?" he asked.

"We've had a big break today. Keep your fingers crossed."

"I will. Good luck."

"Thanks."

Sam went to the pit. "Gonzo, Sergeant Walters found video that puts Robinson in Crestwood on Sunday afternoon. Will you and Matt please go pick him up? The captain is reaching out to Fairfax County for backup."

Gonzo grabbed his jacket and handheld radio. "We're on it."

"Be careful and wear vests. He could be armed."

"Got it."

SAM HAD BARELY GOTTEN to take a breath when Jada Myerson was escorted in by two Patrol officers and a U.S. Marshal.

Sam gasped at the dark bruise on her swollen face. "Thank you all," she said to the other officers. "We'll take it from here." The girl wore a red sweatshirt that was several sizes too big for her, a pair of gray sweatpants and flip-flops.

The female marshal handed Sam a folder. "Medical details."

"Thanks."

"Right this way, Jada. Your dad is eager to see you."

The girl began to cry the minute Sam mentioned her dad.

Sam opened the door to the conference room, and Jada ran to him.

Frank wept as he held his daughter.

Sam stepped into the room and gave them a few minutes before she spoke. Since she no longer considered Elaine's family members suspects, she decided against bringing in Erica Lucas. "I'm so sorry to have to do business at a time like this."

Frank helped his daughter into a chair and then sat next to her.

"Why are you wearing that?" Jada asked of his orange jumpsuit.

"I was detained for obstructing the investigation."

"They *arrested* you? That's what Zoe said was going to happen, that if they couldn't find another suspect, they'd charge us because of all the fighting we did with Mom."

"Is that why she talked you into running away?"

Jada nodded. "She said we could either run or wait to be arrested. She scared me enough that I went along with it."

"You didn't want to?"

"Not really. I'm pretty sure she's the one who did it, but I wouldn't put it past her to stick it on me. I figured if I went, I could keep an eye on her."

"Why is there money missing from both your college funds?" Sam asked.

Jada cast a guilty look at her dad. "We were making plans to move out when Zoe turned eighteen. She was going to petition the court for custody of me."

"Jesus," Frank said. "I was afraid she was using again."

"She's not," Jada said. "She's very determined to stay drug-free. She found out that didn't help anything."

"I can't help but wonder," Sam said, "how you two, who seemed to hate each other, got past that to make plans like these."

"We were desperate," Jada said. "We still don't like each other, but we couldn't live like that any longer."

"How'd you end up left alone in a motel room?"

"I wasn't sure that she didn't kill Mom, so I kept needling her, trying to get her to admit that she did it, but she wouldn't. She kept telling me to shut up and that I didn't know what I was talking about, but I kept it up until she snapped. We got into a fight, and she managed to overpower me. She used a sock to tie my wrists and another to gag me. I couldn't believe they were actually going to leave me there. They fought over that. Zeke thought they should bring me, but Zoe said she'd had enough of my bullshit and that the housekeepers would find me eventually." She hiccupped on a sob. "I was there for a long time before anyone came to the room."

Frank put an arm around her carefully. "Oh God, honey. I'm so sorry you went through that."

"Did you arrest Zoe and Zeke?" Jada asked as she wiped away tears with a tissue Sam had given her.

"No."

"Why not? It's obvious she did it, and he helped her."

"We don't think that's what happened."

Jada glanced at her dad, incredulous. "How could it be anyone else?"

"We've learned that your mom was investigating her sister's murder," Sam said, "and that she recently visited a man she considered a suspect. He took out a restraining order against her to keep her away from him. Our cameras put him in the vicinity of your home on Sunday afternoon, shortly before your mother returned home from doing errands." A new detail clicked into place for Sam as she recited the details.

Sam showed them a photo of the baseball bat that'd been used to kill Elaine.

"Does this look familiar?"

Frank gasped. "That's Zoe's from when she played softball."

"It's possible he snuck into the garage when she opened the door to put her car in and then picked up the bat." That would explain the lack of forced entry.

"It wasn't Zoe?" Jada asked softly.

"We haven't got all the details on the suspect yet, but we don't believe she was involved."

"Oh my God." Jada dissolved into deep, wrenching sobs. "The things I said to her. I accused her of being a monster."

"I was pretty sure she'd done it, too," Frank said. "I hated to think it was possible, but she was so angry with Mom all the time. I thought maybe she and Zeke had decided to get her out of the way."

Jada fell into his arms, sobbing. "I hate her for leaving me in that motel room, but she'll hate me more for what I thought she did."

To Frank, Sam said, "We've located Zoe and Zeke and are working on getting them home."

She left the room and called Zeke's father.

"Greg Bellamy."

"This is Sam Holland. We've found your son, and we're bringing him home."

EPILOGUE

Normally, an arrest that solved two murders would be cause for great celebration. In this case, Sam couldn't shed the sick feeling over how close she'd come to charging an innocent kid with her mother's murder.

If Sergeant Walters hadn't found that file on Elaine's computer, Sam might've ruined the lives of innocent young people.

Thursday evening, she met Lindsey and several of her bridesmaids for the fitting at Shelby's Georgetown studio. What should have been a joyful time with some of her closest friends was anything but as Sam pondered the fine line between success and failure and the consequences of getting it wrong.

Robinson's fingerprints had been a match for those on the baseball bat and a rush of his DNA sample showed a match for the DNA found on Sarah Corrigan's body. He'd been charged with both murders, and more charges would be forthcoming in the next few days. It'd given Sam tremendous satisfaction to call Detective Truehart with the news that the DNA was a match.

"All the credit goes to Elaine," Sam had said. "Robinson never would've been on our radar without her efforts."

"I'm sorry that she didn't bring the info to me," he'd said. "Maybe we could've saved her from such a terrible fate."

"I wish she'd done that, too, but I'm sure she appreciated all your years of hard work on behalf of her sister."

"No family deserves what happened to them."

"I hope you can now enjoy your hard-earned retirement."

"That's the plan. I'm glad I got the chance to meet you, although I wish it had been under different circumstances. I admire your dedication to the job. You remind me of me."

"I'm honored to be compared to you, sir."

"Stay safe, Lieutenant, and don't give the job everything you've got. Save some for yourself and your loved ones."

"I will. Take care, Detective."

"You do the same."

The conversation with Truehart had run through her mind repeatedly in the hours since, as she picked over the scraps of the case and processed an outcome she hadn't expected.

"Everything okay?" Lindsey asked as she came around with a bottle of champagne to refill glasses.

"Absolutely. The dress is gorgeous." Sam had felt sexy in the navy blue dress that left one shoulder bare. "Thank you for not picking something hideous."

"Would I do that to you?"

"Never."

"Congrats on closing two cases for the price of one. I saw Elaine's brother on the news earlier. He was in tears talking about how the same man took both his sisters from him and how thankful he is to you and your team for closing both cases."

"Elaine solved Sarah's case and ended up dead for her efforts. Her family is traumatized, with years of work ahead of them to pick up the pieces. It all feels kind of pointless at the end of the day."

"Not to Elaine's brother. You helped to give him answers that'd eluded his family for decades in Sarah's case. Detective Truehart was interviewed, too. He said now he can finally retire in peace."

"That's the good news, I guess. I still feel sick about how close I came to charging Elaine's daughter."

"You followed the evidence you had to where it led, Sam. Zoe's own father and sister suspected she might be involved. You shouldn't be too hard on yourself."

"When I first told Nick about Juan, I reminded him how things are never as obvious as they appear, and then I didn't take my own advice on this case."

"Everything was pointing to the daughter until it wasn't."

Sam realized she was bringing down Lindsey's festive mood. "Never mind about all that, and don't worry about me. Go enjoy your friends."

"I so appreciate you being here, especially on a day like this one."

Sam hugged Lindsey. "I wouldn't have missed it for anything."

After Lindsey walked away, Shelby came over to Sam, carrying the baby. "Maisie wanted to see her auntie Sam."

Sam took the tiny bundle from Shelby and snuggled her in close as tears stung her eyes. She was an emotional basket case tonight. "She's so beautiful, Tinker Bell. Just like her mama."

"I think she looks like her gorgeous daddy."

"I see both of you in her, which makes her a very lucky girl."

"Are you okay?" Shelby asked. "You're not yourself tonight."

Sam kept her gaze trained on the baby's little face. "I'm much better now after a very challenging week."

"If it makes you feel any better, the dress looked incredible on you."

"Thanks. I like it a lot." Sam kissed the baby's forehead and handed her back to Shelby. "I need to get home to the kiddos since Dad is away."

"Thank you again for the invite to Camp David. We've caved to enormous family pressure to bring baby Maisie to meet everyone since Avery is doing so much better."

"Totally understand. We'll see you Monday at the Easter Egg Roll, if not before?"

"Noah can't wait."

Sam gave Shelby a careful hug around the baby. "Thanks for taking such good care of my beloved Lindsey when it's not really your job to plan weddings anymore."

"Putting together weddings for people I love is a pleasure."

"Have a nice Easter with your family, Tink."

"You, too."

Sam said her goodbyes to Lindsey and the other women and ducked out while they continued the celebration with talk of the upcoming bridal shower and bachelorette outing. Thankfully, that would be just one night and not an entire weekend.

Vernon held the door for her. "Where to?"

"Home, please."

"You got it."

On the ride home, Sam watched the world go by out the window as she contended with a plethora of emotions. Despair over Elaine's murder by the same man who'd killed her sister and the long-term implications for the Myerson family, joy for Lindsey and Shelby. Sadness for herself and Nick and the baby they would've loved to have had together. Loneliness for him and worry over the story over her lies about Juan Rodriguez that refused to let up, though NCIS had finally announced he was alive and well.

They'd charged Goldstein and Wilson with conspiring to commit homicide by hiring someone to murder Juan. Both men had been arraigned in federal court that afternoon, in stunning falls from grace.

So why was it that the only thing the media wanted to talk about was how Sam had questioned Juan's roommate and girlfriend about his murder even though she'd known he was alive?

Agent Truver had confirmed Sam's story that she'd been asked to investigate the case the way she would any other homicide as NCIS worked to make the attempted murder case against Goldstein and Wilson. Sam had done what she'd been asked to do, Truver had said, and shouldn't be held accountable for untruths told as a result of her cooperation with federal authorities.

Nothing anyone said mattered.

The media had decided to brand her a liar, and there was no putting that genie back in the bottle now that it had exploded into the public discourse.

Sam was determined to forget about all of it to focus on her kids. Since they were off from school tomorrow, she'd taken the day off, too, leaving the paperwork and cleanup on the Myerson case to Gonzo, Freddie and the others.

At home, she enjoyed dinner and a movie with the kids, followed by ice cream in the family dining room, four stories for the twins and a later-than-usual bedtime since no one had to get up in the morning.

After Sam and Scotty tucked in the twins, they walked downstairs to let out Skippy and then snuggled up to watch the end of the Capitals game on the sofa in her and Nick's suite.

Nick called just as the game ended with a win for the home team.

"Is that my cue to get the hell out of here?" Scotty asked.

"Hush and say hello to your father."

"Hello, Father. How are you?"

"I'm tired and ready to come home. What goes on there?"

"All the usual stuff, except Mom helped to solve two murder cases with one arrest today."

"I heard about that. Well done, Mom."

"Elaine Myerson gets the full credit. She was investigating her sister's cold case and led us to the guy we arrested."

"That's amazing."

"Thank goodness for her, because I was on my way to charging at least one of her children with murder."

"Everyone has told Mom that she didn't do anything wrong and that she followed the evidence, but she's still beating herself up over it," Scotty said.

"That's because she cares so much."

"I'm going to bed, parentals. You can make kissy faces and other gross things with the child out of the room." He kissed Sam's cheek as he got up. "I'm not gone yet."

Nick laughed. "He's too much."

"He's full of beans lately and such a huge help with the twins."

"I'm calling with very good news."

"I could use some of that. Lay it on me."

"Andy heard back from the grandparents' lawyer. They're dropping their quest for custody."

"Oh, thank God. That was all I could think about tonight when I had them cuddled up to either side of me earlier as we watched *Star Wars* for the nine-hundredth time. Like what would we ever do without them?"

"That's never going to happen. Andy has begun the paperwork for us to adopt the three of them."

Sam's eyes flooded with tears. "I'm *so* happy about that."

"Eli is, too. He said he never imagined he'd want that, but whatever it takes to make our family official."

"Our family... It's a miracle born from multiple tragedies."

"And born from love."

"So much of that. When will you be home? I miss you so much."

"I miss you, too. I'll be there by one o'clock tomorrow afternoon to change and pack for the weekend. My afternoon is free and clear for my family."

"We can't wait."

"Neither can I."

After lunch the next afternoon, Sam was notified that *Marine One* was due to land on the South Lawn at any moment. She gathered the kids and Skippy and went outside to greet their favorite guy.

While they waited, the kids chased each other and Skippy around on the lawn. For a second, Sam could pretend they were like any other family greeting a returning traveler. The presence of Secret Service agents as well as the White House press corps with their long-range lenses trained on Sam and the kids shattered that illusion.

But nothing could dull the elation of seeing *Marine One* come into view, bringing Nick home to them.

Scotty let out a shout of excitement that was echoed by the twins, who were out of their minds with excitement as the big helicopter touched down on the lawn.

Sam held them back until the engine was shut off and the rotors stopped turning.

"Go get him," she said as they ran at full speed toward the chopper.

Sam brought up the rear, which meant she got to see him come down the stairs, salute the Marine who met him and crash into the kids on the lawn in a giant hug that included all three of them, with Skippy in the middle of it all.

With all the cameras recording the reunion, Sam was thankful to know there'd be a record of such a special moment.

It took about ten minutes for Nick to get free of the kids so he could give her a hug and a kiss.

"Welcome home, love. I'm so glad you're here."

"Be it ever so humble, there's no place like home."

Sam laughed, as there was absolutely nothing humble about their home.

Hand in hand, they waved to the gathered media and followed their kids and dog inside.

AFTER *MARINE ONE* delivered them to Camp David later that afternoon, they took a long hike, had dinner and played pool and pinball in the game room. The minute they put the kids to bed, they headed straight for their room, closed and locked their door, tore the clothes off each other and landed in bed in a fiery, passionate embrace that led to some of the fastest sex of their lives together.

It was so fast and so furious that they were left breathless and laughing in the aftermath.

"Welcome home, Mr. President," Sam said as they lay face-to-face, hands joined as they wallowed in the sight of each other. "It's ridiculous how much I missed you. It's like I've got a limb missing, or something equally dramatic, when you're not here."

"I feel the same way. Everything is wrong when you guys are thousands of miles from me, and I can't sleep snuggled up to you."

"Angela had a rough week, and that made me feel guilty for mooning over you being away for a couple of nights."

"I'm sorry to hear that about Ang, but I hope you never stop mooning over me."

"I don't think I ever will. It seems to be a fatal condition."

A smile lit up his gorgeous eyes. "What else did I miss while I was gone, besides you solving two murders with one arrest?"

"I'm not taking the credit for that. Elaine led us to Robinson, and finding him is what got her killed."

"It's all so sad. That poor family."

"I know. I hope Frank and his girls can put their lives back together eventually. He told me they're seeing Elaine's therapist. They thought it would be quicker to go to her since she knows the backstory."

"That's a good idea."

"I also apologized for suspecting them. Zoe said she understood why I did, but she hoped I'd be more empathetic to the families of victims in the future."

Nick winced. "Tell me you know that's not a fair accusation. You're incredibly sensitive in your dealings with them."

"I wasn't this time. I took an immediate dislike to that kid and suspected her from the start. Freddie called me out on it after the first time we met her. I should've listened to him."

"All this proves is that you're still learning, even after so many years on the job."

"Some lessons sting more than others. Such as lying to my colleagues and Juan's loved ones, and then having that made public." The press had been relentless in their coverage of her role in perpetrating a fraud, as they called it. Even after Juan had issued a statement saying that he'd personally asked her to keep the secret, the story showed no sign of dying down. Something else would have to happen to knock it out of the headlines. In the meantime, she was taking a serious beating.

"While I have you all to myself, I need to tell you I heard from Collins Worthy."

Nick was immediately on full alert, the way he got any time his mother intruded into their lives. "What'd he want?"

"To plead her case, to ask you to give her another chance by asking me to talk to her."

"What'd you say?"

"I told him I'd let him know if I was interested, and I asked Neveah to take a deep dive on him to make sure he's on the up-and-up."

"And?"

"He is."

"So what's he doing with her?"

"That was my question, too. I believe he fancies himself in love with her."

Nick made a disgusted face.

"What do you think I ought to do? Should I take the call with her?"

"I don't see what good it would do."

"So call me crazy, but I'm starting to think she sincerely wants to fix things with you—and us."

"Probably because I'm president, and she wants to take full advantage of her proximity."

"I don't know if it's just that. Worthy is a serious family guy. Maybe he's shown her the benefit of having people around who have her back."

He sighed. "I hate the idea of letting her into our lives."

"Then we won't do it."

"Am I a monster for feeling that way?"

"Oh my God, of course not. Anyone would after what she's put you through."

"I just don't believe she's capable of this kind of change."

"We'll let it go for now."

"How'd you leave it with him?"

"That he'd hear from me if I was interested in talking to her."

"Thank you for handling that for me."

"Anything for you." She turned her gaze up to meet his. "There's one more thing you should know about." She filled him in on Scotty and the current-events discussions in social studies.

He cringed. "What the hell do we do about that?"

"Vernon suggested we allow him to use headphones when something comes up that he doesn't want to listen to."

"That's a very good idea."

"I'll pitch it to him and the teacher and see what we can do."

"Look at you handling all the wildfires that break out when I'm not around."

"I like fighting fires better with you than without you."

"Same, babe."

"Tell me the truth. It was pretty cool meeting Thor, right?"

"Did I mention I also met Iron Man?"

"No way! I love RDJ."

"He's pretty cool."

"I'm definitely quitting my job to travel with you if you're going to get to meet all the cool people."

"No, you're not. You'd be bored senseless within a week."

"Being bored is starting to look pretty good to me lately."

"I'm sure it is, but soon enough, you'll be back into another case, and you'll remember why you were put on this earth."

"I was put on this earth to love you and our kids."

"And to catch murderers."

"But mostly to love you."

He pulled her in close to him. "I won't argue with that."

AFTER A PEACEFUL, restful Easter weekend at Camp David, they dressed in their Easter finery to greet hundreds of people on the South Lawn for the annual Easter Egg Roll. Nick had told them the night before that the tradition of kids using large spoons to roll eggs across the South Lawn dated back more than one hundred forty years to President Rutherford B. Hayes, who instituted the event after kids were banned from rolling eggs on the grounds of the Capitol.

"Is that another fact on file you've retained from high school?" Scotty had asked him.

"No, smart aleck, it was in the briefing documents for the event."

"Oh phew, because if you remembered stuff like that from school, I was going to quit while I'm ahead."

"No one is quitting school around here," Nick said.

The Easter Egg Roll was about so much more than eggs, Sam discovered. There were local marching bands, crafts, healthy snacks, stories, games, photos with the White House backdrop and other family-friendly activities.

All the kids in their lives were there—including Sam's nieces and nephews, Gonzo, Christina and their son, Alex, Shelby, Avery, Noah and baby Maisie, Andy and his family, Derek, Roni and Maeve, Leo, Stacy, Brock and Brayden, as well as much of the White House staff and their families.

Vernon brought his wife, daughters and grandchildren over to meet Sam and Nick.

"Thank you so much for sharing him with me," Sam said as she shook hands with each family member.

"He loves working with you," Vernon's wife, Evelyn, said.

She also met Jimmy's pregnant wife, Liz, and family members of other staffers they'd gotten to know since moving to the White House.

"This is amazing," Angela said as she kept watch over Jack and Ella, running wild with the other kids. "Thank you for including us."

"Of course we did. How was Easter?"

"We got through it. What was it like being back at Camp David?"

"We got through it."

"I don't think I could do it."

"It wasn't easy, but it's a great respite away from this place for Nick, so we're trying to give it new mojo."

"I get that. Spence wouldn't want to be the reason it was ruined for you guys."

"He didn't ruin it. We had a nice time, all things considered."

"I'm glad. I'm sorry about the beating you're taking in the media over Juan, especially after you not only solved a murder, but closed a cold case, too."

"Elaine Myerson led us to her killer—and her sister's."

"It's an incredible story. Congratulations on being part of it."

It would never sit well with her to be congratulated for closing Elaine's case after the way she'd treated Frank and his girls, but she'd apologized to them and had decided to try to move on, taking the lessons learned with her. "Thank you."

They rolled the eggs and helped the younger kids with Easter crafts. They ate cupcakes and cookies and posed for photos with Nick and hundreds of other people. When they were rounding up the kids as the event came to an end, Brant, Vernon, Jimmy and several other agents suddenly swarmed them.

"Mr. President, Mrs. Cappuano, please come with us. We need to get you inside right away."

"Why?" Sam glanced back at her sisters and their families, who watched the scene unfold with concern.

"We've received a credible terrorist threat against this event," Brant said, tenser than she'd ever seen him.

"I'm not going anywhere without the kids and the others," Sam said.

Vernon put his arms around her and moved her toward the house while Brant and other agents did the same to Nick. "They'll be right behind us."

AH YES, I did it again! Leaving you with a little nugget to look forward to in the next First Family book, coming in 2025, is so much fun and gives us something to look forward to. This book was bonkers to write—and hopefully to read. I want you to know that my readers inspired the Juan Rodriguez storyline with the genuine outpouring of grief over his "murder" at the end of STATE OF SUSPENSE. You got me to thinking... What if Juan wasn't really dead? Much of this story is the result of that question. So thanks for that!

When you finish reading, join the STATE OF ALERT Reader Group to discuss this story with spoilers allowed and encouraged: *www.facebook.com/groups/stateofalert* and make sure you're a member of the Fatal/First Family Series Reader

Group at *www.facebook.com/groups/FatalSeries* to be among the first to hear about new books and other Sam and Nick news.

Writing their story continues to be the most fun I've ever had as an author. Thank you for your mad love of them and their ongoing adventure. I'm already looking forward to writing the next book... minutes after finishing this one! After every new book, I get concerned questions about whether the series is over. Let me put your minds at ease by saying I plan to write this series for as long as I possibly can. I love it as much as you do!

A very special thank you to Captain Russell Hayes, Newport Police Department (retired), for his amazing input into the investigations. I so appreciate his contributions to all twenty-four of Sam and Nick's full-length books as well as the novellas. I couldn't—and wouldn't—write this series without his involvement. Thank you, Russ, for eighteen years of friendship and some of the details that make these books come alive on the page.

As always, thank you to the team that supports me every day: Julie Cupp, Lisa Cafferty, Jean Mello, Ashley Lopez and Nikki Haley, as well as my editors, Joyce Lamp and Linda Ingmanson, and beta readers, Anne Woodall, Kara Conrad and Tracey Suppo.

Thank you to the First Family Series beta readers: Jennifer, Kelly, Maricar, Karina, Sarah, Kelley, Irene, Gina, Phuong, Juliane and Amy.

And to you, the readers who show up for every new book, thank you so much for giving me the career of my dreams. I appreciate you all so very much!

Xoxo

Marie

ALSO BY MARIE FORCE

Romantic Suspense Novels Available from Marie Force

The First Family Series

Book 1: State of Affairs

Book 2: State of Grace

Book 3: State of the Union

Book 4: State of Shock

Book 5: State of Denial

Book 6: State of Bliss

Book 7: State of Suspense

Book 8: State of Alert

Read Sam and Nick's earlier stories in the Fatal Series!

The Fatal Series*

One Night With You, *A Fatal Series Prequel Novella*

Book 1: Fatal Affair

Book 2: Fatal Justice

Book 3: Fatal Consequences

Book 3.5: Fatal Destiny, *the Wedding Novella*

Book 4: Fatal Flaw

Book 5: Fatal Deception

Book 6: Fatal Mistake

Book 7: Fatal Jeopardy

Book 8: Fatal Scandal

Book 9: Fatal Frenzy

Book 10: Fatal Identity

Book 11: Fatal Threat

Book 12: Fatal Chaos

Book 13: Fatal Invasion

Book 14: Fatal Reckoning

Book 15: Fatal Accusation

Book 16: Fatal Fraud

Contemporary Romances Available from Marie Force

The Wild Widows Series—a Fatal Series Spin-Off

Book 1: Someone Like You

Book 2: Someone to Hold

Book 3: Someone to Love

Book 4: Someone to Watch Over Me

The Gansett Island Series

Book 1: Maid for Love *(Mac & Maddie)*

Book 2: Fool for Love *(Joe & Janey)*

Book 3: Ready for Love *(Luke & Sydney)*

Book 4: Falling for Love *(Grant & Stephanie)*

Book 5: Hoping for Love *(Evan & Grace)*

Book 6: Season for Love *(Owen & Laura)*

Book 7: Longing for Love *(Blaine & Tiffany)*

Book 8: Waiting for Love *(Adam & Abby)*

Book 9: Time for Love *(David & Daisy)*

Book 10: Meant for Love *(Jenny & Alex)*

Book 10.5: Chance for Love, *A Gansett Island Novella (Jared & Lizzie)*

Book 11: Gansett After Dark *(Owen & Laura)*

Book 12: Kisses After Dark *(Shane & Katie)*

Book 13: Love After Dark *(Paul & Hope)*

Book 14: Celebration After Dark *(Big Mac & Linda)*

Book 15: Desire After Dark *(Slim & Erin)*

Book 16: Light After Dark *(Mallory & Quinn)*

Book 17: Victoria & Shannon (Episode 1)

Book 18: Kevin & Chelsea (Episode 2)

A Gansett Island Christmas Novella *(Appears in Mine After Dark)*

Book 19: Mine After Dark *(Riley & Nikki)*

Book 20: Yours After Dark *(Finn & Chloe)*

Book 21: Trouble After Dark *(Deacon & Julia)*

Book 22: Rescue After Dark *(Mason & Jordan)*

Book 23: Blackout After Dark *(Full Cast)*

Book 24: Temptation After Dark *(Gigi & Cooper)*

Book 25: Resilience After Dark *(Jace & Cindy)*

Book 26: Hurricane After Dark *(Full Cast)*

Book 27: Renewal After Dark *(Duke & McKenzie)*

Downeast

Dan & Kara: A Downeast Prequel

The Green Mountain Series*

Book 1: All You Need Is Love *(Will & Cameron)*

Book 2: I Want to Hold Your Hand *(Nolan & Hannah)*

Book 3: I Saw Her Standing There *(Colton & Lucy)*

Book 4: And I Love Her *(Hunter & Megan)*

Novella: You'll Be Mine *(Will & Cam's Wedding)*

Book 5: It's Only Love *(Gavin & Ella)*

Book 6: Ain't She Sweet *(Tyler & Charlotte)*

ABOUT THE AUTHOR

Marie Force is the #1 *Wall Street Journal* bestselling author of more than 100 contemporary romance, romantic suspense and erotic romance novels. Her series include Fatal, First Family, Gansett Island, Butler Vermont, Quantum, Treading Water, Miami Nights and Wild Widows.

Her books have sold more than 13 million copies worldwide, have been translated into more than a dozen languages and have appeared on the *New York Times* bestseller list more than 30 times. She is also a *USA Today* bestseller, as well as a Spiegel bestseller in Germany.

Her goals in life are simple—to spend as much time as she can with her "kids" who are now adults, to keep writing books for as long as she possibly can and to never be on a flight that makes the news.

Join Marie's mailing list on her website at *marieforce.com* for news about new books and upcoming appearances in your area. Follow her on Facebook, at *www.Facebook.com/MarieForceAuthor*, Instagram *@marieforceauthor* and TikTok *@marieforceauthor*. Contact Marie at *marie@marieforce.com*.

Made in United States
North Haven, CT
24 December 2024

63502736R00248